PRAGATI

Pre-higher Primary Scholarship Examination

I0647006

Standard V

English & Mathematics

Paper - I

❑ **SALIENT FEATURES** ❑

* Appropriate Classified chapters will make study very easy and convenient.
* Each Chapter Contains Introductory Information + Model Examples + Examples for Practice with Answers.
* The book will provide perfect guidance to the students.
* For sure success in Pre-higher Primary Scholarship Examination.

▸▸ *By* ◂◂

Mrs. Sandhya Venkatesh   **Dr. Mrs. Mrunal Kothari**

PRAGATI BOOKS

PP003

STD. V : ENGLISH & MATHEMATICS : PAPER - I

First Edition   :   August 2016   ISBN : 978-93-86084-83-5

©   :   Authors

Published by :   Polyplates
NIRALI PRAKASHAN
Abhyudaya Pragati, 1312 Shivaji Nagar,
Off J.M. Road, Pune – 411005,
Phone : 25512336/37/39   Fax : (020) 25511379
Email : niralipune@pragationline.com

DISTRIBUTION CENTERS

PUNE
Nirali Prakashan
119, Budhwar Peth, Jogeshwari Mandir Lane,
Pune - 411002, Maharashtra.
Tel : (020) 24452044, 66022708;
Fax : (020) 2445 1538
Email : niralilocal@pragationline.com

Nirali Prakashan
S. No. 28/27, Dhayari,
Near Pari Company, Pune - 411 041,
Tel - (020) 24690204
Email : dhayari@pragationline.com
bookorder@pragationline.com

MUMBAI
Nirali Prakashan
385, S.V.P. Road, Rasdhara Co-op. Hsg. Society, Girgaum, **Mumbai - 400004**, Maharashtra
Tel : (022) 2385 6339 / 2386 9976, Fax : (022) 2386 9976
Email : niralimumbai@pragationline.com

RETAIL SHOPS

PUNE
Pragati Book Centre
157, Budhwar Peth, Opp. Ratan Talkies,
Pune – 411002, Maharashtra
Tel : 2445 8887 / 6602 2707

Pragati Book Centre
676/B, Budhwar Peth,
Opp. Jogeshwari Mandir,
Pune – 411002, Maharashtra
Tel. : (020) 6601 7784, 2445 2254

PUNE
Pragati Book Centre
Amber Chamber, 28/A, Budhwar Peth,
Appa Balwant Chowk
Pune : 411002, Maharashtra
Tel : (020) 20240335 / 66281669
Email : pbcpune@pragationline.com

Pragati Book Centre
152, Budhwar Peth,
Near Jogeshwari Mandir,
Pune – 411002, Maharashtra
Tel : (020) 6609 2463 / 2445 2254

MUMBAI
Pragati Book Corner
Indira Niwas, 111-A Bhavani Shankar Road,
Dadar (W), **Mumbai** – 400028
Tel : (022) 2422 3525 / 6662 5254
Email : pbcmumbai@pragationline.com

DISTRIBUTION BRANCHES

NAGPUR
Pratibha Book Distributors
Above Maratha Mandir, Shop No. 3, First Floor, Rani Zanshi Square, Sitabuldi,
Nagpur 440012, Maharashtra, Tel : (0712) 254 7129
JALGAON
34, V. V. Golani Market, Navi Peth, Jalgaon 425001, Maharashtra,
Tel : (0257) 222 0395, Mob : 94234 91860
KOLHAPUR
New Mahadvar Road, Kedar Plaza, 1st Floor Opp. IDBI Bank
Kolhapur 416 012, Maharashtra. Mob : 9855046155

PREFACE

Dear Students,

It is good to see you willing to work hard and prepare yourself to be successful in all your activities including studies. The fact that you are holding this book in your hands shows that you are keen to improve your abilities which will hold you in good stead.

This book has been specifically written and published in a format which is easy to understand and help you to prepare thoroughly for the English & Mathematics 5th Standard Scholarship Examination.

Each topic is prepared according to the syllabus and has been kept short but covers all the important guidelines. Model questions with answers are presented according to the examination paper pattern. To help you practice more, carefully developed examples along with answers at the end of each topic are also given.

We believe that the book is prepared with utmost attention to each and every aspect, if studied well and practiced, will enhance confidence of the students. However, we would welcome any suggestions to make it better for the years to come.

We would be very much thankful if any comments, Suggestion Received from Readers.

Thanks to Pragati Books for bringing out this useful book !

Here's wishing you all the best !

- **Authors**

SYLLABUS & CONTENTS

SECTION I : ENGLISH LANGUAGE

SECTION II : MATHEMATICS

WEIGHTAGE FOR QUESTION PAPER

ENGLISH LANGUAGE

Total questions 25, Marks 50

Sr. No	Units	Weightage
1	Vocabulary	16%
2	Word Games	8%
3	Grammar	24%
4	Language Study	4%
5	Creative Writing	16%
6	Reading Skills (Comprehension)	24%
7	Miscellaneous	8%

MATHEMATICS

Total questions 50, Marks 100

Sr. No	Units	Weightage
1	Number work	12%
2	Operations on Numbers	20%
3	Fractions	14%
4	Measurement / Mensuration	20%
5	Applied Mathematics	16%
6	Geometry	14%
7	Pictographs	4%

VOCABULARY

| 1.1 | WORD FORMATION |

✌ INTRODUCTION :

Word formation is the creation of a new word. In linguistics, word formation refers to the ways in which new words are made on the basis of other words.

Q. Changing word forms : Nouns, Verbs, Adjectives.

(A) FORMATION OF NOUNS FROM VERBS

Verbs	Nouns	Verbs	Nouns
learn	Learning/learner	please	Pleasure
think	Thought	refuse	Refusal
grow	Growth	hear	Hearing
succeed	Success	introduce	Introduction
know	Knowledge	draw	Drawing
begin	Beginning	laugh	Laughter
marry	Marriage	describe	Description
tell	Tale	agree	Agreement
attend	Attention	connect	Connection
respond	Response	apply	Application
born	Birth	follow	Following/Follower
try	Trial	reduce	Reduction
wed	Wedding	live	Life
advise	Advice	humble	Humility
impress	Impression	write	Writing
believe	Belief	hate	Hatred
build	Building/Builder	open	Opening
mean	Meaning	serve	Service

(B) FORMATION OF NOUNS FROM ADJECTIVES

Adjectives	Nouns	Adjectives	Nouns
grand	grandeur	great	greatness
happy	happiness	safe	safety
poor	poverty	busy	business
certain	certainty	golden	gold
rich	richness	perfect	perfection
young	youth	firm	firmness
curious	curiosity	honest	honesty
generous	generosity	talkative	talk
proud	pride	deep	depth
free	freedom	moody	mood
tight	tension	new	newness

(C) FORMATION OF VERBS FROM ADJECTIVES

Adjectives	Verbs	Adjective	Verbs
stable	stabilise	able	enable
rich	enrich	poor	impoverish
frustrated	frustrate	new	renew
right	rectify	thick	thicken
proper	appropriate	mean	demean
sick	sicken	wide	widen
different	differentiate	familiar	familiarise
central	centralise	little	belittle
large	enlarge	beautiful	beautify

Model Examples

1. Write the correct suffix for the word 'beauty'.
   ① beautify   ② beautiful
   ③ beaut   ④ beautifully   ❷

2. Write the correct suffix for the word 'free'.
   ① freedomly   ② freed
   ③ freedom   ④ foredom   ❸

●══════ Examples for Practice ══════●

1. Which word is formed by adding the correct suffix for the word 'Canada'.
   ① Canadian   ② Canadel
   ③ Canade   ④ Candia

2. Which word is formed by adding the correct suffix for the word '-ant'.
   ① thermodant   ② psychoant
   ③ deodarant   ④ president

3. Which word is formed by adding the correct suffix for the word '-arian'.
   ① humanity   ② boundary
   ③ agrarian   ④ assistance

4. Which word is formed by adding the correct suffix for the word '-logy'.
   ① Sociology ② Sociologi ③ Social   ④ Satalogy

5. Which word is formed by adding the correct suffix for the word '-scope'.
   ① telescop   ② telepathy
   ③ microscope   ④ friendship

6. Which word is formed by adding the correct suffix for the word '-forfeit'.
   ① forfeiture ② fortified ③ forfeit   ④ forfeity

7. Which word is formed by adding the correct suffix for the word '-ship'.
   ① teleship   ② shipping
   ③ friendship   ④ microship

8. Which word is formed by adding the correct suffix for the word '-ness'.
   ① attendness   ② kindness
   ③ youngsterness   ④ none of these

9. Which word is formed by adding the correct suffix for the word '-ward'.
   ① longward   ② kinward
   ③ backward   ④ none of these

Answers

1.	❶	2.	❸	3.	❸	4.	❶
5.	❸	6.	❶	7.	❸	8.	❷
9.	❸						

❖ ❖ ❖

1.2   HOMOPHONES

✌ INTRODUCTION :

Two words are homophones if they are pronounced the same way but differ in meaning or spelling or both.

For example : Bare and bear

Some more examples of homophones.

1.	be – bee	2.	break – brake
3.	capitol – capital	4.	die – dye
5.	here – hear	6.	I – eye
7.	knot – not	8.	ate – eight
9.	deer – dear	10.	heal - heel
11.	made – maid	12.	no – know
13.	nose – knows	14.	knew – new
15.	mail – male	16.	some – sum
17.	stair – stare	18..	tale – tail
19.	weak – week	20.	write – right
21.	hole – whole	22.	higher – hire
23.	cereal – serial	24.	buy – by – bye
25.	berth – birth		

Examples of sentences :

1. I - eye :
- I went for an <u>eye</u> check-up on Saturday.

2. Knot – not :
- They have <u>not</u> tied the <u>knot</u> yet.

3. Made – maid :
- This pudding has been <u>made</u> by our <u>maid</u>.

4. Knew – new :
- He <u>knew</u> about the <u>new</u> key chain.

5.   Tale – tail :
* Grandma told us a <u>tale</u> about the <u>tail</u> of a monkey.

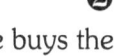
Model Examples

Q. I : Give the meaning of the underlined Homophone.
1. The person who delivered the mail was a young <u>male</u>.
    ① Mainly   ② Opposite of female
    ③ A messaging system   ④ None of these.   ❷
2. The butcher went to <u>meet</u> the farmer from whom he buys the meat.
    ① Come together
    ② Flesh of animals used as food
    ③ Partner   ④ None of these.   ❶

Examples for Practice

Q. I : Give the meaning of the underlined Homophone.
1. His <u>heel</u> will take time to heal.
    ① Cure   ② A body part
    ③ Height   ④ None of these.
2. Yesterday we <u>ate</u> dinner at eight.
    ① Time   ② To eat   ③ To night   ④ None of these
3. He stopped by the grocery shop <u>on</u> the way home to <u>buy</u> some butter.
    ① A preposition   ② To get
    ③ A farewell remark   ④ None of these.
4. The cyclist didn't use his brake in time, causing his bicycle to <u>break</u> when it hit the wall.
    ① Case to stop
    ② Become separated into pieces
    ③ Weak   ④ None of these
5. His most dear memory of their vacation was getting to see some <u>deer</u> in the forest.
    ① A beloved person   ② An animal
    ③ A challenge   ④ None of these.

6. The driver was <u>fined</u> for not being able to find his license.
   ① Penalty of money   ② Get something
   ③ Smooth   ④ None of these.

7. They were planning to pay a higher price to <u>hire</u> the car for a week.
   ① To rise   ② To rent
   ③ To buy   ④ None of these.

8. The <u>knot</u> was not tied well, so it came undone.
   ① Something twisted to form a loop
   ② Negative of a word   ③ A notation
   ④ None of these.

Answers

1.	❷	2.	❷	3.	❷	4.	❷	5.	❷
6.	❶	7.	❷	8.	❶				

❖ ❖ ❖

1.3   *PREFIX - SUFFIX*

✌ INTRODUCTION :

Under this topic we have to build a new word from the given word. Some times you add a suffix or prefixes to any word to make a word.

- **Words created by adding a Prefix :**

1.	appear	disappear	2.	legal	illegal
3.	material	immaterial	4.	national	international
5.	inform	misinform	6.	behave	misbehave
7.	profit	nonprofit	8.	done	outdone
9.	work	overwork	10.	sleep	oversleep

- **Word created by adding Suffix :**

1.	improve	improvement	2.	manage	management
3.	rain	rainfall	4.	happy	happiness
5.	real	realism	6.	confuse	confusion

| 7. leader | leadership | 8. appear | appearance |
| 9. photograph | photography | 10. modern | modernise |

Model Examples

1. Choose the correct prefix for the word 'metre'
   ① diameter   ② diagonal
   ③ kilometre   ④ metre   **❶,❸**

2. Choose the correct suffix for the word 'manage'
   ① manager   ② management
   ③ managed   ④ managtment   **❷**

Examples for Practice

1. Identify the correct suffix for the word 'explore'.
   ① exploit   ② exploration
   ③ expell   ④ expansion

2. Write the suffixed word for accident.
   ① accidents   ② accidental
   ③ accidentals   ④ All are correct

3. Write the correct prefix for the word 'condition'.
   ① conditions   ② conditionally
   ③ precondition   ④ excondition

4. Write the suffix for 'diction'.
   ① dictionally   ② dictation
   ③ dictionary   ④ dictuon

5. Write the correct prefix for the word 'father'.
   ① fathers   ② father's
   ③ forefather   ④ fatherly

6. Write the correct prefix for the world 'rent'.
   ① rental   ② rentals
   ③ non-rent   ④ quasi-rent

Answers

| 1. | ❷ | 2. | ❷ | 3. | ❸ | 4. | ❸ |
| 5. | ❸ | 6. | ❹ | | | | |

❖ ❖ ❖

1.4 ANTONYMS, SYNONYMS

ANTONYMS

✌ INTRODUCTION :

In Scholarship Examination you are given a word and are asked to find the word which is opposite in meaning. Opposite of a word is known as 'Antonym'. Two questions based on this topic will be asked. *Some words having an opposite meaning are given here under for learning.*

• Abiding × Changing	• Ability × Inability
• Absence × Presence	• Abundance × Scarcity
• Acceptance × Rejection	• Accuse × Defend
• Acquisition × Loss	• Active × Inactive, Passive
• Activity × Lethargy	• Admire × Condemn
• Adult × Child	• Adulterated × Pure
• Barbarous × Civilized	• Barren × Fruitful, Fertile
• Beauty × Ugliness	• Beginning × End
• Behave × Misbehave	• Beneficial × Injurious, Unfavourable,
• Blame × Praise	• Birth × Death
• Blunt × Sharp	• Blustering × Gentle
• Boisterous × Calm, Subdued	• Bold × Timid
• Bravery × Cowardice	• Bright × Dull, Dim
• Broad × Narrow	• Calm × Disturbed
• Capable × Incapable, Uneasy	• Careful × Careless, Negligent
• Cautious × Reckless	• Celebrated × Obscure
• Celestial × Terrestrial	• Certain × Probable
• Certainly × Uncertainly	• Check × Accelerate
• Cheerfulness × Dejection, Frustration	• Choose × Reject
• Clean × Dirty	• Clever × Dull

• Cloudy × Clear		• Collect × Distribute	
• Common × Uncommon, Rare		• Compassionate × Merciless	
• Complex × Simple		• Compliance × Refusal	
• Complicate × Simplify		• Composed (Calm) × Restless, Excited	
• Compress × Stretch		• Compulsory × Optional, Voluntary	
• Conceited × Modest		• Concrete × Abstract	
• Deep × Shallow		• Defective × Intact, Perfect	
• Delay × Hurry		• Depression × Elevation	
• Despair × Hope		• Destroy × Construct	
• Different × Same		• Difficult × Easy	
• Dilute × Concentrate		• Diminish × Increase	
• Direct × Indirect		• Disclose × Conceal	
• Disperse × Gather		• Distinguished × Common, Ordinary	
• Distress × Comfort		• Domestic × Wild, Foreign	
• Downfall × Rise		• Dream × Reality	
• Dwarf × Giant		• Earn × Spend	
• Eastern × Western		• Efficient × Inefficient	
• Either × Neither		• Elaborate × Simple	
• Elder × Younger		• Elegance × Ugliness	
• Elementary × Secondary		• Empty × Full	
• Encourage × Discourage		• Enemy × Friend	
• Enjoy × Suffer		• Enslave × Free, Emancipate	
• Enthusiasm × Apathy		• Entrance × Exit	
• Equal × Unequal		• Essential × Unnecessary	
• Evaporate × Consolidate		• Evening × Morning	
• Ever × Never		• Exceedingly × Slightly	
• Expert × Novice		• Exterior × Interior	
• Extravagant × Frugal, Economical		• Fact × Fiction	

•	Fade	× Bloom	•	Fair	× Unfair
•	Falsehood	× Truth	•	Far	× Near
•	Fat	× Thin	•	Fatigue	× Refresh
•	Fear	× Courage	•	Fearless	× Timid
•	Feeble	× Sturdy, Strong	•	Fine	× Coarse
•	Firm	× Loose	•	Flexible	× Rigid
•	Harmful	× Beneficial	•	Harmony	× Discord
•	Haste	× Delay	•	Healthy	× Diseased/sick
•	Heaven	× Hell	•	Heavy	× Light
•	Here	× There	•	Hero	× Villain
•	Honest	× Cunning	•	Honour	× Shame
•	Indulgent	× Harsh	•	Industrious	× Indolent, Lazy
•	Inferior	× Superior	•	Initial	× Final
•	Innocent	× Guilty	•	Insert	× Extract
•	Intentional	× Accidental	•	Known	× Unknown
•	Large	× Small	•	Late	× Early
•	Lawful	× Lawless	•	Legal	× Illegal
•	Lenient	× Strict	•	Less	× More
•	Liberate	× Confine	•	Light	× Heavy, Dark
•	Little	× Much	•	Logical	× Illogical
•	Moderate	× Excess	•	Modern	× Ancient
•	Moral	× Immoral	•	Motion	× Rest
•	Natural	× Artificial	•	Noise	× Silence
•	Numerous	× Few	•	Obey	× Disobey
•	Obligation	× Claim	•	Occasional	× Frequent
•	Offense	× Defence	•	Official	× Private, Unofficial
•	Omission	× Commission	•	Omit	× Include
•	Open	× Close	•	Open	× Secret
•	Optimistic	× Pessimistic	•	Or	× Nor
•	Oral	× Written	•	Order	× Disorder
•	Ordinary	× Rare	•	Partial	× Total, Full, Impartial

•	Patient	× Impatient	•	Peace	× Commotion, War
•	Permanent	× Temporary	•	Physical	× Spiritual
•	Pointless	× Significant, Pointed	•	Possible	× Impossible
•	Precious	× Worthless	•	Predecessor	× Successor
•	Prohibit	× Permit	•	Prompt	× Slow
•	Proper	× Improper	•	Proud	× Humble
•	Shame	× Pride	•	Sharp	× Blunt
•	Similar	× Dissimilar, Different	•	Slippery	× Firm, Solid
•	Smile	× Frown	•	Solemn	× Gay
•	Stern (Serious)	× Lenient	•	Strong	× Frail, Weak
•	Sturdy	× Delicate	•	Suitable	× Unsuitable
•	Swell	× Shrink	•	Tame	× Wild
•	Throne	× Dethrone	•	Tolerance	× Intolerance
•	Top	× Bottom	•	Torrent	× Trickle
•	Tragedy	× Comedy	•	Treacherous	× Loyal, faithful
•	Trifling	× Important	•	True	× False
•	Trust	× Distrust	•	Ugly	× Pretty, beautiful
•	Understand	× Misunderstand	•	Uniform	× Irregular
•	Unique	× Common, Ordinary	•	Universal	× Common, General
•	Unwieldy	× Handy	•	Utility	× Futility
•	Vacant	× Occupied	•	Valuable	× Cheap
•	Victory	× Defeat	•	Virtue	× Vice
•	Voluntary	× Involuntary	•	Wax	× Wane
•	Wrath	× Coolness, Calmness	•	Wreck	× Create

1. List of opposites formed by replacing 'ful' by 'less'.

1.	Careful	× Careless	3.	Painful	× Painless
2.	Shameful	× Shameless	4.	Fearful	× Fearless

2. List of opposites by joining the prefix 'un' to the word.

1.	Fold	× Unfold	16.	Happy	× Unhappy
2.	Safe	× Unsafe	17.	Comfortable	× Uncomfortable
3.	Willing	× Unwilling	18.	Favourable	× Unfavourable
4.	Expected	× Unexpected	19.	Even	× Uneven

5.	Employed	×	Unemployed	20.	Faithful	×	Unfaithful
6.	Equal	×	Unequal	21.	Sure	×	Unsure
7.	Interesting	×	Uninteresting	22.	Holy	×	Unholy
8.	Certain	×	Uncertain	23.	Impressive	×	Unimpressive
9.	Fair	×	Unfair	24.	Due	×	Undue
10.	Desirable	×	Undesirable	25.	Healthy	×	Unhealthy
11.	Grateful	×	Ungrateful	26.	Fit	×	Unfit

3. List of some opposites by joining the prefix 'dis' to the word.

1.	Honest	×	Dishonest	2.	Believe	×	Disbelieve
3.	Order	×	Disorder	4.	Advantage	×	Disadvantage
5.	Cover	×	Discover	6.	Pleased	×	Displeased

Model Examples

Q. Find the word opposite in meaning to the words given below and select the correct answer from the options.

1. Optimist :
   ① Optician ② Courageous ③ Hopeful ④ Pessimist ❹
2. Giant :
   ① Dwarf ② Big ③ Violent ④ Small ❶
3. Willing :
   ① Regular ② Lazy ③ Difficult ④ Reluctant ❹
4. Swell :
   ① Shrink ② Dwell ③ Subvert ④ Succeed ❶
5. Hot :
   ① Warm ② Cold ③ Cool ④ Frozen ❷

Examples for Practice

Q. Find the word opposite in meaning to the word given below and select the correct answer number.

1. Busy
   ① Long ② Empty ③ Bee ④ Idle
2. Arrogant
   ① Boastful ② Humble ③ Gentle ④ Wise

3. Before
   ① Down   ② Noon   ③ Night   ④ After

4. Adversity
   ① Prosperity   ② Advance   ③ University   ④ Town

5. Boastful
   ① Modest   ② Wonderful   ③ Boasting   ④ Offer

6. Alert
   ① Careful   ② Unaware   ③ Learned   ④ Learning

7. Absence
   ① Absent   ② Present   ③ Presence   ④ Presenty

8. Bright
   ① Dull   ② White   ③ Shining   ④ Hot

9. Barren
   ① Borrowed   ② Lended   ③ Greedy   ④ Fertile

10. Admire
    ① Punish   ② Abuse   ③ Scorn   ④ Tease

11. Assemble
    ① Disperse   ② Gather   ③ Talk   ④ Lecture

12. Ancient
    ① Old   ② Marvelous   ③ New   ④ Modern

13. Active
    ① False   ② Passive   ③ Slow   ④ Indifferent

14. Analysis
    ① Separation   ② Synthetic
    ③ Construct   ④ Synthesis

15. Proud
    ① Disappointed   ② Worried   ③ Humble   ④ Disgusted

16. Bankrupt
    ① Break   ② Robbery   ③ Solvent   ④ Tear

17. Ugly
    ① Good   ② Smart   ③ Beautiful   ④ Clever

18. Precious
    ① Jewel   ② Gold   ③ Worthless   ④ Metal

19. Natural
    ① Artist ② Artificial ③ Nature ④ Article
20. Famous
    ① Actress ② Unknown ③ Faulty ④ City

Answers

1.	❹	2.	❷	3.	❹	4.	❶	5.	❶
6.	❷	7.	❸	8.	❶	9.	❹	10.	❸
11.	❶	12.	❹	13.	❷	14.	❹	15.	❸
16.	❸	17.	❸	18.	❸	19.	❷	20.	❷

SYNONYMS

In this section, you are given a word and asked to choose the word which is similar in meaning, i.e. 'Synonyms'. Two questions will be asked based on this topic.

Given below are some words having a similar meaning.

Abandon	=	Leave
Abode	=	Residence, Dwelling
Accommodate	=	Adapt
Accuracy	=	Exact and without error
Accuse	=	Blame
Admirable	=	Praiseworthy
Affectionate	=	Loving
Affluent	=	Rich, Prosperous
Aid	=	Help
Ailment	=	Illness
Alarmed	=	Frightened
Ancient	=	From the very old times
Anger	=	Wrath
Confess	=	Admit, Agree
Convenient	=	Suitable, Fit, Proper
Courage	=	Bravery
Credence	=	Belief, Trust

Criticize	=	Find fault, Indicate fault
Curt	=	Rudely brief
Custom	=	Usage
Cyclone	=	Hurricane
Decease	=	Die
Deceive	=	Cheat
Decide	=	Determine, Settle, Resolve
Delicious	=	Highly pleasant
Devout	=	Having deep religious feeling, earnest
Difficult	=	Hard
Diligent	=	Hardworking, Industrious
Dread	=	Fear, Awe, Fright
Dreadful	=	Fearful, Frightful, Awful
Dunce	=	Dullard
Elude	=	Escape, Avoid
Enemy	=	Foe
Enterprise	=	Adventure, Effort
Surrender	=	Submit, Yield
Synonymous	=	Similar, Same, Like
Temporary	=	Momentary, Brief
Toleration	=	Tolerance, Temperance
Tranquil	=	Peaceful
Transparent	=	Clear
Treacherous	=	Unfaithful, Disloyal, Unreliable
Uncertain	=	Doubtful, Unsettled
Unity	=	Oneness
Universal	=	General
Unwilling	=	Indisposed, Loath
Vanquish	=	Defeat
Versatile	=	Changeable, Inconstant
Vigorous	=	Strong, Energetic

Volunteer	=	Offer
Wealth	=	Riches
Wisdom	=	Prudence
Withdraw	=	Retire, Retract
Wrath	=	Anger
Wretched	=	Miserable
Zenith	=	Climax, Top, Crown

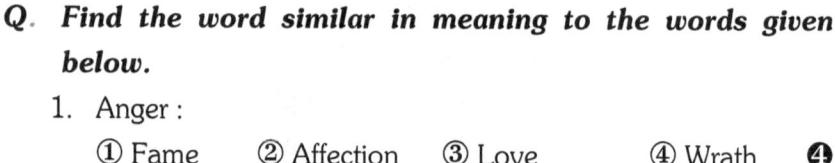

Model Examples

Q. Find the word similar in meaning to the words given below.

1. Anger :
   ① Fame ② Affection ③ Love ④ Wrath ❹

2. Aid :
   ① Avoid ② Medicine ③ Throw ④ Help ❹

3. Error :
   ① Correction ② Correct
   ③ Mistake ④ Incorrect ❸

4. Terror :
   ① Loud ② Tiger ③ Bright ④ Fear ❹

5. Unite :
   ① Join ② Margin ③ Neck ④ Difficult ❶

6. Admiration :
   ① See ② Help ③ Desire ④ Praise ❹

7. Crippled :
   ① Blind ② Deaf ③ Lame ④ Mad ❸

8. Disaster :
   ① Sickness ② Disturbance ③ Calamity ④ Variety ❸

9. Burden :
   ① Bad ② Heavy ③ Sudden ④ Abrupt ❷

Examples for Practice

Q. Find the word similar in meaning to the words given below.

1. Powerful :
   ① Quick   ② Show   ③ Strong   ④ Weak

2. Diligent :
   ① Dignified   ② Hard Working ③ Weak   ④ Idle

3. Rude :
   ① Dangerous   ② Rough
   ③ Impolite   ④ Naughty

4. Little :
   ① Big   ② Title   ③ Small   ④ Baby

5. Conceal :
   ① Vacant   ② Hide   ③ Open   ④ Strong

6. Withdraw :
   ① Purchase ② Roam   ③ Retire   ④ Brush

7. Slender :
   ① Wonder   ② Find   ③ Small   ④ Slim

8. Insolent :
   ① Loyal   ② Instance   ③ Silent   ④ Rude

9. Wealth :
   ① Strong   ② String   ③ Jewels   ④ Riches

10. Insane :
    ① Brilliant   ② Bright   ③ Mad   ④ Mine

11. Annual :
    ① Budget   ② Report   ③ Beast   ④ Yearly

12. Abode :
    ① Dwelling ② Room   ③ Den   ④ Body

13. Cheat :
    ① Talk   ② Short   ③ Deceive   ④ Heat

14. Costume :
    ① Clothes   ② Habit   ③ Roam   ④ Leave

15. Sparkle :
    ① Mixed   ② Spray   ③ Shine   ④ Glitter
16. Blank :
    ① Empty   ② Black   ③ Broad   ④ Long
17. Transparent :
    ① Clear   ② White   ③ Truck   ④ Travel
18. Meager :
    ① Scanty   ② Plenty   ③ Small   ④ Rude
19. Timid :
    ① Courageous   ② Cowardly
    ③ Shy   ④ Terrible
20. Thief :
    ① Robber   ② Cheat   ③ Pirate   ④ Chief
21. Whisper :
    ① Mumble   ② Murmur   ③ Matter   ④ Chatter
22. Gigantic :
    ① Minute   ② Telescope   ③ Huge   ④ Gingetic
23. Rebate :
    ① Discount   ② Interest   ③ Gift   ④ Commission
24. Spin :
    ① Walk   ② Turn   ③ Stable   ④ Round
25. Which out of the following has the same meaning as the given word ?
    STORY :
    ① tale   ② tail   ③ tell   ④ told

Answers

1.	❸	2.	❷	3.	❸	4.	❸	5.	❷
6.	❸	7.	❹	8.	❹	9.	❹	10.	❸
11.	❹	12.	❶	13.	❸	14.	❶	15.	❹
16.	❶	17.	❶	18.	❶	19.	❷	20.	❶
21.	❷	22.	❸	23.	❶	24.	❷	25.	❶

♣ ♣ ♣

1.5   *COMPOUND WORDS*

✌ INTRODUCTION :

Compound words are two little words which are put together to make one larger word. It's just more expressive and less wieldy than using the words separately. The really cool thing about compound words is that they're flexible and changeable.

• airport	• anymore	• anyplace
• anything	• anywhere	• armchair
• backache	• background	• backpack
• basketball	• bathrobe	• bathtub
• battleship	• bedroom	• beeline
• birthday	• blackboard	• bookcase
• booklet	• bookshelf	• bookworm
• briefcase	• buttercup	• butterfly
• campfire	• campground	• candlestick
• cardboard	• carpet	• chopstick
• classmate	• clockwise	• courtyard
• cowboy	• cupboard	• cutlet
• daredevil	• daydream	• dishwasher
• dishwater	• doorbell	• doormat
• doorstep	• doorstop	• doorway
• dragonfly	• droplet	• earache
• earrings	• evergreen	• everybody
• everyday	• eyeball	• fingerprint
• firearm	• firefighter	• fireplace
• fireproof	• fireworks	• fishtail
• football	• footprint	• forecast
• foresee	• forget	• forgive
• fourfold	• friendship	• gentleman

Model Examples

1. Identify the correct compound word from the options.
   ① Woodshed   ② horse-shoe
   ③ red black   ④ none of these   ❶
2. Which is the wrong compound word ?
   ① woodworm   ② watermelon
   ③ toothpaste   ④ charitable   ❹

Examples for Practice

1. Identify the option which is a compound word.
   ① waterproof   ② sea water
   ③ cannot   ④ keylock
2. ① footnote   ② overland
   ③ afterlife   ④ settlement
3. ① uptake   ② newsroom
   ③ performance   ④ cargo
4. ① woodwork   ② weekend
   ③ circulation   ④ supernatural
5. ① shipwreck   ② raining
   ③ seashore   ④ seafood
6. ① sky blue   ② overdue
   ③ playground   ④ playroom
7. ① headlight   ② showmall
   ③ highway   ④ heartbeat
8. ① daydream   ② cupboard
   ③ clockwise   ④ bud-flower

Answers

1.	❶	2.	❹	3.	❸	4.	❸
5.	❷	6.	❶	7.	❷	8.	❹

1.6   ONE WORD FOR MANY

✌ INTRODUCTION :

A single word can explain the meaning of a group of words. There are many words in English, which does the work of numerous words.

Given is the list of some selected words :

1.	Abdicate	:	Formally or by default to renounce power, office etc.
2.	Abolish	:	To do away with
3.	Accelerate	:	To make more rapid in speed
4.	Agenda	:	List of the headings of the business to be transacted at a meeting
5.	Aquatic	:	Growing, living in or near water
6.	Anticipate	:	To look forward to
7.	Annihilate	:	To destroyed completely
8.	Ancestral	:	Belonging to one's forefathers
9.	Anthropology	:	Study of mankind
10.	Archaeology	:	Study of ancient buildings
11.	Medieval	:	Belonging to the middle ages
12.	Linguist	:	Person skilled in many languages
13.	Illiterate	:	Unable to read and write
14.	Edible	:	Fit to be eaten for food
15.	Audible	:	Loud enough to be heard
16.	Autocracy	:	Government by one person
17.	Autobiography	:	Life history of a person written by himself
18.	Botany	:	The science of plant life
19.	Durable	:	Capable of lasting for long
20.	Encyclopaedia	:	Book containing information on all branches of knowledge.
21.	Anonymous	:	(A writing) Whose writer is not known.
22.	Entomology	:	Study of insects

23.	Enunciate	:	To pronounce words distinctly
24.	Pessimist	:	One who takes a dark view of things
25.	Potable	:	That which can be drunk
26.	Contagious	:	Spreading by contact
27.	Contemporary	:	Living in the same period
28.	Transparent	:	That which can be seen through
29.	Popular	:	Liked by people
30.	Epitaph	:	Words inscribed on a tomb
31.	Omnipotent	:	One who is all powerful
32.	Germicide	:	A medicine killing germs
33.	Wardrobe	:	A place where clothes are kept.
34.	Invisible	:	That which can not be seen
35.	Honorary	:	(A post) Which carries no salary
36.	Pseudonymn	:	Fictitious name used by an author
37.	Foreigner/alien	:	A person residing in a country of which he is not a citizen
38.	Extempore	:	A speech made without any preparation
39.	Gullible	:	One who can be easily duped
40.	Velocity	:	The speed at which an object is travelling.
41.	Veteran	:	One who has a long experience.
42.	Improbable	:	Not likely to happen
43.	Eligible	:	Fit to be chosen (selected or elected)
44.	Unanimously	:	With one voice and one mind
45.	Universal	:	Belonging to all parts of the world
46.	Vegetarian	:	One who eats only vegetable food
47.	Verbose	:	Full of words
48.	Equilibrium	:	In a state of perfect balance
49.	Excavate	:	To unearth by digging
50.	Optimist	:	One who looks to the bright side of things
51.	Elocution	:	Art of effective speaking or oral reading

52.	Nostalgia	:	Strong desire to return home (home sickness)
52.	Emphasize	:	To lay special stress on
53.	Eradicate	:	To root out
54.	Fastidious	:	Hard to please
55.	Fragile	:	Easily broken
56.	Incombustible	:	Incapable of being burnt
57.	Inevitable	:	That which cannot be avoided or prevented
58.	Invaluable	:	Above all price

Model Examples

Q. Give one word for the following :

1. That which lasts long.
   ① Endurable   ② Endowable
   ③ Durable   ④ Dribble   ❸

2. That cannot be read :
   ① Intelligible   ② Illegal
   ③ Incorrigible   ④ Illegible   ❹

Examples for Practice

Q. Give one word for the following :

1. One who loves his country.
   ① Patriarch   ② Expatriate   ③ Patron   ④ Patriot

2. Growing, living in or near water :
   ① Aquarium   ② Aquatic
   ③ Aqueous   ④ None of these

3. Fit to be eaten.
   ① Gullible   ② Audible   ③ Capable   ④ Edible

4. The science of plant life.
   ① Physics   ② Botany   ③ Zoology   ④ Chemistry

5. The life story of a man written by himself.
   ① Bibliography   ② Autograph
   ③ Biography   ④ Autobiography

6. With one voice
   ① Graciously   ② Unanimously
   ③ Nicely   ④ Incredible

7. A speech made without any preparation.
   ① Honorary   ② Extempore   ③ Speaker   ④ Debate

8. One who looks at the bright side of things.
   ① Optimist   ② Pessimist   ③ Snob   ④ Cyric

9. That which can be seen through :
   ① Translucent ② Transparent ③ Opaque   ④ Transient

10. The noise which can be heard properly
    ① Autocracy   ② Autograph
    ③ Audible   ④ Autobiography

11. Liked by people
    ① Pessimist   ② Popular   ③ Optimist   ④ Potable

12. Science of animal life.
    ① Zoology   ② Botany   ③ Physics   ④ Chemistry

13. To declare before hard :
    ① Predict   ② Foresee
    ③ Future   ④ None of these

14. Science of mind :
    ① Physics   ② Chemistry
    ③ Psychology   ④ None of these

15. That which can be drunk.
    ① Noteable   ② Potable   ③ Pure   ④ Edible

Answers

1.	④	2.	②	3.	④	4.	②	5.	④
6.	②	7.	②	8.	①	9.	②	10.	③
11.	②	12.	①	13.	①	14.	③	15.	②

1.7	*FIGURATIVE WORDS*

✌ *INTRODUCTION :*

What are Figuratives ? On many occassions, the words may not convey the literal meaning of them. They may convey the indirect meanings which may be just the opposite to their literal meanings. Such symbolical and metaphorical meanings are called Figuratives. They contain the figure of speech. Figurative language helps to make writing or speaking more interesting by making unusual comparisons. These comparisons create pictures in the mind of the reader or listener.

Simile : A simile is when you say that something - a person / place / animal or thing - is **like** something else. We usually do this in order to compare one object or idea with another or suggest that they are alike. A simile always uses the words - "like" or "as".

Example :

"*As fast as the wind*"	=	*with great speed.*
"*Like a mirror*"	=	*shine and glisten.*
"*Busy as a bee*"	=	*a person with no free time.*

Metaphor : A **metaphor** makes an even stronger image in the reader's mind. It states a fact or draws a verbal picture by the use of comparison. When you use a metaphor, you are saying that a person/place/animal or thing "is something else" and "not just like it".

Example : My teacher is an angel. (Kindness of teacher is compared to angel)

Hyperbole : A hyperbole is a statement so exaggerated that no one believes it to be true.

Example : Ravi drank a thousand gallons of water.

Personification : Personification gives animals or inanimate objects human-like characteristics.

Example :

- "The soft voice of the waterfall serenaded me to sleep." (In this sentence, the waterfall has been given the human characteristic of having a "soothing voice" that "serenades" or sings the writer to sleep)

Model Examples

Q. Choose the best ending for the similes below.

1. A soldier fights for our country. A soldier is as brave as a

    _____ .

    ① puppy   ② lion   ③ pigeon   ④ zebra   ❷

2. Reena eats very little, she eats like _____ .

    ① a bird   ② a pig   ③ an ox   ④ a dog   ❶

3. Our English teacher can see the smallest mistake. She has

    eyes like _____ .

    ① a hawk   ② a chicken   ③ a tiger   ④ a bat   ❶

Examples for Practice

Q. 1 to 3 : Choose the correct meanings for the following similes.

1. The simile - "selling like hotcakes" means what ?

    ① you are selling hot pancakes

    ② you are selling sweet pancakes

    ③ you are selling items very quickly

    ④ you are not selling many items.

2. The simile - "She was white as a ghost". means what ?

    ① she dies and became a ghost

    ② she dressed up like a ghost

    ③ she was happy and smiling

    ④ she was nervous and pale looking

3. The simile - "sings like a bird", means what ?

    ① sings softly   ② sings loudly

    ③ sings badly   ④ sings very well

Q. 4 to 6 : Underline the object or animal being personified in the following sentence.

4. I was so hungry that I even ate the plate. What type of figurative language is used in this sentence?

    ① personification   ② metaphor

    ③ hyperbole   ④ simile

5. My father was the sun and the moon to me. What type of figurative language is used in this sentence?
   ① metaphor   ② personification
   ③ hyperbole   ④ simile

6. The rain seemed like an old friend who had finally found us. What type of figurative language is used in this sentence?
   ① simile   ② personification
   ③ onomatopoeia   ④ metaphor

Q. Read the following sentences below and identify the type of figurative language used in each sentence. It could be a Simile/Metaphor/Hyperbole/Personification.

7. Her smile was as sweet as sunshine on a rainy day.
   ① simile   ② metaphor
   ③ hyperbole   ④ personification

8. The snowflakes danced around the green pine trees.
   ① simile   ② metaphor
   ③ hyperbole   ④ personification

9. My dictionary weighed a ton.
   ① simile   ② metaphor
   ③ hyperbole   ④ personification

10. This gift must have cost you more than a million dollars.
    ① simile   ② metaphor
    ③ hyperbole   ④ personification

11. The wooden table was as solid as a rock
    ① simile   ② metaphor
    ③ hyperbole   ④ personification

Answers

1.	❸	2.	❹	3.	❹	4.	❸	5.	❶
6.	❶	7.	❶	8.	❹	9.	❸	10.	❸
11.	❶								

❖ ❖ ❖

1.8   NAME OF YOUNG ONES, SOUNDS AND DWELLING PLACES

✌ INTRODUCTION :

Dwelling, Nursing and Storing : All living things live in some place or the other. The place where they live is called their homes or dwelling place. For example, Man lives in a house, lion lives in a den. In this chapter, we are going to study about the dwelling places or homes of all the living things. As young of human beings are called babies. In the same way babies of animals are also called by different name.

- **Places for Dwelling, Nursing, Storing etc.**

1.	Animals	:	Zoo
2.	Bees	:	Apiary
3.	Birds	:	Aviary
4.	Cars	:	Garage
5.	Aeroplane	:	Hanger
6.	Children	:	Nursery
7.	Clothes	:	Wardrobe
8.	Fish	:	Aquarium
9.	Weapon	:	Arsenal
10.	Wild animals	:	Menagerie, Zoo
11.	Historical relics	:	Museum
12.	Grapes	:	Vineyard
13.	Fruit trees	:	Orchard

- **Here some examples of homes of animals, birds and insects are given.**

1.	Man	:	House	19.	Mouse	:	Hole
2.	Cow	:	Byre, Pen	20.	Dog	:	Kennel
3.	Eagle	:	Aery, Erie, Evry, Aerie	21.	Fox	:	Earth

4.	Horse	:	Stable	22.	Fowl	:	Coop
5.	Prisoner	:	Cell	23.	Nun	:	Convent
6.	King	:	Palace	24.	Peasant	:	Cottage
7.	Squirrel	:	Drey	25.	Bird	:	Nest
8.	Spider	:	Web	26.	Otter	:	Holt
9.	Lunatic	:	Asylum	27.	Parson	:	Parsonage
10.	Soldier	:	Camp, Barracks	28.	Eskimo	:	Igloo
11.	Knight	:	Mansion	29.	Gypsy	:	Caravan
12.	Arab	:	Dower	30.	Tiger	:	Lair
13.	Lion	:	Den	31.	Sheep	:	Pen, hold
14.	Tame rabbit	:	Hutch	32.	Wild rabbit	:	Burrow
15.	Pig	:	Sty	33.	Pigeon	:	Dovecote
16.	Hare	:	Farm	34.	Snail	:	Shell
17.	Wasp	:	Nest	35.	Nobleman	:	Castle
18.	Red Indian	:	Wigwam				

- *Young Ones of Animals :*

For example : A baby of man is called child. A baby of lion is called cub, in the same way a baby of cat is called kitten.

- *Words denoting young ones of Animals are given below.*

1.	Whale	:	Calf	2.	Dog	.	Puppy, Pup
3.	Tiger	:	Cub	4.	Duck	:	Duckling
5.	Horse	:	Colt, Foal	6.	Cow	:	Calf
7.	Cat	:	Kitten	8.	Deer	:	Fawn
9.	Eagle	:	Eaglet	10.	Fox	:	Cub
11.	Frog	:	Tadpole	12.	Goat	:	Kid
13.	Buffalo	:	Calf	14.	Goose	:	Gosling
15.	Hare	:	Leveret	16.	Hen	:	Chick
17.	Owl	:	Owlet	18.	Pig	:	Pigling, Piglet
19.	Sheep	:	Lamb	20.	Wolf	:	Cub
21.	Swan	:	Cygnet	22.	Elephant	:	Calf, Baby
23.	Bear	:	Cub	24.	Man	:	Child
25.	Apes	:	Gibber				

* *Different animals make different sounds. The way we talk or speak, the animals or birds also make different kind of sounds :*

1.	Man	:	Speaks
2.	Cat	:	Mews
3.	Dog	:	Barks
4.	Sparrow	:	Chirps
5.	Lion	:	Roars
6.	Pig	:	Grunts
7.	Duck	:	Quacks
8.	Bear	:	Growls
9.	Monkey	:	Chatters
10.	Elephant	:	Trumpets
11.	Cow	:	Moos
12.	Parrot	:	Speaks
13.	Horse	:	Neighs
14.	Frog	:	Croaks
15.	Sheep	:	Bleats
16.	Goat	:	Bleats
17.	Owl	:	Hoots
18.	Hen	:	Clucks
19.	Mouse	:	Squeaks/Squeals
20.	Bees	:	Hum/Buzz
21.	Snake	:	Hisses
26.	Birds	:	Sing
27.	Blackbird	:	Whistles
28.	Bulls	:	Bellow
29.	Calves	:	Bleat
30.	Deer	:	Bells
31.	Dolphin	:	Chicks
32.	Doves	:	Coo, Moan
33.	Eagle	:	Screams
34.	Falcon	:	Chant
35.	Flies	:	Buzz
36.	Fox	:	Barks, Yelps

Model Examples

Q. Choose the correct word for the dwelling of animals or birds or insects from the choices given below.

1. Spider :
   ① Lair   ② Den   ③ Web   ④ Shell   ❸

2. Pigeon :
   ① Hole   ② Cage   ③ Dovecote   ④ Den   ❸

3. Nun :
   ① Hold   ② Igloo   ③ Cottage   ④ Convent   ❹

4. Tiger :
   ① Lair   ② Cage   ③ Shell   ④ Stable   ❶

5. Soldier :
   ① Lair   ② Camp   ③ Hold   ④ Drey   ❷

6. Lunatic :
   ① Form   ② Asylum   ③ Castle   ④ Hold   ❷

7. Hare :
   ① Drey   ② Farm   ③ Den   ④ Holt   ❷

8. Monk :
   ① Monastery   ② House
   ③ Convent   ④ Hutch   ❶

9. Savage :
   ① Whore   ② Asylum   ③ Hut   ④ Cabin   ❸

Examples for Practice

Q. Choose the correct word for the dwelling of animals or birds or insects from the choices given below.

1. Owl :
   ① Barracks ② Hold   ③ Barn   ④ Burrow

2. Peasant :
   ① Cottage   ② Parsonage ③ Castle   ④ Monastery

3. Fowl :
   ① Byre   ② Hive   ③ Form   ④ Coop

4. Sheep :
   ① Kennel   ② Nest   ③ Pen   ④ Eyrie
5. Mouse :
   ① Asylum   ② Hole   ③ Hut   ④ Caravan
6. Gypsy :
   ① Drey   ② Convent   ③ Caravan   ④ Palace
7. Parson :
   ① Parsonage   ② Pen
   ③ Form   ④ Tree
8. Noble :
   ① Pen   ② Castle   ③ Camp   ④ Hut
9. Arab :
   ① Pen   ② Dower   ③ Ring   ④ Track
10. Otter :
   ① Fold   ② Holt   ③ Hold   ④ House
11. Bird :
   ① House   ② Nest   ③ Drey   ④ Form
12. Eagle :
   ① Sty   ② Eyrie   ③ Nest   ④ Earth
13. Wild rabbit :
   ① Sty   ② Burrow   ③ Hut   ④ Foun
14. Tame rabbit :
   ① Cottage   ② Hutch   ③ Igloo   ④ Cabin
15. Knight :
   ① Hutch   ② Convent   ③ Mansion   ④ Igloo

Q. Choose the name of the young one of the given animals.

16. Whale :
   ① Fawn   ② Kid   ③ Cygnet   ④ Calf
17. Cat :
   ① Chicken   ② Pup   ③ Kitten   ④ Cub
18. Fox :
   ① Cub   ② Whelp   ③ Puppy   ④ Fawn
19. Tiger :
   ① Tigress   ② Cub   ③ Whelp   ④ Pup

20. Owl :
   ① Owlet   ② Kitten   ③ Owlish   ④ Cygnet

21. Bear :
   ① Calf   ② Colt   ③ Cub   ④ Kid

22. Dog :
   ① Kitten   ② Kid   ③ Pup   ④ Calf

23. Buffalo :
   ① Fawn   ② Calf   ③ Child   ④ Kid

24. Man :
   ① Cub   ② Duckling   ③ Kid   ④ Child

25. Deer :
   ① Fawn   ② Pup   ③ Foal   ④ Cub

Q. Choose the correct sound of animals and birds from the given choices below :

26. Flies :
   ① Hum   ② Chant   ③ Buzz   ④ Click

27. Hyenas :
   ① Bray   ② Laugh   ③ Bark   ④ Chatter

28. Doves :
   ① Chirp   ② Coo   ③ Chuck   ④ Quacks

29. Falcons :
   ① Chant   ② Scream   ③ Moan   ④ Yelp

30. Magpies :
   ① Moan   ② Yelp   ③ Chatter   ④ Speak

31. Tiger :
   ① Growl   ② Drone   ③ Bellow   ④ Scream

32. Foxes :
   ① Growl   ② Bray   ③ Snort   ④ Bark

33. Apes :
   ① Chatter   ② Laugh   ③ Gibber   ④ Speak

34. Owl :
    ① Coo   ② Chant   ③ Hoots   ④ Buzz
35. Frog :
    ① Snort   ② Croak   ③ caws   ④ Crows
36. Who lives in an ant-hill ?
    ① Ant   ② Lizard   ③ Honey-bee ④ Rat

Answers

1.	❸	2.	❶	3.	❹	4.	❸	5.	❷
6.	❸	7.	❶	8.	❷	9.	❷	10.	❷
11.	❷	12.	❷	13.	❷	14.	❷	15.	❸
16.	❹	17.	❸	18.	❶	19.	❷	20.	❶
21.	❸	22.	❸	23.	❷	24.	❸,❹	25.	❶
26.	❸	27.	❷	28.	❷	29.	❶	30.	❸
31.	❶	32.	❹	33.	❸	34.	❸	35.	❷
36.	❶								

❖ ❖ ❖

1.9   PROFESSIONS & OCCUPATIONS

✌ INTRODUCTION :

Profession : It is an activity which requires specialized training, knowledge, qualification and skills.

Occupation : It is an activity undertaken by a person to earn livelihood.

- actor
- artisan
- auctioneer
- blacksmith
- carpenter
- chemist
- compositor
- agent
- artist
- banker
- bookbinder
- chauffeur
- compounder
- contractor

- dentist
- engineer
- farmer
- hairdresser
- inspector
- journalist
- milkmaid
- nurse
- painter
- physician
- porter
- publisher
- sanitary inspector
- spectator
- tailor
- tourist
- watchman
- druggist
- examiner
- greengrocer
- helper
- instructor
- merchant
- musician
- operator
- photographer
- plumber
- postman
- reporter
- shoemaker
- surgeon
- teacher
- waiter
- writer

Model Examples

1. Identify the correct professions from Public Services.
   ① Accountant   ② Architect
   ③ Health Inspector   ④ Physician   ❸
2. Choose the correct option for Medical Services.
   ① Lawyers   ② Radiographers
   ③ Linguistics   ④ Economist   ❷

Examples for Practice

1. Select the correct profession from public services.
   ① Accountants   ② Engineers
   ③ Translators   ④ Police Officer
2. Select the correct industrialist profession.
   ① Surveyors   ② Clergy
   ③ Nurses   ④ Psychologist

3. Select the correct academic profession from the options given below :
   ① Professors   ② Photographer
   ③ Dieticians   ④ Pharmacist

4. Select the correct medical profession from the options given below :
   ① Veterinarians   ② Clergy
   ③ Engineer   ④ Health Inspector

5. Select the correct industrialist profession from the options given below :
   ① Lawyers   ② Social workers
   ③ Health Inspector   ④ Accountant

6. Select the correct academic profession from the options given below :
   ① Psychologist   ② Audiologist
   ③ Teacher   ④ Clergy

Answers

1.	❹	2.	❶	3.	❶	4.	❶❹
5.	❹	6.	❸				

❖ ❖ ❖

1.10   JUMBLED SPELLINGS

✌ INTRODUCTION :

In jumbled spellings/words alphabets are placed haphazardly. You are supposed to make a meaningful word by rearranging the alphabets.

For example : 'RWANES' is a particular group of alphabets but has got no meaning. Now, after rearranging we get 'ANSWER' as the correct word.

Rearrange the following words to make meaningful words :

1.	SARGP	→	GRASP
2.	HEWIL	→	WHILE

3.	GTNHI	→	NIGHT
4.	KOCRF	→	FROCK
5.	RREDAE	→	READER
6.	OOWTRROM	→	TOMORROW
7.	TEHORM	→	MOTHER
8.	CCRRENYU	→	CURRENCY
9.	RRYAILB	→	LIBRARY
10.	FMOINUR	→	UNIFORM
11.	IRUCSUO	→	CURIOUS
12.	CREOF	→	FORCE
13.	NCHLRDIE	→	CHILDREN
14.	SSRAILNEECY	→	NECESSARILY
15.	AGPSSAE	→	PASSAGE
16.	NEIESCC	→	SCIENCE
17.	ENNMAR	→	MANNER
18.	HWTSIC	→	SWITCH
19.	UNLEDDSY	→	SUDDENLY
20.	ITCREPU	→	PICTURE
21.	TLGHAOUH	→	ALITHOUGH
22.	DMEOSL	→	SELDOM
23.	LEERFQTYUN	→	FREQUENTLY
24.	TETAAUNRRS	→	RESTAURANT
25.	TTMNIAROP	→	IMPORTANT
26.	EEERSDCA	→	DECREASE
27.	YPALP	→	APPLY
28.	EEASLPRU	→	PLEASURE
29.	NEBLAE	→	ENABLE
30.	TPSPURO	→	SUPPORT

Model Examples

Q. Arrange the jumbled letters to make meaningful words.

1. L A S P E E
   ① PEEASL   ② PLEASE   ③ PLAESE   ④ NONE
2. POSEOP
   ① OPOPSE   ② PPOOSE   ③ OPPOSE   ④ OPOSEP

3. VTNGIALI
   ① VIGIALANI   ② VIGILTANL
   ③ VIGILANT   ④ None of these   ❸

Examples for Practice

Q. *Choose the correct meaningful word given below the jumbled alphabets.*

1. N M A A I L
   ① M A A L I N   ② A N I M A L
   ③ L I N A M A A   ④ None of these.

2. L D E T E A C I L
   ① DELICATE   ② DILECATE
   ③ LIBELTCA   ④ None of these

3. T C D U N O C
   ① CONDOCT ② DONCUCT ③ CUONDCT ④ CONDUCT

4. G H I T T
   ① T I G H T ② T T I G H ③ G H T T I ④ H I G H T T

5. E A P C E
   ① PEEAC   ② CAEPE   ③ PEACE   ④ CEAPE

6. WOPERD
   ① POWER   ② POWDER
   ③ COWARD   ④ None of these

7. TOQUE
   ① QOUTE   ② QUOTE   ③ TEOQU   ④ QEUTO

8. T U I E Q
   ① QUIET   ② QUIETE   ③ QUEIT   ④ QIUET

9. TABELT
   ① BETTLA   ② ATTLEB   ③ BATTLE   ④ EABTTL

10. UFRIELA
   ① FEALIUR   ② FLUREAI   ③ FAILURE   ④ FEILURA

Answers

1.	❷	2.	❶	3.	❹	4.	❶	5.	❸
6.	❷	7.	❷	8.	❶	9.	❸	10.	❸

✣ ✣ ✣

1.11   WORD PUZZLES

✌ INTRODUCTION :

A puzzle or a crossword will be given to test your vocabulary. You will have to find out the answer. One question will be asked based on this topic which will carry two marks.

Model Examples

Q. Find the correct alternative given below :

1. I live in water, I die without water.
   ① Lion   ② Fish   ③ Elephant   ④ Tortoise ❷

2. Find the suitable word for the animal from the letter given below.

   Lion :   S T R E O
              L D E N F
              G A B C K
              L O D E F
   ① Jungle   ② Web   ③ Den   ④ Silk   ❸

Examples for Practice

Q. Find the correct alternative given below :

1. Who am I ? I give you eggs.
   ① Hen   ② Dog   ③ Cow   ④ Rabbit

2. I am a farmer's friend.
   ① Bullock   ② Cow   ③ Earthworm   ④ Horse

3. I am ship of the desert.
   ① Bullock   ② Camel   ③ Horse   ④ Donkey

4. I am useful when it rains or when it is raining.
   ① Coat   ② Shoes   ③ Umbrella   ④ Frock

5. I give you wool for sweaters.
    ① Goat   ② Sweater   ③ Sheep   ④ Ostrich

6. I bring letters for you.
    ① Doctor   ② Nurse   ③ Postman   ④ Engineer

Q. *Find the suitable word for each of the following given below :*

7. Teacher :   A D E F C
                G B O O K
                R A D NC
                A T K L D
    ① School   ② Class   ③ Book   ④ Teach

8. School :   K N D K L
                B E L L K
                A N A F C
                N K T A P
    ① Teacher   ② Bell   ③ Class   ④ Peon

9. Cow :   H L D A P
                N M I L K
                A P A C K
                R A P Q S
    ① Milk   ② Fan   ③ Farm   ④ Animal

10. Father :   F A N I K
                N S I L K
                M O N D C
                R N K L K
    ① Fan   ② Mother   ③ Son   ④ Silk

11.

✪	R	E	A	D
R				
E				
A				
M				

    ① D   ② C   ③ K   ④ B

Q. Find the suitable letter in place of ✪ to form correct words.

12.

✪	A	L	K
O			
O			
D			

① F   ② W   ③ M   ④ P

Answers

1.	❶	2.	❸	3.	❷	4.	❸	5.	❸
6.	❸	7.	❸	8.	❷	9.	❶	10.	❸
11.	❶	12.	❷						

♣ ♣ ♣

1.12   ARRANGE IN ALPHABETICAL ORDER

🖎 INTRODUCTION :

Letters of the alphabets :

A B C D E F G H I J K L M N O P Q R S T U V W X Y Z

This exercise focuses on your knowledge of dictionary. You will be expected to arrange the given group of words in alphabetical order i.e. as they appear in a dictionary.

Model Examples

Q I. Read the given words and the correct alternative answer, which shows its alphabetical arrangement.

1. (a) Goat   (b) Got   (c) Goal   (d) Golf
   ① b, c, d, a   ② c, a, d, b
   ③ a, d, b, c   ④ b, a, d, c   ❷

2. (a) Fan   (b) Fun   (c) Fume   (d) Fair
    ① b, c, d, a   ② c, d, a, b
    ③ d, a, c, b   ④ d, c, b, a   ❸
3. (a) Coal   (b) Coat (c) Comb   (d) Coast
    ① a, d, b, c ② b, d, c, a ③ c, d, b, a ④ a, b, d, c ❶

II. Arrange the words alphabetically and identify the word as instructed :

4. The 2nd word : Run, Rough, Ruin, Roll
    ① Run   ② Rough   ③ Ruin   ④ Roll   ❷
5. The 4th word : Grow, Grave, Grieve, Great
    ① Grow   ② Grave   ③ Grieve   ④ Great   ❸

Examples for Practice

Q. Which is the correct alphabetical order of the following :

1. (a) Ash   (b) Ashare   (c) Assure   (d) Assume
    ① a, b, d, c ② b, c, d, a ③ c, d, b, a ④ a, d, c, b
2. (a) Cry   (b) Crocodile (c) Cucumber(d) Carrot
    ① d, b, a, c ② c, d, b, a ③ d, c, b, a ④ a, b, c, d
3. (a) Brain   (b) Bear   (c) Bottle   (d) Bird
    ① a, b, c, d ② b, c, d, a ③ b, d, c, a ④ c, a, d, b
4. (a) Jaipur   (b) Delhi   (c) Srinagar (d) Kolkatta
    ① c, a, b, d ② b, a, d, c ③ a, b, c, d ④ d, c, b, a
5. (a) Mold   (b) Toad   (c) Tie   (d) Time
    ① c, d, b, a ② b, c, d, a ③ b, d, c, a ④ a, b, c, d

II. Arrange the words alphabetically and identify the word as instructed :

6. The 3rd word : Smile, While, Coil, Spoil
    ① Smile   ② While   ③ Coil   ④ Soil
7. The 2nd word : Call, Fall, Tall, Ball
    ① Call   ② Fall   ③ Tall   ④ Ball

8. The 4ᵗʰ word : Game, Fame, Gamble, Fumble
   ① Game   ② Fame   ③ Gamble   ④ Fumble
9. The 3ʳᵈ word : North, Nest, Neighbour, Number
   ① North   ② Nest   ③ Neighbour ④ Number
10. The 3ʳᵈ word : Shore, Sore, Sir, Sure
   ① Shore   ② Sere   ③ Sir   ④ Sure

Answers

Q.	Ans.	Q.	Ans.	Q.	Ans.	Q.	Ans.
1.	❶	2.	❶	3.	❸	4.	❷
5.	❶	6.	❹	7.	❶	8.	❶
9.	❶	10.	❷					

❖ ❖ ❖

1.13 WORDS DENOTING DIFFERENT SOUNDS

✌ INTRODUCTION :

- Beat of a drum
- Blaring of bands, trumpets
- Blowing of a bugle
- Booming of a gun
- Buzz of a telephone
- Call of a bugle
- Chattering of teeth
- Clanging of chains, hammers, arms
- Clatter of hoofs, plates
- Clinking of glasses, metal, keys
- Crackling of fire
- Crack of a whip
- Creaking of doors or shoes
- Hissing of steam
- Howling of wind
- Jingling of coins
- Lapping of water
- Patter of rain
- Pealing or ringing of bells
- Rattling of windows
- Roaring of guns
- Rustle of silk, leaves

- Shriek of a whistle
- Sizzling of sausages
- Tick of a clock
- Twang of a bow

- Thundering or rumbling of clouds
- Slam of a door
- Toot of a horn
- Whistling, roaring or howling of wind

Model Examples

1. Identify the sound made by 'leaves'.
   ① patterns ② jingle ③ rumble ④ rustle ❹
2. Identify the sound made by 'steam'.
   ① hawling ② jingling ③ hissing ④ lapping ❸

Examples for Practice

1. Identify the sound made by 'trains'.
   ① rumble ② blare ③ rattle ④ creak
2. Identify the sound made by 'doors'.
   ① rumble ② creak ③ bloom ④ tinkle
3. Identify the sound made by 'glasses'.
   ① geak ② clicks ③ clank ④ tinkle
4. Identify the sound made by 'aeroplane'.
   ① chugs ② zooms ③ chime ④ patterns
5. Identify the sound made by 'fireworks'.
   ① ticks ② tinkle ③ crackle ④ rattle
6. Identify the sound made by 'canons'.
   ① booms ② patters ③ bloom ④ creak
7. Identify the sound made by 'whistle'.
   ① shrick ② rustle ③ ratthly ④ twang
8. Identify the sound made by 'water'
   ① jingling ② bloom ③ chive ④ lapping

Answers

1.	❶	2.	❷	3.	❹	4.	❷
5.	❸	6.	❶	7.	❶	8.	❹

✤ ✤ ✤

1.14   *SINGULAR AND PLURALS*

✌ *INTRODUCTION :*

Number is a distinction between nouns to express one thing or more than one thing. There are two types of number.

(i) Singular Number (ii) Plural Number

The Noun that denotes only one person or a thing is said to be in the Singular number. For example : hat, class, mango etc. The noun that denotes more than one person for eg. hats, classes, mangoes etc. is said to be plural. The plural forms are generally formed by adding 's' or 'es' to common nouns.

RULES FOR FORMING THE PLURAL OF NOUN

(1) *Some examples of Plural by adding 's' to the singular*

	Singular	*Plural*		*Singular*	*Plural*
•	Apple	Apples	•	Arm	Arms
•	Book	Books	•	Bee	Bees
•	Cat	Cats	•	Chair	Chairs
•	Dog	Dogs	•	Egg	Eggs
•	Elephant	Elephants	•	Girl	Girls
•	Goat	Goats	•	Horse	Horses
•	Minute	Minutes	•	Monarch	Monarchs
•	Pen	Pens	•	Pencil	Pencils
•	House	Houses	•	Pupil	Pupils
•	Rose	Roses	•	Room	Rooms

(2) *Nouns ending with a consonant 'O' form their Plural by adding 'es' to the singular.*

•	Buffalo	Buffaloes	•	Cargo	Cargoes
•	Echo	Echoes	•	Hero	Heroes
•	Mango	Mangoes	•	Motto	Mottoes
•	Mosquito	Mosquitoes	•	Negro	Negroes

Exceptions				
•	Bamboo	Bamboos	• Ratio	Ratios
•	Photo	Photos	• Cuckoo	Cuckoos
•	Piano	Pianos	• Stereo	Stereos

(3) *Nouns ending with 'f' or 'fe' form their plurals by changing into 'ves'.*

•	Calf	Calves	• Half	Halves
•	Myself	Ourselves	• Knife	Knives
•	Life	Lives	• Sheaf	Sheaves

Exceptions

•	Chief	Chiefs	• Proof	Proofs
•	Clift	Clifts	• Reef	Reefs
•	Dwarf	Dwarfs	• Roof	Roofs
•	Grief	Grief's	• Safe	Saves
•	Gulf	Gulfs	• Root	Roots

(4) *There are few nouns which form their plurals by changing the inside vowel.*

•	Dormouse	Dormice	• Foot	Feet
•	Man	Men	• Mouse	Mice

(5) *By Changing 'Y' into 'i' and adding 'es'*

•	Army	Armies	• Baby	Babies
•	Body	Bodies	• City	Cities
•	Cry	Cries	• Copy	Copies
•	Country	Countries	• Duty	Duties
•	Fairy	Fairies	• Fly	Flies
•	Family	Families	• Gallery	Galleries
•	Library	Libraries	• Lady	Ladies
•	Pony	Ponies	• Remedy	Remedies
•	Story	Stories	• Study	Studies

(6) *There are some nouns which remain unchanged for the plural and for the singular forms.*

•	Deer Deer	•	Sheep Sheep
•	Fish Fish	•	Swine Swine/Swines
•	Heathen Heathen	•	Trout Trout/trouts

(7) *A Compound noun generally turns into plural by adding 's' to the principal word.*

•	Son-in-law	Sons-in-law
•	Father-in-law	Fathers–in-law
•	Daughter-in-law	Daughters-in-law
•	Step daughter	Step daughters
•	Sister-in-law	Sisters-in-law

(8) *Some other words :*

•	Analysis	Analyses
•	Axis	Axes

(9) *By adding 's' to the singular when a noun ending in 'v' has a vowel before it :*

•	Bay	Bays
•	Boy	Boys
•	Chimney	Chimneys
•	Donkey	Donkeys
•	Essay	Essays
•	Journey	Journeys

Model Examples

Choose the correct plurals/singular of the word given :

1. Hobby
   ① Hobbys   ② Hobbyes   ③ Hobbies   ④ Hobby   ❸

2. Horse
   ① Horses   ② Horsess   ③ Horse   ④ Horesh   ❶

3. Reply
   ① Replys   ② Replies   ③ Repply   ④ Replyes   ❷

4. Mango
   ① Mangoo ② Manngo ③ Manggo ④ Mangoes ❹
5. Hero
   ① Heroes ② Herose ③ Heeros ④ Herroes ❶
6. Key
   ① Keeys ② Keys ③ Key ④ Keyess ❷

Examples for Practice

Choose the correct plural/singular of the word given :

1. tooth
   ① Tooth ② Tooths ③ Teeth ④ Teethes
2. Calf
   ① calveses ② calves ③ calfes ④ calfs
3. Roof
   ① Roves ② Roof ③ Roofs ④ Rofes
4. Cry
   ① cry ② Cryes ③ cries ④ cryies
5. Duty
   ① Dutyes ② Dutys ③ Duties ④ Dutyies
6. Body
   ① bodies ② Bodys ③ Bodyes ④ Bodyeses
7. Address
   ① Addresses ② Adressys ③ Adresseys ④ Addressess
8. Dish
   ① Dishes ② Dishe ③ Dishys ④ Dishs
9. Army
   ① Armys ② Armyses ③ Armises ④ Armies
10. Bureau
    ① Bureauses ② Bureaux
    ③ Bureaus ④ Bureauses
11. Dalum
    ① Data ② Datia ③ Datums ④ Datim
12. Fungus
    ① Funguses ② Fungie ③ Fungi ④ Fungii

13. Louse
    ① Louses   ② Lousen   ③ Lice   ④ Lices
14. Mouse
    ① Mice   ② Mouses   ③ Musen   ④ Miceses
15. Hair
    ① Hair   ② Hairs   ③ Haries   ④ Hairees
16. Goose
    ① Giese   ② Geese   ③ Gooses   ④ Goose
17. Wife
    ① Wives   ② Wiefs   ③ Wifs   ④ Wifes
18. Deer
    ① Deers   ② Deeres   ③ Deerese   ④ Deer
19. Chief
    ① Chiefs   ② Chieves   ③ Chiefes   ④ Chief
20. Ox
    ① oxes   ② Oxen   ③ Ox   ④ Oxsses
21. Terminus
    ① Terminia   ② Termini   ③ Terminuss   ④ Terminusis
22. Proof
    ① Proofs   ② Proofs   ③ Proofies   ④ Proofeys
23. Bench
    ① Benchs   ② Benches
    ③ Benchieves   ④ Benchves

Answers

Q.	Ans.	Q.	Ans.	Q.	Ans.	Q.	Ans.
1.	❸	2.	❷	3.	❸	4.	❸
5.	❸	6.	❶	7.	❶	8.	❶
9.	❹	10.	❷	11.	❶	12.	❸
13.	❸	14.	❶	15.	❶	16.	❷
17.	❶	18.	❹	19.	❶	20.	❷
21.	❶	22.	❶	23.	❷		

1.15	PREPARE – SHORT WORDS FROM LONG WORDS

✌ INTRODUCTION :

In each of the questions, some letters from the key-word given in CAPITAL have been used for terming other words. Select the correct options that have letters contained in the key word.

Model Examples

1. TRANSPARENT
   (a) Parent   (b) Spare   (c) Perspire   (d) Transfer
   ① a and b   ② c and d   ③ a and c   ④ b and d ❶

2. FILTERED
   (a) Retire   (b) Diet   (c) Fertile   (d) Fitter
   ① a, b   ② c, d,   ③ b, c   ④ a, d   ❸

Examples for Practice

Q. Find the short words formed out of the long words :

1. DISCRIPTION
   (a) Distil   (b) Ripe   (c) Triple   (d) Script
   ① a, b,   ② b, d   ③ b, c   ④ c, d

2. APPEARANCE
   (a) Reap   (b) Pour   (c) Capper   (d) Reach
   ① a, b   ② b, c   ③ a, c   ④ b, d

3. INTERNATIONAL
   (a) Attire   (b) Alter   (c) Retire   (d) Attrition
   ① a, b   ② b, c,   ③ c, d   ④ b, d

4. BACKWARDS
   (a) Ward   (b) Barren   (c) Dark   (d) Sword
   ① a, b   ② a, c   ③ b, c   ④ c, d

5. AUTOBIOGRAPHICS

   (a) Graphics (b) Broke   (c) Grapes   (d) Graphite

   ① c, d   ② c, b   ③ b, c   ④ a, b

Answers

Q.	Ans.	Q.	Ans.	Q.	Ans.	Q.	Ans.
1.	❷	2.	❸	3.	❶	4.	❷
5.	❶						

❖ ❖ ❖

1.16   *CORRECTLY SPELT WORDS*

✌ INTRODUCTION :

For writing the correct spelling we should know English language. Correct spelling helps the students to get more marks in the examinations.

Following are the examples of correctly spelt words. Students should learn these spellings by heart.

abandon	acceptance
accordance	advertisement
acquiesce	administrator
ambassador	ambiguous
amiable	approximate
architecture	auspicious
autobiography	average
beneficent	bequeath
bereave	besiege
comparable	competition
comprehension	condolence
controversial	cooperation
correspondence	councillor
disguise	drudgery

disciplinarian	dispensary
earnest	eccentricity
exhilarate	explanation
forebode	forecast
foretell	foreword
ferocious	freight
funereal	fruition
guardian	guidance
gymnasium	gypsum
heroine	heterogeneous
hindrance	honorary
honour	hundred
hurricane	hysterical
industrious	interesting
instruction	indefatigable
jealous	jurisdiction
judgement	justice
knowledge	kitchen
liberate	library
litigious	livelihood
luxurious	lottery
maintenance	manoeuvre
manufacture	marvelous
negligence	nineteen
negligible	nephew
nobility	nourish
nowadays	nymph
occurrence	occasion
panacea	panorama
pastime	perceptible
patronage	pension
procession	property
quarreled	querulous
question	quorum
reality	recognise
serviceable	server

separate	signature
supervision	superstition
sympathetic	sympathise
synonym	systematic
transcend	traveller
transcend	transferred
university	upbraid

Model Examples

1. Which of the following spellings is correct ?
   ① license   ② liceanse   ③ licens   ④ lisence ❶
2. Which of the following spellings is correct ?
   ① occassion ② occasioned ③ occasion   ④ ocasion ❸

Examples for Practice

1. Which of the following spellings is correct ?
   ① acomodate   ② accomodate
   ③ acommodate   ④ accommodate
2. Which of the following spellings is correct ?
   ① acknowlegement   ② acknowledgement
   ③ acknowledgment   ④ acknowlgement
3. Which of the following spellings is correct ?
   ① arguement   ② argument
   ③ arguemint   ④ argment
4. Which of the following spellings is correct ?
   ① comitment   ② comitmment
   ③ commitment   ④ committment
5. Which of the following spellings is correct ?
   ① consensus   ② concensus
   ③ consencus   ④ coscenus
6. Which of the following spellings is correct ?
   ① deductible   ② deductable
   ③ deductabel   ④ decductable
7. Which of the following spellings is correct ?
   ① dependant   ② depindant
   ③ dependent   ④ dependunt

8. Which of the following spellings is correct ?
    ① embarras ② embaras ③ embarass ④ embarrass

9   Which of the following spellings is correct ?
    ① existance ② existence ③ excistence ④ existanc

10. Which of the following spellings is correct ?
    ① foreward ② forward ③ forworde ④ don't know

11. Which of the following spellings is correct ?
    ① harass   ② haras   ③ harrass   ④ herrass

12. Which of the following spellings is correct ?
    ① inadvertant   ② inadvartant
    ③ inadvartent   ④ inadvertent

13. Which of the following spellings is correct ?
    ① indispensable   ② indispensible
    ③ indispenable   ④ don't know

14. Which of the following spellings is correct ?
    ① occurrence   ② ocurrance
    ③ occurrance   ④ occurance

15. Which of the following spellings is correct ?
    ① liason   ② liasson   ③ liasone   ④ liaison

Answers

1.	④	2.	②	3.	②	4.	③
5.	①	6.	①	7.	③	8.	④
9.	②	10.	②	11.	①	12.	④
13.	①	14.	①	15.	④		

❖ ❖ ❖

WORD GAMES

2.1   *PUZZLES*

Jumbled Words

In puzzles, words are given, you have to rearrange the alphabets and make a meaningful word.

Model Examples

(I) Rearrange the jumbled letters to make a meaningful words.

1. T C D U N O C
   ① CONDOCT   ② CUONDCT
   ③ CONDUCT   ④ DONCUCT   ❸

2. P O S E O P
   ① OPOPSE   ② OPPOSE
   ③ SEPOOP   ④ SPEOPO   ❷

Examples for Practice

Fill in the blank with suitable alternative

1. NMAAIL
   ① MAALIN   ② ANIMAL   ③ LINAMAA ④ None

2. LDETEACIL
   ① DELICATE   ② DILECATE
   ③ LIDELTCA   ④ NONE

3. LAFNIGNUME
   ① LEAFGUMEN   ② LEGUMELEAF
   ③ MEANLEAFGU   ④ MEANINGFUL

4. GHITT
   ① TIGHT   ② TTIGH   ③ GHTTI   ④ HIGHTT

5. EAPCE
   ① PEEAC   ② CAEPE   ③ PEACE   ④ CEAPE

6. WOPERD
   ① POWER   ② POWDER ③ COWARD ④ NONE

7. TOQUE
   ① QOUTE   ② QUOTE   ③ TEOQU   ④ QEUTO

8. TUIEQ
   ① QUIET   ② QUIETE   ③ QUEIT   ④ QIUET

9. TABELT
   ① BETTLA ② ATTLEB ③ BATTLE ④ EABTH

10. UFRIELA
    ① FEALIUR ② FLUIREAI ③ FAILURE ④ FEILURA

11. for | faults | who | responsible | is | the |?
    ① For faults is responsible who the?
    ② For the faults who is responsible?
    ③ Is responsible for the faults who?
    ④ Who is responsible for the faults?

12. little | milk | is | there| the | in | fridge
    ① Is there little milk in the fridge.
    ② There is little milk in the fridge.
    ③ In fridge there is little milk the.
    ④ There is in the fridge little milk.

13. Taken / to / the / hospital / were / the / injured
    ① To the hospital were injured the taken.
    ② The injured taken to the hospital were.
    ③ The injured were taken to the hospital.
    ④ To the hospital were taken the injured.

14. dress | the | is | very | expensive.
    ① Expensive is very the dress.
    ② Dress is very expensive the.
    ③ Very expensive is the dress.
    ④ The dress is very expensive.

15. student | each | was | given | assignment | an

   ① An student was given each assignment.

   ② Each student was given an assignment.

   ③ Student given was an each assignment.

   ④ Each assignment was given an student.

Answers

1.	❷	2.	❶	3.	❹	4.	❶	5.	❸
6.	❷	7.	❷	8.	❶	9.	❸	10.	❸
11.	❹	12.	❷	13.	❸	14.	❹	15.	❷

❖ ❖ ❖

2.2   *WORD REGISTER*

From standard I to standard V students learn many new words which have relations with each other. Such words are called Word Register. Students should know such Word Registers.

WRITING WORD REGISTER

1. School   : students, teacher, blackboard, chalk, duster, classroom, benches, charts, textbooks, notebooks etc.

2. Bus - stop : bus, driver, conductor, petrol, diesel, passenger, ticket etc.

3. Hospital   : doctor, patient, medicine, injection, tablet, nurse, bed, ambulance, syrup etc.

4. Family: mother, father, relatives, love, small, elder, son, daughter, quarrel, pride, grandfather, grandson, uncle, individual, big, brother-in-law, nephew, niece.

5. **Sports and Game** : ball, baller, bat, cricket, fielder, player, hockey, indoor, outdoor, spirit, team, competition, trophy, kabaddi, football, unity, discipline, win, defeat, draw, racket, goal, umpire, captain, coach, soccer, pitch.

6. **People** : short, brave, kind, tall, small, tribe, black, white, healthy, rich, poor, crowd, group, caste, literate, illiterate, ignorant, country, nation, unity, clever, locality, Negro, crazy, helpful, handsome.

7. **Food** : fresh, hot, rice, wheat, stale, tasty, roti, sweet, delicious, cook, biryani, pavbhaji, ice-cream, healthy, nutritious, diet, boiled, variety, idli, dosa, soyabean, vegetables, fruits, kitchen.

8. **Colours** : green, dark, paint, drawing, white, yellow, red, purple, blue, pink, black, orange, violet, rainbow, faint, deep, pictures, clothes, grey, scarlet, brush, matching.

9. **Sounds** : loud, bell, cry, whisper, silence, listen, dull, low, harsh, noise, song, thunder, horn, pollution, traffic, sweet, soft, loudspeaker, hear, burst, explosion, clear, melodious, volume, pleasing.

10. **Work** : hard, dig, carpenter, painter, busy, workman, factory, office, careful, build, make, slowly, beautiful, industry, salary, money, teacher, clerk, officer, manager, bank.

Model Examples

(I) Identify the word register.

1. Which word is related with the game of cricket.

    ① Racket   ② Net   ③ Stumps   ④ Hockey

2. The following words are given below:

Crop, Plough, Cart, Sickle, Hut, Spade, Wheel

Identify the correct Word Register.

① Farmer   ② Teacher   ③ Doctor   ④ Lawyer **❶**

Examples for Practice

(I) *Identify the word register in the following questions.*

1. Which word is related with classroom?

① Bench   ② Tree   ③ Road   ④ Vehicle

2. Which word is not related with food?

① Roti   ② Salad   ③ Vegetable   ④ House

3. Which word is not related with audio-visual aid?

① Mobile   ② T. V.

③ Projector   ④ Tape recorder

4. Which word is not related to 'office'?

① Computers   ② Chairs

③ Telephone   ④ Bed

5. Which word is not related to 'Garden'?

① Trees   ② Books   ③ Flowers   ④ Birds

6. Which word is not related to 'Temple'?

① Priest   ② Garlands

③ Coconuts   ④ Swimming pool

7. Which word is not related to 'Hospital'?

① Entertainment mall   ② Nurses

③ Watchman   ④ Operation Theatre

8. Which word is not related to 'colour'?

① Yellow   ② Green   ③ Grey   ④ Fast

9. Which word is not related to 'School'?

① Classroom   ② Benches   ③ Blackboard   ④ Music

10. Which word is not related to taste ?

    ① sweet   ② delicious   ③ beautiful   ④ sour

11. Which word is not related to people ?

    ① brave   ② clever   ③ kind   ④ tribe

========= **Answers** =========

Q.	Ans.	Q.	Ans.	Q.	Ans.	Q.	Ans.
1.	❶	2.	❹	3.	❹	4.	❹
5.	❷	6.	❹	7.	❶	8.	❹
9.	❹	10.	❸	11.	❸		

❖ ❖ ❖

2.3   *RELATED WORDS*

Writing familiar related words.

Students are aware of the words that they have learnt from Std. I to Std V. Children should know the related words. Some words are given below.

• Cup – Saucer	• Birds – Animals
• Brother – Sister	• Fairy – Tale
• Summer – Winter	• King – Queen
• Loss – Gain	• Events – Actions
• Table – Tennis	• Car – Road
• Kho – Kho	• Pot – Pan
• Water – Logged	• Duck – tail
• Falling – Leaves	• Top – Bottom
• Golden – House	• Car – Road
• Stars – Shadow	• Read – Write
• Eat - Drink	• Moon – Stars
• Sharp – Claws	• Question – Answer
• Colour – Picture	• Green – Grass

Provide some key of how to do it.

Model Examples

(I) Identify the related words :

1. If Hide – Seek than Green - .... ?
   ① Yellow   ② Grass
   ③ Cold   ④ Long   ❷

2. Hot – Cold than Doctor - ......?
   ① Chair   ② Table
   ③ Patient   ④ Compounder   ❸

Examples for Practice

(I) Identify the related words :

1. If Car – Road then Food - .....?
   ① Bad   ② Tasty   ③ State   ④ Better

2. If Table – Tennis then cricket - ......?
   ① chess   ② football   ③ bat   ④ racket

3. If Eat – Drink then Question ......?
   ① Fingers   ② Pencil
   ③ Sharpener   ④ Answer

4. If King – palace then Monk ......?
   ① Monastery   ② Tree
   ③ House   ④ Garden

5. If Sister – Brother then Niece - .... ?
   ① Sister   ② Nephew
   ③ Aunt   ④ Grandmother

Answers

Q.	Ans.	Q.	Ans.	Q.	Ans.	Q.	Ans.
1.	❷	2.	❸	3.	❹	4.	❶
5.	❷						

2.4   *MATCH THE WORDS AND PICTURES*

Students have learnt various words from Std. I to Std V. They are well aware with different words and their meaning or what it is called.

Model Examples

1. *Identify the place.*

    ① Hospital
    ② Office
    ③ School
    ④ Gym   ❶

2. *Identify the picture.*

    ① Taxi
    ② Rickshaw
    ③ Scooter
    ④ Bus   ❶

3. *Identify the picture.*

    ① Truck
    ② Taxi
    ③ Bus
    ④ Cargo   ❸

4. *Match the following and select the correct option given below :*

Food items	Methods of preservation
(a) Milk	(1) wrap it in a damp cloth
(b) Vegetables	(2) Keeping them in a dry place.
(c) Green coriander	(3) Putting it in a bowl and keeping the bowl in a container with some water.
(d) Chicken and meat	(4) Keeping them in the refrigerator.
	(5) by boiling it.

(1)   (a) – 5,   (b) – 4,   (c) – 1, (d) - 4

(2)   (a) – 5,   (b) – 4,   (c) – 1, (d) - 2

(3)   (a) – 2,   (b) – 4,   (c) – 1, (d) - 4

(4)   (a) – 4,   (b) – 5,   (c) – 1, (d) – 2

Examples for Practice

Q. Look at the picture and identify it or what you can make from it.

1.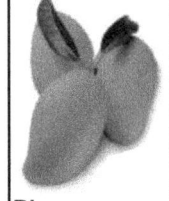

Ripe mangoes

① Jam
② Ketchup
③ Pickles
④ Paneer

2.

Potato

① Pickles
② Chips
③ Paneer
④ Jam

3.

Chilli

① Lady finger
② Potato
③ Green chilli
④ Onion

4.

① Chilli
② Lady finger
③ Brinjal
④ Vegetables

5.

① Telescope
② Microscope
③ Thermometer
④ Vernier Calliper

6.

① Fly
② Mosquito
③ Larvae
④ Moth

7.

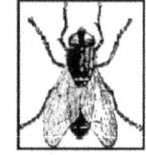

① House fly
② Beetle
③ Grasshopper
④ Bug

8. Who are the persons in the picture?

① Snake Charmer   ② Potter
③ Gambler   ④ Garudi

Answers

Q.	Ans.	Q.	Ans.	Q.	Ans.	Q.	Ans.
1.	❶	2.	❷	3.	❸	4.	❷
5.	❷	6.	❷	7.	❶	8.	❶

✣ ✣ ✣

GRAMMAR

3.1 PARTS OF SPEECH

Sentences are made of words. Words are grouped into various parts of speech according to their use in each and every sentence.

There are eight parts of speech : (1) Noun (2) Pronoun (3) Adjective (4) Verb (5) Adverb (6) Preposition (7) Conjunction (8) Interjection.

We are going to study only about Noun, Pronoun, Adjective, Verb, Adverb and Preposition.

(a) Noun

Naming words are called Nouns. The name of a person, place, thing, animal or feeling is called a noun.

Example

Persons	:	Boy, Girl, Ravi, Rita
Places	:	Pune, hospital, garden
Things	:	Book, pen, chair, cap
Oceans	:	Arctic, Indian
Animals	:	Rat, cat, cow, buffalo
Flowers	:	Rose, jasmine, Marigold, Lotus
Jobs	:	Engineer, doctor, teacher, lawyer
Fruits	:	Apple, mango, banana, orange
Vegetables	:	Carrot, onion, potato.
Buildings	:	Taj Mahal, Red Fort, Kutub Minar
Rivers	:	Thames, Ganga, Amazon, Yamuna
Birds	:	Crow, hen, peacock, pigeon
Relationship	:	Son-in-law, aunt, nephew, uncle
Ideas	:	Truth, honesty, death, beauty
Feelings	:	Joy, sympathy, despise, love

✌ Kinds of Nouns

There are five kinds of nouns : (1) Proper Noun, (2) Common Noun, (3) Collective Noun, (4) Abstract Noun, (5) Material Noun.

(1) Proper Noun

Proper nouns are names given to particular people, places and things. They always begin with a capital letter.

•• The names of people, pets, cities, countries, rivers, oceans and mountains are proper nouns.

Example

Mahatma Gandhi	France
Florence Nightingale	Italy
Mahesh	The river Thames
Geeta	Mount Everest

•• The names of the days of the week, months of the year, festivals and special days are proper nouns.

Example

Tuesday	New Year's day
Monday	Children's day
September	Christmas

•• The names of famous places, buildings, monuments, people who live in a particular country, language and books are also proper nouns.

Example :

the Red Fort	Chinese	Tamil	the Ramayan
the Kutub Minar	Indians	Telugu	the Bible

(2) Common Noun :

A common noun is the name that can be given in common to every person or thing of the same class or kind i.e. words for things, animals, places and types of people are called common nouns.

Example :

pen	calf	school	dancer
box	dog	bank	farmer
helicopter	puppy	airport	magician

(3) Collective Noun

A collective noun is the name of a collection of persons or things taken together and spoken as one whole :

Example

a company of actors	a clutch of eggs
a crowd of people	a fleet of ships
a panel of judges	a fleet of vehicles
a gang of thieves	a pack of cards
a class of school children	a block of flats
a troop of soldiers	a flight of steps

(4) Abstract Noun

An abstract noun is the name of quality, state or action.

Example

1. Honesty is the best policy.
2. Bravery is a great quality.

(5) Material Noun

A material noun is the name of a matter or substance of which things are made.

Example

1. Gold is a precious metal.
2. We make utensils from silver.

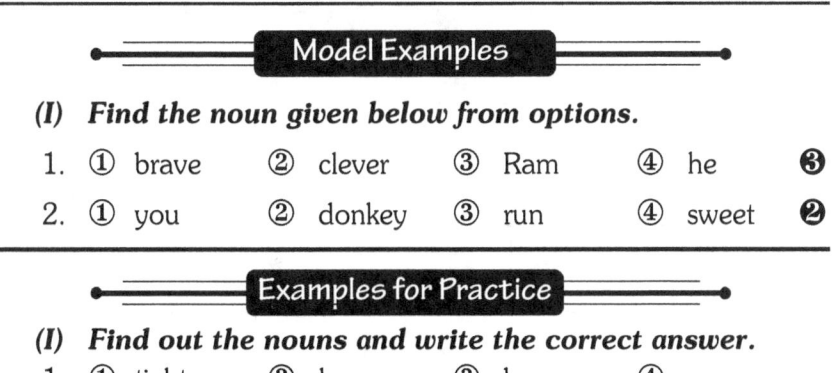

Model Examples

(I) Find the noun given below from options.

1. ① brave   ② clever   ③ Ram   ④ he   ❸
2. ① you   ② donkey   ③ run   ④ sweet   ❷

Examples for Practice

(I) Find out the nouns and write the correct answer.

1. ① tight   ② loose   ③ boy   ④ open
2. ① thin   ② girl   ③ fat   ④ thick

3. Raja was very fat.
   ① was   ② very   ③ Raja   ④ fat

4. Mangoes are very sweet.
   ① very   ② Mangoes ③ are   ④ sweet

5. Everyone praised Radha for her rank.
   ① everyone ② praised ③ rank   ④ Radha

6. The boy is crying.
   ① boy   ② the   ③ is   ④ crying

7. Girls are not weak
   ① weak   ② girls   ③ are   ④ not

8. Computers can solve problems.
   ① computers ② solve   ③ can   ④ problems

9. The elephant trumpeted loudly.
   ① elephant ② the   ③ loudly ④ trumpeted

10. When will Satish come?
   ① will   ② come   ③ when   ④ Satish

11. Raj is very famous.
   ① very   ② famous ③ Raj   ④ is

12. Taj Mahal is very beautiful.
   ① very   ② beautiful ③ Taj Mahal ④ is

Answers

Q.	Ans.	Q.	Ans.	Q.	Ans.	Q.	Ans.
1.	❸	2.	❷	3.	❸	4.	❷
5.	❹	6.	❶	7.	❷	8.	❶
9.	❶	10.	❹	11.	❸	12.	❸

✤ ✤ ✤

(b) The Pronoun

A pronoun is a word that takes the place of a noun.

Example

I, we, he, him, you, she, her, me, they, them, our, who, which, what, this, that, these, mine, their, your, those, it, someone, yourself, herself, themselves, himself, ourselves, myself, itself, my, own, many, few, one, none, all, everybody, each whom.

Model Examples

(I) Find out the pronoun from the words given below :
1. ① Radha   ② Raju   ③ She   ④ Ram   ❸
2. He is a good boy.
   ① is   ② good   ③ boy   ④ he   ❹
3. They talk a lot.
   ① talk   ② lot   ③ they   ④ a   ❸

Examples for Practice

(I) Find the pronoun in the sentences given below.
1. They never could agree about anything.
   ① never   ② they   ③ about   ④ anything
2. Deepen and his ten years old brother Nirupam were flying kites.
   ① Deepen   ② his   ③ brother   ④ Nirupam
3. Here are our sandwiches on the chair.
   ① here   ② sandwiches
   ③ on   ④ our
4. I have seen the caves at Karla.
   ① I   ② have   ③ Karla   ④ caves
5. Ramesh met him at the stand.
   ① at   ② met   ③ stand   ④ him
6. Our blood is mostly made of water.
   ① blood   ② made   ③ water   ④ our
7. My father has six pairs of shoes.
   ① father   ② my   ③ pairs   ④ has

8. They were playing cricket.
   ① were   ② playing   ③ they   ④ cricket
9. These apples are very sweet.
   ① apples   ② these   ③ are   ④ sweet
10. What is your name?
    ① is   ② what   ③ your   ④ name
11. Take care of your health.
    ① care   ② your   ③ health   ④ take
12. My friend sings sweetly.
    ① friend   ② sings   ③ sweetly   ④ my
13. It was a heavy box.
    ① was   ② It   ③ box   ④ heavy
14. She lifted a machine.
    ① lifted   ② a   ③ she   ④ machine
15. This boy is respected.
    ① boy   ② this   ③ respected ④ is

Answers

Q.	Ans.	Q.	Ans.	Q.	Ans.	Q.	Ans.
1.	❷	2.	❷	3.	❹	4.	❶
5.	❹	6.	❹	7.	❷	8.	❸
9.	❷	10.	❸	11.	❷	12.	❹
13.	❷	14.	❸	15.	❷		

(c) Adjective

• An Adjective is a word that is used to add more value or qualities to the Noun.

Example

A <u>beautiful</u> girl, a <u>brave</u> soldier, a <u>tall</u> boy, a <u>smart</u> young man.

Kinds of Adjectives

(1) Adjectives of Quality : They refer to the quality or state of the Nouns.

Examples

(i)   Ram is a clever boy.

(ii) It is a high mountain

(iii) We live under the blue sky.

(iv) She wears a short skirt.

(v)   Rajni is an intelligent girl.

The words 'clever', 'high', 'blue', 'short', 'intelligent' are all Adjectives of Quality.

(2) Adjective of Quantity

They show how much a thing is meant.

Examples

(i)   Give me <u>some</u> mangoes.

(ii) He has too <u>much</u> money

(iii) They take <u>great</u> care

(iv) He ate <u>enough</u> food.

(v)   We drink <u>whole</u> milk.

The words 'some', 'much', 'great', 'enough', 'whole' are all Adjectives of Quantity.

────── **Model Examples** ──────

(I) Find out the adjective from the sentences given below:

1. A wise farmer had a farm.
   ① farmer   ② farm   ③ wise   ④ had   ❸

2. I have a nice frock.
   ① I   ② have   ③ nice   ④ frock   ❸

3. This is a big house.
   ① is   ② big   ③ house   ④ this   ❷

4. Burjh Khalifa is a tall building.
   ① building   ② is   ③ a   ④ tall   ❹

5. Kareena is a beautiful woman

① is   ② beautiful   ③ woman   ④ kareena ❷

Examples for Practice

(I) Find out the adjectives in the sentences given below :

1. My school has a big building.
   ① school   ② building   ③ my   ④ big

2. An old lady was passing by.
   ① old   ② lady   ③ passing   ④ by

3. The fisherman was a huge man.
   ① fisherman   ② huge
   ③ man   ④ the

4. This soap gives a nice smell.
   ① soap   ② smell   ③ nice   ④ gives

5. It was a fine snail.
   ① fine   ② snail   ③ was   ④ it

6. Mohan is a young engineer.
   ① engineer   ② Mohan   ③ young   ④ is

7. The elephant was not cruel.
   ① cruel   ② elephant   ③ was   ④ not

8. Father gave me a new dress
   ① dress   ② father   ③ new   ④ gave

9. Arjun is a good archer.
   ① archer   ② good   ③ Arjun   ④ is

10. Mr. Shinde was a generous farmer.
    ① generous   ② farmer
    ③ Mr. Shinde   ④ was

11. I met an old uncle
    ① met   ② old   ③ uncle   ④ I

12. She has a familiar voice.
    ① has   ② she   ③ voice   ④ familiar

13. We saw a brown bear.
    ① saw   ② brown   ③ we   ④ bear

14. Virat is a skillful player.
    ① Virat   ② player   ③ skillful   ④ a

Answers

Q.	Ans.	Q.	Ans.	Q.	Ans.	Q.	Ans.
1.	❹	2.	❶	3.	❷	4.	❸
5.	❶	6.	❸	7.	❶	8.	❸
9.	❷	10.	❶	11.	❷	12.	❹
13.	❷	14.	❸					

❖ ❖ ❖

(d) The Verbs

A word which describes action is called verb. It is a word which says something about a subject.

Action words are verbs. It tells us what a person or a thing does or what is done to a person or a thing.

Example :
(i) Radha is skipping.
(ii) Raju is playing.
(iii) The cow gives milk.

Model Examples

(I) Find out the verbs in the sentences given below :

1. You can sing song in English.
    ① English ② song   ③ sing   ④ you   ❸
2. The cat caught the mouse
    ① caught ② cat   ③ mouse ④ the   ❶

Examples for Practice

(I) Find out the verbs in the sentences given below :

1. He fell down suddenly
    ① down ② fell   ③ he   ④ suddenly

2. The cow gives milk.
   ① cow   ② milk   ③ gives   ④ the

3. Raju stood before Meena.
   ① stood   ② before   ③ Raju   ④ Meena

4. The window is broken.
   ① window   ② broken   ③ the   ④ is

5. The dog barks loudly.
   ① barks   ② loudly   ③ dog   ④ the

6. The boys are playing football.
   ① football   ② playing   ③ boys   ④ the

7. I saw a cartoon film.
   ① cartoon   ② film   ③ saw   ④ I

8. The boy is crying for toys.
   ① boy   ② is   ③ the   ④ crying

9. I am going to Mahabaleshwar.
   ① I   ② going
   ③ Mahabaleshwar   ④ to

10. Ram polished his shoes.
    ① shoes   ② his   ③ polished   ④ Ram

11. Students are playing kabaddi on the playground.
    ① playing   ② Kabaddi
    ③ playground   ④ students

12. My mother told me a story.
    ① mother   ② story   ③ told   ④ my

13. She teaches us English.
    ① English   ② us   ③ teaches   ④ she

14. The sky grew dark.
    ① sky   ② dark   ③ grew   ④ the

15. The policeman blew his whistle.
    ① policeman ② his   ③ blew   ④ whistle

Answers

Q.	Ans.	Q.	Ans.	Q.	Ans.	Q.	Ans.
1.	❷	2.	❸	3.	❶	4.	❷
5.	❶	6.	❷	7.	❸	8.	❹
9.	❷	10.	❸	11.	❶	12.	❸
13.	❸	14.	❸	15.	❸		

❖ ❖❖

(e) Conjugation

Introduction

It is a variation of form in verb by which the voice, tense, number and person are identified.

Simple Definition of conjugation : The way a verb changes its form to show number, person, tense, etc. : the way a verb is conjugated.

A group of verbs that change in the same way to show number, person, tense, etc. : a set of verbs that are conjugated in the same way.

Conjugated verbs are verbs which have been changed to communicate one or more of the following: person, number, gender, tense, aspect, mood, or voice. Those will be explained in detail in just a moment: but first, here's an example of the verb "break" conjugated in several different ways.

Present Simple
- I, You, We, They : break
- He, She, It : breaks

Present Continuous (Progressive)
- I am breaking
- You, We, They : are breaking

- He, She, It : is breaking

Present Perfect

- I, You, We, They : have broken
- He, She, It : has broken

Past Simple

- I, You, We, They, He, She, It : broke

Past Continuous

- I, He, She, It : was breaking
- You, We, They : were breaking

Past Perfect

- I, You, We, They, He, She, It : had broken

As you can see, each different conjugation changes "break" from its base form to tell us when and by whom the action takes place.

Model Examples

1. For the word 'write' what will be the conjugated sentence in Present Simple.

   ① I write   ② I wrote   ③ I will write   ④ I writes   ❶

2. For the word 'write', what will be the conjugated sentence in Present Continuous.

   ① I write   ② I will write

   ③ I am writing   ④ I writes   ❸

3. For the word 'write', what will be the conjugated sentence in Present Perfect.

   ① I wrote   ② I am writing

   ③ I writes   ④ I have written   ❹

4. For the word 'write', what will be the conjugated sentence in Past Simple Tense.

   ① I wrote   ② I am writing

   ③ I writes   ④ I have written   ❶

5. For the word 'write', what will be the conjugated sentence in Past Continuous.

   ① I am writing   ② I was writing

   ③ I will write   ④ I have written   ❷

Examples for Practice

(I) Write conjugated sentences.

1. For the word 'Break', what will be conjugated sentence in Present Simple.
   ① You break   ② You broke
   ③ You breaks   ④ You are breaking

2. For the word 'Break', what will be the conjugated sentence in Present Continuous.
   ① He break   ② He is breaking
   ③ He broke   ④ He has broken

3. For the word 'Break', what will be the conjugated sentence in Present Perfect.
   ① She broke   ② She breaks
   ③ She has broken   ④ She was breaking

4. For the word 'Break', what will be the conjugated sentence in Past Simple.
   ① They break   ② They are breaking
   ③ They have broken   ④ They broke

5. For the word 'Break', what will be the conjugated sentence in Past Continuous.
   ① He is breaking   ② He was breaking
   ③ He broke   ④ He has broken.

Answers

Q.	Ans.	Q.	Ans.	Q.	Ans.	Q.	Ans.
1.	❶	2.	❷	3.	❸	4.	❹
5.	❷						

❖ ❖ ❖

(I) ***Action (main) verbs*** : An action verb is a verb that expresses physical or mental action. The action verb tells us what the subject of our clause or sentence is doing-physically or mentally.

If you're having trouble deciding if a particular word is an action verb or not, go through every word in the sentence and ask yourself, "Is this something a person or thing can actually do?"

Model Examples

(I) ***Find out the action verbs in the sentences given below :***

1. Sheela walked to school.

   ① walked   ② Sheela   ③ school   ④ to   ❶

2. Rakshit thought about the math problem.

   ① maths   ② Rakshit   ③ thought   ④ problem ❸

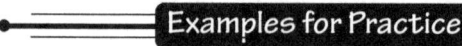

Examples for Practice

(I) ***Find out the action verbs in the sentences given below:***

1. Raj and Debu ride the bus to school each morning.

   ① ride   ② bus   ③ morning   ④ night

2. Reena wants a horse for her birthday.

   ① horse   ② wants   ③ Reena   ④ birthday

3. Dilip reads a chapter in his book each night.

   ① book   ② chapter   ③ night   ④ reads

4. Do you think it will rain today?

   ① think   ② rain   ③ you   ④ today

5. I believe in fairies and unicorns.

   ① fairies   ② unicorns ③ believe   ④ in

6. Will you help me with my homework?

   ① homework ② help   ③ me   ④ will

7. Please call your mom.
   ① call   ② your   ③ fireworks   ④ night

8. The chicken strutted across the road.
   ① chicken   ② across   ③ strutted   ④ road

Answers

Q.	Ans.	Q.	Ans.	Q.	Ans.	Q.	Ans.
1.	❶	2.	❷	3.	❹	4.	❶
5.	❸	6.	❷	7.	❶	8.	❸

(II) Auxiliary verbs

A verb used in forming the tenses, moods, and voices of other verbs. The primary auxiliary verbs in English are be, do, and have ; the modal auxiliaries are can, could, may, might, must, shall, should, will and would.

Auxiliary (or Helping) verbs are used together with a main verb to show the verb's tense or to form a negative or question. The most common auxiliary verbs are have, be and do.

Example :

Does Raj write all his own reports?

The secretaries haven't written all the letters yet.

Rashmi is writing an e-mail to a client at the moment.

Examples for Practice

(I) **Find out the verbs in the sentences given below :**

1. .... you want tea?
   ① Have   ② Do   ③ Could   ④ Would

2. I .... go now.
   ① shall   ② can   ③ may   ④ do

3. I ...... have thought so.
   ① shall   ② will   ③ might   ④ should

4. If he studied harder, he .... pass this course.
   ① could   ② have   ③ should   ④ would

5. She .... be my advisor next semester.
   ① can   ② may   ③ should   ④ could
6. Humidity .... ruin my hairdo.
   ① have   ② could   ③ will   ④ shall
7. I didn't used to ...... like him.
   ① have   ② be   ③ might   ④ may
8. ...... you attend the school?
   ① Do   ② May   ③ Would   ④ Shall

Answers

Q.	Ans.	Q.	Ans.	Q.	Ans.	Q.	Ans.
1.	❷	2.	❶	3.	❹	4.	❶
5.	❷	6.	❸	7.	❷	8.	❶

(g) Adverbs

An adverb is a word that describes a verb. It modifies the meaning of a verb.

Generally, adverbs end in 'ly' when 'ly' is added to an adjective it becomes an adverb.

Example :

(i)   Radha spoke <u>loudly</u>.

(ii) The car was moving <u>slowly</u>.

(iii) Ravi writes <u>neatly.</u>

(iv) Sam was feeling <u>lonely</u>.

(v)   The plane landed <u>safely</u>.

Kinds of Adverbs

Adverbs are of four kinds :

(1) Adverb of Manner   (2) Adverb of Time

(3) Adverb of Place   (4) Adverb of Frequency

Examples :

(1) Adverb of Manner

They show how an action is done.

(i)   The soldiers fought <u>bravely.</u>   (ii) They work <u>hard</u>.

(iii) The rabbit runs <u>fast</u>.   (iv) Tortoise walks <u>slowly</u>.

(v)   The infant slept <u>soundly</u>.

(2) Adverb of Time.

They show when an action is done.

(i)   We read newspaper <u>daily</u>

(ii) They will finish the work <u>today</u>.

(iii) Children will go to the park <u>tomorrow</u>.

(iv) They left for Europe <u>yesterday</u>.

(v)   She has <u>already</u> finished her homework.

(3) Adverb of Place

They show where an action is done.

(i)   Ravi is waiting <u>outside</u>.   (ii) Come and sit <u>here</u>.

(iii) Don't go <u>there</u>.

(iv) His father looked for him <u>everywhere.</u>

(v)   She is sitting <u>inside</u> the cab.

(4) Adverb of frequency

They show how often an action is done.

(i)   You are <u>always</u> late.   (ii) She helped her <u>once</u>.

(iii) The shops are <u>often</u> very busy.

(iv) I visited her <u>twice</u>.   (v)   John <u>Seldom</u> comes here.

Model Examples

(I) Find out the adverb from the following :

1. I could not find my pen anywhere.

    ① find   ② pen   ③ anywhere ④ could   ❸

2. The train has already left.

    ① already   ② left   ③ train   ④ has   ❶

Examples for Practice

(I) Find out the adverbs in the sentences given below :

1. The sun always rises in the east.

    ① sun   ② always   ③ east   ④ rises

2. The postman has already left.
   ① already   ② postman   ③ left   ④ has
3. They live in a house nearby.
   ① live   ② house   ③ nearby   ④ they
4. I will never make that mistake again.
   ① will   ② make   ③ never   ④ again
5. Sam plays the guitar skillfully.
   ① plays   ② guitar   ③ skillfully   ④ Sam
6. He was driving carelessly.
   ① was   ② carelessly   ③ driving   ④ He
7. Is she working today?
   ① She   ② today   ③ Is   ④ working
8. The sun is extremely hot.
   ① sun   ② hot   ③ extremely   ④ The
9. The monkey looked up.
   ① monkey   ② up   ③ looked   ④ The
10. I have rarely seen better work.
    ① rarely   ② have   ③ seen   ④ better
11. I hardly know what to do.
    ① know   ② hardly   ③ what   ④ do
12. He often talks nonsense.
    ① often   ② talks   ③ he   ④ nonsense
13. Have you looked everywhere?
    ① everywhere   ② looked
    ③ Have   ④ you
14. He usually gets up at six.
    ① six   ② at   ③ usually   ④ He

Answers

Q.	Ans.	Q.	Ans.	Q.	Ans.	Q.	Ans.
1.	❷	2.	❶	3.	❸	4.	❸
5.	❸	6.	❷	7.	❷	8.	❸
9.	❷	10.	❶	11.	❷	12.	❶
13.	❶	14.	❸					

(h) Prepositions

A preposition is a word that shows the relation between a noun or a pronoun and some other word in a sentence. Most prepositions are little words like in, an, at etc.

The Use of Prepositions

1. At, in :

With reference to time, 'at' is used for a point of time, 'in' for a period of time in which something happens; as

(i)   School starts at nine O'clock.

(ii) He lives in Pune.

(iii) I met him at Kothrud in Pune.

(iv) He was born in 1983.

(v)   In this month many celebrities were born.

➺   Also, 'At' is used for small places and 'In' is used for large places.

2. In, Within :

'In' is used to denote the end of a period of time in the future, whereas, 'at' is used to denote before the end of a period of time in the future :

(i)   John will return in a month. (i.e. at the close of)

(ii) Ravi will return within a month. (in less than)

3. By, with :

'With' is used with the instrument. 'By' is used after a verb in the passive voice.

(i)   Sharpen the pencil with a sharper.

(ii) He was punished by his teacher.

4. On, Upon :

Generally, 'On' is used in speaking of things at rest; 'upon' is used in speaking of things in motion; as,

(i)   Together, we sat on the floor.

(ii) The monkey sprang upon the roof.

5. In, into :

'In' implies a state of rest or position inside anything while 'into' denotes motion towards the inside of anything; as

(i)   He is in his room

(ii) He fell into the river.

6. For, Since :

'For' is used to denote a period of time; 'since' is used to denote a point of time.

    (i)   It has been raining for two hours

    (ii)   They have been dancing since morning.

7. Between, Among :

'Between' is used with two persons or things; 'among' with more than two.

    (i)   Share the food between the two of you.

    (ii)   She was standing among the people.

8. Till, By :

'Till' means 'up to', By means 'not later than'.

    (i)   She waited till seven O'clock.

    (ii)   Remember to return by six O'clock.

Model Examples

(I) Insert the appropriate preposition.

1. You must finish the work ...... Friday.

    ① by   ② at   ③ upon   ④ from   ❶

2. We are going to the zoo ...... Saturday.

    ① for   ② on   ③ in   ④ at   ❷

Examples for Practice

Insert the appropriate Preposition.

1. He was placed ..... the two girls.

    ① among   ② into   ③ between   ④ for

2. He is not ..... home just now.

    ① at   ② in   ③ into   ④ on

3. We must enquire ...... the matter.

    ① by   ② about   ③ in   ④ for

4. Someone is knocking ..... the door.

    ① in   ② on   ③ at   ④ by

5. Distribute the mangoes ..... the children.

    ① between   ② among   ③ in   ④ by

6. Tom has been ill ..... Tuesday last.
    ① for   ② on   ③ since   ④ from

7. The sun will not rise ..... an hour
    ① in   ② from   ③ since   ④ for

8. He lives ..... London.
    ① in   ② from   ③ into   ④ at

9. They will come ..... a month.
    ① in   ② within   ③ after   ④ at

10. Finish the work ..... two o'clock.
    ① by   ② at   ③ on   ④ for

11. She will visit us ..... Sunday next.
    ① by   ② for   ③ on   ④ with

12. He is ..... the office.
    ① in   ② on   ③ at   ④ by

13. We travel ...... one place to another.
    ① by   ② on   ③ from   ④ within

Answers

Q.	Ans.	Q.	Ans.	Q.	Ans.	Q.	Ans.
1.	❸	2.	❶	3.	❷	4.	❸
5.	❷	6.	❸	7.	❹	8.	❶
9.	❷	10.	❶	11.	❶	12.	❸
13.	❸						

(i) Conjunction

In this topic the following sub-topics related to the concept of conjunctions are covered :

Types of Conjunctions.

A conjunction is a word that "joins". A conjunction joins two parts of a sentence. Conjunctions are linking words.

You use conjunctions to join words together. The commonest conjunctions are 'and', 'but' and 'or'.

For example :
- We buy eggs *and* rice at the supermarket.
- Say your name loudly *and* clearly.

You can use the conjunction *'but'* to link words that have different or contrasting meaning.

For example :
- The elephant is a large *but* gentle animal.
- Ants are small *but* strong.

✌ Types of Conjunction

(1) Conjunctions of Time : Here are some more conjunctions that you use to say when something happens. They are called conjunctions of time.

Notice that there are two verbs, one on each side of the conjunction.

For example :
- Look both ways *before* you cross the road.
- Dad was frowning *as* he came in.

(2) Conjunctions of Reason : The conjunctions 'as', 'because', 'since' and 'in case' are called *conjunctions of reason.*

They are used to say why something happens, or why somebody does something, or why you are suggesting something.

For example :
- *As* it's late we'd better take a taxi.
- I bought an ice cream *because* I was hungry.

(3) Conjunctions of Purpose : The conjunctions 'so', 'so that', 'in order that', 'so as to' and 'in order to' are called conjunctions of purpose.

They are used to say what is the purpose of doing something.

For example :
- Stand still *so that* I can brush your hair.

- *In order that* everyone gets a piece of cake, please take only one piece each.

(4) Conjunctions of Condition : The conjunctions 'if', 'as long as' and 'unless' are called conjunctions of condition. You use them to say what follows a certain happening, or what must come first before a certain thing happens.

For example :

- I'll tell you some news, *as long as* you agree to keep it secret.
- *Unless* you all stop talking, you would not hear what I'm saying.

(5) Conjunctions of Comparison : The conjunctions 'as .... as' and 'than' are called conjunctions of comparison. You use them for comparing.

For example :

- The sky is almost *as dark as* it is at night.
- I can swim much *further than* my little brother can.

✌ *Kinds of Conjunction*

There are two kinds of conjunctions :

(1) Co-ordinating Conjunctions : There are four kinds of co-ordinating conjunctions.

(A) Alternative Conjunctions : When there is choice or alternative between two statements, the conjunctions is called alternative conjunction.

For example : 'either .... or'; 'neither ...... nor'; 'whether .... or'; 'otherwise', 'or' etc.

- *Whether* he *or* she has asked my permission.
- *Either* my mother *or* father will do the work.

(B) Copulative Conjunction : A conjunction that addresses one statement or fact to the other one is called a copulative conjunction.

For example : • She was *both* a cheat *and* a liar.

• Saroj *as well as* Manoj has to go to the jungle.

(C) Adversative Conjunction : When a conjunction has two opposite statements, it is called an adversative conjunction.

For example : 'but', 'still', 'yet', 'nevertheless', 'while', etc.

• I am studying hard *but* my brother is lazy.

• Your uncle is rich *but* he is also a miser.

(D) An Illusive Conjunction : It joins two sentences to express inference.

For example : 'therefore', 'so', 'consequently', 'for', etc.

• He had committed a crime *therefore* he was imprisoned.

• My brother will get the target *for* he is studying day and night.

(2) Sub-ordinating Conjunction : A conjunction that joins a Principal and Sub-ordinate clause is called a sub-ordinating conjunction.

Sub-ordinating Conjunction of	**Example**
time	after, since, until, till, before, etc.
place	where, wherever, etc.
reason	that, since, because, as, etc.
purpose	so that, lest, etc.
concession	though, although, even though, etc.

──────────── Model Examples ────────────

Q. Choose the correct conjunction in the following sentences :

1. Four ………. four make eight.
   ① unless   ② and   ③ that   ④ if   ❷
2. Write it down ………. you don't forget.
   ① so that   ② since   ③ although   ④ When   ❶

──────────── Examples for Practice ────────────

1. The bus stopped……..the man got off.
   ① but   ② and   ③ or   ④ so

2. I wanted to buy a book ....didn't have enough money.
    ① or   ② and   ③ but   ④ so

3. Do you want tea .....coffee ?
    ① and   ② but   ③ so   ④ or

4. I am hungry .... I don't want to eat.
    ① and   ② but   ③ so   ④ or

5. He will eat .... he gets home.
    ① or   ② because   ③ and   ④ when

6. I would have told you ....I had known.
    ① and   ② unless   ③ so   ④ if

7. He ate........he was hungry.
    ① if   ② or   ③ because   ④ so

8. Sita will not succeed unless she works harder.
    ① will   ② she   ③ unless   ④ not

9. He is poorer than us.
    ① he   ② us   ③ is   ④ than

10. Reach there before I come.
    ① there   ② before   ③ I   ④ come

11. Although he is very naughty I like him.
    ① he   ② like   ③ although   ④ him

12. Are you ok? You look as if you have a problem.
    ① you   ② as if   ③ have   ④ look

Answers

Q.	Ans.	Q.	Ans.	Q.	Ans.	Q.	Ans.
1.	❷	2.	❸	3.	❹	4.	❷
5.	❹	6.	❹	7.	❸	8.	❸
9.	❹	10.	❷	11.	❸	12.	❷

❖ ❖ ❖

3.2   THE ARTICLES

The words 'a', 'an', 'the' are commonly called Articles. 'A' and 'An' are called the Indefinite article because they do not refer to any particular person or thing, as :

I saw a boy in the theatre.

It is an orange ball.

'The' is called the 'Definite Article' because it points out to show particular person or thing, as :

The earth moves round the sun.

The Ganga is a holy river for the Hindus.

Use of 'A', 'An'

'A' is used before words beginning with a consonant sound, and 'An' before words beginning with a vowel sound.

Example :

- ❖ A bird, a pen, a man, a cow, a union, a unit, a university, a useful animal, a B. A., a B-Tech.
- ❖ An eye, an inkpot, an orange, an apple, an elephant, an umbrella, an M. A. an heir, an honest man.

As a general rule, an Article is used before a common noun in the singular number, as :

Here is a pen for you.

Buy an inkpot.

The Ganga is a sacred river.

'The' Definite Article 'the' is used when we speak of a particular person or thing.

The pen you gave me is lost.

The teacher of this school is very hard working.

'The' is used with superlatives as the darkest cloud has a silver lining.

Honesty is the best policy.

'The' is used when a singular countable noun is meant to represent a whole class, as :

The cow is a useful animal.

The rose is the sweetest of all flowers.

'The' is used with the names of rivers, seas, gulfs, oceans, groups of islands, mountain ranges, ships, trains, newspapers, races, holy books, etc.

The Persian Gulf, The Bay of Bengal.

The Ganga is a holy river for the Hindus

The Indian Ocean, The Red Sea.

The Himalays lie to the north of India.

The Vedas the Puranas, The Ramayan, The Mahabharata.

The Hindustan Times, The statesman.

The Titanic, The Deccan Queen.

'The' is used before common nouns which are names of things unique of their kind, as :

The sun rises in the east.

The earth moves round the sun.

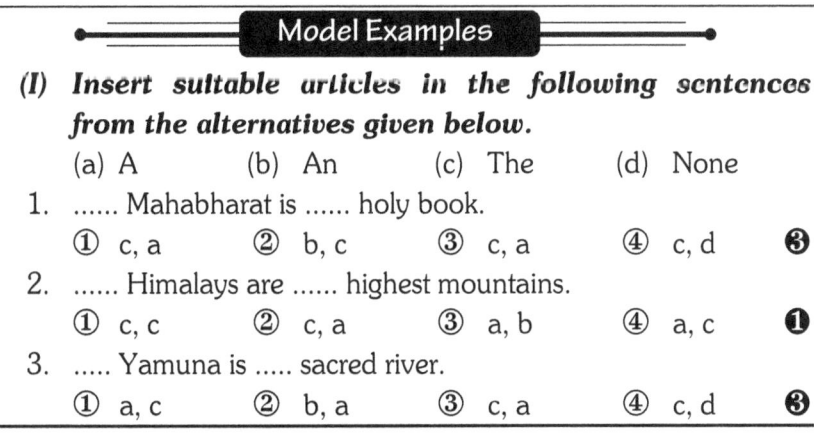

Model Examples

(I) Insert suitable articles in the following sentences from the alternatives given below.

    (a) A   (b) An   (c) The   (d) None

1. ...... Mahabharat is ...... holy book.

    ① c, a   ② b, c   ③ c, a   ④ c, d   ❸

2. ...... Himalays are ...... highest mountains.

    ① c, c   ② c, a   ③ a, b   ④ a, c   ❶

3. ..... Yamuna is ..... sacred river.

    ① a, c   ② b, a   ③ c, a   ④ c, d   ❸

Examples for Practice

(I) Find the correct option for the sentences given below:

1. ..... English defeated ...... French.

    ① The, a   ② a, an   ③ The, the ④ a, a

2. ...... honest man is ...... noblest work of God.

    ① The, the   ② An, the   ③ A, the   ④ A, An

3. He is ..... Indian but his wife is ..... European.

    ① an, a   ② the, a   ③ an, an   ④ an, the

4. There is ..... union of domestic servants also.

    ① an   ② a   ③ the   ④ none

5. Sri Lanka is ..... island in ..... Indian ocean.

    ① the, an   ② an, the   ③ a, the   ④ an, a

6. ..... aeroplane flies in .... sky.

    ① an, the   ② the, a   ③ the, the   ④ an, a

7. He is ..... honour to his profession.

    ① an   ② the   ③ a   ④ none

8. ...... accident took place in ..... Mall yesterday.

    ① an, the   ② an, a   ③ a, an   ④ the, a

9. .... people of Agra are very fond of visiting ..... Taj.

    ① an, a   ② The, a   ③ an, the   ④ The, the

10. English is ...... language of ..... people of England.

    ① a, the   ② the, a   ③ the, the   ④ an, the

11. ...... honest man will speak out ..... truth.

    ① An, the   ② as, the   ③ the, the   ④ An, a

12. Where there is ..... will there is ...... way.

    ① a, a   ② the, a   ③ a, the   ④ an, a

13. This is ..... most interesting book an history.

    ① the   ② a   ③ an   ④ none

14. Rajdhani Express is ..... fastest train in India.

    ① a   ② the   ③ An   ④ A

15. ..... flying Mail was ..... hour and ..... half late.

    ① The, an, a   ② A, the, an

    ③ The, a, an   ④ A, a, a

Answers

Q.	Ans.	Q.	Ans.	Q.	Ans.	Q.	Ans.
1.	❸	2.	❷	3.	❶	4.	❷
5.	❷	6.	❶	7.	❶	8.	❶
9.	❹	10.	❸	11.	❶	12.	❶
13.	❶	14.	❷	15.	❶		

✌ *Vowels and Consonants*

The Alphabets can be written both in Capital Letters and in Small Letters. And the Alphabets can be classified into Vowels and Consonants.

Vowels : A vowel is a letter of the alphabet (*a, e, i, o, u,* and sometimes *y*) that represents a speech sound created by the relatively free passage of breath through the larynx and oral cavity. Letters that are not vowels are consonants.

Words with Vowel Letters : Absorb, enjoy, idea, open, uneasy, each, idiot, etc.,

Words with Vowel Sound : why, shy, sky, dry, cry, fry, fly, wry, etc.,

Special Vowel Words : dialogue, education, adulteration, equation, behaviour, nefarious, pandemonium, precaution, etc.

(i) One or more vowels are found in almost all English Words.

(ii) Though there are words without vowels, they usually end with vowel sound.

No English word is there without either a vowel or a vowel sound.

Consonants : A ***consonant*** is a speech sound that is not a ***vowel***. It also refers to letters of the alphabet that represent those sounds: Z, B, T, G and H are all ***consonants***. Consonants are all the

non-vowel sounds or their corresponding letters: A, E, I, O, U and sometimes Y are not consonants. B, C, D, F, G, H, J, K, L, M, N, P, Q, R ,S, T, V, W, X, Y and Z

3.3   *PARTS OF A SENTENCE*

A sentence is a group of words which makes complete sense. Sentences usually have a **Subject** and a **Verb**.

A sentence begins with a capital letter and ends with a full stop.

Example :

Subject	Verb
He	is writing
Fish	swims
The sun	sets in the west

Kinds of sentences

Sentences are of four kinds :

1. A sentence can make a statement;

   (i)   They play volleyball.

   (ii)   Ravi does not play volleyball.

   (iii)   The sun rises in the East.

   (iv)   It is raining.

A sentence that makes a statement or assertion is called a **Declarative or Assertive** sentence.

2. A sentence can ask a question; as

   (i)   How are you?

   (ii)   Where have they gone?

   (iii)   Who is talking to Reena?

   (iv)   Is it raining?

A sentence that asks a question is called an **interrogative sentence.** (Question)

An interrogative sentence ends with a question mark.

3. A sentence can express a command or a request. This kind of sentence usually does not have a subject.

    (i)   Please be quiet.

    (ii)   All of you stand up.

    (iii)   Speak up.

    (iv)   Keep your shoes in place.

A sentence that expresses a command or a request is called an **Imperative sentence.**

4.   A sentence can express a feeling, a wish or a prayer : as

    (i)   What a beautiful rose is this!

    (ii)   May, God bless you!

    (iii)   That's an excellent idea!

    (iv)   What an opportunity!

A sentence that expresses sudden feeling, a wish or a prayer is called an **Exclamatory Sentence.** It shows a strong feeling like surprise, anger or happiness. An exclamatory sentence ends with an exclamation mark (!) instead of a full stop.

✌ Subject and Predicate

A complete sentence must contain a subject and a Predicate. A group of words cannot be called a sentence without these essential elements.

When we make a sentence we name some person or thing and say something about the subject. The Predicate tells us something about the subject.

Example :

Subject	Predicate
Children	like sweets
The policeman	catches thieves
Ritu	dances
An aeroplane	flies in the air
She	likes to read book

Note : Assertive sentences can be divided into subject and predicate but Imperative sentences do not have a subject. The subject is generally understood.

Example

(You) shut up

(You) sit down

Note :

A sentence can be Positive as well as Negative.

Example

(i) Ram is a lazy boy. (Positive)

Ram is not a lazy boy. (Negative)

(ii) He smokes. (Positive)

He does not smoke. (Negative)

(iii) Cattle eat hay. (Positive)

Cattle do not eat hay. (Negative)

Model Examples

Q. Find out the type of sentence.

1. My name is Radha.

① Interrogative   ② Imperative

③ Assertive   ④ Negative   ❸

2. Who is the writer of this lesson?

① Assertive   ② Interrogative

③ Imperative   ④ Exclamatory   ❷

Examples for Practice

Q. Find out the type of sentence given below :

1. "Ooh, my teeth! They've come off.

① Imperative   ② Interrogative

③ Assertive   ④ Exclamatory

2. Do you mean Radha Iyer?

① Interrogative   ② Exclamatory

③ Assertive   ④ Negative

3. My son Ram often makes tea for me.

① Imperative   ② Assertive

③ Exclamatory   ④ Interrogative

4. A dictionary tells us what a word means.
   ① Assertive   ② Interrogative
   ③ Imperative   ④ Negative

5. "Give me the answer at once".
   ① Interrogative   ② Imperative
   ③ Negative   ④ Exclamatory

6. And how is little Sonu?
   ① Assertive   ② Interrogative
   ③ Exclamatory   ④ Imperative

7. We know that the sun gives us light and warmth.
   ① Interrogative   ② Imperative
   ③ Assertive   ④ Negative

8. Rohan, come here immediately.
   ① Interrogative   ② Assertive
   ③ Imperative   ④ Exclamatory

9. Sir, could you please tell me where the Post Office is?
   ① Interrogative   ② Exclamatory
   ③ Assertive   ④ Negative

10. How handsome I look!
    ① Exclamatory   ② Imperative
    ③ Negative   ④ Assertive

11. A hailstorm can damage crops and plants.
    ① Interrogative   ② Imperative
    ③ Exclamatory   ④ Assertive

12. May I see your book, please?
    ① Assertive   ② Imperative
    ③ Exclamatory   ④ Interrogative

13. You must eat everything that's on your plate.
    ① Assertive   ② Exclamatory
    ③ Imperative   ④ Interrogative

14. Hey! Great News!
    ① Exclamatory   ② Assertive
    ③ Imperative   ④ Interrogative

15. Do your work with a good will.
    ① Assertive   ② Imperative
    ③ Exclamatory   ④ Interrogative

Q. *Fill in the gaps with appropriate words*

16. Make a positive sentence.
    He .... throw sticks and stones at us.
    ① could not ② shall   ③ shall not   ④ would

17. Make a negative sentence.
    We .... fond of children.
    ① are   ② are not   ③ is   ④ is not

18. Make a positive sentence.
    We .... going to learn letter writing today.
    ① are   ② are not
    ③ will not   ④ is

19. Make a positive sentence.
    When I .... old, I .... eat grass.
    ① was not, could not   ② because, loved to
    ③ was, could   ④ will be, will not

20. Make a negative sentence.
    I .... forgotten my mother's advice.
    ① have   ② will not   ③ have not   ④ will

Answers

1.	❹	2.	❶	3.	❷	4.	❶	5.	❷
6.	❷	7.	❸	8.	❸	9.	❶	10.	❶
11.	❹	12.	❹	13.	❶	14.	❶	15.	❷
16.	❹	17.	❷	18.	❶	19.	❸	20.	❸

✌ *Wh Questions*

Introduction

Under this topic, you are supposed to find the correct WH question for the underlined word.

Model Examples

(I) Find the correct WH question for the underlined word.

1. Aesop lived hundreds of years ago in a country called <u>Greece</u>.

   ① Who lived in Greece?

   ② Which country did Aesop live in?

   ③ How many years ago did Aesop live?

   ④ Where did Aesop live?

2. The sun shines brightly and the temperature is high in <u>summer</u>.

   ① What happens in summer?

   ② When does the sun shine brightly and the temperature is high?

   ③ When is it very hot?

   ④ How does the sun shine in summer?   ❷

Examples for Practice

(I) Find the correct WH question for the underlined word.

1. <u>Radha</u> went to Calcutta.

   ① How did Radha go?   ② Where did Radha go?

   ③ When did Rahul go?   ④ Who went to Calcutta?

2. Soumya was reading a <u>novel.</u>

   ① Who was reading a novel?

   ② What was Soumya doing?

   ③ What was Soumya reading?

   ④ Where was Soumya?

3. Rama was <u>cleaning</u> his bicycle.

   ① Who was cleaning the bicycle?

   ② What was Rama cleaning?

   ③ Where was Rama going?

   ④ What was Rama doing to his bicycle?

4. <u>Raghav</u> was preparing for his test.
   ① Who was preparing for the test?
   ② How was Raghav preparing?
   ③ What was Raghav doing?
   ④ What was Raghav preparing?

5. Taj Mahal is in <u>Agra</u>.
   ① What is in Agra?   ② Where is Taj Mahal?
   ③ Who is in Agra?   ④ Where is Agra?

6. <u>Chen Yaazi</u> was an archer.
   ① Who was Chen Yaazi?   ② Who was an archer?
   ③ What was Chen Yaazi?   ④ How was Chen Yaazi?

7. The <u>Treasure Valley</u> belonged to three brothers.
   ① What belonged to three brothers?
   ② Whom did the treasure valley belong to?
   ③ Where was the Treasure Valley?
   ④ What did the three brothers have?

8. Schwartz threw a <u>rolling pin</u> at Gluck.
   ① Where did Schwartz throw the rolling pin?
   ② Who threw the rolling pin?
   ③ What did Schwartz throw at Gluck?
   ④ Who threw the rolling pin as Gluck?

9. Encyclopaedia are books that give lot of <u>information.</u>
   ① What gives lot of information?
   ② What does encyclopaedia mean?
   ③ What kind of a book is encyclopaedia?
   ④ Who is enclyclopaedia?

10. Gandhiji gave a lot of <u>importance</u> to truth, simplicity and non – violence.
    ① What did Gandhiji give to truth, simplicity and non – violence?
    ② Who gave importance to truth, simplicity and non – violence?
    ③ What is truth, simplicity and non – violence?
    ④ Who is truth, simplicity and non – violence?

11. <u>Ryokan</u> was a monk who lived in Japan.

    ① Who was Ryokan?   ② Who was a monk?

    ③ What was the name of the monk who lived in Japan?

    ④ Where did Ryokan live?

12. Gluck did not have any <u>water</u> himself.

    ① What did Gluck not have?

    ② Who did not have water?

    ③ What was the name of the person who did not any water?

    ④ What did Gluck have?

13. <u>Androcles</u> was a kind, gentle and courteous man.

    ① Who was Androcles?

    ② Who was kind, gentle and courteous?

    ③ What was Androcles?   ④ How was Androcles?

14. The king of Russia decided to hold a grand <u>feast</u>.

    ① Who decided to hold a grand feast?

    ② What type of feast was decided?

    ③ What did the king of Russia decide to hold?

    ④ How was the feast which the king of Russia decided to hold?

15. A <u>diamond</u> is a brilliant stone.

    ① Which is a brilliant stone?

    ② Who is a brilliant stone?

    ③ What is a diamond?

    ④ What kind of stone is a diamond?

Answers

1.	❹	2.	❸	3.	❹	4.	❶	5.	❷
6.	❷	7.	❶	8.	❸	9.	❸	10.	❶
11.	❸	12.	❶	13.	❷	14.	❸	15.	❶

✌ *Verbal Questions*

Verbal Reasoning section that is composed of two different kinds of questions: synonyms and sentence completions. Both kinds of questions test your vocabulary and reasoning ability.

Strategies:

*   Read each sentence to get the overall meaning.
*   Focus on key words or clue words in the question to help you determine the correct answer.
*   Mentally fill in the blank with your own answer and then find the answer choice that is closest in meaning to your own answer.
*   Remember that there is almost always a word or phrase that obviously points to the correct answer.

Model Examples

Q. Identify the correct option :

1. Poles : Magnet :: ? : Battery
    ① Cells   ② Power   ③ Terminals   ④ Energy   ❸
2. Cassock : Priest :: ? : Graduate
    ① Cap   ② Tie   ③ Coat   ④ Gown   ❹

Examples for Practice

Q. Identify the correct option :

1. Paw : Cat :: Hoof : ?
    ① Lamb   ② Elephant   ③ Lion   ④ Horse
2. Ornithologist : Bird :: Archealogist : ?
    ① Islands   ② Mediators   ③ Archealogy ④ Aquatic
3. Peacock : India :: Bear : ?
    ① Australia   ② America   ③ Russia   ④ England
4. Carbon : Diamond :: Corundum : ?
    ① Garnet   ② Ruby   ③ Pukhraj   ④ Pearl

5. Conference : Chairman :: Newspaper : ?

   ① Reporter   ② Distributor   ③ Printer   ④ Editor

6. Safe : Secure :: Protect : ?

   ① Lock   ② Sure   ③ Guard   ④ Conserve

7. Microphone : Loud :: Microscope : ?

   ① Elongate   ② Investigate   ③ Magnify   ④ Examine

8. Melt : Liquid :: Freeze : ?

   ① Ice   ② Condense   ③ Solid   ④ Force

9. Race : Fatigue :: Fast : ?

   ① Food   ② Laziness   ③ Hunger   ④ Race

10. Tiger : Forest :: Otter : ?

    ① Cage   ② Sky   ③ Nest   ④ Water

Answers

1.	❹	2.	❸	3.	❸	4.	❷	5.	❹
6.	❸	7.	❸	8.	❸	9.	❹	10.	❹

❖ ❖ ❖

Language Study

| 4.1 | **PUNCTUATION MARK** |

✌ *INTRODUCTION :*

Punctuation means the right use of putting in points or stops in writing. The following are the principle points or stops.

(1)	Full stop	: (.)
(2)	Colon	: (:)
(3)	Semicolon	: (;)
(4)	Comma	: (,)
(5)	Question mark	: (?)
(6)	Exclamation	: (!)
(7)	Dash	: (–)
(8)	Quotation mark	: (" ") Inverted commas
(9)	Apostrophe	: (')
(10)	Hyphen	: (-)

(1) The full stop is used to mark the end of a sentence. e.g. Mumbai is a big city. The full stop is also used to mark *abbreviation* and *initials* as, M. A. = [Master in Arts], S. M. = (Sunil Manohar).

(2) The semicolon is used when two short sentences are joined by conjunction as 'He tried his best; but failed to get success.'

(3) The comma represents the shortest pause and is used to separate a series of words or short sentences as (a) Meena, Beena, Rekha, Usha and Sheela are going back today. (b) He came, he saw, he conquered. The comma is also used while addressing a person or a thing as, 'Father, tell me a new story'.

(4) The quotation marks (Inverted Commas) are used to enclose the exact words of the speaker as "When are you coming back, my son ?"

(5) The mark of exclamation is used after interjection and after phrases and sentences expressing sudden emotion or wish, as, (a) Alas !, (b) Oh dear !

(6) For quotations, proverbs, books, titles etc. single inverted commas are used as 'Health is Wealth', 'Discovery of India'.

(7) Capital letters are used : (a) To begin a sentence. (b) To begin each fresh line. (c) To begin all proper nouns.

Some Examples : Punctuate the following.

1. Oh What a beautiful picture
   – Oh ! What a beautiful picture !
2. Whose book is this
   – Whose book is this ?
3. The Madam asked what day was yesterday
   – The Madam asked, "What day was yesterday ?"

Model Examples

Q. State which punctuation mark is to be used in the given sentence.

1. You must study
   ① question mark   ② inverted commas
   ③ full stop   ④ exclamatory mark   ❸

2. When are you going to the school
   ① full stop   ② question mark
   ③ inverted commas   ④ exclamatory mark   ❷

3. Add the appropriate punctuation mark to the following sentence :
   How beautiful the scene was
   ① !   ② ?   ③ .   ④ ;   ❶

Examples for Practice

Q. State which punctuation mark should be given in the following sentence.

1. "What are you doing"
   ① question mark   ② full stop
   ③ exclamatory mark   ④ comma.

2. Minu said, "I want to play with you.
   ① exclamatory mark   ② comma
   ③ full stop   ④ inverted commas.
3. "May I play with you"
   ① full stop   ② question mark
   ③ exclamatory mark   ④ inverted comma
4. Hi, What a pleasant surprise
   ① full stop   ② exclamatory mark
   ③ comma   ④ question mark
5. Vegetables are fresh
   ① question mark   ② full stop
   ③ exclamatory mark   ④ comma

Answers

Q.	Ans.	Q.	Ans.	Q.	Ans.	Q.	Ans.
1.	❶	2.	❹	3.	❷	4.	❷
5.	❷						

❖ ❖ ❖

4.2   CONTRACTED FORMS

✌ INTRODUCTION :

In grammar a contracted form is a shortened form of a word or group of words, with the missing letters usually marked by an apostrophe.

Standard Contractions in English

- aren't   are not
- couldn't   could not
- doesn't   does not
- hadn't   had not
- haven't   have not

- he'll   he will; he shall

- can't   cannot
- didn't   did not
- don't   do not
- hasn't   has not
- he'd   he had; he would

- he's   he is; he has

- I'd — I had; I would
- I'm — I am
- isn't — is not
- let's — let us
- mustn't — must not
- she'd — she had; she would
- she's — she is; she has
- that's — that is; that has
- they'd — they had; they would
- they're — they are
- we'd — we had; we would
- we've — we have
- what'll — what will; what shall
- what's — what is; what has; what does
- where's — where is; where has
- who'll — who will; who shall
- who've — who have
- wouldn't — would not
- you'll — you will; you shall
- you've — you have

- I'll — I will; I shall
- I've — I have
- it's — it is; it has
- mightn't — might not
- shan't — shall not
- she'll — she will; she shall
- shouldn't — should not
- there's — there is; there has
- they'll — they will; they shall
- they've — they have
- we're — we are
- weren't — were not
- what're — what are
- what've — what have
- who'd — who had; who would
- who's — who is; who has
- won't — will not
- you'd — you had; you would
- you're — you are
-

Model Examples

Q. *Write the Contracted form in following Examples*

1. These are not Bananas.

    ① are not   ② aren't   ③ ardent   ④ are

2. Do they have Material to make thing
    ① have   ② they have   ③ They've   ④ They have ❸

━━━━━━━ **Examples for Practice** ━━━━━━━

Q. Write the Contracted form of the word in following sentences :

1. I have my own pen to write.
    ① have   ② I have   ③ I've   ④ I
2. I do not want to go.
    ① do not   ② do   ③ not   ④ don't
3. I am busy now.
    ① am   ② I am   ③ I   ④ I'm
4. I cannot stand now.
    ① can   ② not   ③ can't   ④ cannot
5. We are going to park.
    ① we're   ② We are   ③ We   ④ Are
6. Where is a temple ?
    ① where   ② Where is   ③ Is   ④ Where's

━━━━━━━ **Answers** ━━━━━━━

Q.	Ans.	Q.	Ans.	Q.	Ans.	Q.	Ans.
1.	❸	2.	❹	3.	❹	4.	❸
5.	❶	6.	❹				

✤ ✤ ✤

4.3	**EXPANDED FORMS**

✍ *INTRODUCTION :*

In grammar expanded form is long form of word or group of words.

Expanded Forms

- are not   aren't   • could not   couldn't

- did not   didn't   • does not   doesn't
- do not   don't   • have not   haven't
- shall not   shan't   • should not   shouldn't
- what are   what're   • what is   what's
- where is   where's   • who is   who's
- will not   won't   • you will   you'll
- you are   you're

Model Examples

Q. Choose the correct expanded form of word in the following sentences.

1. They aren't coming.
   ① are   ② not   ③ are not   ④ aren't   ❸

2. He doesn't have car.
   ① does not   ② does   ③ not   ④ doesn't   ❶

3. I don't have a balloon.
   ① do   ② not   ③ don't   ④ do not   ❹

Examples for Practice

Q. Choose the correct expanded form of word in the following sentences.

1. What're they doing there.
   ① what're   ② are   ③ what are   ④ what is

2. Where's the temple ?
   ① where   ② where is   ③ where're   ④ is

3. I won't be able to go to the market.
   ① will   ② not   ③ will go   ④ will not

4. This shouldn't be the way.
   ① should not   ② should
   ③ not   ④ should be

5. You're my best friend.
   ① you   ② are
   ③ yours   ④ you are

Answers

Q.	Ans.	Q.	Ans.	Q.	Ans.	Q.	Ans.
1.	❸	2.	❷	3.	❹	4.	❶
5.	❹						

❖ ❖ ❖

4.4   *IDIOMS, PHRASES AND PROVERBS*

✌ *INTRODUCTION :*

Proverb means a short saying which is meaningful and expresses wisdom of years as common sense, truth and useful thought. A proverb is a wise saying which conveys a universal truth.

Some proverbs are given below together with their meanings.

1. An apple a day keeps the doctor away   :   Eat fresh fruits and be healthy.

2. All that glitters is not gold   :   Things that are attractive are not always the best

3. As you sow, so you shall reap   :   You get good or bad fruit according to your good or bad deed

4. All roads lead to Rome   :   All well directed efforts achieve the same goal

5. A burnt child dreads the fire   :   Man learns by experience

6. We live in deeds, not in years : Our life is measured by our good deeds and not by the span of our life

7. It is easier said than done : It is very easy to speak than to act

8. Charity begins at home : One should start doing good things from oneself

9. The early bird catches the worm : To get benefit one should start work very early

10. Every dog has its day : Every person has his favourable period

11. The dog that bites does not bark : One who acts does not make loud noise

12. Where there is smoke there is fire : Behind every happening there is some reason

13. Slow and steady wins the race : For achieving success one should act patiently and calmly

14. Old is gold : Things of the past are always precious

15. Too many cooks spoil the broth : Too many experts make a mess of the job

16. Better late than never : It is better to do a thing even after delay rather than not do it at all

17. Cut your coat according to the cloth : Live within your income or make your plans fit the circumferences

18. Rome was not built in a day : Great things cannot be achieved in short span of time

19. Where there is a will, there is a way : If you have the will to do, you will also find a way to do it

20. A hard nut to crack : A difficult problem to solve

21. A friend in need is a friend indeed : A friend who helps another friend when he needs it is a true friend.

22.	A stitch in time saves nine	: A problem must be resolved at its initial stage or later it may become so bad that it will out of control.
23.	Birds of a feather flock together	: People of similar characters and tastes associate with one another.
24.	Do not judge a book by its cover	: Appearances are often misleading and deceptive.
25.	The dog that bites does not bark	: One who acts does not make loud noise.
26.	Work is worship	: There is no better way to worship than lay doing hard and sincere work.
27.	Haste makes waste	: Making hurry in doing things is wasting it altogether.
28.	A bad workman blames his tools	: An inefficient person always grumbles.
29.	Don't cross bridge before you come to it	: Don't worry about the difficulties untill they actually occur.
30.	Look before you leap	: Be careful before you take any action.
31.	Man proposes God disposes	: Man's efforts are sometimes shattered to reasons not known.
32.	Necessity is the mother of invention	: Need gives an inspiration to create new things.
33.	People who live in glass house should not throw stones at others	: People who are guilty should not accuse others for their sins.
34.	Sin and sorrow go together	: Who does a bad deed loses peace of mind.
35.	Well begun is half done	: A satisfactory beginning is half the work, for it is easy to go through it once it has been begun.

36.	Empty vessels make the most noise	:	Those who know or have little, often shout the loudest.
37.	Let bygones be bygones	:	Forget past quarrels and hatreds, however bitter, and make a fresh start in friendship, affection etc.
38.	Spare the rod and spoil the child	:	The surest way of spoiling a child is by allowing his faults to go unpunished, or by withdrawing him from parental authority.
39.	Every cloud has a silver lining	:	In every trouble and difficulty there is hope or expectation of an improvement is the circumstances
40.	Take things as they came	:	Accept every event that happens to you with calmness and without complaint even if it is unpleasant.
41.	A man is known by the company he keeps	:	A man's character can be judged by the people with whom he lives or associates.

SOME IMPORTANT IDIOMS

An idiom is a beautiful way of expressing thoughts. Idiom is a mode of expression makes a language more colourful and effective.

Some useful idioms with their meanings :

1.	Most recent	:	up to date
2.	To walk arm in arm	:	To walk in a friendly manner
3.	To keep at arm's length	:	To keep at a distance
4.	To back out	:	To dropout; to get out of
5.	To keep the ball rolling	:	To continue or maintain, some process eg. conversation
6.	In favour with	:	In good books of
7.	To got into hot water	:	To get into trouble

8.	A hard nut to crack	:	A difficult problem to solve
9.	Half the battle	:	Half of the difficulty overcome
10.	To bear in mind	:	To retain in one's memory or to remember
11.	To bear the brunt of	:	To bear the full ferce or to face the major difficulty of.
12.	To bear with	:	To tolerate, endure, put up with
13.	To beat about the bush	:	To convey one's meaning in a roundabout fashion.
14.	Bent upon	:	Determined to (take a certain action)
15.	To make one's point	:	To make one's opinions or feelings known.
16.	To play with fire	:	To take foolish or dangerous risks
17.	To kill two birds with one stone	:	With one action to accomplish two different purposes.
18.	A birds eye view	:	A wide perspective or a general survey such as a flying bird may obtains
19.	To bite off more than one can chew	:	To undertake more than one is able to perform
20.	A bolt from the blue	:	A sudden, unexpected misfortune.
21.	Within a stone's throw	:	At a short distance from
22.	To break open	:	To open by force.
23.	To call a spade a spade	:	To be very frank
24.	To bell the cat	:	To do something full of risk or danger.

25.	To eat one's words	:	To take back what one has said
26.	Once in a blue moon	:	Very rarely.
27.	To gain ground	:	To become more general or popular
28.	To give ear to	:	To listen to
29.	To take in account	:	To consider
30.	To bring to light	:	To make known, to reveal
31.	Out of the way	:	Strange
32.	Man of his words	:	A trustworthy man
33.	To hit the mail on the head	:	To say or do exactly the right thing.
34.	To take one's breath away	:	To make one breathless with surprise, delight etc.
35.	To come across	:	Accidentally to meet, encounter
36.	To carry out (or through)	:	To complete
37.	To carry on	:	To continue
38.	To take the bull by the horns	:	Boldly to face and tackle a difficulty.
39.	To get the hang of a thing	:	To understand the meaning of it.
40.	To turn down	:	To refuse or to reject
41.	To take to heart	:	To be seriously affected
42.	To roll up one's sleeves	:	To get ready for a fight or an effort.
43.	A slip of the tongue	:	A verbal error made in speaking.
44.	At sixes and sevens	:	In confusion or in disagreement
45.	To keep an eye on	:	To watch over
46.	Off and on	:	Now and then, occasionally
47.	To give ear to	:	To listen to
48.	A man of straw	:	Worthless or useless fellow
49.	To stand one's ground	:	To maintain one's position
50.	To take in account	:	To consider

Model Examples

Q. *Choose the proverbs having the closest meaning to the following.*

1. Good health is a real treasure

   ① No news is good news   ② Health is wealth

   ③ A stitch in time saves nine

   ④ Pen is mightier than a sword   ❷

2. One should start doing good things from oneself

   ① A cat has nine lives

   ② The darkest cloud has a silver lining

   ③ Don't make a pig of yourself

   ④ Charity begins at home   ❹

3. Behind every happening there is some reason

   ① Wisdom is too high for a fool

   ② Where there is smoke there is fire

   ③ Too many cooks spoil the broth

   ④ Time and tide wait for no man   ❷

Examples for Practice

Q. *Choose the proverbs having the closest meaning to the following.*

1. A man cannot satisfy too many at a time

   ① Rome was not built in a day

   ② No man can serve two masters

   ③ A rolling stone gathers no moss

   ④ A stitch in time saves nine

2. Don't be greedy

   ① The early bird catches the worm

   ② To err is human

   ③ Every dog has its day

   ④ Don't make a pig of yourself

3. Health of body and mind depends upon your good habits
   ① Full many flowers is born to blush unseen
   ② Fortune favours the brave
   ③ Fools rush in where angels fear to tread
   ④ Early to bed and early to rise makes one healthy and wise

4. Correct yourself as soon as you discover the mistake
   ① It never rains but pours
   ② It is never too late to mend
   ③ It is easier said than done
   ④ The ill wind that blows does no good to anyone

5. To make mistake is in human nature
   ① Early to bed and early to rise makes one healthy and wise
   ② A friend in need is a friend indeed
   ③ Fortune favours the brave
   ④ To err is human

6. Eat fresh fruit and be healthy
   ① A bad workman blames his tools
   ② Borrowed garments never fit well
   ③ As you sow, so you shall reap
   ④ An apple a day keeps the doctor away

7. Man's efforts are sometimes shattered due to reasons not known
   ① Man proposes and God disposes
   ② No man can serve two masters
   ③ New broom sweeps well
   ④ Nothing succeeds like success

8. Things of the past are always precious
   ① A rolling stone gathers no moss
   ② Old is gold
   ③ Prevention is better than cure
   ④ Pen is mightier than a sword

9. Absence of noise gives mental peace
   ① Still water runs deep
   ② Silence is golden
   ③ Sin and sorrow go together
   ④ Spare the rod and spoil the child

10. Something is better than nothing
    ① Half bread is better than no bread
    ② Blood is thicker than water
    ③ Cleanliness is next to godliness
    ④ Fortune favours the brave

11. Be careful before you take any action
    ① Make hay while the sun shines
    ② Look before you leap
    ③ Nature is the best physician
    ④ New broom sweeps well

12. Too many experts make mess of the job
    ① A thunderstorm often makes milk sour
    ② Time makes worst enemies friends
    ③ Time and tide wait for no man
    ④ Too many cooks spoil the broth

13. Every person has his favourable period
    ① Nothing venture, nothing have
    ② Early bird catches the worm
    ③ Every dog has its day
    ④ After the storm comes the calm.

14. Even little efforts achieve great success
    ① Little strokes fell great oaks
    ② Let not the pot call the kettle black
    ③ It is an evil wind that blows nobody good
    ④ It is easier said than done

15. You get good or bad fruit according to your good or bad deed
    ① Charity begins at home
    ② As you sow, so you shall reap
    ③ Blood is thicker than water
    ④ All that glitters is not gold

Q. *Find out the proper meaning of idioms given below.*

16. To move heaven and earth
    ① To travel between heaven and earth
    ② To make choice between good and bad
    ③ To make every possible effort
    ④ To bring heaven and earth together

17. To see eye to eye
    ① To examine eyes by an expert
    ② To be in complete agreement
    ③ To view correct picture
    ④ To look through other's eye

18. At sixes and sevens
    ① Between six and seven o'clock
    ② At the age of six and seven
    ③ In an orderly arrangement
    ④ In a disorder or confusion

19. Ins and outs
    ① Full details   ② Joys and sorrows
    ③ Correct meaning   ④ Insiders and outsiders

20. To keep the wolf from the door
    ① To be prepared for any danger
    ② To ward off starvation   ③ To be on the just side
    ④ To keep away extreme poverty

21. To worship the rising sun
    ① To make a salutation to the rising sun
    ② To honour a man who attends office
    ③ To honour promising young people
    ④ To welcome coming events

22. To make room for
    ① To dispose off   ② To spoil
    ③ To make a building   ④ To make place for
23. To pocket an insult
    ① To ignore insults   ② To take it to bread
    ③ To bear insult without resentment
    ④ To insult others
24. A hard nut to crack
    ① To take it to heart
    ② To know no bounds
    ③ A fish out of water
    ④ A difficult problem to solve
25. Select the correct meaning of the phrase : 'Stand by' :
    ① to stand at the side   ② to stand behind
    ③ to watch   ④ to help or support

Answers

Q.	Ans.	Q.	Ans.	Q.	Ans.	Q.	Ans.
1.	②	2.	④	3.	④	4.	②
5.	④	6.	④	7.	①	8.	②
9.	②	10	①	11.	②	12.	④
13	③	14.	①	15.	②	16.	③
17.	②	18.	④	19.	①	20.	②
21.	③	22.	④	23.	③	24.	④
25.	④						

✣ ✣ ✣

4.5   SLOGANS

✌ INTRODUCTION :

A slogan is an advertising tag line or phrase that advertisers create to visually express for the benefit of product or event.

Some Slogans

1. "Jai Hind" - Netaji Subhash Chandra Bose.
2. "Vande Mataram" - Bankim Chandra Chatopadhyay.
3. "Swaraj Mera Janam Siddh Adhikar Hai", Main Ise Lekar Rahunga" - Bal Gangadhar Tilak.
4. "Jai Jawan Jai Kisaan" - Lal Bahadur Shastri.
5. "Satyamev Jayate" - Pandit Madan Mohan Malaviya.
6. "Inquilaab Zindabad" - Bhagat Singh.
7. "You cannot believe in God until you believe in yourself" - Swami Vivekanand.
8. "Aaram Haraam Hai" - Pandit Jawaharlal Nehru.
9. "Go Green to Keep this World Clean."
10. "Save Water before its Too Late".
11. "Save Water Save Life".
12. "Education is the most Powerful Weapon that can change the World".
13. "Think Different" - Apple.
14. "Nothing is Impossible" - Adidas.
15. "Have a break, have a kit kit".
16. "Each One Plant One".
17. "Education is a Path not a Pedestrian".
18. "Its better late than never".
19. "Safety First is Safety Always".
20. "Be the change you want to see in the world - Mahatma Gandhi.
22. "Give Blood Save Life".

Model Examples

(I) *Find out the correct slogan writer in the following.*

1. "Jai Jawan Jai Kisaan", who has said this slogan ?
   ① Bal Gangadhar Tilak   ② Lal Bahadur Shastri   ❷
   ③ Mahatma Gandhi   ④ Pandit Jawaharlal Nehru

2. "Go Green to keep this World Clean", above slogan is related to what ?
   ① Water   ② Safety
   ③ Environment   ④ Tree   ❸

3. Laughter is the best ......
   ① Health   ② Practice
   ③ Exercise   ④ Medicine   ❹

4. "Satyamev Jayate" slogan was given by whom ?
   ① Pandit Madan Mohan Malaviya
   ② Bankim Chandra Chatopadhyay
   ③ Netaji Subhash Chandra Bose
   ④ Lal Bahadur Shastri   ❶

Examples for Practice

Fill in the blank with suitable alternative

1. "Aaram Haraam Hai", who gave this slogan ?
   ① Mahatma Gandhi
   ② Lal Bahadur Shastri
   ③ Pandit Jawaharlal Nehru
   ④ Netaji Subhash Chandra Bose

2. "Save Water Save Life" slogan is for what ?
   ① Environment   ② Water
   ③ Cleanliness   ④ Life

3. "Think Different" is a slogan of which company ?
   ① Microsoft   ② Samsung   ③ Apple   ④ Google

4. "Each One ...... One.
   ① Tree   ② Water   ③ Flower   ④ Plant

5. "Be the change you want to see in the world" given by whom?
   ① Pandit Jawaharlal Nehru
   ② Lal Bahadur Shastri
   ③ Mahatma Gandhi
   ④ Netaji Subhash Chandra Bose
6. An Apple a Day Keep ...... Away.
   ① Medicine　② Disease　③ Hospital　④ Doctor

Q.	Ans.	Q.	Ans.	Q.	Ans.	Q.	Ans.
1.	❸	2.	❷	3.	❸	4.	❹
5.	❸	6.	❹					

❖ ❖ ❖

4.6 FOLLOW INSTRUCTIONS / ROAD SIGNS

✌ INTRODUCTION :

Speed Limit

Speed limits would be varying in various states and it can be according to the vehicles as well. These Maximum Speed Limit of Motor Vehicles are set through the local government and people are required to follow all of them.

Road Safety

The renowned organization, RSC provides as the nodal organization for planning and managing initiatives of all Govt., Social and Business companies in our group for distributing attention about Street Protection. It is well known today that the internalization of road guidelines and road self-discipline by the motorists is a crucial precondition

Indian Traffic Rules and Signs

Basic Rules of the Road : There are certain rules that have been prepared for the benefit of people and the idea of preparing these rules is not that they should be understood by the drivers, but it should also be understood by the cyclists, pedestrians and other people. It is essential to follow all the rules and regulation and they are clearly listed here. People are recommended that they should be carefully observing all the rules and regulation and it is effectual to be careful, considerate and patient.

Traffic Signals

Traffic signals or stop lights are positioned on the road intersection and they are used for indicating that whether it is safe to walk or not. People are recommended that they should follow all the Traffic signs and they would be required to understand this information that is displayed through colour code.

Road Signals

These signs have got the very prominent role to play in the traffic system and they are made for the safety of people. According to the congress of Indian Roads, these signs and Traffic symbols have been categorized into 3 different categories

Model Examples

(I) ***Find out the correct answer in the following.***

1. Which sign is used for No U turn ?   ❹

   ① ② ③ ④

2. Which sign is used for No Overtaking ?   ❸

   ① ② ③ ④

Examples for Practice

Fill in the blank with suitable alternative

1. Which sign is used for Horn Prohibited ?

①  ②  ③ ④

2. Which sign is used for No Parking ?

①  ②  ③  ④

3. Which sign is used for turn right ahead ?

①  ②  ③  ④

Answers

Q.	Ans.	Q.	Ans.	Q.	Ans.
1.	④	2.	②	3.	④

❖ ❖ ❖

4.7   *PHRASES*

✌ INTRODUCTION

A phrase is a group or words that expresses a concept and is used as a unit within a sentence. Eight common types of phrases are: noun, verb, gerund, infinitive, appositive, participial, prepositional, and absolute.

✌ Noun Phrases

A noun phrase consists of a noun and all its modifiers.

Here are some examples :

- The bewildered tourist was lost.
- The senile old man was confused.

- The lost puppy was a wet and stinky dog.
- It was a story as old as time.

✌ Verb Phrases

A verb phrase consists of a verb and all its modifiers.

Here are some examples :

- He was waiting for the rain to stop.
- She was upset when it didn't boil.
- You have been sleeping for a long time.
- He was eager to eat dinner.

✌ Gerund Phrases

A gerund phrase is simply a noun phrase that starts with a gerund.

Here are some examples :

- Taking my dog for a walk is fun.
- Walking in the rain can be difficult.
- Getting a promotion is exciting.
- Signing autographs takes time.
- Going for ice cream is a real treat.

✌ Infinitive Phrases

An infinitive phrase is a noun phrase that begins with an infinitive.

Here are some examples :

- Everybody loves to watch movies.
- To make lemonade, you have to start with lemons.
- I tried to see the stage, but I was too short.
- She organized a boycott to make a statement.
- To see Niagara Falls is mind-boggling.
- He really needs to get his priorities in order.

✌ Appositive Phrases

An appositive phrase restates a noun and consists of one or more words.

Here are some examples :

- My favourite pastime, needlepoint, surprises some people.
- Her horse, an Arabian, was her pride and joy.

- My wife, the love of my life, is also my best friend.
- A cheetah, the fastest land animal, can run 70 miles an hour.

✌ Participial Phrases

A participial phrase begins with a past or present participle.

Here are some examples :

- Washed with my clothes, my cell phone no longer worked.
- Knowing what I know now, I wish I had never come here.
- I am really excited, considering all the people that will be there.
- We are looking forward to the movie, having seen the trailer last week.

✌ Prepositional Phrases

A prepositional phrase begins with a preposition and can act as a noun, an adjective or an adverb.

Here are some examples :

- The book was on the table.
- We camped by the brook.
- He knew it was over the rainbow.
- She was lost in the dark of night.

✌ Absolute Phrases

An absolute phrase has a subject, but not an acting verb, so it cannot stand alone as a complete sentence. It modifies the whole sentence, not just a noun.

Here are some examples :

- His tail between his legs, the dog walked out the door.
- Picnic basket in hand, she set off for her date.
- Their heads hanging down, the whole group apologized.

Model Examples

Q. Identify the correct phrase.

1. He always behaves in a good manner.

    ① He   ② in a good manner

    ③ always   ④ behaves

2. A boy from America won the race ❷
   ① A boy   ② from America
   ③ won   ④ the race

─────────── Examples for Practice ───────────

Q. *Find out the type of sentence.*

1. He is wearing a nice red shirt.
   ① He   ② is
   ③ wearing   ④ a nice red shirt

2. She brought a glass full of water.
   ① She   ② brought
   ③ glass   ④ a glass full of water

3. The boy with brown hair is laughing.
   ① The boy   ② is
   ③ The boy with brown hair ④ laughing

4. A man on the roof was shouting.
   ① A man   ② A man on the roof
   ③ was   ④ shouting

5. A boy on the roof is singing a song.
   ① A boy   ② on the roof
   ③ is singing   ④ a song

6. The man in the room is our teacher.
   ① The man   ② in the room
   ③ is our   ④ teacher

7. She is shouting in a loud voice.
   ① She   ② in a loud
   ③ is shouting   ④ in a loud voice

─────────── Answers ───────────

Q.	Ans.	Q.	Ans.	Q.	Ans.	Q.	Ans.
1.	❹	2.	❹	3.	❸	4.	❷
5.	❷	6.	❷	7.	❹		

❖ ❖ ❖

4.8   *ELEMENTS IN STORY*

✌ INTRODUCTION :

A story has five basic but important elements. These five components are the characters, the setting, the plot, the conflict, and the resolution. These essential elements keep the story running smoothly and allow the action to develop in a logical way that the reader can follow.

✌ CHARACTER

The characters are the individuals that the story is about. The author should introduce the characters in the story with enough information that the reader can visualize each person. This is achieved by providing detailed descriptions of a character's physical attributes and personality traits. Every story should have a main character. The main character determines the way the plot will develop and is usually who will solve the problem the story centers upon. However, the other characters are also very important because they supply additional details, explanations, or actions. All characters should stay true to the author's descriptions throughout the story so that the reader can understand and believe the action that is taking place and perhaps even predict which character may do what next.

✌ SETTING

The setting is the location of the action. An author should describe the environment or surroundings of the story in such detail that the reader feels that he or she can picture the scene. Unusual settings (such as a fantasy world) can be interesting, but everyday settings can help a reader to better visualize the story and feel connected to the plot!

✌ PLOT

The plot is the actual story around which the entire book is based. A plot should have a very clear beginning, middle, and end with all the necessary descriptions and suspense, called exposition so that the reader can make sense of the action and follow along from start to finish.

✌ CONFLICT

Every story has a conflict to solve. The plot is centered on this conflict and the ways in which the characters attempt to resolve the problem. When the story's action becomes most exciting, right before the resolution, it is called the climax

✌ RESOLUTION

The solution to the problem is the way the action is resolved. For example, Pranita often resolves a conflict by finding a compromise for two fighting characters or helping fix any mistakes she made while switcheroo into someone else. It is important that the resolution fit the rest of the story in tone and creativity and solve all parts of the conflict. Below is given a small story/drama.

Read the story and answer the questions given below it.

Although Sherri was only seven years old, people always wanted to know what she wanted to be when she grew up. Her response was easy, a teacher. She had the perfect picture in her mind what her classes would look like and how they would behave. The only problem was that she didn't have any worksheets or materials to give to her imaginary class.

In class she watched the teacher walk over to her file cabinet and throw mounds of unused worksheets in the trash. "What a waste! "Sherri murmured to herself. An idea suddenly blossomed in her head. She would use the worksheets that had ended up in the trash. After school, when the halls were clear of students and teachers, she sneaked into Mrs. Shaikh's class, her first grade classroom and grabbed the discarded worksheets. Feeling confident that she had accomplished her mission, she walked around the corner with the new teaching materials under her arms. A loud, booming voice startled her as the janitor yelled, "What are you doing here ? Go home !"

Sherri didn't wait to respond to his questions as she ran out of the schools front doors. As she walked home, she kept looking behind her to see if the janitor had followed her.

Safely home, she closed her bedroom door and announced to her imaginary students, "Good morning students. Today you are going to learn about nouns and verbs. I am going to pass out a few worksheets and explain the assignment to you."

1. The feeling or atmosphere created when reading a story is called the ....
    ① mood
    ② conflict
    ③ climax
    ④ setting

2. The plot of a story starts off with a ....
    ① climax
    ② rising action
    ③ conflict
    ④ theme

3. The most exciting part of a story is called the ....
    ① conflict
    ② falling action
    ③ resolution
    ④ climax

4. The moral or lesson to be learned in a story is called the ....
    ① conflict
    ② mood
    ③ sequencing
    ④ theme

5. Sherri searched in the trash for ....
    ① her homework
    ② her lunch
    ③ money
    ④ unused worksheets

6. Sherri can be best described as ....
    ① goal orientated
    ② shy
    ③ angry
    ④ moody

7. Sherri's imaginary class is located in ....
    ① dinning room
    ② school
    ③ library
    ④ her bedroom

8. What was the last event of the story ?
    ① The janitor yelled at her
    ② She ran out of the school
    ③ She walked home
    ④ She greeted her imaginary class.

9. Sherri's conflict at the beginning of the story is ....
   ① She doesn't have any teaching material.
   ② She doesn't know what she wants to do when she grows up.
   ③ That the janitor catches her sneaking into the trash.
   ④ That her teacher doesn't recycle.
10. Which one of the following is a major character ?
    ① Mrs. Shaikh   ② Sherri
    ③ Imaginary class   ④ Janitor

Answers

Q.	Ans.	Q.	Ans.	Q.	Ans.	Q.	Ans.
1.	❶	2.	❸	3.	❹	4.	❹
5.	❹	6.	❶	7.	❹	8.	❶
9.	❷	10.	❷				

❖ ❖ ❖

4.9   TENSES : PRESENT, PAST, FUTURE

✌ INTRODUCTION :

The time of a verb when the action takes place is called its tense. i.e. The Tense of a verb shows the time of an action or event.

Example :

     (1)   I <u>like</u> Mangoes   (Present time)

     (2)   I <u>liked</u> mangoes   (Past time)

     (3)   I <u>shall like</u> mangoes.   (Future time)

Thus,

1. A verb that refers to the Present Time is said to be in the Present Tense, as,

     I play   I go   I write

2. A verb that refers to the Past Time is said to be in the Past Tense, as,

     I played   I went   I wrote

3. A verb that refers to the Future Time is said to be in the future tense; as

> I will/shall play   I shall go   I shall write

So, there are three main tenses

    (1)   The Present Tense
    (2)   The Past Tense
    (3)   The Future Tense

Further, to know more about the terms of tenses of verbs study the following sentences :

The Present Tense :

    (i)   I write   (Simple Present Tense)
    (ii) I am writing   (Present continuous Tense)
    (iii) I have written   (Present Perfect Tense)
    (iv) I have been writing   (Present Perfect continuous Tense)

The Past Tense :

    (i)   I wrote   (Simple Past Tense)
    (ii) I was writing   (Past continuous Tense)
    (iii) I had written   (Past Perfect Tense)
    (iv) I had been writing   (Past Perfect continuous Tense)

The Future Tense :

    (i)   I shall write   (Simple future Tense)
    (ii) I shall be writing   (Future continuous Tense)
    (iii) I shall have written   (Future Perfect Tense)
    (iv) I shall have been writing   (Future Perfect continuous Tense)

Tense	Simple	Continuous	Perfect	Perfect continuous
PRESENT	I write	I am writing	I have written	I have been writing
PAST	I wrote	I was writing	I had written	I had been writing
FUTURE	I shall write	I shall be writing	I shall have written	I shall have been writing

✌ *Use of Tense*

(1) The simple present tense is expressed in two ways: as

(i) verb + '– s' or verb + '-es'

i.e.   play   plays

take   takes

go   goes

cross   crosses

Study the following table carefully

First Person	I go/play	We go/play
Second Person	You go/play	You go/play
Third Person	He/She/It goes/plays	They go/play

Simple Present Tense is used :

(i) To express what is actually taking place at the present moment; as,

See how it rains !

She looks beautiful.

(ii) To express universal truth; as

The sun rises in the east.

The earth is round.

Where there is a will, there is a way.

(iii) To express habitual action; as

He takes exercise every morning.

He gets up early in the morning.

(2) The Present Continuous Tense is used to express an action going an at the time of speaking, as,

The girls are dancing

They are running.

Formation : Present form of verb 'be' + verb + ing

(3) The Present Perfect Tense expresses an action begun in the Past and completed at the present time, as,

The train arrived.

The girls have learnt their lesson

Present Perfect Tense

First Person	I have spoken	We have spoken
Second Person	You have spoken	You have spoken
Third Person	He has spoken She has spoken Raj has spoken	They have spoken The children have spoken

Note :

(i) He has lived here for four years, means that he is still living here.

(ii) He lived here for four years, means that he is no longer living here.

Formation : 'has' or 'have' + the past participle form of the verb

(4) The Present Perfect continuous Tense is used to indicate an action which began in the past and is still going on; as,

I have been working for two hours.

Note :

In the Present Perfect Continuous Tense, we use 'since' to indicate 'point of time' and 'for' to indicate 'period of time'.

example :

Since morning, Since last night, Since Tuesday last, Since December last, Since 1962 etc.

For a long time, for six months, for five years, etc.

I have been waiting for you for half an hour.

We have been playing football since 8 o'clock.

Formation : 'has' or 'have' + been + verb + ing

(5) The Simple Past tense is used : To express an action that took place in the past times, as,

I met him yesterday.

I failed last year.

Formation : 'verb' + 'ed' (mainly)

(6) The Past Continuous Tense denotes : An action begun and continuing in the past time, as

He was singing when I called upon him.

They were playing when we saw them.

Formation past form of the verb 'be' + verb + ing

   i.e. be + verb + ing

      Was   saying

      were   running

(7) The Past Perfect Tense expresses : An action completed at some point in past time before another action was begun, as,

The train had left when I reached the railway station.

They had completed their work before I reached.

Formation : 'had' + the past participle form of the verb

Note : The verb expressing the previous action is put into Past Perfect Tense.

(8) The Past Perfect continuous tense is used to express an action which was completed at definite past time, but which had been going on till then, as,

      It had been raining .....

      We had been writing ......

Formation : 'had' + been + verb + ing

(9) The Simple Future Tense is used to express some future action, as

      I shall see you tomorrow.

      They will meet us on Tuesday.

Formation : I/we + shall do

      He/she/it/Ram will do

(10) The Future Continuous Tense expresses : An action going on at some point in future time, as,

      He will be going tonight

      I shall be visiting us next month.

Formation : 'shall be' or 'will be' + verb + 'ing'.

(11) The Future Perfect Tense denotes : An action that will be completed at some point in future time; as

      I shall have finished this exercise by 6 o'clock

      I shall have done my work before you come.

Formation : 'will have' + the past participle form.

(12) The Future Perfect Continuous Tense is used to express : An action continuing beyond a point of time in future; as,

Ashok will have been living in Jaipur for ten years.

By the end of this month.

We shall have been playing for three hours when you come here.

Formation : 'will have' + 'been' + verb + 'ing'

Model Examples

(I) **Find out the tense of the verb in the following.**

1. Ram is writing.
   - ① past
   - ② future
   - ③ present
   - ④ simple past   ❸
2. If you study, you will pass
   - ① future
   - ② past
   - ③ Present
   - ④ simple past   ❶

Examples for Practice

Fill in the blank with suitable alternative.

1. The sun ...... set.
   - ① has
   - ② is
   - ③ has been
   - ④ will be
2. They ..... arrived.
   - ① has
   - ② have
   - ③ have been
   - ④ are
3. Ravi ..... to wear blue trousers.
   - ① has liked
   - ② like
   - ③ liking
   - ④ likes
4. I ...... leave for Shimla on Monday.
   - ① shall
   - ② shall be
   - ③ shall have
   - ④ have been
5. John will .... meeting his father.
   - ① be
   - ② been
   - ③ being
   - ④ bee

   Find the tenses of the following
6. Ajay was an actor.
   - ① Present
   - ② Past
   - ③ Future
   - ④ Simple present

7. I am going to Mumbai.
   - ① past
   - ② present
   - ③ simple future
   - ④ future

8. I have done my homework.
   - ① future
   - ② past
   - ③ present perfect
   - ④ simple present

9. She was reading a book.
   - ① present
   - ② past
   - ③ simple future
   - ④ future

10. The dog barked at me.
   - ① past
   - ② future
   - ③ present
   - ④ simple present

11. Radha was skipping.
   - ① past
   - ② future perfect
   - ③ present
   - ④ simple future

12. John performed various activities.
   - ① simple present
   - ② past perfect
   - ③ simple future
   - ④ simple past

13. The train will be late by two hours.
   - ① future perfect
   - ② simple present
   - ③ present continuous
   - ④ simple future

14. Mary sings a sweet song.
   - ① present perfect
   - ② simple present
   - ③ simple past
   - ④ past perfect

15. The bus will be arriving soon.
   - ① simple future
   - ② future continuous
   - ③ simple past
   - ④ past perfect

Answers

Q.	Ans.	Q.	Ans.	Q.	Ans.	Q.	Ans.
1.	❶	2.	❷	3.	❹	4.	❶
5.	❶	6.	❷	7.	❷	8.	❸

9.	❷	10.	❶	11.	❶	12.	❹
13.	❹	14.	❷	15.	❷		

❖ ❖ ❖

4.10 | *MAKE MEANINGFUL SENTENCES*

A meaningful sentence is one that adds value to a paragraph by bringing in information. The sentence delivers a logical fact in addition to good subject-verb agreement, spelling and grammar. Every sentence must be written for a purpose, specifically to provide supporting facts.

The content of the sentence must add meaning. When a sentence lacks significance to the story and the reader, it does not convey the purpose for which it is written. It is always good for one to read a sentence for clarity, purpose and meaning, to ensure that it makes sense. In long essays, it is desirable to hire a proof-reader to go though the work before publishing it.

 Model Examples

1. has / Susie / lessons / her / learned
   ① Susie has learned her lessons
   ② Susie learned her lessons
   ③ Susie has learn her lessons
   ④ None of these   ❶

2. There I six o'clock got to have be
   ① I have there by six o'clock
   ② I have to be there by six o'clock
   ③ I went there by six o'clock
   ④ I have to by six o'clock

Examples for Practice

1. Waiting we for have ages been.
   ① I have waiting for ages.
   ② We have been waiting for ages.
   ③ I wait there by ages.
   ④ Have I been working for ages.
2. Their they in have already work handed.
   ① I have already handed in their work.
   ② They have already handed in their work.
   ③ I will already handed in their work.
   ④ They have handed their work.
3. Working Supriya has for been us years for twenty.
   ① Supriya has been working for us for twenty years.
   ② Supriya has been working to us for twenty years.
   ③ She has been working to us for twenty years.
   ④ All are correct.
4. Your have you breakfast had?
   ① Have you had breakfast.
   ② Have your completed breakfast.
   ③ Have you had your breakfast.
   ④ Do you complete breakfast.
5. Start decided to a has business Emily.
   ① Emily decided to start a business.
   ② Emily has decided to start a business.
   ③ Emily decided starting a business.
   ④ Emily had decided to start a business.

Answers

Q.	Ans.	Q.	Ans.	Q.	Ans.	Q.	Ans.
1.	❷	2.	❷	3.	❶	4.	❸
5.	❷						

CREATIVE WRITING

UNIT 5

| 5.1 | GIVE TITLES, CAPTIONS AND HEADLINES ON NEWS, STORIES, PICTURES & CARTOONS |

✌ INTRODUCTION :

Creative writing is any writing that goes beyond the lines of normal professional, journalistic, academic or technical forms of literature, normally identified by an emphasis on narrative craft, character development, and the use of literary tropes or with different traditions of poetry and poetics. Due to the looseness of the definition, it is possible for writing such as feature stories to be considered creative writing, even though they fall under journalism, because the content of features is specifically focused on narrative and character development. Both fictional and non-fictional works fall into this category, including such forms as novels, biographies, short stories, and poems. In the academic setting, creative writing is typically separated into fiction and poetry classes, with a focus on writing in an original style, as opposed to imitating pre-existing genres such as horror.

Writing for the screen and stage—screenwriting and playwriting—are often taught separately, but fit under the creative writing category as well.

Creative writing can be considered any writing of original composition. In this sense, creative writing is a more modern and process-oriented, a name for what has been traditionally called literature, including the variety of its genres.

✌ WHAT IS THE MEANING OF TITLE, CAPTION & HEADLINE?

Title is an identifying name given to a book play, film, musical composition, or other work. It is also a descriptive or distinctive appellation, especially one belonging to a   person by right of   rank, office, attainment, etc.

A caption is a short explanation that accompanies an article, photograph or illustration. It is also a line displaying the dialogue and description of action situations along the bottom of the screen for a movie or television show. In the legal world, a caption is the title of a document. The word also describes the process of creating one of these labels or titles.

A Headline is a head of a newspaper story or article usually printed in large type and giving the gist of the story or article that follows. A headline's purpose is to quickly and briefly draw attention to the story. It is generally written by a copy editor, but may also be written by the writer, the page layout designer, or other editors.

✌ *NEWS* :

News is   packaged information about current   events happening somewhere else. News moves through many different media, based on word   of   mouth, printing, postal   systems, broadcasting,   and electronic communication.

Model Examples

(1)   A spell of heavy showers that lashed parts of the city on Tuesday afternoon brought much-needed relief from the rising temperature over the last two days.

In its latest forecast, the India Meteorological Department has said spells of light rainfall are expected in the city till August 1, followed by moderate rainfall in the range of 10-15 mm. "As per the monthly long range forecast for August, there is good rainfall in store for the city," DS Pai, scientist at the IMD, Pune, said, adding that the country is expected to get 104% rainfall.

"Another cyclonic circulation is prevalent over Marathwada and adjoining regions. Feeble off-shore trough continues from Konkan and Goa to Kerala coast, but these systems will not cause much rainfall over Pune," said an IMD official.

Pune has received 275.7mm of rainfall in July, so far, which is 14.0 mm less than the average. While the IMD has forecast heavy rainfall over isolated places over north central Maharashtra on July 27th, there will be only moderate rainfall thereafter.

Q. Choose an appropriate Headline from the following Options

① Light Showers in Store till August 1st
② Heavy Rains till August 1st
③ No Rains till August   ④ None of the Above.   ❶

(2)   A team of birdwatchers that went out looking for birds in India's eastern-most district have discovered the existence of a new species of primate (primate are a group of mammals to which humans belong too) in India. The White-cheeked Macaque was spotted in Anjaw district of Arunachal Pradesh by a group of wildlife experts and photographers who were visiting the area to bird-watch. The macaque, which is a kind of monkey, has a hairless tail with hair on its neck and chin that creates a white-cheek effect. The White-cheeked Macaque is itself a new species to the world as it was discovered in Tibet only in 2015. The Anjaw district, where the Indian population is found, borders Tibet.

Q. Choose an appropriate Headline from the following Options

① New Species Found
② New Primate Species Discovered in India
③ New Animals Discovered in India
④ None of the above   ❷

Examples for Practice

April 23rd we recall Shakespeare Literature as we observe World Book and Copyright Day. This day, UNESCO seeks to promote reading, publishing and the protection of intellectual property through copyright. On 23rd April, great personalities, Cervantes, Shakespeare and Inca Garcilaso de la Vega all died. It is also the date of birth or death of other prominent authors such as Maurice Druon, K. Laxness, Vladimir Nabokov, Josep Pla and Manuel Mejía Vallejo.

The idea for this celebration originated in Catalonia where on 23rd April, Saint George's Day, a rose is traditionally given as a gift for each book sold. The original idea of World Book Day was of the Valencian writer Vicente Clavel Andres as a way to honour the author Miguel de Cervantes, who died on April 23rd. The date is also the anniversary of the death of William Shakespeare and Inca Garcilaso de la Vega.

1. Choose an Appropriate Headline from the following Options
    ① Book Day   ② Copy Right Day
    ③ World Book Day and Copyright Day
    ④ None of the Above

A cool new range of products for girls 6-12 called DC Super Hero Girls to be launched by joint force of DC Comics, Warner Bros, Mattel and Random House Children's Books. The universe features the iconic female superheroes and villains of the DC universe, including Wonder Woman, Batgirl, Supergirl, Poison Ivy, Bumble Bee and Katana. The twist is that this universe shows the women in their formative years, before they found out they have super powers.

Each character will have her own story which will be told over a number of platforms. The program kicks off in the fall of 2015 with what DC calls "an immersive digital experience." There will be original digital content which will be interactive. There will be games, as well. In 2016 the program really ramps up, with TV specials, original videos, clothing, books and toys.

Random House Books for Young Readers will do all the book publishing for the line. Random House will publish a series of books in the DC Super Hero Girls line. The books will roll out in the spring of 2016. They will coordinate with original graphic novels that DC Entertainment will publish. LEGO Group will create building sets which will feature the young superheroes. This means Girls can be Super Heros – why the only label for Boys? It seems to be a fantastic option with the Super Girls stories and the colorful Graphics to attract with the books and digital experience.

2. Choose an appropriate Headline from the following options
   ① Digital Experience to be given to D.C Super Hero Girls Comics
   ② D.C Super Hero Girls Comics
   ③ Digital Experience for the Comics
   ④ None of the Above

Answers

Q.	Ans.	Q.	Ans.
1.	❸	2.	❶

❖ ❖ ❖

❧ STORIES :

A story is a simulation that allows the reader to experience what the protagonist goes through. But how do we get the reader to empathize with the people we are helping, with the cause they represent? By letting them feel what they feels.

Model Examples

There was a Mogul Emperor in India, Akbar The Great (1542-1605). His full name was Jalaluddin Mohammed Akbar and he ruled India from 1560 to 1605. He himself was illiterate, but he invited several learned people in his court. Among these people, nine were very famous and were called Nav Ratna (Nine Jewels of the Mogul Crown) of his court. Among these nine jewels, five people were more famous - Tansen, Todarmal, Abul Fazal, Maan Singh and Birbal.

On the basis of this story answer the following Questions:

1. Choose an appropriate Title from the following options :

1. ① Akbar the Great   ② The Mughal King
   ③ The Famous King   ④ None of the Above   ❶
2. How many famous people were in his court?
   ① Seven   ② Nine
   ③ Eight   ④ Five   ❷

3. By what name were these people called?
   ① Asta Pradhan   ② Parliament
   ③ Nav Ratna   ④ Famous Nine   ❸

Devan was a clever thief. He robbed the rich and gave all to the sick and the needy. The other thieves were jealous of him. They planned to get rid of him. They challenged to steal the King's Pyjamas.

Deven accepted the challenge. After that he prepared to execute the new challenge. He charted out a plan to steal the King's Pajamas. He prepared himself mentally to carry out a plan. He went to the King's Palace. He found the King sleeping. He opened a bottle of red ants on the bed. The King was badly bitten. He cried for help. The servants rushed in. They pretended to look for ants. Deven removed the King's Pyjamas and escaped. Other thieves were dumb founded. They accepted Deven as their leader.

---

1. Choose an appropriate Title from the following options
   ① Deven the Thief   ② The Clever Thief
   ③ The Thief   ④ None of the Above   ❷

2. What challenge was given to Devan?
   ① to steal the king's crown
   ② to steal the king's cloths
   ③ to steal the king's Pyjamas
   ④ to seal the king's things.   ❸

Examples for Practice

(1) There was an old owl that lived in an oak. Every day he saw incidents happening around him. Yesterday he saw a boy helping an old man to carry a heavy basket. Today he saw a girl shouting at her mother.

The more he saw the less he spoke. As he spoke less, he heard more. He heard people talking and telling stories. He heard a woman saying that an elephant jumped over a fence. He also heard a man saying that he had never made a mistake. The old owl had seen and heard about what happened to people. Some became better and some became worse. But the old owl had become wiser each and every day.

1. Choose an appropriate Title from the following options
    ① The Owl   ② The Old Wise Owl
    ③ The Old Owl   ④ None of the Above
2. Choose an appropriate Caption from the following options
    ① The great Old wise Owl!   ② The Rich Owl
    ③ The old Owl   ④ None of the Above
3. Choose an appropriate Headline from the following options
    ① The Owl   ② The Owl Who was Wise
    ③ The Intelligent Owl   ④ None of the Above

---

(2)   There lived many mice in a grocer's shop. They ate plenty of grains and the grocer suffered heavy loss. So, he brought a fat cat to catch the mice. The mice were worried. They held a meeting to drive away the cat.

A smart-looking mouse suggested that the cat moved softly and swiftly. They decided to tie a bell round its neck. So that when the cat moves, the mice would become aware of the cat. All the mice agreed to this decision. The old mouse said, "Can you tell me who is to bell the cat?" There was no reply. Their decision is not yet executed.

---

4. Choose an appropriate Title from the following options.
    ① The Cat   ② Belling the Cat
    ③ Bell the Cat   ④ None of the Above
5. Choose an appropriate Caption from the following options.
    ① 'Can you tell me who is to bell the cat'?
    ② 'Who will bell the cat'?
    ③ The Mouse and the cat
    ④ None of the Above
6. Choose an appropriate Headline from the following options
    ① The Wise Mouse's Idea to Bell the Cat
    ② Belling the Cat
    ③ The Idea to Bell the Cat
    ④ None of the Above

Answers

Q.	Ans.	Q.	Ans.	Q.	Ans.	Q.	Ans.
1.	❸	2.	❶	3.	❷	4.	❸
5.	❸	6.	❶					

❖ ❖ ❖

✌ PICTURES AND CARTOONS :

A cartoon is a form of two-dimensional illustrated visual art. While the specific definition has changed over time, modern usage refers to a typically non-realistic or semi-realistic drawing or painting intended for satire or humour, or to the artistic style of such works. An artist who creates cartoons is called a cartoonist.

Model Examples

Q. Give an appropriate Caption for the following cartoons.

① Let's get Clean
② Sorry, Son.... There is no App for That
③ Wow! So much Snow
④ None of the Above   ❷

① Jai Hind   ② Tribute
③ Salute!   ④ None of the Above   ❸

Examples for Practice

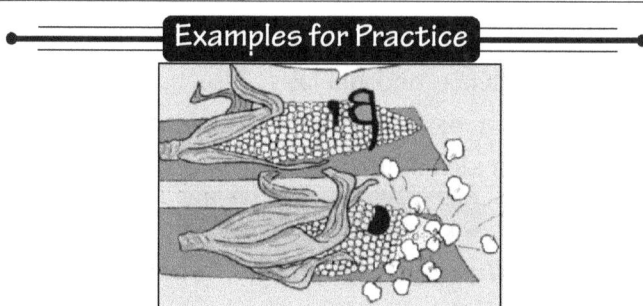

1. Choose an appropriate Caption from the following Options
   ① What a Lovely Day!   ② Sunscreen is a Must
   ③ 'Didn't I tell you to apply Sunscreen'
   ④ None of the Above

2. Choose an appropriate Caption from the following options
   ① What a Snow!
   ② 'I told you cigarettes were bad for you'
   ③ Sleepy Lazy Boy   ④ None of the Above

Answers

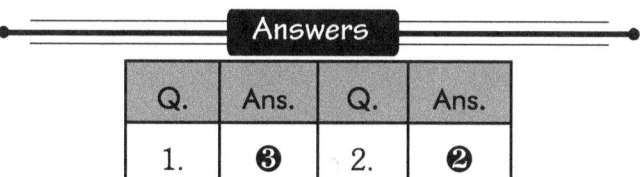

Q.	Ans.	Q.	Ans.
1.	❸	2.	❷

❖ ❖ ❖

5.2 PARAGRAPH WRITING, STORIES, PROCESSES, EVENTS, EXPERIMENTS

✍ PARAGRAH WRITING :

A clear and effective paragraph is constructed like an essay. Just as an essay has a main idea (thesis statement) that is developed and supported with evidence and analysis in the body paragraphs, a paragraph needs to focus on a single idea that is developed and supported with evidence and analysis. Also, just as an essay ends with a conclusion, a paragraph should close by linking the topic sentence to the main idea in the next paragraph.

Model Examples

Q. Read the following paragraphs, each containing five sentences and fill in the gaps using the appropriate words given to make it a meaningful paragraph. Write the numbers given for the options as answers.

(1)

1. Prakash bought a .... ticket.
   ① railway   ② lottery   ③ bus   ④ drama   ❷

2. He brought the ticket .... with great care.
   ① school   ② bazaar   ③ theatre ④ home   ❹

3. Next day he saw the number in the ....
   ① newspaper   ② book
   ③ magazine   ④ weekly   ❶

4. He was declared a ....winner.
   ① medal   ② award   ③ prize   ④ shield   ❸

5. "Hey, I have won!" he ....
   ① sighed   ② begged
   ③ exclaimed   ④ cried   ❸

(2)

1. It was a very .... experience having dinner with the young musician, Amit Dutta in a Kolkata restaurant.
   ① amusing   ② boring
   ③ disturbing   ④ scary   ❶

2. We had some .... about one of his recent music albums and later he asked me to have lunch with him at Trinca's.
   ① discussion   ② appointment
   ③ differences   ④ arguments   ❶

3. I arrived at Trinca's around half past eleven and found him waiting looking a little ....
    ① impatient   ② nervous   ③ angry   ④ dull ❶

4. I didn't know what he was .... about, but I did not worry about it.
    ① looking   ② curious
    ③ thinking   ④ nervous   ❸

5. I ordered some .... for lunch.
    ① rupees   ② rice   ③ wine   ④ water   ❷

─────────────── **Examples for Practice** ───────────────

Read the below given passages and answer the questions given below the passages.

The questions are provided with four alternative answers. Select the correct answer from the alternatives.

Once upon a time the King of France decided to hold a grand feast. He invited princes, rich merchants, brave warriors and all the other important people in his kingdom.

On the night of the feast, the king and his guests sat together at a long table in the dining hall. They talked and laughed and everyone was happy.

Suddenly a huge animal burst into the hall. It was a horrible looking dragon. It was as tall as a tree, as abroad as a house, with teeth like spikes and claws like knives. The skin was hard and scaly and the eyes were red. Red flames shot forth from his mouth and his nostrils belched out black smoke.

Now, the dragon was a very mean creature. It walked straight to the head of the table and sat between the king and the queen. Everyone became scared and stopped talking. However, Ivan the brave warrior stood up and said angrily, "What a rude and impolite creature you are!"

1. Who decided to hold a grand feast?
    ① King of India   ② King of Prussia
    ③ King   ④ King of France

2. Suddenly a huge .... burst into the hall.
   ① crowd   ② bird   ③ animal   ④ worm
3. Red flames shot forth from his mouth and black smoke from his ....
   ① ears   ② nostrils   ③ eyes   ④ mouth
4. Who exclaimed "What a rude and impolite creature you are!"
   ① King   ② Queen   ③ Ivan   ④ Guest

━━━━━━━━━━━━━━━ **Answers** ━━━━━━━━━━━━━━━

Q.	Ans.	Q.	Ans.	Q.	Ans.	Q.	Ans.
1.	❹	2.	❸	3.	❷	4.	❸

✤✤ ✤

When coffee was first introduced in Europe during the second part of the 17th century, there was a great deal of controversy about it. Many learned doctors announced that coffee was a strong poison and should be prohibited. Others insisted it was a good thing to drink coffee and very soon coffee houses sprang up everywhere.

Coffee actually acts as a poison when it is given in large doses to animals in laboratory tests. It can also produce toxic effects in small children. However, for adults drinking it in moderation, it is definitely not poison.

The coffee bean contains one percent of a substance known as caffeine which is always combined with acids. Most people believe that it is caffeine which produces all the effects that coffee has on the body, but the other substances in the coffee bean are involved too.

Here are some of the things that happen when someone drinks coffee. The colour of the coffee itself produces stimulating effects in various parts of the body. The blood vessels in the brain are dilated so that circulation is improved and this removes some of the fatigue toxins from the brain.

1. There was a great deal of controversy about coffee. This statement means.....

   ① all agreed that coffee was a good drink.

   ② all agreed that coffee was a bad drink.

   ③ some doctors announced that people should prefer coffee to tea.

   ④ some agreed that coffee was a good drink and some said it should not be consumed.

2. Coffee is certainly not a poison when it is given.....

   ① in large doses to animals.

   ② to children on a large scale.

   ③ to adults in moderation.

   ④ mixed with tea to anyone.

③ In the above passage, the term 'learned doctors' is used. Here it means .....

   ① the doctors who are well read in the field of science.

   ② the students learning in a medical college.

   ③ the doctors who give importance to learning only.

   ④ the doctors who were only learning about side effects of coffee on the body.

4. Coffee should be prohibited. If we change this sentence into 'active voice' it will be....

   ① Coffee should be prohibited by them.

   ② Let the coffee be prohibited.

   ③ Coffee must not be prohibited.

   ④ They should prohibit coffee.

Q.	Ans.	Q.	Ans.	Q.	Ans.	Q.	Ans.
1.	❹	2.	❸	3.	❶	4.	❹

Answers

❖ ❖ ❖

There was one particular type of animal that lived in a particular period of the Earth's history. This was the 'dinosaur', a word derived from Greek words meaning 'terrible lizard'. It lived about 225 million years ago to 100 million years ago. On our twenty-four hour clock of the Earth's history, dinosaurs disappeared about twenty-five million minutes ago and existed for about ten million minutes.

There were several types of dinosaurs as seen by the shape of their skeletons. Some types were amphibious, that is, they could live on both land and in water. The other types lived entirely on land. Some were herbivorous eating only plants; others were carnivorous eating other animals. All were reptiles, that is, creatures that crawled on the ground as lizards and snakes do today. They were also 'cold blooded' needing heat to warm their blood and make them active. If it was cold, they were dull and slow; if it was too hot, they had to find somewhere to cool off!

1. Choose the most suitable title for the passage.
   ① Earth's History
   ② The Scientists
   ③ Fish and Birds
   ④ Terrible Lizards

2. How long did dinosaurs last on Earth?
   ① 10 million years
   ② 125 million years
   ③ 325 million years
   ④ 35 millions years.

3. Four statements are given below. Pick out the correct one.
   ① Cats and cows are herbivorous animals.
   ② Lions and zebras are carnivorous animals.
   ③ Frogs and fish are amphibious animals.
   ④ Dinosaurs were amphibious, herbivorous and carnivorous.

4. In the above passage, the term cold blooded means needing heat to warm the body. What is another meaning of the term cold blooded?
   ① Dishonest
   ② Sympathetic
   ③ Cruel
   ④ Harmless

Answers

Q.	Ans.	Q.	Ans.	Q.	Ans.	Q.	Ans.
1.	❹	2.	❷	3.	❹	4.	❸

✌ STORY WRITING :

Story writing is an art. While some are born with this artistic gift, anyone can develop this art by gradual practice. The aspects of correct and good language and the skill of narrating events and happenings in a systematic and regular flow are vital for good story writing.

The following points must always be kept in mind when writing a story.

1. The plot.
2. Systematic narration.
3. Simple language.
4. Not changing the main part of the story.
5. The sequence of events.
6. Major points of interest and the moral of the story.
7. Appropriate heading.

Model Examples

My Family

I love my family. There are five people in my family. I have one brother and one sister. My brother is seven and my sister is two. My mother and father make the rules for my family. My little sister gets in trouble sometimes. Our favourite thing to do as a family is to play games together.

Answer the questions about the story.

1. How many people are in the family? _____
   ① four   ② three   ③ two   ④ five   ❹

2. How old is the sister? _____
   ① one year   ② two years
   ③ three years   ④ six years   ❷

3. Who gets in trouble sometimes? _____
   ① my sister   ② my brother
   ③ my mother   ④ my father   ❶

4. Who makes the rules?
   ① father   ② brother
   ③ sister   ④ mother and father   ❹

5. What does the family like to do best?
    ① eat   ② pray
    ③ talk   ④ play games   ❹

The Greedy Farmer

> Once there lived a farmer in a village. He was very poor. A saint visited the village and took pity on the farmer. He gave the farmer a wonderful hen that gave one golden egg every day.
>
> The farmer grew richer and richer. But he also started becoming greedy. He wanted to get all the golden eggs at once. He took out a knife and cut the hen's stomach to extract all the golden eggs once for all. However, he could find nothing.
>
> The farmer was very sad and disappointed. But it was no use repenting. He could get no more gold and hence became poor again.

Answer the questions about the story.

1. Where did the farmer live?
    ① village   ② town   ③ town   ④ city   ❶
2. Who visited the village where the farmer lived?
    ① friend   ② saint   ③ soldier   ④ king   ❷
3. What did the saint gift the farmer?
    ① cat   ② dog   ③ cow   ④ hen   ❹
4. What happened to the hen?
    ① given away   ② died
    ③ went missing   ④ stomach cut open   ❹
5. What is the moral of the story?
    ① greed is a curse   ② become rich
    ③ become poor   ④ happy   ❶

Examples for Practice

A Picnic

> Last week I went with some close friends to Lonavala for a picnic. We decided to go on our motorcycles. The other arrangements had already been done in advance. We set out when the weather was pleasant. The sky was cloudy and a cool wind was blowing. We were all feeling a little cold.

Moreover it looked like it would rain. We left our motorcycles under a tree and started trekking. When we reached the banks of the canal we spread a big carpet on the ground and started playing a game of cards. After a few games, we decided to dance and sing songs.

Soon it was time for lunch. We decided to go swimming before having lunch. After a good swim we became very hungry and decided to have our lunch. All in all we had a great time and all of us enjoyed the picnic very much.

Answer the questions about the story.

1. To which place did they go for the picnic?
    ① Mathura   ② Lonavla
    ③ Sinhagad   ④ Matheran
2. What mode of transport was used for the picnic?
    ① bicycle   ② motorcycle
    ③ taxi   ④ auto-rickshaw
3. How was the weather?
    ① sky was cloudy   ② hot
    ③ humid   ④ rainy
4. Where were the motorcycles parked?
    ① in the garage   ② under a tree
    ③ banks of the canal   ④ on the road
5. When did they have their lunch?
    ① after swimming   ② before swimming
    ③ after playing games   ④ after dancing

Answers

Q.	Ans.	Q.	Ans.	Q.	Ans.	Q.	Ans.
1.	❷	2.	❷	3.	❶	4.	❷
5.	❶						

2. King Richard

King Richard was an able and intelligent king of England many centuries ago. He was known for his valour and agility in battle with swords and spears.

One day he decided to go hunting with his daughter Mary. They rode on a horse with Mary sitting on her father's back.

After travelling for a while they reached the banks of a river. Just then they were attacked by a gang of dacoits. Since his daughter was with him, the king decided not to fight and instead flee from the place. He decided to swim across the river but was unable to do so since his daughter was on his back.

Being an expert spear thrower, he tied his daughter to his spear and hurled it with all his strength to the other side of the river. After doing so, he dived into the river and swam across to the other side.

This unexpected action by the king amazed the dacoits and they gave up the chase.

Answer the questions about the story.

1. What was King Richard known for?
   ① valour and agility   ② kindness
   ③ cruelty   ④ compassion
2. What was the king's daughter's name?
   ① Camille   ② Mary   ③ Yvonne   ④ Daisy
3. Who were they attacked by?
   ① dacoits   ② thieves
   ③ friends   ④ enemies
4. What did the king do to save his daughter?
   ① made her swim   ② tied her to his spear
   ③ left her behind   ④ dive
5. Why did the dacoits give up the chase?
   ① amazement   ② surprise
   ③ confusion   ④ shock

Answers

Q.	Ans.	Q.	Ans.	Q.	Ans.	Q.	Ans.
1.	❶	2.	❷	3.	❶	4.	❷
5.	❶						

✌ PROCESSES :

Introduction : There are some steps involved in creative writing for any particular project or projects.

The 5 step for writing process are as follows

1. Prewriting :   Getting your thoughts and writing on paper.
2. Thesis   :   Finding the main point, you want to write.
3. Outline   :   Organise your idea to make writing easier.
4. Drafting   :   Converting you ideas into full sentences.
5. Revision   :   Reworking of your writing.

Model Examples

1. What are the steps or process in paragraph or story writing sequentially ?

①   Pre-writing, Thesis, Outline, Drafting, Revision
②   Thesis, Prewriting, Outline, Drafting, Revision
③   Drafting, Thesis, Pre-writing, Revision
④   Pre-writing, Revision, Outline, Thesis   ❶

2. State the steps related to Good Paragraph writing.

①   Decide, Develop, Demonstrate, Meaning, Conclusion, Proof Reading
②   Develop, Demonstrate, Conclusion, Meaning, Proof Reading
③   Develop, Demonstrate, Conclusion, Meaning, Proof Reading, Develop
④   Develop, Demonstrate, Meaning, Develop, Proof Reading, Conclusion   ❶

✌ EVENTS :

In writing of events, it is about the details of events and its. Objective when it take place, schedule and details of entire event.

Steps in event are :

(1)   Event name   (2)   Objective
(3)   Date/time   (4)   Venue/place
(5)   Schedule   (6)   Conclusion

Model Examples

Q. Find out the type of sentence.

1. In event writing, which is the first step?
    ① Event objective   ② Event name
    ③ Event schedule   ④ Event conclusion   ❷
2. Event writing ends with......
    ① Objective   ② Schedule
    ③ details   ④ Conclusion   ❹
3. Which steps show where events is happening
    ① Date/time   ② Objective
    ③ Venue/Place   ④ Schedule   ❸

5.3 AUTOBIOGRAPHY, SHORT AUTOBIOGRAPHY OF A THING OR OBJECT

✌ AUTOBIOGRAPHY :

An autobiography is a written account of the life of a person written by that person. In other words it is the story that a person writes about themselves.

Model Examples

A short autobiography of a story book

My name is 'Flying Carpet'. I am a colourful and attractive book. I was printed in Singapore and was later shipped to India. It was a long and tiring journey. As soon as I reached Mumbai port in India, I was taken to a bookshop called Higginbottoms. I was displayed on a shelf with other new books. Soon I met and befriended a book entitled 'The Orchid'.

One day a few girls entered the shop. They laughed and joked amongst themselves. They were browsing through the books and one of the girls picked me up. She was attracted to me and bought me immediately. She took me to her house and placed me on a bookshelf in her bedroom. She took great care of me. After she finished reading me, she would always place me carefully on the shelf.

One day her naughty cousin visited her. He entered her bedroom without her permission and started tearing and throwing her books around. Soon, to my anguish, he picked me up and was about to tear my pages when my owner stormed into the room and rescued me. She smoothed my crumpled pages and soon I was good as new. Till today, I am with her giving her satisfaction through my stories.

Answer the following questions.

1. What is my name?
   ① Magic Wand ② Flying Carpet
   ③ Magic Bus ④ Blue Bell ❷

2. Where was I printed?
   ① America ② England
   ③ India ④ Singapore ❹

3. Who bought me from the bookshop?
   ① girl ② boy ③ man ④ woman ❶

4. Who tried to tear my pages?
   ① cousin ② aunt
   ③ uncle ④ nephew ❶

5. Who rescued me?
   ① my owner ② mother ③ father ④ friend ❶

A short autobiography of a tree

I am a tree of a small village. Proud and firm I stand on sandy ground. I like all the village folk for the care and concern they show me. I readily and happily offer shelter to their goats and sheep. Their children play under my care and protection. I owe them my life.

It was long ago, when I was young and slim. I cared only for my desire to grow up. One day, I saw a gang of the king's axe men sharpening their axes to cut me down. I became highly anxious. I trembled with fear. Suddenly, a loud voice echoed through the village. "Do not cut our trees. They are the breath of our life."

It was Mamta, my neighbour. I never knew that she loved me so much. She hugged my trunk so tightly that three axe men were not able to tear her away from me. "Chop me first," she cried. "Take my life but leave my trees alone." I was moved by her affection but had no means to express my feelings. I could only shed a few of my leaves on her to show my gratitude.

The axe men were surprised at her protest, but they were trained to obey orders. They tore her away from me and threw her on the ground. Mamta got up quickly and hugged me again. She cried and wept badly.

Suddenly, hundreds of villagers, old and young, rushed towards me and other trees. Each one hugged one of us. The king's axe men were unable to touch any tree. They beat and arrested several men and women. It terrified me. At least seven villagers hugged my trunk to save me from the axes. I shed hundreds of my leaves on them.

The king heard of the intense public protest. He rushed to the spot. He stood under me when the villagers begged for mercy on trees. The king ordered that this village would never be called upon to provide timber to his men nor would any hunting be permitted here. Today even after two centuries, the greenery of this village is intact. The village is an oasis in the region that is almost a desert.

Answer the following questions.

1. As a tree, I grow in a _____
   ① town   ② village   ③ city   ④ state   ❷
2. To whom do I owe my life?
   ① villagers   ② drivers   ③ people   ④ women ❶
3. Who tried to save my life from the king's axemen?
   ① Sushila   ② Mamta   ③ Rani   ④ Asmita ❷
4. How many villagers tried to save me?
   ① eleven   ② eight   ③ seven   ④ nine   ❸
5. The greenery of the village is intact even after _____
   ① two centuries   ② 100 years
   ③ ten days   ④ five hours   ❶

Examples for Practice

1. A short autobiography of a clock

Hi, my name is Tic-Tock the clock. I don't know what you want to know about me, but here goes. I sit in the same boring place on the same dark wall every single day. I feel incredibly lonely, you see, because nobody ever talks to me or even pays attention to me. There are moments when people gawk at me and then they suddenly become flustered. Am I scary? Well, I don't remember.

There used to be a small mirror on the wall opposite from me but the fat woman took it down. That was so long ago that I have forgotten what I look like. While we're on the topic of my memory and cognitive abilities, I must tell you about the incessant ticking in my head that never ceases. It hasn't stopped from the moment I was born. What is it? Why is it there? Tic... Tock... Tic... Tock... It's enough to drive a lonely-old clock just plain crazy.

Answer the following questions.

1. What is my name?
   ① Tic-Tock
   ② Bing-Bong
   ③ Ding-Dong
   ④ none of these

2. Where am I kept?
   ① dark wall
   ② living room
   ③ bedroom
   ④ wardrobe

3. Who took away the mirror?
   ① a thin woman
   ② a fat man
   ③ a fat woman
   ④ a thin man

4. What is that never ceases in my head?
   ① whistling sound
   ② banging sound
   ③ incessant ticking
   ④ no sound

5. What does this incessant sound do?
   ① drives me crazy
   ② makes me sad
   ③ makes me happy
   ④ no feelings

Answers

Q.	Ans.	Q.	Ans.	Q.	Ans.	Q.	Ans.
1.	❶	2.	❶	3.	❸	4.	❸
5.	❶						

2. A short autobiography of a car

I carry people from one place to another. They drive me to go to work, shopping, school, picnics, and extra-curricular activities. People come to purchase me at showrooms to choose from the different models, colours, sizes, and designs I am marketed in.

They bring their family and friends to help them make the right decision. They spend thousands of rupees on me, and take me home.

My presence grows their self esteem, saves their time, provides them with independence, mobility and convenience. As much as they are happy to have me in their home, with all the benefits I provide to them, I am often misused.

The first year I had a beautiful experience with the family. I was provided with extra care and attention. I was kept in the garage to protect me from the rain, and snow, so that rust does not build up on me. Kids were not allowed to have any food or drinks while being seated in me. They installed a freshener in me, so I always stay fresh and fragrant. Frequently, I was either taken to a car wash or washed at home, and maintenance was done on a timely basis. I was so glad to be part of the family.

Soon things started to change. I was starting to feel unwanted. I could not recollect the last time I was taken to a car wash or even washed at all. Dust and pollution has accumulated on me. You may even notice a bird's poo on one of my passenger windows.

They no longer care to have a freshener put in me. The one currently installed has been there for over six months, and doesn't smell any different than the entire car. On the rear seats, you will find papers, documents, files which need organisation but have been there for over two weeks. Once they are picked up, new ones take their place.

On the floor, you will notice wrappers, chips, and an empty box of juice. My storage compartment is filled with CDs, manuals, receipts, parking tickets, and a whole lot more.

I want to look good again; I want to be treated right. I often envy other cars, whose owners keep them spick and span, and spend time cleaning and taking good care of them.

Answer the following questions.

1. Where do people come to purchase me?
   ① showrooms   ② malls
   ③ theatres   ④ garage

2. My presence provides _____ to the family.
   ① pride   ② love
   ③ self-esteem   ④ no feelings

3. Where was I kept to protect me from the elements?
   ① garage   ② mechanic shop
   ③ home   ④ road

4. How much do people spend to buy me?
   ① hundreds of rupees   ② thousands of rupees
   ③ none of these

5. Why do I envy other car owners?
   ① they take good care   ② ignore their cars
   ③ none of these

Answers

Q.	Ans.	Q.	Ans.	Q.	Ans.	Q.	Ans.
1.	❶	2.	❸	3.	❶	4.	❷
5.	❶						

✣ ✣ ✣

5.4   INFORMAL LETTER (FORMAT OR COMPLETE THE LETTER)

✌ INFORMAL LETTERS :

A delightful form of composition, which is very much a part of our daily lives, is letter writing. We often write letters to our friends and relatives especially when they are far away from us. The style of a letter is dependent on the nature of the correspondence. Letters are generally of two types, that is, formal and informal. Informal letters (private letters) are those that are written to friends, parents, and relatives and are more in a conversational style.

Model Examples

(1) Your friend Robert has got the first prize in the in the inter-school essay competition. Congratulate him by completing the following informal letter.

> 3244, Sarita Colony
> Mumbai 400032
> 25th July, 2016

Dear Robert,

    Heartiest ____1____! I am extremely ____2____ to know that ____3____ in the inter-school essay competition. You have proved ____4____ constant practice always ____5____ sweet rewards.

May you ____6____ in all your ventures!

Please do convey my regards to your parents.

Yours sincerely,

    John

1. ① congratulation   ② congrat
   ③ congratulations   ④ greetings   ❸
2. ① saddened   ② exhausted
   ③ delighted   ④ excited   ❸
3. ① You have stood first
   ② you have won the first prize
   ③ you bagged the first prize
   ④ any one of these   ❹
4. ① if   ② that   ③ what   ④ then   ❷
5. ① brings   ② brought
   ③ is bringing   ④ have brought   ❶
6. ① succeeded   ② succeeds
   ③ succeed   ④ get succeed   ❸

(2) Write a letter to your uncle thanking him for the birthday present.

> 14, Nav Kavita Society
> DP Road
> Pune 411007
> 26th July, 2016

My dear uncle,

I just cannot _____1____ you enough for the wonderful ____2_____
present (money paid by you) which ____3_____ me to go on this
lovely trekking expedition.

We ____4_____ yesterday after a tour of ten days. It was a thrilling
and ____5_____ experience having to carry our own things,
____6____ our own food and sharing our joys and sorrows.

With respect to dear aunt.

Your affectionate nephew,
  Roshan

1.	① thank	② curse	③ happy	④ sad	❶
2.	① best	② bad	③ birthday	④ wedding	❸
3.	① allowed	② sent	③ made	④ enabled	❹
4.	① got	② returned	③ went	④ came	❷
5.	① disgusting		② crazy		
	③ educative		④ non-educative		❸
6.	① carry	② cook	③ buy	④ steal	❷

━━━━●━━━━ **Examples for Practice** ━━━━●━━━━

(1) Write a letter to your friend inviting him for your
brother's wedding.

A-203, 1ˢᵗ Floor
Ajmera Housing Society
Pimpri, Pune 411018
27ᵗʰ July 2016

Dear Keira,
How are you and family ____1_____ ?
As you might be aware, my elder brother Roger is getting ____2____
next month, that is, on August 20ᵗʰ, 2016.

I ___3___ be very happy if you and family can ___4___ the wedding. Please___5___ this as a personal invitation. The official ___6___ follows.

With love,

Derek

1. ① going   ② doing   ③ well   ④ coming
2. ① married   ② separated   ③ divorced   ④ together
3. ① could   ② should   ③ would   ④ cannot
4. ① attend   ② come   ③ ignore   ④ not come
5. ① make   ② consider   ③ get   ④ ignore
6. ① call   ② receipt   ③ invitation   ④ bill

Answers

Q.	Ans.	Q.	Ans.	Q.	Ans.	Q.	Ans.
1.	❷	2.	❶	3.	❸	4.	❶
5.	❷	6.	❸					

(2) Write a letter to your friend, sharing your joy of having a puppy at home.

A-35, Dream Apartments

Karol Bagh

New Delhi

27th July, 2016

Dear Gary,

    I hope this letter of mine finds you in best of ___1___ and prosperity. I was glad to receive a letter from you ___2___week.

    I am very ___3___ to share my joy with you as we got a cute puppy yesterday. He is just 2-3 weeks old and he's a pug.

I have named him Boxer. When I return home from school, the first thing I do is to ___4___with him. I love him a lot and he's the best ___5___ I ever got.

I am sure when you will meet him, you too will ___6___ him. Don't forget to give my regards to your parents and lots of love to your sister.

Yours lovingly,

Rita

1. ① health   ② wealth   ③ belt   ④ dealt
2. ① first   ② second   ③ third   ④ last
3. ① sad   ② bitter
       ③ disappointed   ④ happy
4. ① hit   ② tease   ③ play   ④ throw
5. ① tree   ② cat   ③ bat   ④ gift
6. ① hate   ② love   ③ disgust   ④ ignore

Answers

Q.	Ans.	Q.	Ans.	Q.	Ans.	Q.	Ans.
1.	❶	2.	❹	3.	❹	4.	❸
5.	❹	6.	❷				

✤ ✤ ✤

Reading Skills (Comprehension)

6.1   PASSAGES

✌ Passage 1

Read the passage carefully and answer the questions given below it. Select the correct answer from the options.

Helen was born in 1880 in a small town in the southern U.S.A. At 18 months, when she was beginning to talk, she suddenly became terribly ill and very nearly died. When she recovered she was completely deaf and blind.

It is very difficult for a deaf child to learn to talk. Most babies learn by hearing other people talking. But the deaf child cannot hear anyone so how can she know what talking sounds like? Many deaf people learn to lip read and they become very clever at understanding what other people are saying by watching them. But Helen could not see what other people were doing. She remembered a few words she had known before she was ill, for instance, she went on calling water 'waa-waa'. But she had to make signs for most things. She would shake her head for 'No', and nod for 'Yes'. Apull meant 'come', and a push, 'Go'. But of course she could say very little like this and she depended entirely on other people. Yet Helen had an active mind and a clever brain and wanted to do and say everything any other child would.

Questions :

1. In which year was Helen born?
   ① 1879   ② 1880   ③ 1830   ④ 1920

2. Deaf people learn to ....
   ① lip read   ② face read
   ③ hand touch   ④ None of these.

3. What sign Helen would make for 'No'?
   ① Nod   ② Push
   ③ Shake her head   ④ Pull

4. What was the age of Helen when she was ill?
   ① 16 months   ② 19 months
   ③ 18 months   ④ 16 months

Answers

Q.	Ans.	Q.	Ans.	Q.	Ans.	Q.	Ans.
1.	❷	2.	❶	3.	❸	4.	❸

✌ Passage 2

Read the passage carefully and answer the questions given below it. Select the correct answer from the options.

The information on the net is stored and made available in a systematic way on websites. Websites are places on the net. Each website has its own address. Using this address, you can visit a website, that is you can read or view the information stored on it. The thousands of websites on the net together form the World Wide Web (WWW).

There are special computer programme known as search engines which help you to find the different websites on the World Wide Web. If you type the word or subject on which you want information, the search engine shows on your screen, a list of websites that have the information. You can then go to that website. Looking at the various websites is known as browsing or surfing the net.

Questions :

1. Where are websites placed?
   ① In computers   ② On the net
   ③ Search engines   ④ Browsing

2. What is known as browsing?
   ① Network of computers   ② Looking at the internet
   ③ looking at the various websites
   ④ Search engine

3. Thousands of the websites on the net together form the ....
   ① Internet   ② World Wide Web (WWW)
   ③ Search engine   ④ Network

4. Special computer programmes are known as ....
   ① Network   ② Internet
   ③ Websites   ④ Search Engine

Answers

Q.	Ans.	Q.	Ans.	Q.	Ans.	Q.	Ans.
1.	❷	2.	❸	3.	❷	4.	❹

✌ Passage 3

Read the passage carefully and answer the questions given below it. Select the correct answer from the options.

At once, a hundred men climbed up on to my body and marched up to my mouth, carrying food. The bread was as small as bullets. So I ate two or three loaves at a time and cries of surprise rose from the Lilliputians that I should eat so quickly and so much. The Lilliputians were no longer afraid of me. They danced upon my body and ran to and fro. I could have caught at least forty of them with my hands and thrown them down. But I remembered my promise to remain quiet. Indeed, I was surprised at their bravery for I must have seemed the greatest giant in the world.

Later I was taken to the city where the king lived. A great cart was made by joining many carts.

Hundred men on to the cart which was drawn by fifteen hundred of the king's finest horses. The city was just half a mile away but the journey took almost a full day.

Questions :

1. Why were the Lilliputians surprised?
   ① Because Gulliver could eat so much and so fast.
   ② Because Gulliver could eat so much to and fro.
   ③ They can ran to and fro.
   ④ No idea.

2. What promise did Gulliver give?
   ① To eat little   ② To remain quiet
   ③ To save purple   ④ To returns back

3. How much time it took for a journey of half a mile?
   ① 12 hours   ② 2 day
   ③ 3 days   ④ Full day

4. How many horses were tied to the cart ....
   ① Sixteen hundred   ② Fourteen hundred
   ③ Seventeen hundred   ④ Fifteen hundred

Answers

Q.	Ans.	Q.	Ans.	Q.	Ans.	Q.	Ans.
1.	❶	2.	❷	3.	❹	4.	❹

✍ Passage 4

Read the passage carefully and answer the questions given below it. Select the correct answer from the options.

Saturday, 15th August 1936. It was the day of the Hockey finals during the Olympic events held in Berlin, Germany. Germany had defeated several teams to enter the finals against the Indian team.

They were the hosts of the Olympics, and they were sure of their victory. Perhaps that was the reason why their ruler Hitler had himself come to watch the match. About forty thousand people had gathered in the hockey stadium to cheer Germany against India. The Maharaja of Baroda State, the Prince of Bhopal and a few other Indians had also come to support the Indian Team.

The match started exactly at 11 am. The German team had adopted a novel strategy of using the Indian technique of short distance passes against the Indian team itself. They had resorted to a very offering an equally strong resistance. No team could make a goal during the first half hour. During the 32nd minute, Roop Singh scored the first goal, hitting the ball towards the goalpost from a difficult angle.

Questions :

1. Which two teams qualified for the final match ?
   ① Berlin and India   ② Bhopal and Berlin
   ③ Germany and India   ④ Germany and Berlin
2. Who scored the first goal?
   ① Dhyan Chand   ② Prince of Bhopal
   ③ German team captain ④ Roop Singh
3. At what time did the final match start?
   ① 10 a.m.   ② 11 a.m.
   ③ 2 p.m.   ④ 4 p.m.
4. Who were the host of Olympic Games?
   ① India   ② Berlin
   ③ Germany   ④ Olympia

Answers

Q.	Ans.	Q.	Ans.	Q.	Ans.	Q.	Ans.
1.	❸	2.	❹	3.	❷	4.	❸

✌ Passage 5

Read the poem carefully and answer the questions given below it. Select the correct answer from the options.

Count your garden by the flowers
 Never by the leaves that fall
Count your days by golden hours;
 Don't remember clouds at all.

> Count the nights by stars, not shadows;
>   Count your life by smiles, not tears;
> And with joy on every birthday,
>   Count your age by friends, not years.

Questions :

1. How will you count the nights?
   ① by shadows   ② by years
   ③ by leaves   ④ by stars

2. How will you count the garden?
   ① by leaves   ② by flowers
   ③ by clouds   ④ by years

3. Identify the correct rhyming pairs in the option given below.
   ① shadows-tears   ② friends - years
   ③ night - stars   ④ tears - years

4. How will you count your life?
   ① by tears   ② by years
   ③ by smiles   ④ by clouds

Answers

Q.	Ans.	Q.	Ans.	Q.	Ans.	Q.	Ans.
1.	❹	2.	❷	3.	❹	4.	❸

Passage 6

Read the poem carefully and answer the questions given below it. Select the correct answer from the options.

> In our little boat to glide
> On the water blue and wide,
> While the sky is smooth and bright,
> What could give us more delight?
>   See the ripples, how they run,
>   Twinkling brightly in the sun,

> While reflected we can see
> Shadows of each hill and tree.
> See the lilies, round and large,
> Floating near the reedy marge,
> Where the bulrush has its place
> And the heavy water-mace.

Questions :

1. Identify the correct rhyming pairs.
   - ① ripples - twinkling
   - ② large - marge
   - ③ water - mace
   - ④ reflected - shadow

2. Where are the lilies floating?
   - ① Near reedy marge
   - ② Near water mace
   - ③ Near the boat
   - ④ Near the shadows

3. How do the ripples run alike?
   - ① round and large
   - ② twinkling brightly in the sun
   - ③ where the bulrush has its place
   - ④ like heavy water mace

4. Select the proper synonym for the word 'bright'.
   - ① Dark
   - ② Blithe
   - ③ Radiant
   - ④ Cheerful

Answers

Q.	Ans.	Q.	Ans.	Q.	Ans.	Q.	Ans.
1.	❷	2.	❶	3.	❷	4.	❸

✻ Passage 7

Read the poem carefully and answer the questions given below it. Select the correct answer from the options.

> Lark bird, lark-bird, soaring high
> Are you never weary?
> When you reach the empty sky

> Are the clouds not dreary?
> Don't you sometimes long to be
>   A silent goldfish in the sea?
> Goldfish, goldfish, diving deep,
>   Are you never sad, say?
> When you feel the cold waves creep
>   Are you really glad, say?
> Don't you sometimes long to sing
>   And be a lark-bird on the wing?

Questions :

1. What does the poet say to the lark bird?
   ① Are you not happy for soaring high.
   ② Are you not tired for flying so high.
   ③ Are you not satisfied for flying so high.
   ④ None of these.

2. What does the gold fish do ?
   ① It dives deep
   ② It feels the cold waves
   ③ It sometimes longs to sing
   ④ none of these

3. Identify the correct rhyming pair
   ① lark - wing   ② during - deep
   ③ deep – creep   ④ weary - empty

4. Identify the antonym for the word 'Deep'.
   ① Depth   ② Shallow
   ③ Contract   ④ Beneath

Answers

Q.	Ans.	Q.	Ans.	Q.	Ans.	Q.	Ans.
1.	❷	2.	❶	3.	❸	4.	❷

✌ *Passage 8*

Read the poem carefully and answer the questions given below it. Select the correct answer from the options.

> Hundreds of stars
>   in the pretty sky
> Hundreds of shells
>   on the shore together
> Hundreds of birds
>   that go singing by,
> Hundreds of lambs
>   in the sunny weather
> Hundreds of dewdrops
>   to greet the dawn,
> Hundreds of bees
>   in the purple clover
> Hundred of butterflies
>   on the town
> But only one mother
>   the wide world over.

Questions :

1. Where are hundreds of butterflies?
   - ① In the sunny weather
   - ② On the shore
   - ③ In the purple clover
   - ④ On the town

2. Identify the correct rhyming pair from the options
   - ① lawn – dawn
   - ② world - over
   - ③ shells – shore
   - ④ stars - sky

3. Identify the synonym in the word 'pretty'/
   - ① charming
   - ② Cheerful
   - ③ Happy
   - ④ Beautiful

4. Where are hundred of shells together?
   - ① on the lawn
   - ② on the shore
   - ③ in the purple clover
   - ④ none of these

Q.	Ans.	Q.	Ans.	Q.	Ans.	Q.	Ans.
1.	❹	2.	❶	3.	❶	4.	❷

✣ ✣ ✣

6.2   NEWS ITEMS/ ADVERTISEMENT / LEAFLET

News is packaged information about current events happening somewhere else. News moves through many different media, based on word of mouth, printing, postal systems, broadcasting and electronic communication.

Common topics for news reports include war, politics and business as well as athletic events, quirky or unusual events and the doings of celebrities. Government proclamations, concerning royal ceremonies, laws, taxes, public health and criminals, have been dubbed news since ancient times.

Prepare a news on each of the following

(1)   Fee Hike :

Ace News Service Pune : 2ⁿᵈ Aug.

Universities decision to hike fees brought several students on the street to protest against the unjustified fee hike. It was first started by Welcome College and soon enough other colleges joined. Traffic was badly affected and the police promptly diverted the traffic to alternate roads. Sensing more trouble as the students gradually became violent the Police Commissioner ordered extra forces to control the mob and quickly disposed them.

Other college gates were closed to prevent more students from joining the agitating students. Mild lathi charge had to be used to prevent students from damaging public property, shops, vehicles etc. Water canons were used to scatter away the students.

Several students were rounded up in vans and taken away. Those injured in the 'lathi charge' were either given treatment and discharged or some admitted in government hospital. Quick action by police prevented further damage.

Students Union Leader, condemned the attack by police on innocent students, who he said, were justified in protesting against the unwarranted fee hike. He said the students would continue to agitate till their demands were met.

(2) No Parking Boards Fail to Clear Traffic :
Nashik, 18ᵗʰ Aug :

Traffic chaos continues to haunt the public with no police action in sight. It seems, No Entry - No Parking Boards seems to have no effect on the erring drivers. They merrily flaunt these rules by parking the vehicles just below the no parking board.

One follows the other and sooner enough vehicles are parked in a row. Similarly, vehicles enter No Entry roads one after another, as if no board exists there. This causes lot of hardships to those who follow these rules. Tempers run high and as there are bottlenecks on junction with no policeman in sight. Shopkeepers also join in protesting as their business is affected. By the time one or two policemen arrive on the scene there is complete chaos as no one can move back or forward with pedestrians and cyclist adding to the woe. Unless there is strict action against erring drivers this situation will continue to be so with the situation going from bad to worse.

The Traffic department must wake up and start penalizing these openly violating traffic rules, heavily, if they want to enthuse some discipline among the drivers - both educated and uneducated. Only then will there be some sanity on city roads.

3) Write a brief newspaper report on the following headline :

Sachin Tendulkar Receives Bharat Ratna :

Sachin Ramesh Tendulkar is the youngest recipient of Bharat Ratna Award. This award was presented to him by the honourable President Pranav Mukharjee.

Prior to this Award, he has received Arjun Award, Rajiv Gandhi Khel Ratna Award, Padma Shri, Maharashtra Bhushan and Padma Vibhushan Award. Sachin in his speech thanked all the people who had helped him in his life – his parents, family members, relatives, his coach, doctors, trainers and media people who had supported him. His achievement in the play of cricket is unimaginable and he had set the World Record for having the highest number of world records.

Questions : You are Rashmi Patil staff correspondent of Times of India you have just covered state level school exhibition in Mumbai, on "Best Out of Waste", and following is your report. Choose from the options given below.

| 1 |

| 2 |

Students from twenty states participated in a national level exhibition and displayed articles made out of waste to create awareness about environment friendly products.

The event was organised by D.P.S. Raipur, in association with Save Environment Centre, New Delhi. One student designed a projector out of waste car-board, mirror pieces and lenses.

The chief guest, Mr. Patel praised the participants for their efforts. The exhibition was really an eye opener!

| 3 |

1. An appropriate heading for the report would be "............".
   ① The Useless Become Useful ② The Useless Things
   ③ Waste Products   ④ Using Waste Products

2. What would come in place of ②̲ given in the letter ?
   ① Venue
   ② Date/place/name of the correspondent
   ③ Date
   ④ Place
3. What would come in place of ③̲ given in the letter ?
   ① Name of the newspaper   ② The writer's signature
   ③ Name of the event   ④ None of the above

Answers

Q.	Ans.	Q.	Ans.	Q.	Ans.
1.	❹	2.	❷	3.	❹

❖ ❖ ❖

ADVERTISEMENT

Definition : Paid, non-personal, public communication about causes, goods and services, ideas, organisations, people, and places, through means such as direct mail, telephone, print, radio, television and internet. An integral part of marketing, advertisements are public notices designed to inform and motivate. Their objective is to change the thinking pattern (or buying behaviour) of the recipient, so that he or she is persuaded to take the action desired by the advertiser. When aired on radio or television, an advertisement is called a commercial.

1. You are a member of Young India Club of your town. You have arranged a rally for the Blind Relief Fund (BRF). Prepare a handout appealing to the public for generous donations. (i) Use slogans (ii) Declare gifts (iii) Time of the rally (iv) Famous personality to lead rally (v) Make an appeal (vi) Add your own ideas.

Grand (BRF) Blind Relief Fund Rally

An Eye for an Eye
Come One ! Come All !
Fabulous gifts to be Won !
To
Conference Hall,
Image Academy, Gole Colony, Nashik
on
21st June, 2016

Satishrao Deshmukh will lead the rally.

**Donate Generously ! Donate Generously !
To the Noble Cause !**

Make this rally a grand success for the blind
and be a light to those in the dark.

2. *Draft an advertisement for a cleanliness drive that your village is organising.*

DAHIWAD VILLAGE

Announces

CLEANLINESS WEEK

[15th August 2016 to 22nd August 2016]

Here's what we have to do :

☞ *Always use a dustbin. Do not litter.*

☞ *Keep your locality clean.*

☞ *Don't spit on roads and walls.*

☞ *Clean private and public toilets regularly.*

**Cleanliness keeps you healthy
which is next to Godliness**

3. *Prepare a handout appealing to the public to be aware of 'Saving our Environment.' Make use of the following points : (i) Use an attractive slogan (ii) Make persuasive appeal, (iii) Inform about different programmes (iv) Ask for contribution, (v) Tell about importance to save the environment, (vi) Add your own ideas.*

Save Our Environment

If you kill Environment, she shall kill you !

Experts warn that by 2016 every 6 out of 10 persons will suffer from some kind of chest disease.

The killer of course will be Pollution !

WHOM TO BLAME ? YOU AND I !

Can pollution be avoided ?
Yes, if you wish !
Stop deforestation.
Plant more trees.
Stop city - growth.
Use auto - vehicles only when most necessary.
Make villages clean and pleasant.

Keep the Environment Clean :

1. Plant trees.
2. Save trees.
3. Avoid pollution in your surrounding area.

VANDEVI FOUNDATION has undertaken to help you to do the above. Contribute liberally. Even a small amount is welcome.

Send Cheque / DD / M.O. To

VANDEVI FOUNDATION

Post Box - 21, Shivaji Nagar, Pune.

AWAKE, ARISE, ACT OR FOREVER BE POLLUTED !

---

4. Prepare an appeal making the public aware of the need of 'Eye Donation'. Make use of the following points :

(i) Prepare an attractive slogan. (ii)Make persuasive appeal. (iii) Tell about the need for eye donation (iv) Add your own ideas.

OFFER SIGHT TO THE BLIND EYE DONATION

- Let a blind person experience the joy of light.
- Let his world be clearly seen by him.
- Your Eye Donation can make a blind man see the world and enjoy life.
- He can get greatest happiness because of your kindness.

Won't you offer him a Chance to See ?

Donate Eyes ! Donate sight, to the blind !!

Come forward – Be generous

---

5. Prepare an appeal in the form of a handout about how the people in the vicinity can come together for donating blood. Red Cross Society is in urgent need of blood. Draft an advertisement appealing for Blood Donors.

Every Drop Can Save a Life

The need is indeed great!
Millions die for lack of adequate blood
Millions die for lack of timely blood. Help to prevent this.
Have no fear...Donating blood doesn't bring weakness
Donate your blood generously.
If you desire to be of service to others, act now !
We invite you cordially. Call now, before it is too late.

• Visit •
Red Cross Society, Bhagat Singh Road,
Mumbai – 400 001. Tel No. 22012345.

6. Create an advertisement on 'Save Animals' for your annual day in your school.

STOP ! THINK ! ACT !

(Before it is too late)

"Wake up to the cruelty against animals."

Stop killing animals for:

* Fur, ivory and meat
* Their use in laboratories
* Entertainment and sports

What a shame and disgrace !

* Humans kill animals
* Humans beat animals
* Humans mistreat animals

They are God's gift to man

SAVE ANIMALS

Animal Welfare Society

Model Examples

Observe the following advertisement given above carefully and answer the questions that follow :

1. By whom has this poster been supported?
   - ① Save Animals !
   - ② Animal Welfare Society
   - ③ Humans
   - ④ None of these

2. Why do men kill animals?
   - ① For fur, ivory and meat
   - ② For their use in laboratories
   - ③ For entertainment and sports
   - ④ All of these

3. What is the message of the poster?
   - ① Be cruel to animals
   - ② Get costly things from animals
   - ③ Feel shame
   - ④ Stop cruelty against animals

4. Who or what are God's gift to man?

  ① Ducks   ② Frogs

  ③ All animals   ④ None of these

Answers

Q.	Ans.	Q.	Ans.	Q.	Ans.	Q.	Ans.
1.	❷	2.	❹	3.	❹	4.	❸

Q. *Read and Observe the poster carefully and answer the following questions :*

KROOT PUBLIC SCHOOL

Presents

PUPPET SHOW

AT 11.00 A.M.

On 10 February 2016

in the

Mrunal Memorial Auditorium

Tickets : ₹ 20/-   ₹ 50/-   ₹ 100/-

Tickets available at the school library.

❀ Supported by ❀

Students of Class VI

1. Who is organising the puppet show?

  ① Devi   ② Auditorium

  ③ Kroot Public School   ④ None of the above

2. When will the show be organised?

  ① 20th January   ② 10th February 2016

  ③ 15th February   ④ None of these

3. Name the venue of the show

  ① Students of Class V   ② Fruits Public School

  ③ Mrunal Memorial Auditorium

  ④ None of the above

4. Where can you purchase tickets from?

   ① From the school office   ② From the school library

   ③ From the auditorium   ④ None of the above

5. When will the puppet show begin?

   ① At 10.50 a.m.   ② At 11.30 p.m.

   ③ At 10.15 a.m.   ④ At 11.00 a.m.

Answer the given questions based on the picture below :

UFO SPOTTED OVER ANDHRA PRADESH ARTISTS IMPRESSION

6. What is UFO

   ① Union Foreign Office

   ② Unidentified Force Object

   ③ Unidentified Flying Object

   ④ Unidentified Forced Object

7. What is the meaning of 'spotted'?

   ① Draw   ② Seen   ③ Placed   ④ Pin pointed

8. What according to you is the object in the picture?

   ① A cricket ball   ② A red ball

   ③ A flying object   ④ A planet

Answers

Q.	Ans.	Q.	Ans.	Q.	Ans.	Q.	Ans.
1.	❸	2.	❷	3.	❸	4.	❷
5.	❹	6.	❸	7.	❷	8.	❸

The following is the layout of a 'postcard' (of one side). Fill in the blanks by choosing from the options given below :

1. What will come in place of ① ?
   - ① Pincode
   - ② Receiver's address
   - ③ Contents
   - ④ Left blank

2. What will come in place of ② ?
   - ① Sender's name/signature
   - ② Sender's address
   - ③ Most important information
   - ④ None of the above

3. What will come in place of ③ ?
   - ① Receiver's address
   - ② Sender's address
   - ③ Most important information
   - ④ Contents

4. What will come in place of ④ ?
   - ① Sender's photo
   - ② Receiver's photo
   - ③ Sender's stamp
   - ④ Postal stamp

5. What will come in place of ⑤ ?
   - ① City/state
   - ② Pin code
   - ③ House number
   - ④ Country code

Answers

Q.	Ans.	Q.	Ans.	Q.	Ans.	Q.	Ans.	Q.	Ans.
1.	❸	2.	❶	3.	❶	4.	❹	5.	❷

❖ ❖ ❖

$$\boxed{\textbf{\textit{Leaflets}}}$$

Tourism

Tourism today is an important economic sector contributing effectively to the GDP of many countries in the world. It is playing a successful role in the development of national resources and creation of employment opportunities, in addition to its laudable role in the social and cultural advancement.

Objectives of tourism are not limited to the aspects of entertainment alone, although this constitutes one of the important aims. The new concept of tourism, which is adopted and led by the government, considers tourism as a sector of multiple benefits, including economic, cultural, social, heritage and environmental benefits as related to different segments of the society. Hence, it is evident that, this sector has a set of nested dimensions and aspirations that are in the service of the individual and the society.

Q. 1   *Write a short tourist leaflet about any Historical place you like. Take the help of the following points :*

  • *How to go there ?*

  • *Where to stay there ?*

  • *What to see there ?*

  • *Any specialty of the place.*

TOURIST LEAFLET

Shivgad is a small town in Maharashtra.

✦ **Road** : Journey takes five hours (210 km) from Mumbai. Government buses, private buses and taxies ply regularly

✦ **Stay** : You can stay at any one of the hostels. Hotels cost ₹ 400 to 1500 per head. You can get one, which can suit your pocket.

✦ ***Spots to Visit :***

➡ ***Shivgad :*** A fort built by King Shivaji. Partly in ruins but in grandeur. Sound and light shows are held on every Tuesday and Friday.

➡ ***Kali Temple :*** An ancient temple. People believe in the power and mystery of the goddess.

➡ ***Beaches :*** Shivgad is full of clean and delightful beaches. There is facility for boating and swimming.

✦ ***Specialty :***

➡ Ganesh Chaturthi is celebrated on a grand scale.

➡ Winter is the best season to visit the place.

➡ Fish and rice preparation is the speciality of this region.

Q. 2 ***Prepare a tourist leaflet of Kolhapur based on the information given below. You can take the help of the following framework.***

-   ***Location***   • ***How to go : Rail, Road, Air***
-   ***Where to stay***   • ***Cuisine***
-   ***Places to see (in the city)***
-   ***Excursions***   • ***Shopping***
-   ***Art and Craft***

Ans.

TOURIST LEAFLET

Kolhapur is a beautiful city nestling amid the Sahyadris on the banks of the Panchganga river. It was known as Karveernagari in ancient times.

Road : Journey takes six hours (260 km) from Mumbai. Government buses, private buses and taxies ply regularly. Mahalaxmi Express and other trains are available.

Stay : You can stay in one of the private hotels, lodges, circuit house, tourist bungalows *etc.* Hotels cost Rs. 500 to 5000 per head. You can get one, which can suit your pocket.

Spots to Visit :

(a) **The New Palace :** A magnificent structure built in 1818 for the Maharaja along with its museum.

(b) **Mahalaxmi Temple :** Built in black stone. The deity is said to be Swayambhu, self created or naturlaly formed and not sculpted.

(c) The Shalini Palace, The Town Hall, The Museum and other old palaces.

Cuisine :

Veg : Missal, Goli Pulao, Bharleli Vangi, Greens, Pickels and Chutneys with Jowar bhakris.

Non-veg : Mutton sukka, mutton loncha, kombdi masala, pandhara rassa and tamda rassa, the two signature gravies.

Excursions :

• To Hupri (20 km from Kolhapur) for silver anklets and toe rings.
• To the Panchagana river.
• To the Circuit house.

Shopping :

• Kolhapuri chappal from chappal galli.
• Kolhapuri jewellery – the saj and the thushi, the royal neckware.

Art and Craft :

• Silver anklets and toe rings.
• Handcrafted chappals.

You are always welcome to Kolhapur.

Model Examples

1. Which one of the following is a pact of adventure tourism

① Swimming   ② Bowling

③ Bungee Jumping   ④ Chess   ❶

2. The typical feature of tourism is that
   ① The tourist spot is neat, clear and attractive
   ② Tourists have to pay lots of money to visit various tourist spots.
   ③ The tour operator helps its customers
   ④ Tourists have to be physically transported to tourist spots.
   ❹

3. Recreation is a
   ① Product   ② Service
   ③ Privilege of a tour operator
   ④ Privilege of a tour guide   ❷

4. A traveller, who visits Mecca for the purpose of performing Hajj is a/an
   ① Excursionist   ② Religious Tourist
   ③ Tourist   ④ Both A and B   ❷

5. A Dharmashala is suitable for
   ① Those businessman who can stay in graded hotels
   ② Low income families
   ③ Only rich merchants
   ④ All the above   ❷

Examples for Practice

1. Which one of the following is not a place of religious significance?
   ① Puri   ② The Vatican
   ③ Jerusalem   ④ Riyadh

2. The mode of transport to be used by the tourist would depend upon.
   ① The availability of transport network to reach the tourist spot
   ② His financial Prowess
   ③ His willingness to use a particular mode of travel
   ④ All of these

3. If you are moving in a sanctuary and learning more about migratory birds you are in all probability a/an
   ① Tourist   ② Explorer
   ③ Eco-Tourist   ④ Researcher

4. If you to enjoy a Camel Safari you would have to go to
   ① Rann of Kutch   ② Pilani
   ③ Shri Ganganagar   ④ Jaisalmer

5. Which state is called the cradle of Buddhism?
   ① Sikkim   ② Bihar
   ③ Uttar Pradesh   ④ Madhya Pradesh

6. The Konark temple in Orissa is dedicated to
   ① Lord Indra   ② Lord Rama
   ③ The Sun God   ④ None of these

7. The depictions in Ajanta Caves display the
   ① Incidents in the life of Buddha
   ② Incidents pertaining to Mahavira's life
   ③ Legends of Vikramadithya
   ④ Epic incidents

8. The most populous city in India is
   ① Calcutta   ② Delhi
   ③ Chennai   ④ Mumbai

9. Which one of the following is not a part of the infrastructure of Tourism
   ① Natural sports
   ② Sarais
   ③ Rope Ways
   ④ Government Owned factories

10. Chhatrapati Shivaji Terminus is situated in ....
    ① Mumbai   ② Chennai
    ③ Delhi   ④ Agra

Answers

Q.	Ans.	Q.	Ans.	Q.	Ans.	Q.	Ans.
1.	❹	2.	❹	3.	❸	4.	❸
5.	❹	6.	❸	7.	❶	8.	❹
9.	❹	10.	❶				

❖ ❖ ❖

6.3 *INTERVIEW*

✌ *Interview*

Success of a candidate in getting employment depends largely upon how he/she has fared in the interview. Personality of the candidates appearing at interview plays a very important role as a deciding factor. Personality does not mean that the person is looking good. Personality is the sum of confidence, a positive attitude, good manners and will power.

The qualities are very important to be successful in life. The interviewers have certain expectations from the candidates. They study the candidates eagerness to learn new things. They give preference to such candidates who have ambition to rise to a high position through hard work and grit.

Questions asked in Interview

(1) Introduce yourself.

(2) Why you wish to choose academics as your career ?

(3) What do you enjoy most about teaching students ?

(4) What are your strengths and weaknesses ?

(5) What competition do you see, if you take up this job ?

(6) What would be your teaching methodology?

Model Examples

(I) Choose the correct answers

1. Interview is a .... way of communications.
   - ① Two way
   - ② Three way
   - ③ One way
   - ④ None of these   ❶

2. .... is a process of selecting candidates.
   - ① Group Discussion
   - ② Conference
   - ③ Interview
   - ④ All are correct   ❸

Examples for Practice

1. In Interview, what types of questions are asked?
   - ① Personal and Educational
   - ② Professional and Previous experience
   - ③ Preference and General Knowledge
   - ④ All are correct

2. Interviews and Resume or Bio-data are ....
   - ① different
   - ② one and same
   - ③ part of interview
   - ④ None of these

3. .... is a very important part of selection procedure.
   - ① conference
   - ② E-mail
   - ③ Interview
   - ④ Internet

4. The knowledge of .... is required in interview.
   - ① English language
   - ② Mother tongue
   - ③ local language
   - ④ All are correct

5. Nowadays interviews are held on ....
   - ① e-conference/online
   - ② telephone
   - ③ face to face
   - ④ None of these

Answers

Q.	Ans.	Q.	Ans.	Q.	Ans.	Q.	Ans.
1.	❹	2.	❸	3.	❸	4.	❶
5.	❶						

MISCELLANEOUS

7.1 NUMBERS (CARDINALS AND ORDINALS)

✌ INTRODUCTION :

Cardinals :

1	One	30	Thirty
2	Two	31	Thirty-one
3	Three	33	Thirty-three
4	Four	34	Thirty-four
5	Five	39	Thirty-nine
6	Six	40	Forty
7	Seven	41	Forty-one
8	Eight	44	Forty-four
9	Nine	49	Forty-nine
10	Ten	50	Fifty
11	Eleven	55	Fifty-five
12	Twelve	59	Fifty-nine
13	Thirteen	60	Sixty
14	Fourteen	66	Sixty-six
15	Fifteen	69	Sixty-nine
16	Sixteen	70	Seventy
17	Seventeen	77	Seventy-seven
18	Eighteen	79	Seventy-nine
19	Nineteen	80	Eighty
20	Twenty	88	Eighty-eight
21	Twenty-one	89	Eighty-nine

22	Twenty-two	90	Ninety
23	Twenty-three	99	Ninety-nine
29	Twenty-nine	100	Hundred

101	Hundred and one
102	Hundred and two
200	Two hundred
202	Two hundred and two
300	Three hundred
303	Three hundred and three
400	Four hundred
500	Five hundred
600	Six hundred
754	Seven hundred and fifty-four
832	Eight hundred and thirty-two
919	Nine hundred and nineteen
999	Nine hundred and ninety-nine
1000	Thousand
2000	Two thousand
2001	Two thousand and one
1111	One thousand one hundred and eleven
2222	Two thousand two hundred and twenty-two
10 000	Ten thousand
10 001	Ten thousand and one
10 987	Ten thousand nine hundred and eighty-seven
1 00 000	Hundred thousand /One lakh
10 00 000	Million/Ten lakh
1 00 00 000	Ten million/One Crore
10 00 00 000	Hundred Million/Ten Crore
1 00 00 00 000	Thousand Million
10 00 00 00 000	Billion

Ordinals :

1st	First	40th	Fortieth
2nd	Second	44th	Forty-fourth
3rd	Third	49th	Forty-ninth
4th	Fourth	50th	Fiftieth
5th	Fifth	52nd	Fifty-second
6th	Sixth	59th	Fifty-ninth
7th	Seventh	60th	Sixtieth
8th	Eighth	61th	Sixty-first
9th	Ninth	69th	Sixty-ninth
10th	Tenth	70th	Seventieth
11th	Eleventh	73th	Seventy-third
12th	Twelfth	79th	Seventy-ninth
13th	Thirteenth	80th	Eightieth
14th	Fourteenth	88th	Eighty-eighth
15th	Fifteenth	89th	Eighty-ninth
16th	Sixteenth	90th	Ninetieth
17th	Seventeenth	94th	Ninety-fourth
18th	Eighteenth	99th	Ninety-nine
19th	Nineteenth	100th	Hundredth
20th	Twentieth	101st	Hundred and first
21th	Twenty first	102nd	Hundred and second
22nd	Twenty-second	103rd	Hundred and third
23rd	Twenty-third	206th	Two hundred and sixth
24th	Twenty-fourth	309th	Three hundred and ninth
30th	Thirtieth	1000th	Thousandth
34th	Thirty-fourth	1001st	Thousand and first
35th	Thirty-fifth	1002nd	Thousand & second

Model Examples

1. How will you write 13th in Ordinal numbers ?

    ① 13th ②   Thirteenth

    ③   13   ④   One and three

2. How will you write 1000 in ordinal numbers ?

   ①　1000ᵗʰ   ②　1000

   ③　Thousandth   ④　Thousand   ❸

Examples for Practice

1. How will you write 102 in cardinal numbers ?

   ①　102   ②　Hundred and two

   ③　Hundred, two   ④　102ᵗʰ

2. How will you write 1111 in cardinal numbers ?

   ①　One thousand one hundred and one

   ②　One thousand eleven

   ③　One thousand one hundred and eleven.

   ④　1000ᵗʰ

3. How is Thousand and Second written in ordinal numbers ?

   ①　1000ᵗʰ   ②　1002ⁿᵈ   ③　1000ˢᵗ   ④　102ⁿᵈ

4. How is hundred thousand written in Cardinal numbers

   ①　10000   ②　100000   ③　1000000   ④　1000

Answers

Q.	Ans.	Q.	Ans.	Q.	Ans.	Q.	Ans.
1.	❷	2.	❸	3.	❷	4.	❷

❖ ❖ ❖

7.2   *NON-ENGLISH WORDS*

•⋄ *Let us see some Non English Words*

- African- banana, jumbo, yam, zebra
- Chinese - ketchup, pekoe, shanghai
- French - catalogue, essence, gourmet, justice, massage, perfume, regret, terror
- Japanese - anime, karaoke, tycoon, hibachi, sushi
- Norwegian - fjord, krill, ski, slalom

- Tagalog – boondocks, manila, ylang ylang (a flower)
- Welsh - corgi (dog), crag, penguin

Here is a collection of curious and interesting words. Here are a few with the language of origin and the definition:

- **Alarm** : Italian - to arms
- **Ballot** : Italian - small pebble or ball, people would vote by casting a pebble into a box
- **Cantelope** : Italian - singing wolf, a town in Italy where the melon was grown
- **Companion** : from both Spanish and French, but with a Latin root : one with whom you would eat bread
- **Denim** : French - the cloth was developed in Nimes and called Serge di Nimes, later shortened to di Nimes, then to denim. It was also made in Genoa, Italy, hence the name "jeans"
- **Genuine** : Italian - placed on the knees. In Rome, a father placed a newborn on his knee to legally claim it as his
- **Muscle** : Latin - little mouse, when you flex a muscle, it was called a little mouse that runs beneath your skin
- **Night** : German - first meant "day" because the day began at sunset, like many other ancient civilizations
- **Ostracize** : Greek - pottery, if someone was a danger to the town, the people would write their vote on chunks of pottery to decide to banish him or not
- **Slogan** : Celtic - two words together that mean battle cry
- **Victim** : Latin - an animal that was to be sacrificed
- **Worm** : Old English - dragon
- **Abacus** : Comes from the Greek word abax, which means "sand tray." Originally, columns of pebbles were laid out on the sand for purposes of counting. See calculate and exchequer.
- **Allegory** : From Greek allos meaning "other" and agora meaning gathering place (especially the marketplace

- ***Apple (Eng.)/ Pomme (Fr.) / Manzana (Sp.)*** : These words, which all mean the same thing, should be explained one at a time, as they come from different sources.
- ***Apricot*** : This term, which comes from the French abricot-- and was aubercot until the Fifteenth Century.
- ***Addict*** : Slaves given to Roman soldiers to reward them for performance in battle were known as addicts. Eventually, a person who was a slave to anything became known as an addict.
- ***Alarm*** : From the Italian, "All'arme" -- "To arms!"
- ***Alcohol***
- ***Algebra***
- ***Algorithm***
- ***Appendix*** : In Latin it means "the part that hangs." A human appendix hangs at the end of the large intestine; appendices come at the end of books.
- ***Assassin*** : From the old Arabic word "hashshshin," which meant, "someone who is addicted to hash," that is, marijuana. Originally refered to a group of warriors who would smoke up before battle.
- ***Asthma*** : From the Latin, "asthma," meaning both "asthma" and "oppression." The Latin was derived from the Greek meaning the same.
- ***Avocado*** : From "awa guatl," a South American Indigenous word for testicle. The Spanish took this term and used to to refer to what we now call the avocado.
- ***Ballot*** : Italian term for "small ball or pebble." Italian citizens once voted by casting a small pebble or ball into one of several boxes.
- ***Barbarian*** : From the Greek "barbaroi," meaning "babblers," used to mean non-Greeks, i.e., people who didn't speak Greek; from the sound that the Greeks thought they were making: "bar bar bar bar..."
- ***Bead*** : From the Old English "gebed," meaning, "prayer."

- **Beserk** : Beserk most likely comes from the Old Icelandic "berserkr," meaning "bear shirt."
- **Big Apple** : "The term, the Big Apple, was first used by in the early '20s by stablehands to refer to the New Orleans race track, then the king of race tracks.
- **Biscuit** : From the mediaeval French 'Bis + cuit' meaning 'cooked twice'
- **Boudoir** : Literally, "a place to sulk in" from the French "bouder," to pout.
- **Boulevard** : (French) Boulevard; and Bulwark : From the Old Dutch word, "bolwerk," a type of fortification: a "Bulwark." The word changed in French from, "boullewerc" to "bollewerc" to "boulever" and, ultimately, to "boulevard."
- **Broke** (In the sense of having no money)
- **Bucolic** : From the Greek "boukolos," meaning "herdsman," from "bous," meaning "ox."
- **Bulimia** : From the Greek "bous" meaning "ox" and "limos," meaning "hunger," presumably because one with Bulimia has the appetite of an ox.
- **Cab (as in. Taxicab)**
- **Cantar (Spanish) To Sing** : From the Latin "Cantare," meaning, "to sing again and again." The Latin "Canere" mean just "to sing."
- **Carnival**
- **Catharsis**
- **Dibbs**
- **Dollar**
- **Elite**
- **Escape** : In Latin, escape means "out of cape." The ancient Romans would often avoid capture by throwing off their capes when fleeing

---

Model Examples

Q. Identify the odd one out.

1. ① Ginger   ② Ketchup
   ③ Alarm   ④ Box

2. ① Potato   ② Lady finger
    ③ Brinjal   ④ Yam   ❹

Examples for Practice

1. Which word has five vowels.
    ① voyage   ② queueing
    ③ keenness   ④ roomate
2. Find the odd one.
    ① Addict   ② Alcohol   ③ Apricot   ④ Banana
3. Below given words are related with Maths. Identify the odd one.
    ① Abacus   ② Algebra   ③ Algorithm   ④ Appendix
4. Identify the odd one.
    ① Barbarian   ② Beserk   ③ Biscuit   ④ Marry
5. Identify the odd word.
    ① Candidate   ② chaos
    ③ Choose   ④ Campus

Answers

Q.	Ans.	Q.	Ans.	Q.	Ans.	Q.	Ans.
1.	❷	2.	❹	3.	❹	4.	❹
5.	❸						

7.3   READ MAPS

•• A direction is what leads you to a place where you want to go. The north direction is shown with the help of an arrow. The four directions shown on the compass are called cardinal points. A compass is an instrument with a magnetic needle which always points to the north. Look at any map you will find North direction towards the top. Opposite to North is South. When you face the map to your left is West and to right is East.

- To locate a place on the map various signs and symbols are used. We can identify a place on the map with the help of these symbols. Various symbols are used for Dams, Rivers, Village, Post office, Bus stop, Zilla Parishad, Telephone Exchange, Hospitals etc.
- An index is given for every map which help us to identify the places and objects.
- Some maps give knowledge of districts, talukas, state, nations and so on

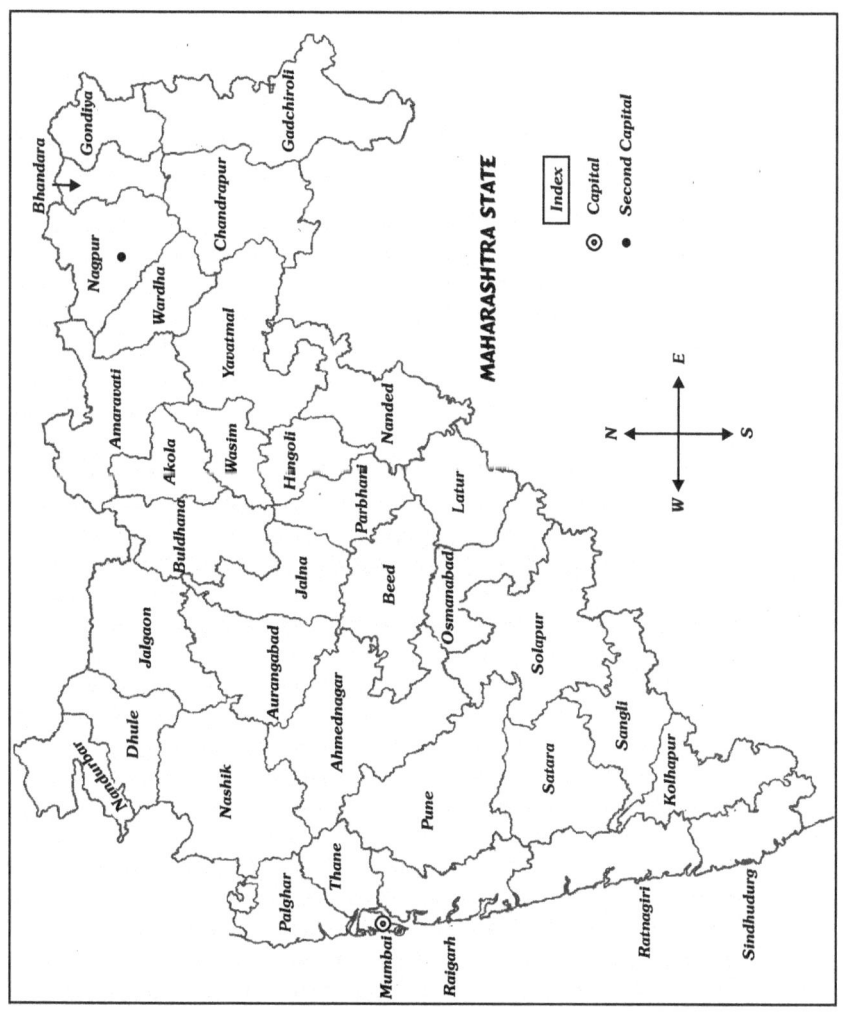

◆◆ The East, West, North and South are the four major directions. There are four sub-directions. They are South-East, South-West, North-West and North-East.

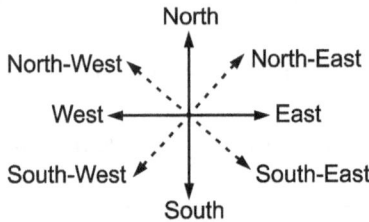

◆◆ When we talk of a particular place being near some place or away from it, we are talking about the distance between them. Distance is measured in units such as centimetre, metre, kilometre etc. When we tell our address, we tell the location of our house. In the same way we can tell the location of our town, taluka, district and even our country.

◆◆ Directions are always parallel to the ground. That is why a map must always be aligned to the local direction. This makes it easier for us to understood the map and the region.

◆◆ Direction and sub-direction have been determined by man on the basis of the rising and setting of the sun. Thus, nature can be our guide.

Examples for Practice

Q. Refer to the map and answer the questions.

1. Which district is near Pune ?
   - ① Osmanabad
   - ② Beed
   - ③ Satara
   - ④ Jalgaon

2. Which state is to the north west of Maharashtra ?
   - ① Goa
   - ② Gujarat
   - ③ Karnataka
   - ④ Andhra Pradesh

3. Which district is attached to Kolhapur ?
   - ① Chandrapur
   - ② Sangli
   - ③ Ahmednagar
   - ④ Nashik

4. Which sea is to the West of Maharashtra ?

   ① Arabian sea   ② Indian ocean

   ③ Bay of Bengal   ④ Pacific ocean

5. What symbol is used for Second Capital ?

   ① •   ② ⊙   ③ ....   ④ _ . _ . _

6. Directions are always .... to the ground.

   ① clockwise   ② anticlockwise

   ③ straight   ④ parallel

7. Map must always be aligned to the .... directions.

   ① state   ② local

   ③ international   ④ national

8. Which district is to the north of Ahmednagar ?

   ① Mumbai   ② Pune

   ③ Nashik   ④ Aurangabad

9. Which district is to the east of Solapur ?

   ① Osmanabad   ② Sangli

   ③ Satara   ④ Pune

10. Which district is to the west of Pune ?

   ① Ahmednagar   ② Raigad

   ③ Satara   ④ Thane

11. Which district is to the south of Parbhani ?

   ① Beed   ② Nanded   ③ Jalna   ④ Latur

12. .... is the most important part of a map.

   ① Attractiveness   ② Index

   ③ Sub-directions   ④ None of these

Answers

Q.	Ans.	Q.	Ans.	Q.	Ans.	Q.	Ans.
1.	❸	2.	❷	3.	❷	4.	❶
5.	❶	6.	❹	7.	❷	8.	❸
9.	❶	10.	❷	11.	❹	12.	❷

7.4   *CHARTS*

◦◦ Using a chart to present data for a school project or work presentation can help ensure the significance of the information is conveyed to the audience. A variety of chart types can present data -- pie charts, line charts, bar graphs -- in different ways. However, the overall consideration of using a chart to present data has its own advantages and disadvantages. A person considering a chart should weigh those before making one.

◦◦ ***Visually interesting :*** One of the greatest advantages of using a chart is that it makes information visually interesting to the audience. A table full of numbers may contain exactly the same information as a chart, but it is more difficult for an audience to easily absorb and comprehend. In contrast, a chart provides a quick, direct way to present information, in a way that is visually dynamic and of interest to the audience.

◦◦ ***Direct emphasis :*** Another advantage of using a chart is that, depending on the type chosen, it can directly empharise the key findings of the data for the audience. For example, if the data indicates how much of a certain product is sold in the store, a pie chart could make that readily apparent. If a pie chart shows one section, which represents one product, accounting for the vast majority of the whole, the audience will immediately perceive that and absorb its implications. In contrast, a table of data may also indicate high sales for that particular product, but it will not drive home the significance of that information like a chart would.

◦◦ ***Charts should be:***
- be clear, easy to understand and easy to find.

- display content that is current and supports increasingly complex skills.
- have a clear purpose.
- include steps for how to do specific strategies or procedures.
- have visuals including symbols, pictures, and or photos to go with words.

• ➤ ***Lack of precision*** *:* A disadvantage of using a chart is that, by design, a chart will likely not be as precise as the raw data. The data that would make up the chart includes the numbers that make up the data, which is as accurate as it gets. However, when you transfer that information into a chart, it decreases the specificity of that information. A bar graph can quickly indicate that one category exceeds another, but exactly how much one exceeds the other will not be as apparent as it would be with the raw data.

• ➤ ***Simplicity*** *:* One disadvantage to charts is that it can simplify the information, making some of its more complicated aspects less apparent. A chart is more visually interesting and makes apparent the significant portions of the data, but it does so by emphasising particular features of the data. While charts excel at presenting the data in certain ways, it also means that charts struggle to highlight various aspects of the data for which they are not designed.

Model Examples

1. A chart is also called a ....
   - ① Data
   - ② Method
   - ③ Graph
   - ④ Illustration   ❸

2. A chart should be ....
   - ① easy to understand
   - ② complex
   - ③ purposeful
   - ④ None of these   ❶

Examples for Practice

Q. Look at pie chart and answer the following questions.

1.

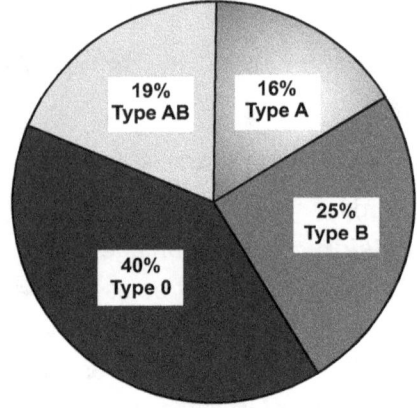

1. How many people, in this group, have blood type AB?
    ① 40 %   ② 19 %   ③ 48 %   ④ 28 %

2. How many people, in this group, do not have blood type O?
    ① 60 %   ② 30 %   ③ 50 %   ④ 90 %

3. How many people, in this group, have blood types A or B?
    ① 56 %   ② 72 %   ③ 62 %   ④ 92 %

The pie chart shows the percentages of types of transportation used by 800 students to school.

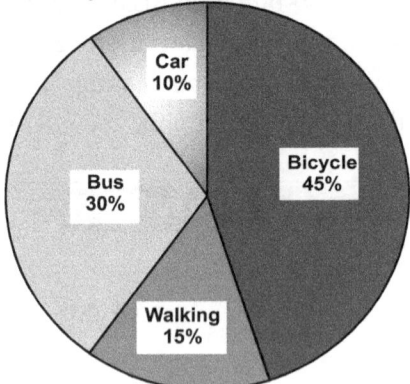

4. How many students, in the school come on bicycle?
    ① 360   ② 200   ③ 340   ④ 400

5. How many students do not walk to school?

    ① 680   ② 360   ③ 280   ④ 480

6. How many students come to school by bus or in a car?

    ① 180   ② 320   ③ 400   ④ 340

Answers

Q.	Ans.	Q.	Ans.	Q.	Ans.	Q.	Ans.
1.	❷	2.	❶	3.	❶	4.	❶
5.	❶	6.	❷				

❖ ❖ ❖

7.5   STOCK EXPRESSIONS

●◆ A phrase frequently or habitually used by a person or group, and thus associated with them.

●◆ ***Introductions :*** I'm so pleased to meet you – have you just been introduced to a new person and you want to tell them how nice it is meeting them? Well, this is just the right phrase to use on such an occasion!

●◆ I've heard so much about you – in case the person you're being introduced to is well known, this is just the right English small talk phrase to tell them during the introduction!

It's good to have you here! – sometimes you may want to make the new person feel welcome at the party or event, so this is what you tell them to make them feel included.

●◆ I'd like you to meet someone! – this is a typical way of introducing a new person to one or more people.

●◆ It's good to see you again! – this is how you recognize the presence of an old friend or acquaintance when you meet them after a while.

Conversation Starters & Greetings

- How are you getting on? – just another way of saying 'how are you?'
- You doing OK? – asked when the person has had some tough experience recently and you want to ask politely if they're OK.
- Hi, …! What's new? – this is a very informal way of greeting a close friend or anyone who you see on a regular basis and you want to ask has anything happened since you last met.
- Hi, …! What's up? – the same as above with a difference that you're probably not that interested in what news the other person might have.
- Is everything OK? – this is what you'd say to a person when you see that they're distressed and obviously not OK. Normally you'd ask this to a close friend or a work colleague – but you can also say this to a stranger you meet in the street and if it's obvious that person needs help.

Departure Phrases

- OK, I'm sorry but I have to leave now! – used when your chat partner has clear intentions of continuing the conversation but you just need to go so you're making it clear that you need to go.
- See you later! – used when you know that you'll be seeing each other again sometime.
- See you around! – the same as above
- See you in a couple of minutes! – this phrase is typically used when you're leaving the other person for a short while during an event, for example.
- Keep in touch! – a good-bye phrase meaning you want the other person to get in touch with you every now and then and that you've the same intentions.

Christmas and Happy New Year wishes

- ➽ May you have a Prosperous New Year.
- ➽ Wishing you a New Year filled with happiness and good fortune.
- ➽ I wish you happiness in the year to come.
- ➽ Let the year ahead be the one where all your dreams come true.
- ➽ May the coming year bring success to you.

Congratulations

- ➽ ***Congratulations on or for.***
- ➽ Congratulations on your marriage!
- ➽ Congratulations on your new baby!
- ➽ Congratulations on your promotion!
- ➽ Congratulations on winning the lottery!
- ➽ Congratulations can be offered as praise for someone's achievement. In that context, the preposition to use is for:
- ➽ Congratulations for completing 100 days without an accident!
- ➽ Congratulations for leading the Scouts to safety!
- ➽ Congratulations for saving the farm from foreclosure!

Model Examples

1. Raj, "The teacher has been looking for Anil since morning and he is hiding from her."
    Vijay : "I know they are .... since morning."
    ① In the school somewhere
    ② looking for each other
    ③ going to talk about the test.
    ④ playing cat and mouse.   ❹

2. Jaya: "......................"
    Raj : "Hey I'm sorry. I pressed the wrong button, I guess. I'll fix it, don't worry".
    ① Who goofed up the machine?
    ② The machine is malfunctioning.
    ③ Why is this machine faulty?
    ④ They gave us a broken machine.   ❶

●═════════ Examples for Practice ═════════●

1. Sally : "Why know, the school has closed the back gate permanently".
    ① I know, permanently means forever and ever
    ② Our teacher said we need to come early
    ③ Ravi! That's news to me. I didn't know that
    ④ That's the thing everyone is telling us to do

2. Kapil : "Hey Nitin, I'm free now, my friend. What do you want?"
    ① It would be very kind of you to get me some bread
    ② I would be grateful if you would get me some bread
    ③ Do me a favour, will you? Get me some bread
    ④ I would really appreciate if you could get me bread.

3. Millie : "Hey, what's up?"
    Amit : ".............."
    ① I am fine, thank you
    ② Thank you for asking.
    ③ Nothing much. What about you?
    ④ Very well. How about you?

4. Seema : "How was the birthday party last night?"
    Mohan : "The party was great. We had a ..... . We really enjoyed it".
    ① Balloon   ② present
    ③ cake   ④ ball

5. Rajesh : "Do you know that boy who lives in that house?"
    Gul : "I don't know him very well. He's just a/an.........acquaintance."
    ① great   ② casual   ③ average ④ careless

6. Sanjay : "What's that noise outside? I'm scared."
    Mandy : ".............."
    ① It sounds like someone is trying to open the lock.
    ② Does anyone know that you don't live there anymore?
    ③ Just let it go. You are always too upset with me.
    ④ Sometimes it makes noise all the time, it needs oiling.

7. Rubin : How was the English exam?"

    Sonu : " .... "

    ① English is very easy   ② It was a piece of cake

    ③ Exam was in another class

    ④ I had prepared for History instead

8. " .... ! This soup is out of this world. I can eat it everyday.

    ① Yuck   ② Uh

    ③ Yippee   ④ Mmm

Answers

Q.	Ans.	Q.	Ans.	Q.	Ans.	Q.	Ans.
1.	❸	2.	❸	3.	❸	4.	❸
5.	❷	6.	❶	7.	❷	8.	❹

❖ ❖ ❖

7.6   ABBREVIATIONS

❧ INTRODUCTION :

◦◦ Abbreviations are short forms of lengthy expressions. Abbreviations are in use in almost every discipline and area of life from commonly used abbreviations like names, for instance Mr. for Mister or Sgt. for Sergeant, to less commonly used abbreviations, such as the shortened version of abbreviation itself, which is abbr.

Examples:

- B.A. : Bachelor of Arts
- B.Sc. : Bachelor of Science
- M.A. : Master of Arts
- M.Phl or M.Phl : Master of Philosophy
- J.D. : Juris Doctor
- D.C. : Doctor of Chiropractic
- P.A. : Personal Assistant

- M.D. : Managing Director
- V.P. : Vice President
- SVP : Senior Vice President
- EVP : Executive Vice President
- CMO : Chief Marketing Officer
- CFO : Chief Financial Officer
- CEO : Chief Executive Officer

❖ *Latin Abbreviations:*

Abbreviations	Full Form	Meaning	Use
A.D.	Anno Domini	In the year of our lord	Used to show years after the birth of Jesus Christ -1600 A.D
a.m.	Ante Meridian	Before midday	Used for the hours after midnight and before noon - 10a.m, 2a.m
c. / ca.	Circa	Approximately	Used for years/months when not sure of exact date - ca. 1500
C.V.	Curriculum Vitae	Course of Life	A document summarizing a person's education and experience.
e.g.	Exempli gratia	For example	To give an example or instance of something - different cities, e.g. New York, Delhi, Beijing etc.
Et al.	Et All	And others	Used to show that there are more names that are unmentioned on a list - Tom, Jane, Jack et al.

Abbreviations	Full Form	Meaning	Use
Etc.	Et cetera	And other things	Used to signify similar things that are unmentioned on a list - milk, cheese, yoghurt etc.
i.e.	Id est	In other words / That is	Used in sentences to rephrase or show a connection between clauses - Jack, i.e. the most popular senior, likes Beth.
p.a.	Per Annum	Through the year	Used to show something in the manner of 'yearly' - He earns 2 million dollars p.a.
p.m.	Post meridian	After midday	Used to show the hours after midday and before midnight - 10p.m, 2p.m
P.S.	Post Scriptum	Something written after the main text was finished.	Used mainly in letters to add something extra after the signoff - Yours Shirley, P.S. - I'll be in Canada for 2 weeks.
R.I.P.	Requiescat in pace	May he/she rest in peace	Used as a prayer for someone who has died - May Janet R.I.P.
Stat	Statim	Immediately	Used most often in the medical fields - This man needs a bypass stat.

☞ *Abbreviations Related to Names*

Abbreviation	Meaning	Use
Dr.	Doctor	Dr. Smith was also invited.
Gen.	General (army)	Gen. Luke ordered them to fire at the enemy.
Hon.	Honorable	Hon. James Smith gave away the prizes.
Mr.	Mister	Mr. Hall is in office at the moment.
Mrs.	Mistress	Mrs. Hall is waiting for her car.
Ms.	Miss	Ms. Jane Watson is here to see you.
Prof.	Professor	Prof. Jain is a popular faculty in college.
Rev.	Reverend (clergyman)	Rev. Jones blessed the house today.
Sr. / Jr.	Senior / Junior	Bates Sr. and Harry Bates Jr. were inspecting the grounds.
St.	Saint	St. Patrick is one of the most popular Irish saints.

☞ *General Abbreviations*

Abbreviations	Meaning	Use
Assn.	Association	They named their club Assn. of Low and Highs.
Ave.	Avenue	They said they would be waiting at Lexington Ave.
Dept.	Department	The Arts Dept. is holding a bake sale.
Est.	Established	Annabel's est. 1963 in London, England.
Fig.	Figure	Look to fig. 8 to see how the process takes place.

Abbreviations	Meaning	Use
Hrs.	Hours	We will reach the next camp at 1500hrs.
Inc.	Incorporated	Apple Inc. was founded in the 1970s by Steve Jobs and Steve Wozniak.
Mt.	Mount	Mt. Everest is the tallest mountain on earth.
No.	Number	The address is House no. 64, Mulberry Lane.
Oz.	Ounces	The recipe needs 34 oz. of honey.
Sq.	Square	The rent is 100 dollars per sq. inch.
St.	Street	The shop is located at Xyza St. near the intersection.
Vs. or Vr.	Versus	The final match is going to be Australia vs. India.

➻ **Abbreviations of Grammar :**

Abbreviation	Meaning
Abbr.	Abbreviation / Abbreviated
Adj.	Adjective
Adv.	Adverb
Obj.	Objective
Pl.	Plural
Poss.	Possessive
Prep.	Preposition
Pron.	Pronoun
Pseud.	Pseudonym

Abbreviation	Meaning
Sing.	Singular
Syn.	Synonym
Trans.	Translation
V. / Vb.	Verb

⊸ **List of Acronyms:**

General Acronyms

Acronym	Full Form	What It Is
ATM	Automated Teller Machine	A computerised cash dispenser
BPO	Business Process Outsourcing	The outsourcing of specific functions of a business to a third party.
CAT	Common Admission Test	An ability-based admission test conducted by the Indian Institute of Management.
DNA	Deoxyribonucleic Acid	The molecule in any living being that contains all the genetic data of the living being.
DVD	Digital Versatile Disk	A compact optical storage disk, used for storing videos and other information.
FAQ	Frequently Asked Questions	A common section in most sites containing common queries from the visitors.
HR	Human Resources	The workforce of any organisation can also refer to the department that is in charge of human resources.

Acronym	Full Form	What It Is
LCD	Liquid Crystal Display	A type of video display panel
LED	Light Emitting Diode	A glowing light source used in indicators.
PC	Personal Computer	A computer whose size, price and capabilities are useful for individual use.
RAM	Random Access Memory	A way/disk to store data on a computer
SONAR	Sound Navigation And Ranging	A technique that uses echoes to navigate or communicate usually used in submarines.
USP	Unique Selling Proposition	A term used to show how one product or service is different and unique from another.
VIP	Very Important Person	A person who gets special privileges due to their status or importance.
WWW	World Wide Web	Interlinked web documents accessed by the internet

•◦ Acronyms of Names

Acronym	Full Form	What It Is
AIDS	Acquired Immuno Deficiency Syndrome	A disease of the immune system caused by the HIV.
ASEAN	Association of Southeast Asian Nations	A political and economic organisation based on geographical location.

Acronym	Full Form	What It Is
CERN	Conseil Européen pour la Recherche Nucléaire - European Organization for Nuclear Research	An international organisation that operates the largest particle physics laboratory
FIFA	Federation Internationale de Football Association	Organisation in charge of international association football.
InterPol	International Criminal Police Organization.	An international organisation helping police cooperation across countries.
NASA	National Aeronautics and Space Administration	An American government agency handling space research.
NASCAR	National Association for Stock Car Auto Racing.	A family-owned business sanctioning auto-racing events.
SARS	Severe Acute Respiratory Syndrome	A respiratory disease in humans which is fatal.
UN	United Nations	An international organisation for inter-country cooperation.
UNICEF	United Nations Children's Education Fund	A UN program that provides humanitarian help to children.
YMCA	Young Men's Christian Association	A worldwide association that helps to put Christian principles into action.
HIV	Human Immuno deficiency Virus	The virus that causes AIDS.

Model Examples

1. Write the abbreviated form of : 'AEC'

   ①   Atomic Energy Commission

   ②   Atomic Energy

   ③   Audit Education Centre

   ④   Asian Electic Commission   ❶

2. Write the abbreviated form of : 'AITUC'

   ①   All India Trade under Commission

   ②   All India Trade Union Congress

   ③   Air India Trade under Commission

   ④   Air Andia Travel under Commission.   ❷

Examples for Practice

1. Write the abbreviated form of : 'CID'

   ①   Captain of Indian Department

   ②   Criminal Intelligence Department

   ③   Captain of Intelligence Department

   ④   None of these.

2. Write the abbreviated form of : 'DIG'

   ①   Deputy Investigation General

   ②   Department of Intelligence General

   ③   Deputy Inspector General

   ④   District Inspector General

3. Write the abbreviated form of : 'ECG'

   ①   Electro Cardiogram

   ②   Electric Circuit

   ③   European Centre Geophysical

   ④   Excellency in Centre of Gravity

4. Write the abbreviated form of : 'IAA'

   ①   Indian Agriculture Agency

   ②   International Agro Agency

   ③   Indian Agency Association

   ④   Indian Airports Authority

5. Write the abbreviated form of : 'MEd'

   ①   Master of Electric Department

   ②   Master of Education

   ③   Merit of Education

   ④   Madras Educational Department

Answers

Q.	Ans.	Q.	Ans.	Q.	Ans.	Q.	Ans.
1.	❷	2.	❸	3.	❶	4.	❹
5.	❷						

❖ ❖ ❖

KNOWING NUMBERS

UNIT

1.1 INTERNATIONAL NUMERALS AND ROMAN NUMERALS

(A) INTERNATIONAL NUMERALS

✌ INTRODUCTION :

The numbers 0, 1, 2, 3, 4, 5, 6, 7, 8, 9 are used to in English write. These numbers are called as international numerals.

The number ०, १, २, ३, ४, ५, ... are used in Marathi, Sanskrit, those numbers are called as Devnagari numbers. The international numerals and the corresponding Devnagari numerals are given in following table.

International Numerals	0	1	2	3	4	5	6	7	8	9
Devnagari Numerals	०	१	२	३	४	५	६	७	८	९

Model Examples

1. Rewrite the following numbers in the Devnagari Script :

(a) 894 :

① ८५४   ② ८३४   ③ ८९४   ④ ८८४   ❸

(b) 12 :

① २९   ② ३१   ③ ११   ④ १२   ❹

2. Rewrite the following number in International Numerals :

६६ :

① 36   ② 56   ③ 66   ④ 16   ❸

(2.1)

3. Rewrite the 42 in Devnagari Script :

     ① १२   ② ४२   ③ ४४   ④ २४   ❷

4. How to write the following in international numeral ?

Two hundred five.

     ① 2005   ② 205   ③ 2055   ④ 25   ❷

Examples for Practice

(a) Rewrite the following numbers in Devnagari Script :

1. 794 :

     ① ७९४   ② ९७४   ③ ४७९   ④ ७९४

2. 98 :

     ① ९८   ② ८९   ③ ९९   ④ ८८

3. 507 :

     ① ५७०   ② ५०७   ③ ५००   ④ ५७८

4. 31 :

     ① २१   ② ३२   ③ ३१   ④ १३

5. 642 :

     ① ६४४   ② ६४२   ③ ६४   ④ ६२

6. 26594 :

     ① २६५४९   ② २५६९४   ③ २६५९४   ④ २६५९

7. 31,609 :

     ① ३१६०९   ② ३१६९   ③ ३०१६९   ④ ३६१०९

8. 19307 :

     ① १३९७०   ② १३९०७   ③ १९३७०   ④ १९३०७

9. 47995 :

     ① ४९९७५   ② ४७९९५   ③ ४७५९९   ④ ४७९९६

10. 85890 :

     ① ८९८५०   ② ८८५९०   ③ ८५८९०   ④ ८५९८०

(b) Rewrite the following numbers in International Script :

1. २२ :

     ① 22   ② 92   ③ 2.2   ④ 11

2. ५०८ :

     ① 805   ② 508   ③ 500   ④ 805

3. ६६६ :
   ① 667   ② 666   ③ 366   ④ 336
4. ९०९ :
   ① 505   ② 509   ③ 905   ④ 909
5. १२८ :
   ① 281   ② 821   ③ 218   ④ 128
6. ९५८१२३ :
   ① 985213   ② 958123   ③ 958231   ④ 985123
7. ४५६७२ :
   ① 45627   ② 45682   ③ 47652   ④ 45672
8. २३८९ :
   ① 2389   ② 2589   ③ 2489   ④ 2379
9. ८५६४३ :
   ① 75643   ② 87643   ③ 85643   ④ 85463
10. ६३०१ :
    ① 6031   ② 6301   ③ 6302   ④ 7302

Q.11 to 14   Write the following numbers in international numbers.

11. २५४
    ① 254   ② 245   ③ 425   ④ 542
12. ७,५४३
    ① 7,534   ② 5,437   ③ 7,453   ④ 7,543
13. ८०१
    ① 104   ② 401   ③ 410   ④ 41
14. ५५
    ① 77   ② 55   ③ 45   ④ 35

Q15 to 17   Write the following numbers Devnagri Script

15. 375
    ① ३७५   ② ३५७   ③ ५३७   ④ ५७३
16. 8,050
    ① ८५०   ② ८,५००   ③ ८,०५०   ④ ८,००५

17. 4,051

①૫,૮૦૧   ② ૪,૪૦૫   ③ ૪,૪૫૦   ④ ૪,૦૫૧

Q18 to 21 Fill in the balnks with correct alternative

18. ૬૪૨ = ☐ 52

① 7   ② 5   ③ 6   ④ 4

19. 8,441 = ૮૪ ☐ ૧

① 1   ② 4   ③ 3   ④ 8

20. ૮,૦૫૮ = ☐ 05 ☐

① 5   ② 8   ③ 6   ④ 4

21. ૮૦ ☐ ૧ = 8,051

① 8   ② 5   ③ 6   ④ 4

Answers

(a)	1.	④	2.	❶	3.	❷	4.	❸	5.	❷
	6.	❸	7.	❶	8.	④	9.	❷	10.	❸
(b)	1.	❶	2.	❷	3.	❷	4.	❸	5.	④
	6.	❷	7.	④	8.	④	9.	❸	10.	❷
	11.	❷	12.	④	13.	❷	14.	❷	15.	❶
	16.	❸	17.	④	18.	❶	19.	❷	20.	❷
	21.	❷								

✤ ✤ ✤

(B) ROMAN NUMBERS

✌ INTRODUCTION :

The Roman Numeral System has its origin in ancient Rome and uses combination of letters from the Latin alphabet to signify values. The letter 'I' was the symbol used for 1, 'V' for 5 and 'X' for 10. In this method, there is no symbol for 0 (zero) that means it does not include zero also the value of a symbol does not change its place. There are a certain rules for writing numbers using the Roman numerals.

✌ *Rule 1 :*

If any of the symbol I or X is written consecutively two or three times, their sum total is the number they make.

For example, :

$$II = 1 + 1 = 2$$
$$III = 1 + 1 + 1 = 3$$
$$XX = 10 + 10 = 20$$

✌ *Rule 2 :*

The symbol 'I' or 'X' an be repeated maximum for three times. The numeral 'V' can never be or is never repeated consecutively.

✌ *Rule 3 :*

When either 'I' or 'V' is written on the right of the symbol of a bigger number, its value is added to the value of the bigger number.

For example :

$$VI = 5 + 1 = 6$$
$$XI = 10 + 1 = 11$$
$$XV = 10 + 5 = 15$$
$$VIII = 5 + 1 + 1 + 1 = 8$$
$$XII = 10 + 1 + 1 = 12$$
$$XVII = 10 + 5 + 1 + 1 = 17$$
$$XIII = 10 + 1 + 1 + 1 = 13$$

✌ *Rule 4 :*

When I is written to the left of 'V' or 'X', the value is subtracted from the value of 'V' or 'X'. However, the symbol 'I' is not written more than once (or only one) before 'V' or 'X'.

For example : $IV = 5 - 1 = 4$
$$IX = 10 - 1 = 9$$

Apart from 'I', 'V' and 'X' we also use 'L', 'C', 'D' and 'M' as Roman numerals.

Roman numerals	I	V	X	L	C	D	M
Numbers	1	5	10	50	100	500	1000

Model Examples

Q. Choose the correct international numbers for the below mentioned roman numbers.

1. VII :

    ① 5   ② 7   ③ 8   ④ 6   ❷

    Explanation : VII $\Rightarrow$ V = 5, I = 1, I = 1 $\therefore$ 5 + 1 + 1 = 7

    $\therefore$ Alternative ❷ is the correct answer.

2. XVI :

    ① 14   ② 15   ③ 16   ④ 26   ❸

    Explanation : XVI $\Rightarrow$ X = 10, V = 5 and I = 1

    $\therefore$ XVI = 10 + 5 + 1 = 16

    $\therefore$ Alternative ❸ is the correct answer.

3. IX :

    ① 9   ② 11   ③ 8   ④ 21   ❶

    Explanation : IX $\Rightarrow$ I = 1, X = 10 $\therefore$ IX = 10 – 1 = 9

    $\therefore$ Alternative ❶ is the correct answer.

4. XIX :

    ① 29   ② 21   ③ 12   ④ 19   ❹

    Explanation : XIX $\Rightarrow$ X = 10, I = 1, X = 10 and

    IX = 10 – 1 = 9 $\therefore$ XIX = 10 + 9 = 19

    $\therefore$ Alternative ❹ is the correct answer.

Examples for Practice

(I) Choose the correct roman numerals for the below mentioned International Numbers :

1. 61

    ① LVI   ② LXVI   ③ LXI   ④ LIX

2. 40

    ① LX   ② XXXX   ③ LXX   ④ XL

3. 26

    ① XXVI   ② LVI   ③ XXIV   ④ XXXVI

4. 58

① XXXXXVIII   ② LVIII

③ XLVIII   ④ LXVIII

5. 100 :

① D   ② L   ③ C   ④ M

6. 49 :

① XLIX   ② LXIX   ③ XXXXIX   ④ LXXI

(II) *Choose the correct Hindu Arabic or Roman numerals in the following statements.*

1. There are XXIV students in my class.

① 26   ② 24   ③ 14   ④ 24

2. My birthday is on XXIX of January.

① 19   ② 30   ③ 29   ④ 31

3. My mother gave me XLVIII chocolates for my birthday.

① 67   ② 58   ③ 38   ④ 48

4. I scored 96 marks in Science in this examination.

① XCVI   ② CXVI

③ LXXXXVI   ④ XCIV

5. Our team nceded 19 more runs to win the match.

① XXIX   ② XIX   ③ IXX   ④ XXI

6. How much is XX + IX + VI + L = ?

① 95   ② 45   ③ 85   ④ 75

7. How much is XL – XIX = ?

① XI   ② XXXI   ③ XXIX   ④ XXI

(III) *Choose the correct roman numerals for the below mentioned International Numbers :*

1. 37

① XXXVIIII   ② XXXVII   ③ XXXIV   ④ XXVII

2. 19

① IXX   ② XXI   ③ XIX   ④ XXIX

3. 87 :

① XXXLVII   ② LXXVII   ③ LXXIIV   ④ LXXXVII

4. 501 :

① DI   ② CI   ③ MI   ④ LI

(IV) *Choose the correct Hindu Arabic or Roman numerals in the following statements.*

1. The symbols V, L and D in Roman numerals are never repeated.

① True   ② False   ③ may be   ④ don't know

2. In Roman numerals we have zero.

① True   ② False
③ 1 and 2 correct   ④ All the true

3. A smaller value symbol after a greater value symbol means ....

① subtraction   ② multiplication
③ addition   ④ division

4. No letter is used more than .... terms in a row in roman numerals.

① two   ② four   ③ one   ④ three

Answers										
1.	1.	❸	2.	❹	3.	❶	4.	❷	5.	❸
	6.	❸								
2.	1.	❷	2.	❸	3.	❶	4.	❸	5.	❷
	6.	❸	7.	❹						
3.	1.	❷	2.	❸	3.	❹	4.	❶		
4.	1.	❶	2.	❷	3.	❸	4.	❹		

1.2   *READING AND WRITTING NUMBERS UP TO TEN DIGITS*

✌ INTRODUCTION :

To write any number we use 1, 2, 3, 4, 5, 6, 7, 8, 9 and 0. This means all the numbers are prepared using this 10 digits i.e. 1 – 10. Any number without its place value is of no importance.

For example : Write in words 2, 08, 204 : We must first fix-up the value of each number by writing its value on top. i.e.

L TTh Th H T U
2 0   8 2 0 4   answer is two lakhs eight thousand two hundred and four.

───── Model Examples ─────

Write in words the following figure :

1. 1,08,102 :
   ① One lakh eight thousand one hundred and two.
   ② Eighteen thousand one hundred and two.
   ③ Ten thousand eighty one hundred and two.
   ④ Ten lakh eight thousand one hundred and two.   ❶

               L TTh Th H T U
   Explanation : 1 0   8 1 0 2 .

   ∴ Alternative ❶ is the correct answer.

2. 9,05,125 :
   ① Nine lakh five thousand one hundred twenty five.
   ② Ninety five thousand one twenty five.
   ③ Nine lakh fifty thousand one twenty five.
   ④ Ninety thousand five hundred twenty five.   ❶

               L TTh Th H T U
   Explanation : 9 0   5 1 2 5 .

   ∴ Alternative ❶ is the correct answer.

3. 2,50,094 :
   ① Twenty five thousand ninety four.
   ② Twenty five hundred ninety four.
   ③ Two lakh fifty thousand ninety four.
   ④ None of the above.   ❸

Explanation : We need to write the place value and then

L   TTh   Th   H   T   U
2   5   0   0   9   4 ⋅

∴ Alternative ❸ is the correct answer.

4. 8,53,413 :
   ① Eighty five hundred thirteen.
   ② Eight thousand fifty three thousand four hundred thirteen.
   ③ Fifty three thousand four hundred thirteen.
   ④ Eight lakh fifty three thousand four hundred thirteen   ❹

Explanation :

L   TTh   Th   H   T   U
8   5   3   4   1   3 ⋅

∴ Alternative ❹ is the correct answer.

5. 5,41,727 :
   ① Fifty four thousand seventeen hundred twenty seven.
   ② Fifty four thousand seven hundred twenty seven.
   ③ Fifty four lakh one thousand seven hundred twenty seven only.
   ④ Five lakh forty one thousand seven hundred twenty seven.   ❹

Explanation :

L   TTh   Th   H   T   U
5   4   1   7   2   7

∴ Alternative ❹ is the correct answer.

●══════ Examples for Practice ══════●

Write in words the following figures :

1. 8,88,888
   ① Eighty thousand eight hundred and eighty eight.
   ② Eighty eight hundred and eighty eight.
   ③ Eight lakh eighty eight thousand eight hundred and eighty eight.
   ④ Eighty eight hundred and eighty eight.

2. 1,20,303
    ① One lakh twenty thousand three hundred and thirty.
    ② One lakh twenty thousand three hundred and three.
    ③ One lakh two thousand three hundred and three.
    ④ One lakh twenty lakh and three hundred.

3. 6,13,256
    ① Six lakh thirteen thousand two hundred and fifty six.
    ② Six lakh thirteen thousand two hundred and six.
    ③ Six lakh thirteen thousand two hundred and sixty five.
    ④ Sixty one lakh three thousand two hundred fifty six.

4. 5,32,484
    ① Five lakh thirty thousand two four hundred and eighty four.
    ② Thirty two thousand and eight four.
    ③ Three thousand two hundred and eighty four.
    ④ Five lakh thirty two thousand four hundred and eighty four.

5. 9,65,083
    ① Nine lakh sixty five thousand and eighty three.
    ② Nine lakh sixty thousand five hundred and eighty three.
    ③ Nine lakh sixty five thousand eight hundred and three.
    ④ Nine lakh sixty five thousand and three.

6. How will you write 56,301 in words ?
    ① Five six three hundred and one.
    ② Fifty six thousand three hundred ten.
    ③ Fifty six thousand three hundred and one.
    ④ Fifty thousand sixty three hundred one.

7. Ten thousand and ten. Write in numbers.
    ① 10,100 ② 10,101   ③ 10,001   ④ 10,010

8. $(5 \times 100) + (6 \times 1,000) + (8 \times 10,000) + (11 \times 1)$
    ① 86,511 ② 56,011   ③ 86,115   ④ 58,611

9. Which of the following is true representation of the number 5,328 ?
    ① 5 thousand + 3 hundred + 28 tens + 8 units.
    ② 5 thousand + 21 tens + 7 units.
    ③ 4 thousand + 13 hundred + 7 units.
    ④ 5 thousand + 3 hundred + 20 tens + 8 units.

10. 31,15,765 :
    ① Thirty two thousand fifteen lakhs seven hundred and sixty five.
    ② Thirty one lakhs fourteen thousand seven hundred and fifty six.
    ③ Thirty one lakhs fifteen thousand seven hundred and sixty five
    ④ Thirty two lakhs fifteen hundred and sixty five

11. 73,03,988 :
    ① Seventy three lakhs thirty thousand eight hundred and ninety eight.
    ② Seventy three lakhs three thousands nine hundred and eighty eight.
    ③ Seventy three thousand three hundred and ninety eight.
    ④ Seventy three lakh nine hundred and eighty eight.

12. 48,00,600 :
    ① Forty eight thousand and six hundred
    ② Forty eight lakhs and six thousand
    ③ Forty eight lakhs and six hundred
    ④ Forty eight thousand and six

13. 57,39,461 :
    ① Five crores seventythree lakhs ninety four thousand and sixty one.
    ② Fifty lakhs seventy three thousands ninety four hundred and sixty one.
    ③ Fifty seven lakhs thirty nine thousands six hundred and forty one.
    ④ Fifty seven lakhs thirty nine thousands four hundred and sixty one.

14. 70,20,000 :
    ① Seventy lakhs twenty thousands
    ② Seven lakhs and two thousands
    ③ Seven crores and two lakhs
    ④ Seven lakhs and twenty thousand

15. Write in numbers :
    Eight lakh nine thousand and forty three.
    ① 890043 ② 800943   ③ 89043   ④ 809043

16. Eighteen lakh thirty two thousand five hundred and fifteen
    ① 1,80,32,515   ② 18,32,515
    ③ 18,23,515   ④ 18,32,551

17. Ninety five lakhs seven thousand two hundred and one.
    ① 95,07,210   ② 95,00,721
    ③ 95,07,201   ④ 95,70,201

18. Eighty lakhs thirty thousand three hundred and thirteen
    ① 8003313   ② 8030313
    ③ 8300313   ④ 8030331

19. Five lakh fifty nine thousand seventy three.
    ① 559073   ② 505973
    ③ 5059703   ④ 550973

20. Sixty two lakhs seven thousand four hundred and nine
    ① 6270409   ② 6027409
    ③ 627409   ④ 6207409

Answers

1.	❸	2.	❷	3.	❶	4.	❹	5.	❶
6.	❸	7.	❹	8.	❶	9.	❹	10.	❸
11.	❷	12	❹	13.	❹	14	❶	15.	❹
16.	❷	17.	❸	18.	❷	19.	❶	20.	❹

♣ ♣ ♣

1.3 FACE VALUE, PLACE VALUE OF A DIGIT AND EXPANDED FORM OF A NUMBER

✌ INTRODUCTION :

Place value of every digit in any number is on the basis of place occupied by the digit. There are only ten digits such as : 0, 1, 2, 3, 4, 5, 6, 7, 8, 9.

- Numbers from 1 to 9 are all one digit numbers.
- Numbers from 10 to 99 are two digit numbers.
- Numbers from 100 to 999 are three digit numbers.
- Numbers from 1000 to 9999 are four digit numbers.
- Numbers from 10,000 to 99,999 are five digit numbers.
- Numbers from 1,00,000 to 9,99,999 are six digit numbers.
- Numbers from 10,00,000 to 99,99,999 are seven digit number.
- Numbers from 1,00,00,000 to 9,99,99,999 are eight digit number.

For example : 1,67,43,269

Digit	Place of Digit	Place Value of Digit
9	units	$9 \times 1 = 9$
6	tens	$6 \times 10 = 60$
2	hundreds	$2 \times 100 = 200$
3	thousands	$3 \times 1000 = 3,000$
4	ten thousands	$4 \times 10,000 = 40,000$
7	Lakhs	$7 \times 1,00,000 = 7,00,000$
6	ten lakhs	$6 \times 10,00,000 = 60,00,000$
1	Crore	$1 \times 1,00,00,000 = 1,00,00,000$

Face Value : The face value of a digit in a number is the number itself and does not depend on its place in the number. For example, : 9456. The place value of '5' in this number is $5 \times 10 = 50$ whereas the face value is '5'.

Model Examples

Q. Choose the correct answer.

1. 500 units : How many tens ?

   ① 50   ② 5   ③ 500   ④ 5000   ❶

   Explanation :   1 unit = 1

   $$500 \text{ unit} = 1 \times 500$$
   $$1 \text{ ten} = 10$$
   $$\therefore \qquad 500 \div 10 \text{ or } \frac{500}{10} = 50$$

   ∴ Alternative ❶ is the correct answer.

2. 99,999 : Write this number in words.

   ① Ninety thousand nine hundred and ninety nine.

   ② Ninety nine thousand and ninety nine.

   ③ Ninety nine thousand nine hundred and ninety nine.

   ④ Ninety nine hundred and ninety nine.   ❸

   ∴ Alternative ❸ is the correct answer.

3. 4 ten thousands = ... hundreds.

   ① 4   ② 40   ③ 400   ④ 4000   ❸

   Explanation : 4 ten thousands $= 4 \times 10,000$
   $$= 40,000 \div 100$$
   $$= 400 \text{ hundreds}$$

   ∴ Alternative ❸ is the correct answer.

4. 800 tens = ... hundreds.   ❸

   ① 8,000   ② 800   ③ 80   ④ 8

   Explanation :   800 tens $= 800 \times 10$
   $$= 8,000$$
   $$= 80 \times 100$$
   $$= 80 \text{ hundred}$$

   ∴ Alternative ❸ is the correct answer.

5. Nine thousands + Ninety hundreds + Ninety tens + Ninety units.

   ① 19,990   ② 18,990   ③ 19,090   ④ 1,990   ❷

Explanation : The sum of the given numbers is :

9000 + 9000 (90 × 100) + 900 (90 × 10) + 90 (90 × 1) = 18,990.

∴ Alternative ❷ is the correct answer.

6. (5 × 100) + (3 × 1000) + 32 = ?

① 3532   ② 35,032   ③ 5,332   ④ 3,325   ❶

Explanation : 5 × 100 = 500 ! 3 × 1000 = 3,000

The sum = 500 + 3000 + 32 = 3532

∴ Alternative ❶ is the correct answer.

7. What is the product of the place values of the digit 2 in the number 4202.

① 400   ② 8404   ③ 2222   ④ 4222   ❶

Explanation : The place values of the digit 2 in the given number are 200 and 2. The product is 400.

∴ Alternative ❶ is the correct answer.

8. Seventy hundreds + two hundred tens + one thousand.

① 17,210   ② 10,000   ③ 70,212   ④ 71,202   ❷

Explanation :

70 × 100 + 200 × 10 + 1000 = 7000 + 2000 + 1000

= 10,000

∴ Alternative ❷ is the correct answer.

9. (3 × 1000) + (9 × 100) + (7 × 10) + 0

① 3,907   ② 3,397   ③ 3,970   ④ 9,370   ❸

∴ Alternative ❸ is the correct answer.

━━━━━ Examples for Practice ━━━━━

(I) *Solve the following examples and write the correct answer.*

1. 10 thousand = ………… hundreds.

① 1,000   ② 100   ③ 10,000   ④ 10

2. 20,000 = ………… tens.

① 2,000   ② 20,000   ③ 200   ④ 20

3. What is the difference between the place value 3 and 1 in the number 43,018 ?
    ① 2,990   ② 2,980   ③ 2,030   ④ 3,990

4. Twelve and a quarter hundred write in number.
    ① 12,075   ② 1,225   ③ 1,250   ④ 1,275

5. 8 thousand and 3 quarter hundred write in number.
    ① 8,375   ② 8,150   ③ 8,250   ④ 8,075

6. In which of the following numbers has the digit 8 the greatest place value :
    ① 84,764   ② 48,764   ③ 72,380   ④ 62,728

7. State the place value of underlined digit : 89760
    ① 8,000   ② 80,000   ③ 80   ④ 800

8. 72178 – State the place value of underlined digit.
    ① hundreds ② units   ③ tens   ④ thousand

9. What is the sum of the place values of the digit 3 in the number 30003 ?
    ① Three   ② Three lakh one
    ③ Three ten lakh   ④ Thirty thousand and three

10. In which of the following numbers is the place value of the digit 2 the least ?
    ① 2,001   ② 42,819   ③ 48,872   ④ 9,025

11. 14 Th + 14 H + 14 T + 14
    ① 15,554   ② 14,14,414 ③ 14,14,14 ④ 14,014

12. Thirty six and three quarter thousand is written in figures as :
    ① 36,250   ② 36,500   ③ 36,750   ④ 36,075

13. $(8 \times 1000) + (0 \times 100) + (4 \times 10) + (9 \times 1) = ?$
    ① 8049   ② 8149   ③ 8490   ④ 8491

14. Write the correct number of the given number name :
    Ninety nine thousand nine hundred and ninety nine.
    ① 99,909   ② 99,999   ③ 90,909   ④ 9,999

15. Smallest five digit number having 5 at tens place is ....
    ① 20,495   ② 40,549   ③ 20,459   ④ 50,249

16. Largest five digit number having 0 at thousands place is ......
    ① 95,002   ② 94,250   ③ 05,042   ④ 90,542

17. 100 tens =
    ① 1 lakh   ② 1 thousand   ③ 100 thousand   ④ one hundred

18. 7000 + 700 + 0 + 1 = ?
    ① 70701   ② 7701   ③ 70071   ④ 70017

19. 7 thousand 9 hundred is same as :
    ① 70,900   ② 7,900   ③ 70,090   ④ 7,009

20. Seven and a half thousand : Write in number.
    ① 7,050   ② 7,005   ③ 6,500   ④ 7,500

21. Twenty nine and three quarter hundred.
    ① 29,175   ② 29,075   ③ 2,975   ④ 20,975

22. What is the place value of underlined digit ?
    7<u>6</u>94356
    ① lakh   ② thousand
    ③ ten thousand   ④ ten lakh

23. What is the sum of the place values of the digit 7 in the
    number 7,69,74,727 ?
    ① 70070707   ② 70007707
    ③ 70700707   ④ 70707007

24. State the place value of underlined digit : <u>9</u>896740.
    ① 90000000   ② 9000000
    ③ 900000   ④ 90000

25. What is the difference between the place value 7 and 9 in the
    number 6700904 ?
    ① 6,98,100   ② 6,19,100   ③ 6,99,100   ④ 7,00,100

26. In which of the following numbers is the place value of the
    digit 4 the least ?
    ① 1,86,946   ② 73,46,958   ③ 65,39,489   ④ 5,64,79,89

27. Biggest 8 digit number having 6 at tens place is
    ① 48,476,940   ② 9,46,75,432
    ③ 34,796,430   ④ 4,74,65,960

28. 17L + 17TTh + 17 Th + 17H + 17
    ① 18,80,717   ② 18,88,717
    ③ 10,88,717   ④ 18,08,717
29. State the place value of underlined digit 56̲94895
    ① thousand   ② ten thousand
    ③ lakh   ④ ten lakh
30. 9̲895670
    ① ten lakh   ② lakh
    ③ crore   ④ ten thousand

(II) Write the correct number from the given expanded form.

31. 90000000 + 8000000 + 70000 + 6000 + 90 + 9
    ① 9,87,06,909   ② 9,80,76,099
    ③ 9,87,06,099   ④ 9,08,76,099
32. 70,00,000 + 40,000 + 9,000 + 300 + 20
    ① 70,43,920   ② 74,09,320
    ③ 7,49,320   ④ 70,49,320
33. 60,00,000 + 9,00,000 + 80,000 + 5,000 + 700 + 90 + 1
    ① 69,85,791   ② 69,58,791
    ③ 69,87,591   ④ 69,87,591

(III) Write the numbers in their expanded form :

34. 5,49,634 :
    ① 5,00,000 + 40,000 + 9,000 + 600 + 4
    ② 5,00,000 + 90,000 + 4,000 + 600 + 30 + 4
    ③ 5,00,000 + 40,000 + 9,000 + 600 + 30 + 4
    ④ 50,000 + 40,000 + 9,000 + 600 + 30 + 4
35. 3,52,749 :
    ① 30,000 + 5,000 + 2,000 + 700 + 40 + 8
    ② 3,00,000 + 50,000 + 2,000 + 700 + 40 + 9
    ③ 30,00,000 + 50,000 + 2,000 + 700 + 40 + 9
    ④ 3,00,000 + 5,00,000 + 2,000 + 700 + 40 + 9

(IV) Write the place name of the underlined digits.

36. 357̲050
    ① Hundred   ② thousand
    ③ ten thousand   ④ lakh
37. 2̲579899
    ① ten lakh   ② lakh
    ③ ten thousand   ④ crore

38. 48,07,659
① thousand   ② ten thousand
③ ten lakh   ④ lakh

39. 1,92,32,992
① ten thousand   ② lakh
③ ten lakh   ④ crore

40. 2785089
① thousand ② tens   ③ hundred   ④ one

1.	❷	2.	❶	3.	❶	4.	❷	5.	❹
6.	❶	7.	❷	8.	❶	9.	❹	10.	❸
11.	❶	12.	❸	13.	❶	14.	❷	15.	❸
16.	❹	17.	❷	18.	❷	19.	❷	20.	❹
21.	❸	22.	❹	23.	❶	24.	❷	25.	❸
26.	❶	27.	❹	28.	❷	29.	❸	30.	❶
31.	❷	32.	❹	33.	❶	34.	❸	35.	❷
36.	❷	37.	❶	38.	❹	39.	❸	40.	❷

1.4 MAKING THE SMALLEST AND GREATEST NUMBERS FROM GIVEN DIGITS

✌ **INTRODUCTION :**

1. Using each of the digits 6, 5 and 3 only once we can write six different numbers. These are 563, 653, 635, 536, 365 and 356 of these numbers 653 is the greatest number.

    Observe the number 653, 6 > 5 > 3.

    While forming the greatest number, arrange the given digit in their descending order.

2. In the number 356, 3 < 5 < 6 of the six number formed by using the digits 3, 5 and 6 only once. We get smallest number 356. While forming the smallest number, arrange the given digits in their ascending order.

3. We have to form the smallest four digit number using the digit 6, 0, 1, 7 only once. As per the instruction given in (2) above $0 < 1 < 6 < 7$. Hence, the number formed is 0167. But 0167 is not a four digit number because the digit 0 written in the first place has no value. Therefore, the smallest four digit number will be 1067.

	Smallest Number	**Greatest Number**
One digit	1	9
Two digit	10	99
Three digit	100	999
Four digit	1,000	9,999
Five digit	10,000	99,999
Six digit	1,00,000	9,99,999
Seven digit	10,00,000	99,99,999
Eight digit	1,00,00,000	9,99,99,999

While deciding the smaller or greater between the two numbers. Some signs are used. Put a proper sign $>$, $<$, $=$

4 ☐ 8 we use $<$ because 8 is greater than 4 and 4 is smaller than 8.

12 ☐ 12 we use $=$ sign because both numbers are same.

──────── Model Examples ────────

Solve the following examples and write the answer in circle.

1. Form the greatest number using the digits 7, 9, 4, 8 only once.

   ① 7948   ② 9874   ③ 8974   ④ 9784   ❷

   Explanation : The given digits are arranged in descending order. i.e. $9 > 8 > 7 > 4$.

   ∴ Alternative ❷ is the correct answer.

2. Form the smallest number using the digits 6, 4, 3, 1 only once.

   ① 3146   ② 1436   ③ 1346   ④ 6431   ❸

Explanation : The given digits are arranged in ascending order 1, 3, 4, 6.

∴ Alternative ❸ is the correct answer.

3. Using the digits 2, 3, 0, 1 only once form the smallest number.

    ① 1023   ② 0123   ③ 2013   ④ 3210   ❶

    Explanation : The given digits are arrange in ascending order and 0 is placed after the smallest digit 1, 0, 2, 3.

    ∴ Alternative ❶ is the correct answer.

4. Using the digits 2, 7, 5, 3 and 0 only once form the greatest five digit number.

    ① 70532   ② 75320   ③ 75032   ④ 70523   ❷

5. Using the number 8, 9, 2 only once, how many maximum 3 digit number can be made ?

    ① 4   ② 5   ③ 8   ④ 6   ❹

6. Using the digits 2, 8, 1, 0 and 9 only once form the greatest even number.

    ① 98102   ② 98210   ③ 92108   ④ 98012   ❷

7. What should be added to the greatest two digit number to get the smallest three digit number ?

    ① 0   ② 100   ③ 101   ④ 1   ❹

8. Which one of the following is the smallest five digit number ?

    ① 29111   ② 21111   ③ 10001   ④ 10000   ❹

9. Which one of the following statement is correct ?

    ① $7 \times 12 < 8 \times 4$ ② $7 \times 7 + 0 = 0$
    ③ $9 + 8 = 8 + 9$ ④ $8 + 3 < 2 + 3$ ❸

10. Insert the proper sign in the box.

    $6 \times 7 \div 2 \boxed{} 25 - 6$

    ① >   ② =   ③ <   ④ ^   ❶

12. If the numbers 89256, 98256, 86,925, 98652 and 86952 arranged in descending order, which will be the middle number ?

    ① 89256   ② 98256   ③ 86925   ④ 98652   ❶

Explanation : 98652, 98256, 89256, 86952, 86925. We arrange the numbers in descending order and the number 89256 comes in middle.

∴ Alternative ❶ is the correct answer.

13. What is the digit in the units place of the sum of the greatest even number and the smallest odd number formed using the digits 8, 2, 7, 4 each only once.

    ① 6   ② 0   ③ 9   ④ 7   ❸

14. Which one of the following set of numbers is arranged in ascending order ?

    ① 2538, 1027, 1392, 2983

    ② 1548, 1957, 2007, 3921

    ③ 1995, 2007, 1727, 5297

    ④ None of these   ❷

15. Successor of largest 4 digit number is :

    ① 10000   ② 9999   ③ 9998   ④ 1000   ❶

Put the proper sign and write down the answer in the circle given.

1. $7 + 8$ ☐ $6 + 8$

    ① =   ② >   ③ <   ④ v   ❷

2. 8×7 ☐ 7×9

    ① <   ② >   ③ v   ④ =   ❶

3. 18.25 ☐ 18.75

    ① >   ② <   ③ =   ④ ^   ❷

4. $16810 + 20$ ☐ $16830 - 20$

    ① <   ② >   ③ =   ④ v   ❷

5. $108 \div 12$ ☐ 13×5

    ① =   ② >   ③ v   ④ <   ❹

6. $(2000 + 300 + 3)$ ☐ $(3000 + 200 + 3)$

    ① >   ② <   ③ =   ④ ^   ❷

7. 75.07 ☐ 75.70

   ① >   ② =   ③ <   ④ ^   ❸

8. Six thousand + 8 hundred ☐ 8 hundred + six thousand

   ① =   ② <   ③ >   ④ ^   ❶

Examples for Practice

(a) Solve the examples and write the correct alternative.

1. One less than 10,000 is :
    ① 99999   ② 9009   ③ 9999   ④ 10009

2. Which one of the following is greatest number ?
    ① 23189   ② 32189   ③ 31289   ④ 31218

3. 8, 9, 7, 0 by using each digit only one time. Which number will be the greatest number ?
    ① 9870   ② 8970   ③ 7809   ④ 7980

4. Using the digits 1, 2, 0, 4 each only once. Form the smallest four digit number ?
    ① 4210   ② 0124   ③ 1024   ④ 1240

5. Greatest five digit even number is :
    ① 99999   ② 88888   ③ 99888   ④ 99998

6. Four digit smallest number ÷ two digit smallest number = ?
    ① 10   ② 100   ③ 1   ④ 9

7. Greatest three digit number ÷ greatest one digit number = ?
    ① 111   ② 11   ③ 1   ④ 100

8. Greatest five digit number – Smallest five digit number = ?
    ① 9000   ② 1000   ③ 98999   ④ 89999

9. Which of the following is smallest number ?
    ① 0789   ② 1078   ③ 1230   ④ 7089

10. Which number has the place value always equal to its own value ?
    ① 1   ② 0   ③ 2   ④ 5

11. Find the number which shows the difference between the number 36,481 and the number by reversing the order of the digits in it.

    ① 18,018   ② 18,463   ③ 28,135   ④ 28,028

12. How many two digit numbers are there in between 1 to 100 ?

    ① 9   ② 91   ③ 19   ④ 90

13. By using each digit once which greatest number is formed from 5, 9, 6, 1 ?

    ① 5,619   ② 1,569   ③ 9,651   ④ 6,951

14. By using each digit once which smallest number is formed from 5, 9, 6, 1 ?

    ① 5,619   ② 1,569   ③ 9,651   ④ 6,951

15. By using each digit once which greatest five digit number is formed from the given series 4, 2, 7, 3, 0 ?

    ① 74,320   ② 42,730   ③ 73,402   ④ 24,730

16. By using each digit once which smallest five digit number is formed from the given series 4, 2, 7, 3, 0 ?

    ① 42,730   ② 74,320   ③ 23,470   ④ 20,347

17. Using each of the digits 2, 0, 4, 1 only once, how many numbers more than 2000 can be formed ?

    ① 6   ② 18   ③ 24   ④ 12

18. Using the numbers 4, 6 and 8 only once, how many maximum 3 digit numbers can be made ?

    ① 4   ② 6   ③ 9   ④ 5

19. By using the digits 8, 4, 0, 6, 1 only once, if the smallest five digit number is made, what would be the digit in the ten thousands place ?

    ① 8   ② 0   ③ 1   ④ 6

20. Using the numbers 7, 0, 2, 3, 4 once each, write the smallest even five digit number.

    ① 23,740   ② 20,374   ③ 20,347   ④ 20,734

21. How many two digit numbers can be formed by using 2, 0, 5, 8 only once without repetition ?
    ① 18   ② 9   ③ 6   ④ 24

22. Which one of the following is five digit number ?
    ① 00,729   ② 07,290   ③ 70,290   ④ 00,029

23. Which one of the following is the smallest four digit number ?
    ① 2,010   ② 1002   ③ 1100   ④ 1,000

24. From the statements given below, pick-up the statement indicating the smallest number.
    ① A quarter of 240   ② A half of 160
    ③ Three quarters of 100   ④ Double of 45

25. Which number will be in the middle, if the following numbers are arranged in an ascending order ? 6804, 6721, 6591, 6903, 6328
    ① 6,721   ② 6,591   ③ 6,804   ④ 6,328

26. If the following numbers are written in descending order, which number will be the middle one ? 7504, 7450, 7540, 5740, 5407.
    ① 5,740   ② 7,504   ③ 7,540   ④ 7,450

27. If the following numbers are written in descending order, what will be the middle digit of the middle number ? 421, 493, 444, 417, 439.
    ① 2   ② 1   ③ 3   ④ 4

28. By using each digit once which six greatest number is formed from 2, 3, 0, 6, 7, 1
    ① 763021   ② 762301   ③ 763120   ④ 763210

29. Using the following digit and form the greatest seven digit number ?
    9, 4, 3, 8, 0, 6, 7
    ① 98,76,430   ② 98,76,340
    ③ 98,76,403   ④ 98,76,304

30. By using digit 7, 6, 4, 3, 01, 2 once make the smallest seven digit number ?
    ① 10,23,476   ② 10,23,674
    ③ 10,23,467   ④ 10,24,367

31. By using the given digit 1, 4, 6, 7, 5, 0, 2, 3 once make the smallest eight digit number ?
    ① 1,02,34,576   ② 1,02,34,567
    ③ 0,12,34,567   ④ 1,02,34,657

32. Which of the following is the smallest six digit number ?
    ① 1,00,099   ② 1,00,001   ③ 9,99,999   ④ 1,00,000

33. Which of the following is the smallest eight digit number ?
    ① 1,00,00,000   ② 0,00,00,001
    ③ 0,10,00,000   ④ 1,00,00,001

34. What is a half of one lakh ?
    ① 20,000   ② 50,000   ③ 25,000   ④ 75,000

35. From the statement given below, pick-up the statement indicating the smallest number ?
    ① A quarter of 10,000   ② A half of 7,000
    ③ Three quarters 10,000   ④ A double of 1500

36. Greatest eight digit number – smallest six digit number ?
    ① 9,98,99,000   ② 9,00,00,000
    ③ 9,98,99,000   ④ 9,98,99,999

37. What is the sum of greatest seven digit number and smallest four digit number ?
    ① 99,98,999   ② 10,00,999
    ③ 1,00,00,999   ④ 9,98,999

38. Six digit greatest number ÷ three digit greatest number ?
    ① 10001   ② 1001   ③ 1001.01   ④ 1010

39. What should be added to greatest four digit number to get the smallest six digit number ?
    ① 1,00,000   ② 900001
    ③ 10001   ④ 90001

40. What is the digit in the units place of the greatest even number and the smallest odd number formed using the digits 9, 4, 6, 7, 5, 3 each only once ?

① 6   ② 3   ③ 4   ④ 5

(b) Put a proper sign in the square :

1. $9 \times 4 + 2$ ☐ $7 \times 4 + 4$

    ① >   ② <   ③ =   ④ ∨

2. $36 - 3 \times 6 + 26 \div 2$ ☐ $45 \div 9 \times 4 + 2$

    ① >   ② =   ③ <   ④ ∧

3. $99 + 1 + 999$ ☐ $1000 + 99$

    ① >   ② <   ③ ∧   ④ =

4. $5999 - 99$ ☐ 6250

    ① <   ② >   ③ =   ④ ∨

5. Smallest four digit number ☐ greatest five digit number-one.

    ① <   ② =   ③ >   ④ ≥

6. $10 + 5$ ☐ $6 + 8$

    ① >   ② <   ③ =   ④ ≠

7. 6×5 ☐ 3×10

    ① >   ② <   ③ =   ④ ≤

8. 4×5 ☐ 5×5

    ① >   ② <   ③ =   ④ ≠

9. Which one of the following statement is true ?

    ① $8 + 18 > 13 - 6$ ② $6 + 6 \times 01 = 0$
    ③ $3 \times 18 < 9 \times 5$ ④ $6 + 0 > 3 \times 13$

10. Which one of the following statements is true ?

    ① $77 > 7 + 7 \times 11$ ② $413 > 528$
    ③ $217 > 171$ ④ $55 = 11 \times 5 + 5$

11. What should be the sign in the square in the statement 16.05 ☐ 16.50 ?

    ① >   ② =   ③ <   ④ ≥

12. What sign will you use to fill the square in the statement given below ?

    6,760 + 27 ☐ 1,079 + 5,830

    ① >   ② <   ③ =   ④ ≠

13. In 27,015 ☐ 27,105 which sign replaces ☐

    ① <   ② =   ③ >   ④ None of these

14. 6705 ☐ 6750 which sign replaces ☐ ?

    ① ≤   ② =   ③ >   ④ <

Q. Which sign replaces ☐ in

15. 3534304 ☐ 3534404

    ① <   ② >   ③ =   ④ ≤

16. 480009 ☐ 4800009

    ① =   ② >   ③ <   ④ ≤

17. 88,88,888 ☐ 8,88,888

    ① <   ② >   ③ =   ④ ≥

18. 33,84,706 ☐ 32,84,706

    ① >   ② =   ③ ≤   ④ <

19. 356980 ☐ 396850

    ① ≤   ② >   ③ <   ④ =

20. 1269894 ☐ 1269994

    ① ≤   ② >   ③ =   ④ <

21. 45,12,806 ☐ 45,21,806

    ① <   ② >   ③ =   ④ ≥

22. 4000000 + 800000 + 90000 + 7000 + 300 + 50 + 2

    ☐

    4000000 + 80000 + 90000 + 7000 + 300 + 50 + 2

    ① =   ② ≤   ③ >   ④ <

23. 5129370 ☐ 5119370

    ① <   ② >   ③ ≤   ④ =

24. 9999900 ☐ 9999990

     ① =   ② >   ③ ≤   ④ <

25. 1000009 ☐ 100009

     ① >   ② <   ③ ≥   ④ =

Answers

(a)

1.	❸	2.	❷	3.	❶	4.	❸	5.	❹
6.	❷	7.	❶	8.	❹	9.	❶	10.	❷
11.	❶	12.	❹	13.	❸	14.	❷	15.	❶
16.	❹	17.	❹	18.	❷	19.	❸	20.	❷
21.	❷	22.	❸	23.	❹	24.	❶	25.	❶
26.	❹	27.	❸	28.	❹	29.	❶	30.	❸
31.	❷	32.	❹	33.	❶	34.	❷	35.	❶
36.	❹	37.	❸	38.	❷	39.	❹	40.	❷

(b)

1.	❶	2.	❶	3.	❹	4.	❶	5.	❶
6.	❶	7.	❸	8.	❷	9.	❶	10.	❸
11.	❸	12.	❷	13.	❶	14.	❹	15.	❶
16.	❸	17.	❷	18.	❶	19.	❸	20.	❹
21.	❶	22.	❸	23.	❷	24.	❹	25.	❶

♣ ♣ ♣

1.5 ASCENDING & DESCENDING ORDER OF NUMBERS AND COMPARISON

✌ INTRODUCTION :

Ascending order means to climb. i.e. to go from a smaller number to bigger number. Descending order means come down i.e. to go from bigger to smaller number.

Example : 28, 38, 86, 68, 18.

Ascending Order : 18, 28, 38, 68, 86.

Descending Order : 86, 68, 38, 28, 18.

In order to find out the ascending or descending order of the numbers given first,

- See if the numbers have the same number of digits.
- If so, compare them digit by digit starting from the left.
- The greatest number will have the greater digit first.
- The smallest number will have the smaller digits first.
- If the numbers on the extreme left are the same then proceed to the next digit and compare the numbers.

For example : (1) 57968, 79658, 67589

The greater numbers will have the greater digits in the extreme left i.e. $7 > 6 > 5$

∴   Ascending order will be 57968, 67589, 79658

Descending order will be 79658, 67589, 57968

Model Examples

1. Write the following number in Ascending and Descending Order.

   796, 5084, 3891, 68

   ① A. O. : 796, 68, 3891, 5081   D. O. : 3891, 5081, 68, 796
   ② A. O. : 68, 796, 3891, 5084   D. O. : 5084, 3891, 796, 68
   ③ A. O. : 68, 796, 5081, 3891   D. O. : 3891, 68, 796, 5081
   ④ A. O. : 5081, 3891, 68, 796   D. O. : 68, 796, 3891, 5084   ❷

2. Write the smallest number from given numbers.

   94,000   27,535   84,110   48025

   ① 48,025   ② 27,535   ③ 84,110   ④ 94,000   ❷

3. Write the greatest number from given numbers.

   74150, 47025, 110350, 87025

   ① 110350   ② 47025   ③ 74150   ④ 84025   ❶

4. Write the following numbers in Ascending Order.

   84015, 97135, 89245, 47140

   ① 89245, 84125, 97135, 47140
   ② 47140, 84015, 89245, 97135
   ③ 97135, 89245, 84015, 47140
   ④ 84015, 89245, 97135, 47150   ❷

5. Write the following number in Descending Order.
    105490, 28430, 13540, 48295
    ① 13540, 28430, 48295, 105490
    ② 105490, 48295, 13540, 28430
    ③ 28430, 13540, 48295, 105490
    ④ 105490, 48295, 28430, 13540   ❹

━━━━━━━━━ **Model Examples** ━━━━━━━━━●

Write the following in Ascending and Descending Order.

1. 7109, 7190, 7091
    ① A.O. : 7091, 7109, 7190   ② A.O. : 7109, 7190, 7091
       D.O. : 7190, 7109, 7091   D.O. : 7091, 7190, 7109
    ③ A.O. : 7190, 7091, 7109   ④ A.O. : 7109, 7190, 7091
       D.O. : 7091, 7190, 7109   D.O. : 7091, 7109, 7190

2. 826, 682, 286
    ① A.O. : 826, 286, 682   ② A.O. : 286, 682, 826
       D.O. : 682, 286, 826   D.O. : 826, 682, 286
    ③ A.O. : 682, 286, 826   ④ A.O. : 826, 862, 286
       D.O. : 826, 286, 682   D.O. : 286, 682, 826

3. 699, 2699, 1699
    ① A.O. : 699, 1699, 2699   ② A.O. : 1699, 699, 2699
       D.O. : 2699, 1699, 699   D.O. : 2699, 699, 1699
    ③ A.O. : 2699, 1699, 699   ④ A.O. : 2699, 699, 1699
       D.O. : 699, 1699, 2699   D.O. : 699, 2699, 1699

4. 349, 358, 344
    ① A.O. : 358, 349, 344   ② A.O. : 349, 344, 358
       D.O. : 344, 349, 358   D.O. : 344, 358, 349
    ③ A.O. : 344, 358, 349   ④ A.O. : 344, 349, 358
       D.O. : 349, 344, 358   D.O. : 358, 349, 344

5. 2,013; 3,012; 2,031
    ① A.O. : 3,012; 2,013; 2,031   ② A.O. : 2,013; 2,031; 3,012
       D.O. : 2,031; 2,013; 3,012   D.O. : 3,012; 2,031; 2,013
    ③ A.O. : 2,031; 3,012; 2,013   ④ A.O. : 3,012; 2,031; 2,013
       D.O. : 2,013; 3,012; 2,031   D.O. : 2,013; 2,031; 3,012

6. 1,500; 2,500; 1,300

① A.O. : 1,500; 1,300; 2,500 ② A.O. : 1,300; 1,500; 2,500

  D.O. : 2,500; 1,300; 1,500   D.O. : 2,500; 1,500; 1,300

③ A.O. : 2,500; 1,500; 1,300 ④ A.O. : 1,500;1,300; 2,500

  D.O. : 1,300; 1,500; 2,500   D.O. : 2,500; 1,300;1,500

7. 7,820; 3,920; 9,320

① A.O. : 3,920; 9,320; 7,820 ② A.O. : 9,320; 3,920; 7,820

  D.O. : 9,320; 3,920; 7,820   D.O. : 3,920; 9,320; 7,820

③ A.O. : 7,820; 9,320; 3,920 ④ A.O. : 3,920; 7820; 9,320

  D.O. : 9,320; 3,920; 7,820   D.O. : 9,320; 7,820; 3,920

8. 6,800; 5,737; 2,329

① A.O. : 2,329; 6,800; 5,737 ② A.O. : 2,329; 6,800; 5,737

  D.O. : 6,800; 2,329; 5,737   D.O : 6,800; 5,737; 2,329

③ A.O. : 2,329; 5,737; 6,800 ④ A.O. : 2,329; 5,737; 6,800

  D.O. : 6,800; 2,329; 5,737   D.O. : 6,800; 5,737; 2,329

9. 2,119; 5,500; 4,909

① A.O. : 4,909; 2,119; 5500 ② A.O. : 2,119; 4,909; 5,500

  D.O. : 5,500; 2,119; 4909   D.O. : 5,500; 4,909; 2,119

③ A.O. : 2,119; 4,909; 5,500 ④ A.O. : 4,909; 5500; 2,119

  D.O. : 4,909; 2,119; 5,500   D.O. : 2,119; 4,909; 5,500

10. Write the given numbers in descending order : 5238, 6890, 5600, 6500.

① 6890, 6500, 5238, 5600 ② 6890, 6500, 5600, 5238

③ 6500, 6890, 5600, 5238 ④ None of these.

11. 169543, 179543, 169953, 169853

① A.O. : 169543, 169853, 169953, 179543

  D.O. : 179543, 169953, 169853, 169543

② A.O. : 179543, 169543, 169853, 169953

  D.O. : 169953, 169853, 169543, 179543

③ A.O. : 169543, 169853, 179543, 169953

  D.O. : 179543, 169953, 169543, 169853

④ A.O. : 169543, 169953, 169853, 179543

  D.O. : 179543, 1698543, 169953, 169543

12. 154361, 144361, 143461, 153461
     ① A.O. : 153461, 154361, 144361, 143461
        D.O. : 144361, 143461, 153461, 154361
     ② A.O. : 144361, 143461, 153461, 154361
        D.O. : 153461, 154361, 144361, 143461
     ③ A.O. : 143461, 144361, 153461, 154361
        D.O. : 154361, 153461, 144361, 143461
     ④ A.O. : 143461, 153461, 144361, 154361
        D.O. : 153461, 154361, 144361, 143461

13. Write the descending order of the given number.
     9889432, 9869423, 9969423, 9979432
     ① 9979432, 9969423, 9869423, 9889432
     ② 9979432, 9889432, 9969423, 9869423
     ③ 9889432, 9979432, 9969423, 9869423
     ④ 9979432, 9969423, 9889432, 9869423

Answers

1.	❶	2.	❷	3.	❶	4.	❹	5.	❷
6.	❷	7.	❹	8.	❹	9.	❷	10.	❷
11.	❶	12.	❸	13.	❹				

❖ ❖ ❖

1.6   QUESTIONS BASED ON NUMBERS FROM 1 - 100

✌ INTRODUCTION :

1 to 100 numbers are divided into the following different types :

	Total Numbers	Smallest Number	Largest Number	Even Numbers	Odd Numbers
One digit number	9	1	9	4	5
Two digit number	90	10	99	45	45
Three digit number	900	100	999	450	450

- There are 10 numbers from 1 - 100 that have zero at the unit's place.

  i.e. 10, 20, 30, 40, 50, 60, 70, 80, 90 and 100.

- There are ten numbers that have any of the digits from 1 - 9 in the unit's place.

  i.e. 1, 11, 21, 31, 41, 51, 61, 71, 81, 91

  i.e. 2, 12, 22, 32, 42, 52, 62, 72, 82 and 92.

- There are nine numbers that have the same digits in the unit's and ten's place.

  i.e. 11, 22, 33, 44, 55, 66, 77, 88, 99

  All these are divisible by 11.

- There are eight numbers that are multiples of twelve.

  i.e. 12, 24, 36, 48, 60, 72, 84, 96.

- There are seven numbers which are multiples of 13 and 6 numbers which are multiples of 15 and 16.

- In the numbers from 1 - 100

  - The digit 0 occurs eleven times.
  - The digit 1 occurs twenty one times.
  - Other digits occur 20 times each.
  - The digits 1 - 9 occur 19 times in all.

- There are 90 numbers having two digits.

- There are 45 odd and 45 even numbers.

- The digit '0' occurs 11 times and other digits occurs 19 times.

The numbers in between 1 to 100 are divided as follows :

Digit of the number	0	1	2	3	4	5	6	7	8	9
No. from 1 to 100	10	21	20	20	20	20	20	20	20	20
No. from 10 to 99	9	19	19	19	19	19	19	19	19	19

Model Examples

1. Write a single number digit in between 1 to 100.

   ① 90   ② 9   ③ 10   ④ 100

   ∴ Alternative ❷ is the correct answer.

2. In two digit numbers, how many times do you find the digit 5 ?
   ① 20   ② 21   ③ 19   ④ 18   ❸
   ∴ Alternative ❸ is the correct answer.

3. What is the difference between the two digits smallest and largest number ?
   ① 88   ② 90   ③ 89   ④ 98   ❸
   ∴ Alternative ❸ is the correct answer.

4. How many one digit even number are there ?
   ① 9   ② 5   ③ 4   ④ 8   ❸
   ∴ Alternative ❸ is the correct answer.

5. Write how many times the digit 1 will be used in the number 1 to 100.
   ① 21   ② 19   ③ 20   ④ 18   ❶
   ∴ Alternative ❶ is the correct answer.

Examples for Practice

1. Write how many times the digit 4 will appear in the numbers 1 to 100.
   ① 21   ② 20   ③ 19   ④ 11

2. In two digit numbers how many times the digit 1 will appear ?
   ① 19   ② 18   ③ 20   ④ 21

3. Write how many odd numbers in two digit numbers.
   ① 90   ② 45   ③ 50   ④ 40

4. In two digit number how many numbers will be formed by using one digit only one time ?
   ① 90   ② 81   ③ 80   ④ 99

5. Which is the largest one digit even number ?
   ① 9   ② 10   ③ 8   ④ 12

6. By using 0, how many two digit numbers will be formed ?
   ① 10   ② 12   ③ 9   ④ 8

7. How many times 4 will be appear in between the numbers 41 to 50 ?
   ① 10   ② 9   ③ 8   ④ 11

8. How many times 2 will be appear in between the numbers 21 to 40 ?

① 11   ② 10   ③ 12   ④ 9

9. How many odd numbers are there between 20 and 30 ?

① 5   ② 4   ③ 2   ④ 1

10. Which is the odd number after 44 ?

① 46   ② 45   ③ 43   ④ 47

Answers

1.	❷	2.	❶	3.	❷	4.	❷	5.	❸
6.	❸	7.	❶	8.	❶	9.	❶	10.	❷

❖ ❖ ❖

1.7   EVEN AND ODD NUMBERS, PRIME AND COMPOSITE NUMBERS, SQUARE NUMBERS

✌ INTRODUCTION :

• The numbers which are completely divisible by 2 are called even numbers. Numbers which have any of the digits 0, 2, 4, 6, 8 in their unit place are called as even numbers.

For Example : 28, 30, 324, 9998 are all even numbers.

• The numbers which are not completely divisible by two are called odd numbers. Numbers which have any of the digits 1, 3, 5, 7, 9 in their unit place are called odd numbers.

For Example : 25, 69, 57, 897.

• The sum of two odd numbers is always an even number.

For Example : 23 + 67 = 90 is even number on unit place.

• The sum of two even numbers is always an even number.

For Example : 12 + 48 = 60.

• The sum of an odd number and an even number is always odd number :

For Example : 17 + 62 = 79.

- The product of two odd numbers is always an odd number :

For Example : $13 \times 17 = 221$.

- The product of two even numbers is always an even number.

For example : $16 \times 22 = 352$.

- The product of an odd number and an even number is always an even number.

For example : $7 \times 12 = 84$.

- **Consecutive numbers :** The numbers that go on increasing by 1 are called consecutive numbers.

For example : (a) 1, 2, 3, 4, ... (b) 57, 58, 59, 60, 61

- **Consecutive even numbers :** The numbers that start with an even number and go on increasing by two are called consecutive even numbers.

For example : (a) 2, 4, 6, 8, 10, 12, 14, ... (b) 20, 22, 24, 26, .

- **Consecutive odd numbers :** The numbers that start with one odd number and go on increasing by two are called consecutive odd numbers.

For example : (a) 1, 3, 5, 7, 9, ... (b) 21, 23, 25, 27, 29, 31,..

- The sum of five consecutive odd or even numbers is equal to 5 times the middle number.

For example : (a) $2 + 4 + 6 + 8 + 10 = 30$

- The middle number in this series is 6. Therefore, $5 \times 6 = 30$.

For example : (b) $1 + 3 + 5 + 7 + 9 = 25$

The middle number is 5. Therefore, $5 \times 5 = 25$

- **Prime numbers :** A **prime number** (or a **prime**) is a natural number greater than 1 that has no positive divisor other than 1 and itself.

For example : 1, 2, 3, 5, 7, 11, 13, 17, 19, 23, 29, 31, 37, 41, 43, 47, 53, 59, 61, 67, 71, 73, 79, 83, 89, 97

A natural number greater than 1 that is not a prime number is called a composite number. For example, 5 is prime because 1 and 5 are its only positive integer factor, whereas 6 is composite because it has the divisors 2 and 3 in addition to 1 and 6.

- **Square number** : The product of a number multiplied by itself,

  For example : $4 \times 4 = 16$

- **Composite Numbers** : A whole number that can be divided evenly by numbers other than 1 or itself. For Example : 9 can be divided evenly by 3 (as well as 1 and 9), so 9 is a composite number.

- **Twin Prime Numbers** : A twin prime is a prime number that is either 2 less or 2 more than another prime number

  For example : The twin prime pair (41, 43). In other words, a twin prime is a prime that has a prime gap of two. Sometimes the term twin prime is used for a pair of twin primes; an alternative name for this is prime twin or prime pair.

- **Co-Prime Numbers** : A set of numbers which do not have any other common factor other than 1 are called co-prime or relatively prime numbers. This means those numbers whose HCF is 1.

- **Triangular Numbers** : Triangular number or triangle number counts the objects that can form an equilateral triangle, as in the diagram on the right. The nth triangular number is the number of dots composing a triangle with n dots on a side, and is equal to the sum of the n natural numbers from 1 to n. The sequence of triangular numbers starting at the 0th triangular number, is 0, 1, 3, 6, 10, 15, 21, 28, 36, 45, 55, 66, 78, 91, 105, 120, 136, 153, 171, 190, 210, 231, 253, 276, 300, 325, 351, 378, 406 …

The triangle numbers are given by the following explicit formulas:

Tringular Number = (n * (n+1))/ 2

Base of Triangular Number can be define as : for the two consecutive natural numbers the first natural number is called as base of natural number. It is denoted by 'N'.

For example,

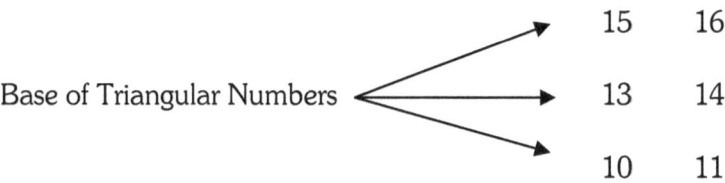

This is the triangular number sequence.

1, 3, 6, 10, 15, 21, 28, 36, 45

This sequence is generated from a pattern of dots which form a triangle. By adding another row of dots and counting all the dots we can find the next number of the sequence.

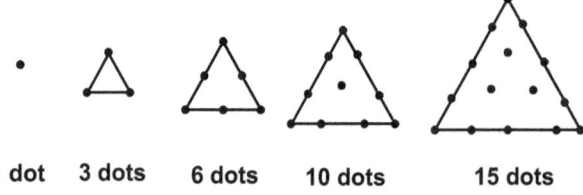

1 dot   3 dots   6 dots   10 dots   15 dots

We can make a, 'Rule', so we can calculate any triangular number. First rearrange the dots and give each pattern a number 'n' like this :

```
n =    1       2         3         4          5
       •       •         •         •          •
               • •       • •       • •        • •
                         • • •     • • •      • • •
                                   • • • •    • • • •
                                              • • • • •
```

Then double the number of dots and form them into a rectangle.

n =   1   2   3   4

5

The rectangles are n high, n + 1 wide and X_n is how many dots in the triangle (the value of the Triangular Number 'n').

For example :

$$2\,X_n = n(n + 1)$$

$$\therefore\ X_n = \frac{n(n + 1)}{2}$$

Rule is $\longrightarrow X_n = \frac{n(n + 1)}{2}$

- **Square Number** : The number we get after multiplying an integer (not a fraction) by itself.

  Example : $4 \times 4 = 16$, so 16 is a square number.

  For Example,

$$0\ (=0\times0)$$
$$1\ (=1\times1)$$
$$4\ (=2\times2)$$
$$9\ (=3\times3)$$
$$16\ (=4\times4)$$
$$25\ (=5\times5)$$

Model Examples

Answer the following :

1. Which of the following is an odd number ?

    ① 7128   ② 3874   ③ 2198   ④ 5257   ❹

    Explanation : 525$\underline{7}$ on unit place the number 7 is not. Completely divisible by 2 so it is an odd number.

    ∴ Alternative ❹ is the correct answer.

2. Which of the following is an even number ?

   ① 4463   ② 4448   ③ 4447   ④ 4441   ❷

   Explanation : 4448. 8 is unit place and 8 is completely divided by 2 so it is even number.

   ∴ Alternative ❷ is the correct answer.

3. What is the sum of the odd numbers between 20 to 30 ?

   ① 125   ② 225   ③ 100   ④ 150   ❶

   Explanation : Odd numbers between 20 to 30 are 21 + 23 + 25 + 27 + 29 = 125.

   ∴ Alternative ❶ is the correct answer.

4. Which is the 13th odd number coming after 22 ?

   ① 52   ② 43   ③ 47   ④ 45   ❸

   Explanation : Odd number next to 22 is 22 + 1 = 23 we have to find the 13th odd number after 13. i.e. 23 + (12 × 2) = 23 + 24 = 47.

   ∴ Alternative ❸ is the correct answer.

5. x is a even. What will be the fifth even number after x ?

   ① x + 4   ② x + 5   ③ x – 5   ④ x + 10   ❹

6. Find the sum of odd numbers between 230 and 236.

   ① 689   ② 932   ③ 466   ④ 699   ❹

   Explanation : The odd numbers between 230 and 236 are 231 + 233 + 235 = 699.

   ∴ Alternative ❹ is the correct answer.

7. x is an odd number. What is the next consecutive odd number ?

   ① (x + 1)   ② (x + 2)   ③ (x – 2)   ④ (x + 3)   ❷

   Explanation : Consecutive odd numbers go on increasing by 2. So the next consecutive odd number is x + 2.

   ∴ Alternative ❷ is the correct answer.

8. How many two digit even number are there ?

   ① 49   ② 45   ③ 84   ④ 20   ❷

Explanation : Two-digit are from 10 to 99 are in all 90. Half of them must be odd and half must be an even. So half of 90 is 45.

∴ Alternative ❷ is the correct answer.

9. ……….. is prime number.
   ① 2   ② 8   ③ 15   ④ 27   ❶

10. 10 is a ……….. number.
   ① prime   ② square   ③ composite ④ odd   ❸

11. The square of 14 is ………..
   ① 186   ② 196   ③ 166   ④ 176   ❷

12. Which one of the following number is a perfect square……….
   ① 622   ② 393   ③ 5778   ④ 625   ❹

13. From the following numbers find which number is not a perfect square ?
   ① 81   ② 100   ③ 72   ④ 64   ❸

   Explanation : From given alternative it is clear that 81, 100 and 64 are the perfect squares i.e.

   $81 = 9 \times 9 = $ Square of 9
   $100 = 10 \times 10 = $ Square of 10
   $64 = 8 \times 8 = $ Square of 8
   72 is not a square number.

   ∴ Alternative ❸ is the correct answer.

14. Find the Triangular number whose base is 25.
   ① 325   ② 352   ③ 235   ④ 253   ❶

   Explanation : Base is given i.e. 25 the next number of 25 is 26 to find triangular number we use formula.

   $$\frac{n \times (n+1)}{2}$$

   ∴ $$\frac{25 \times 26}{2} = 325$$

   ∴ Alternative ❶ is the correct answer.

15. If 78 is a triangular number then find it's base
   ① 22   ② 24   ③ 12   ④ 11   ❸

Explanation :

Step 1 : Multiply by 2 to given triangular number

Step 2 : Find the perfect square number before the answer obtained and take square root of it

Square root is the base

∴ $78 \times 2 = 156$

∴   144 is the perfect square before 156

∴ $\sqrt{144} = 12$

∴   Base = 12

∴ Alternative ❸ is the correct answer.

16. Find the 4ᵗʰ Triangular number after the number 66

    ① 120   ② 130   ③ 140   ④ 150   ❶

Explanation :

Step 1 : First find the base of given triangular number by the procedure mentioned in above example .

∴ $66 \times 2 = 132$

∴ 121 is the perfect square before 132

∴ $\sqrt{121} = 11$

∴   Base = 11

Step 2 : If we add next number in base we get new base.

∴ $11 + 4 = 15$

∴   New base if 15

Step 3 : We want to find 4ᵗʰ triangular number

∴ $\dfrac{15 \times 16}{2} = 120$

∴   120 is the fourth triangular number after 66

∴ Alternative ❶ is the correct answer.

17. If n= 5 then Find $X_n = $ ......

    ① 18   ② 15   ③ 16   ④ 12   ❷

Explanation : $X_n = \dfrac{n(n + 1)}{2}$

∴ $X_5 = \dfrac{5(5 + 1)}{2}$

$$\therefore \qquad X_5 = \frac{5 \times 6}{2}$$

$$\therefore \qquad X_5 = \frac{30}{2} = 15$$

$\therefore$ Alternative ❷ is the correct answer.

18. What is the 21st triangular number?

    ① 231   ② 462   ③ 230   ④ 331   ❶

    Explanation : $X_n = \dfrac{n(n + 1)}{2}$

$$\therefore \qquad X_{21} = \frac{21(21 + 1)}{2}$$

$$\therefore \qquad X_{21} = \frac{462}{2}$$

$$\therefore \qquad X_{21} = 231$$

$\therefore$ Alternative ❶ is the correct answer.

Examples for Practice

Solve the following examples.

1. Which one of the following is an even number ?

   ① 5779   ② 5977   ③ 5970   ④ 5971

2. Which one of the following is an odd number ?

   ① 8681   ② 8682   ③ 8684   ④ 8680

3. Which one of the following numbers when divided by 4 leaves remainder 1 ?

   ① 81216   ② 4896   ③ 2832   ④ 3445

4. What is the sum of the even numbers from 40 to 50 ?

   ① 200   ② 270   ③ 225   ④ 180

5. Find the 6th even number coming serially after 63.

   ① 74   ② 75   ③ 73   ④ 72

6. What is the sum of odd numbers from 81 to 91 ?

   ① 526   ② 344   ③ 430   ④ 516

7. Which of the following is first even number after 999 ?

   ① 100   ② 1002   ③ 1000   ④ 998

8. At which place could the place value of a digit be an odd number ?
    ① Thousands place   ② Units place
    ③ Hundreds place   ④ Tens place

9. Which statement is wrong in the following ?
    ① Sum of two odd numbers is always an even number.
    ② Sum of two even numbers is always an even number.
    ③ Sum of an odd number and an even number is always an even number.
    ④ Product of two even numbers is always an even number.

10. Which is the even prime number ?
    ① 4   ② 2   ③ 6   ④ 8

11. Which of the following is an even number ?
    ① 44,453   ② 55,554   ③ 3,333   ④ 5,765

12. Which of the following is an even number ?
    ① 315   ②390   ③ 481   ④ 299

13. Which of the following is an even number ?
    ① 168   ② 207   ③ 9,999   ④ 99,777

14. Which of the following is an even number ?
    ① 4,132   ② 1,297   ③ 8,765   ④ 6,789

15. Which of the following is an even number ?
    ① 176   ② 671   ③ 167   ④ 183

16. Which of the following is an odd number ?
    ① 2,730   ② 3,254   ③ 577   ④ 112

17. Which of the following is an odd number ?
    ① 19   ② 90   ③ 164   ④ 32

18. Which of the following is an odd number ?
    ① 212   ② 324   ③ 576   ④ 111

19. Which of the following is an odd number ?
    ① 2,130   ② 3,954   ③ 677   ④ 322

20. Which of the following is an odd number ?
    ① 890   ② 862   ③ 936   ④ 971

21. Which of the following digit does even number bears at its unit place ?

    ① 3   ② 6   ③ 9   ④ 1

22. Which of following digit does odd number bears at its unit place ?

    ① 2   ③ 4   ③ 6   ④ 9

23. Which is the third odd number after 7001 ?

    ① 7,003   ② 7,005   ③ 7,007   ④ 7,009

24. Which of the following is first even number after 9999 ?

    ① 1000   ② 100   ③ 990   ④ 10000

25. Which of the following odd number comes before the smallest 4 digit even number ?

    ① 999   ② 99   ③ 1001   ④ 997

26. What is the sum of all even numbers between 50 and 60 ?

    ① 220   ② 270   ③ 330   ④ 240

27. Find the prime number 2, 3, 5, 7... 31, ...,41

    ① 33   ② 35   ③ 37   ④ 39

28. Find the composite number ,.............

    ① 1   ② 5   ③ 13   ④ 15

29. The total of prime number from 20 – 35 is ,.............

    ① 83   ② 110   ③ 116   ④ 81

30. The total of composite number from 21 – 32 is ,.............

    ① 236   ② 235   ③ 203   ④ 214

31. Which is the prime number after 31 and before 41?

    ① 33   ② 39   ③ 37   ④ 35

32. How many composite number are there between 20 – 35 including both numbers ?

    ① 10   ② 12   ③ 11   ④ 13

33. How many prime numbers are there between 50 – 100?

    ① 12   ② 10   ③ 11   ④ 9

34. Square of 9 is ,.............

    ① 82   ② 87   ③ 81   ④ 91

35. Square of 21 is ,.............
    ① 422   ② 442   ③ 441   ④ 421

36. .... is the square of 18.
    ① 289   ② 324   ③ 361   ④ 196

37. The sum total of square of 14 and square of 16 is ....
    ① 452   ② 752   ③ 652   ④ 352

38. Prime number is a number which is divisible by .... or number ....
    ① 1, itself   ② 2, 1   ③ 0, 1   ④ itself, 1

39. 1 – 100 are .... numbers.
    ① Prime   ② Composite   ③ Natural   ④ square

40. Square number means the product of numbers .... by itself.
    ① added   ② multiplied   ③ divided   ④ subtracted

41. .... prime numbers are there from 20 – 50.
    ① 5   ② 8   ③ 7   ④ 6

42. What would be the total or sum if you add composite numbers from 25 – 40?
    ① 389   ② 375   ③ 360   ④ 384

43. .... is the product of 13 and 7.
    ① 71   ② 91   ③ 81   ④ 101

44. 667 is the product of 23 and ....
    ① 29   ② 37   ③ 31   ④ 17

45. Square of 24 is ....
    ① 529   ② 484   ③ 576   ④ 441

46. There are .... prime numbers from 1 – 100.
    ① 27   ② 24   ③ 26   ④ 25

47. There are .... composite numbers from 1 – 100.
    ① 75   ② 76   ③ 74   ④ 73

48. Composite numbers has ....
    ① more than two factors   ② infinite factors
    ③ one factor   ④ two factors

49. Largest composite number less than 40 is ....
    ① 31   ② 37   ③ 33   ④ 39

50. The two numbers which have only '1' as the common factor are called ....
    ① prime numbers   ② composite numbers
    ③ primary numbers   ④ co-prime numbers

51. The product of two prime numbers is...................
    ① composite number   ② prime number
    ③ odd number   ④ even number

52. Check which of the following is a not a perfect square ....
    ① 81000   ② 8100   ③ 900   ④ 6250000

53. Which of the following perfect square numbers, is the square of an odd number? 289, 400, 900, 1600
    ① 289   ② 400   ③ 900   ④ 16005

54. Which of the following perfect square numbers, is the square of a even number? 361, 625, 4096, 65536
    ① 361   ② 625   ③ 4096   ④ 2601

55. How many natural numbers lie between squares of 12 and 13.
    ① 22   ② 23   ③ 24   ④ 25

56. Find the 4th triangular number before the triangular number 91.
    ① 45   ② 46   ③ 40   ④ 42

57. What is the base of triangular number 276.
    ① 276   ② 32   ③ 23   ④ 20

58. Find the triangular number whose base is 13.
    ① 78   ② 91   ③ 65   ④ 98

59. What it the base of triangular number 36.
    ① 2   ② 8   ③ 6   ④ 4

60. If base = 42, then the triangular number is ....
    ① 903   ② 882   ③ 861   ④ 908

61. The 28th triangular number is ....
    ① 406   ② 415.5   ③ 415   ④ 402

62. The 56th triangle number is ....
    ① 1595.5   ② 1594   ③ 3192   ④ 1596

63. The .... triangular number is 2211.
    ① 67   ② 66   ③ 68   ④ 56

64. The 15th triangular number is ....
   ① 110   ② 220   ③ 120   ④ 240

65. The 11th triangular number is ....
   ① 66   ② 60.5   ③ 65   ④ 64

66. The 41st triangular number is ....
   ① 860.5   ② 862   ③ 860   ④ 861

67. The .... triangular number is 91.
   ① 14   ② 13   ③ 12   ④ 13.5

68. The .... triangular number is 1035.
   ① 44   ② 46   ③ 45   ④ 44.5

Answers

1.	❸	2.	❶	3.	❹	4.	❷	5.	❶
6.	❹	7.	❸	8.	❷	9.	❸	10.	❷
11.	❷	12.	❷	13.	❶	14.	❶	15.	❶
16.	❸	17.	❶	18.	❹	19.	❸	20.	❹
21.	❷	22.	❹	23.	❸	24.	❹	25.	❶
26.	❶	27.	❸	28.	❹	29.	❶	30.	❷
31.	❸	32.	❹	33.	❷	34.	❸	35.	❸
36.	❷	37.	❶	38.	❹	39.	❸	40.	❷
41.	❸	42.	❷	43.	❷	44.	❶	45.	❸
46.	❹	47.	❶	48.	❸	49.	❹	50.	❹
51	❶	52.	❶	53.	❶	54.	❸	55.	❸
56.	❶	57.	❸	58.	❶	59.	❷	60.	❶
61.	❶	62.	❹	63.	❷	64.	❸	65.	❶
66.	❹	67.	❷	68.	❸				

❖ ❖ ❖

OPERATIONS ON NUMBERS

UNIT 2

2.1 ADDITION (UP TO SEVEN DIGIT NUMBERS) WITH CARRYING, WORD PROBLEMS

✌ INTRODUCTION :

For performing the operation of addition fast and accurate, follow the following points very carefully.

- Addition should be practised horizontally.
- Take proper care while adding vertically. Write units below units, tens below tens, hundreds below hundreds and so on.
- Sum of two digits must be done mentally.

Model Examples

Solve the following examples :

1. 100 + 0 =
    ① 1000 ② 100 ③ 10 ④ 101 **❷**

2. 999 + 1 =
    ① 10,000 ② 998 ③ 1,000 ④ 990 **❸**

3. 8573 + 1422 =
    ① 9995 ② 9997 ③ 9097 ④ 9999 **❶**

4. 9,999 + 0 =
    ① 9,999 ② 999 ③ 99 ④ 9 **❶**

5. 10,000 + 1 =
    ① 11,000 ② 10,001 ③ 1,001 ④ 101 **❷**

6. 2,450 + 2,400 =
    ① 4,850 ② 2,45,024 ③ 5,02,424 ④ 4,800 **❶**

7. 713 + 0 = 713 + ?

    ① 0   ② 11   ③ 713   ④ 1   ❶

8. 48724 + 12710 = ?

    ① 61434   ② 60434   ③ 61430   ④ 51434   ❶

    Explanation :

TTh	Th	H	T	U
1	1			
4	8	7	2	4
+ 1	2	7	1	0
6	1	4	3	4

    ∴ Alternative ❶ is the correct answer.

9. 153257 + 451769 = ?

    ① 504026   ② 604026   ③ 603926   ④ 605026   ❹

    Explanation :

L	TTh	Th	H	T	U
1		1	1	1	
1	5	3	2	5	7
+ 4	5	1	7	6	9
6	0	5	0	2	6

    ∴ Alternative ❹ is the correct answer.

10. 623569 + 696 + 46093 =

    ① 679358   ② 670358   ③ 670354   ④ 660358   ❷

Explanation :

L	TTh	Th	H	T	U
	1	1	2	1	
6	2	3	5	6	9
+			6	9	6
	4	6	0	9	3
6	7	0	3	5	8

∴ Alternative ❷ is the correct answer.

Examples for Practice

Solve the following examples :

1. 240 + 230 =
   ① 460   ② 470   ③ 490   ④ 450

2. 8711 + 0088 =
   ① 8787   ② 8789   ③ 8799   ④ 8790

3. 35 + 300 + 3330 =
   ① 3665   ② 3995   ③ 3985   ④ 3330

4. 51051 + 4141 =
   ① 54092   ② 59059   ③ 49059   ④ 55192

5. 4000 + 400 + 40 + 4 =
   ① 4400   ② 4444   ③ 40444   ④ 4044

6. 33 + 420 + 5050 =
   ① 5503   ② 4583   ③ 5834   ④ 345

7. 435 + 25 =
   ① 450   ② 460   ③ 470   ④ 445

8. 9909 + 90 =
   ① 1000   ② 99999   ③ 9999   ④ 9990

9. 25 + 24 =
   ① 39   ② 59   ③ 40   ④ 49

10. 300 + 5 =
    ① 35   ② 350   ③ 305   ④ 53

11. 120 + 78 =
    ① 200   ② 196   ③ 198   ④ 190

12. 1,334 + 6,214 =
    ① 7,448   ② 7,548   ③ 7,648   ④ 7,048

13. 29 + 170 + 100 =
    ① 299   ② 300   ③ 289   ④ 279

14. 3,000 + 200 + 40 + 2 =
    ① 2,443   ② 3,242   ③ 3,042   ④ 3,142

15. $71,142 + 6,701 + 2,003 =$
    ① 78,846   ② 77,846   ③ 79,846   ④ 76,846

16. $32,610 + 10,342 + 3,011 =$
    ① 45,963   ② 44,962   ③ 45,962   ④ 45,964

17. $4,501 + 1,472 =$
    ① 5,873   ② 5,773   ③ 5,973   ④ 5,903

18. $45,510 + 12,370 =$
    ① 57,870   ② 57,860   ③ 58,880   ④ 57,880

19. $5,431 + 407 + 2,010 =$
    ① 7,848   ② 7,748   ③ 7,858   ④ 7,868

20. $41,010 + 14,070 =$
    ① 54,080   ② 55,080   ③ 56,080   ④ 55,070

21. $25 + 250 + 200 =$
    ① 450   ② 475   ③ 400   ④ 425

22. $2,463 + 3,201 =$
    ① 5664   ② 5464   ③ 5466   ④ 5646

23. $9673 + 6985 =$
    ① 16558   ② 16658   ③ 15658   ④ 16668

24. $34653 + 48379 =$
    ① 83302   ② 82330   ③ 83203   ④ 83032

25. $1245 + 6742 =$
    ① 9877   ② 7987
    ③ 7897   ④ None of these.

26. $4236908 + 2324607 = ?$
    ① 6560515   ② 6551515   ③ 6561505   ④ 6561515

27. $58961223 + 30275781 = ?$
    ① 89237004   ② 89237904
    ③ 89137004   ④ 89236004

28. $2567321 + 3934517 = ?$
    ① 6510838   ② 6401838   ③ 6501838   ④ 6591838

29. $4326908 + 2496752 + 46902 = ?$
    ① 6807562   ② 6850562   ③ 6870552   ④ 6870562

30. 9100345 + 328361 + 23690 = ?
    ① 9452296 ② 9452396 ③ 9451396 ④ 9441396
31. 3640 + 51369 + 703698 = ?
    ① 758707 ② 757907 ③ 758907 ④ 757507
32. 49 + 839 + 6146380 = ?
    ① 6046268 ② 6147258 ③ 6147268 ④ 6147158
33. 44 + 8057 + 594684 = ?
    ① 602685 ② 592185 ③ 602775 ④ 602785
34. 2518638 + 1806725 = ?
    ① 4314363 ② 4325353 ③ 4325363 ④ 3325363
35. 5694368 + 6850394 = ?
    ① 12544762   ② 12544752
    ③ 12544652   ④ 12444762
36. 3464521 + 5314346 = ?
    ① 8777861 ② 8778867 ③ 8788867 ④ 8778857
37. 4324360 + 5653526 = ?
    ① 9977880 ② 1977886 ③ 19977886 ④ 9977886
38. 153206 + 12510 + 2013410 = ?
    ① 2078126 ② 2079126 ③ 2179126 ④ 2178126
39. 6943206 + 1034102 + 56201 = ?
    ① 8033509 ② 7933509 ③ 8023509 ④ 7023509
40. 432102 + 32601 + 1001 = ?
    ① 455704 ② 465704 ③ 465074 ④ 465740
41. 16643610 + 25396439 + 13004231 = ?
    ① 55944280   ② 54944280
    ③ 55044270   ④ 55044280

Answers

1.	❷	2.	❸	3.	❶	4.	④	5.	❷
6.	❶	7.	❷	8.	❸	9.	④	10.	❸
11.	❸	12.	❷	13.	❶	14.	❷	15.	❸

16.	❶	17.	❸	18.	❹	19.	❶	20.	❷
21.	❷	22.	❶	23.	❷	24.	❹	25.	❷
26.	❹	27.	❶	28.	❸	29.	❹	30.	❷
31.	❶	32.	❸	33.	❹	34.	❸	35.	❶
36.	❷	37.	❹	38.	❸	39.	❶	40.	❷
41.	❹								

WORD PROBLEMS ON ADDITION

✌ INTRODUCTION :

Under this topic word problems based on addition are to be asked. After reading the question carefully select the correct answer from the given options.

Model Examples

Solve the following examples.

1. There were three bags full of money. The first bag had ₹ 5806, the second bag had ₹ 2,109 and third bag had ₹ 389. What was the total sum of money in the bags ?
   ① 8304   ② 5815   ③ 7420   ④ 8204   ❶

2. A factory made 7579 pencil boxes in the morning. 2064 pencil boxes in the afternoon and 987 pencil boxes in evening. How many pencil boxes were made in a day ?
   ① 10600   ② 10830   ③ 10630   ④ 10720   ❸

3. In my school there are 192 teachers, 1872 boys and 1768 girls. How many people are all altogether ?
   ① 2064   ② 3832   ③ 3640   ④ 3720   ❷

4. During the polio eradication campaign, 517789 children were given the polio vaccine in one city and 3078747 children in another. Altogether, how many children got the vaccine ?
   ① 826526   ② 811536   ③ 826427   ④ 826536   ❹

Explanation :

L	TTh	Th	H	T	U
	1	1	1	1	
5	1	7	7	8	9
+ 3	0	8	7	4	7
8	2	6	5	3	6

∴ Alternative ❹ is the correct answer.

5. For the first day of a cricket match 43,567 tickets were sold while 24,979 tickets were sold for the second day. How many tickets were sold in all ?

① 68446   ② 68436   ③ 67446   ④ 68445   ❶

Explanation :

TTh	Th	H	T	U
	1	1	1	
4	3	5	6	7
+ 2	4	9	7	9
6	8	5	4	6

∴ Alternative ❶ is the correct answer.

Examples for Practice

1. For a cricket match at Sharjah on 2608 tickets were sold the first day. 4896 tickets the second day and 3102 tickets were sold on the third day. How many tickets were sold in all ?

① 10006   ② 16000   ③ 10600   ④ 10606

2. Our school library has 2384 Hindi books and 1598 English books. How many books are there in the library ?

① 3982   ② 3882   ③ 4082   ④ 4982

3. On Monday Arun drove 167 miles. On Tuesday he drove 68 miles and on Saturday he drove 73 miles. Approximately how many miles did he drive in three days ?
   ① 100 miles ② 200 miles ③ 308 miles ④ 400 miles

4. What is the sum of three thousand + two thousand + twenty four
   ① 5524 ② 5024 ③ 5240 ④ 5004

5. Add the greatest four digit number to the smallest three digit number.
   ① 10990 ② 10099 ③ 1990 ④ 19900

6. There were 3625 girls and 2785 boys who appeared for 4th scholarship from one district. So how many children were there altogether ?
   ① 6410 ② 6140 ③ 6440 ④ 6014

7. Add the place values of the same digits in number 375879.
   ① 7007 ② 70070 ③ 70007 ④ 77000

8. Add the smallest three digit number to the smallest four digit number.
   ① 1010 ② 1110 ③ 1100 ④ 1001

9. Write the successor of the number 54328.
   ① 54329 ② 54327 ③ 54322 ④ 54326

10. There were 3621 girls and 2783 boys in a school. How many students were there altogether ?
    ① 6044 ② 6440 ③ 6004 ④ 6404

11. What will be the sum of the smallest and largest eight digit number ?
    ① 109999990 ② 10099999
    ③ 10999999 ④ 109999999

12. Rambhau bought a truck for ₹ 10,87,949 and a tractor for ₹ 9,07,960. How much money did he spend altogether ?
    ① ₹ 1995808 ② ₹ 1995909
    ③ ₹ 1984909 ④ ₹ 1985909

13. In the state election last year, 15879396 men and 17798539 women cast their votes. How many votes were polled altogether ?
   ① 3,36,77,935   ② 3,26,77,935
   ③ 33,577,935   ④ 3,36,77,835

14. If the NGO donated books worth of ₹ 57,89,698 and tracing aids worth ₹ 23,25,796 to government schools, what is the total amount spent altogether on both ?
   ① ₹ 71,15,494   ② ₹ 81,15,484
   ③ ₹ 81,15,494   ④ ₹ 80,15,494

15. A company made a profit of ₹ 18,56,900 in 2010, ₹ 26,78,500 in 2011 and ₹ 32,95,569 in 2012. How much did the company earn as profit in these three years ?
   ① ₹ 78,31,969   ② ₹ 76,30,969
   ③ ₹ 68,30,969   ④ ₹ 78,30,969

16. The annual fees collection of a city school was ₹ 87,65,985 in 2014 and ₹ 1,98,89,568 in 2015. What was the total amount collected in these two years ?
   ① ₹ 3,76,11,553   ② ₹ 2,86,55,553
   ③ ₹ 2,76,55,553   ④ ₹ 2,86,55,543

17. Raja booked a two BHK flat for ₹ 55,69,596 and bought a SUV for ₹ 19,79,599. What is the total amount spent by Raja ?
   ① ₹ 75,49,195   ② ₹ 74,49,195
   ③ ₹ 75,49,185   ④ ₹ 75,48,115

18. Hamidbhai bought 4 acres of land for ₹ 4,59,63,700 in 2012 and 5 acres of land for ₹ 4,98,73,969 in 2013. How much did he spend in all ?
   ① ₹ 9,58,37,769   ② ₹ 9,48,37,669
   ③ ₹ 9,58,36,669   ④ ₹ 9,58,37,669

19. Maganlal won the lottery of ₹ 69,59,000 in 2009 and he got a gift of ₹ 79,58,798 from his uncle. How many rupees he has in all with him ?
   ① ₹ 1,48,17,798   ② ₹ 1,49,17,798
   ③ ₹ 1,39,17,798   ④ ₹ 1,49,07,718

20. Children's movie Jungle book earned ₹ 59,85,950 in the first week and ₹ 89,96,789 in the second week. How much did it earn in all ?

① ₹ 1,49,72,739   ② ₹ 1,49,82,639

③ ₹ 1,49,82,739   ④ ₹ 139,82,739

1.	❹	2.	❶	3.	❸	4.	❷	5.	❷
6.	❶	7.	❷	8.	❸	9.	❶	10.	❹
11.	❹	12.	❷	13.	❶	14.	❸	15.	❹
16.	❷	17.	❶	18.	❹	19.	❷	20.	❸

❖ ❖ ❖

2.2 SUBTRACTION (UPTO 7 DIGIT NUMBERS) BY BORROWING, WORD PROBLEMS

✌ INTRODUCTION :

Subtraction should be practiced horizontally.

Take care while copying the number for subtraction.

Model Examples

Solve the following examples.

1. 90,000 – 20,000

   ① 30,000 ② 11,000   ③ 7,000   ④ 70,000   ❹

2. 384 – ☐ = 290

   ① 94   ② 84   ③ 104   ④ 74   ❶

3. ☐ – 78 = 124

   ① 102   ② 202   ③ 32   ④ 42   ❷

4. 5999 – 4888

   ① 1111   ② 1010   ③ 2222   ④ 2020   ❶

5. $80,000 - 80,000 =$

① 772 ② 872 ③ 88 ④ 0 ❹

6. $3,750 - 750 =$

① 3,775 ② 4,750 ③ 3000 ④ 300 ❸

7. $88 - \square = 70$

① 168 ② 160 ③ 28 ④ 18 ❹

8. $672 - \square = 600$

① 72 ② 1,272 ③ 6,72,600 ④ 720 ❶

9. $4,800 - \square = 800$

① 5,600 ② 4,000 ③ 8,400 ④ 800 ❷

10. $10,000 - 1,000 =$

① 900 ② 9,000 ③ 90,000 ④ 9,00,000 ❷

11. $64293 - 26536 = ?$

① 32757 ② 47757 ③ 47767 ④ 37757 ❹

Explanation :

TTh	Th	H	T	U
5	13	1	8	1
6	4	2	9	3
− 2	6	5	3	6
3	7	7	5	7

∴ Alternative ❹ is the correct answer.

12. $7560321 - 5460310 = ?$

① 2100111 ② 2100011 ③ 13020631 ④ 2100001 ❷

Explanation :

TL	L	TTh	Th	H	T	U
		5	3	1	8	1
7	5	6	0	3	2	1
− 5	4	6	0	3	1	0
2	1	0	0	0	1	1

∴ Alternative ❷ is the correct answer.

13. 2879879 – 2143567 = ?

    ① 736322   ② 736311   ③ 736312   ④ 733612   ❸

Explanation :

TL	L	TTh	Th	H	T	U
2	8	7	9	8	7	9
– 2	1	4	3	5	6	7
0	7	3	6	3	1	2

∴ Alternative ❸ is the correct answer.

14. 345678 – 162054 = ?

    ① 183624   ② 183024   ③ 123624   ④ 283624   ❶

Explanation :

L	TTh	Th	H	T	U
2	1				
3	4	5	6	7	8
– 1	6	2	0	5	4
1	8	3	6	2	4

∴ Alternative ❶ is the correct answer.

15. 623300 – 526304 = ?

    ① 93946   ② 96996   ③ 96904   ④ 1,03,004   ❷

Explanation :

L	TTh	Th	H	T	U
5	1	2	2	9	1
6	2	3	3	0	0
– 5	2	6	3	0	4
0	9	6	9	9	6

∴ Alternative ❷ is the correct answer.

Examples for Practice

Solve the following examples.

1. 9874 – 8763 =

    ① 1000   ② 900   ③ 1111   ④ 1010

2. $7322 - 5022 =$
    ① 2200   ② 2000   ③ 1820   ④ 2300

3. $999 - 898 =$
    ① 101   ② 100   ③ 110   ④ 1000

4. $4225 - \boxed{} = 225$
    ① 3225   ② 4000   ③ 4225   ④ 225

5. $425 - 0 =$
    ① 0   ② 1   ③ 425   ④ 420

6. $1009 - 9 =$
    ① 1001   ② 1010   ③ 1018   ④ 1000

7. $7054 - 3050 =$
    ① 4004   ② 4000   ③ 4050   ④ 4006

8. $7425 - \boxed{} = 7425$
    ① 1   ② 7425   ③ 0   ④ 1000

9. $2{,}345 - \boxed{} = 234$
    ① 2,111   ② 1,111   ③ 111   ④ 11

10. $80 + 0 - \boxed{} = 80$
    ① 80   ② 160   ③ 0   ④ 20

11. $458 - 235 =$
    ① 22   ② 223   ③ 323   ④ 123

12. $2{,}796 - 1{,}542 =$
    ① 1,254   ② 1,354   ③ 1,454   ④ 1,554

13. $176 - 0 =$
    ① 176   ② 0   ③ 1,760   ④ 76

14. $1{,}942 - \boxed{} = 1{,}942$
    ① 0   ② 1   ③ 10   ④ 3,884

15. $2{,}000 - \boxed{} = 0$
    ① 0   ② 1   ③ 2,000   ④ 2

16. $8{,}094 - 3{,}062 =$
    ① 5,302   ② 5,203   ③ 5,002   ④ 5,032

17. $9,364 - 2,004 =$

① 7,359   ② 7,360   ③ 7,340   ④ 7,350

18. $9,999 - 6,090 =$

① 3,909   ② 3,809   ③ 3,999   ④ 3,989

19. $39100345 - 2492836 = ?$

① 37507509 ② 37607509 ③ 36607179 ④ 36607509

20. $4345827 - 1265938 = ?$

① 3179889   ② 3120111   ③ 3079889   ④ 3079111

21. $1419518 - 1006424 = ?$

① 413094   ② 413114   ③ 403094   ④ 403114

22. $6935602 - 2458823 = ?$

① 4323221   ② 4476779   ③ 4477779   ④ 4467779

23. $47058 - 23649 = ?$

① 23509   ② 24409   ③ 23409   ④ 24419

24. $345778 - 182659 = ?$

① 163129   ② 263119   ③ 163129   ④ 163119

25. $8012645 - 2865548 = ?$

① 5147097   ② 6147097   ③ 5247097   ④ 6247097

26. $4902214 - 4756759 = ?$

① 255455   ② 145455   ③ 145465   ④ 245455

27. $34106763 - 12100078 = ?$

① 22006685 ② 22006785 ③ 22006585 ④ 22007685

28. $2512000 - 1618236 = ?$

① 893664   ② 1104236   ③ 893764   ④ 11093764

29. What must be added to 36978949 to get a sum that is the greatest number of eight digits ?

① 63011500 ② 63021500 ③ 63011050 ④ 63021050

30. What must be subtracted from 3434700 to get a balance that is the smallest seven digit number ?

① 2434007   ② 2434700   ③ 2434070   ④ 2443700

Answers

1.	❸	2.	❹	3.	❶	4.	❷	5.	❸
6.	❹	7.	❶	8.	❸	9.	❶	10.	❸
11.	❷	12.	❶	13.	❶	14.	❶	15.	❸
16.	❹	17.	❷	18.	❶	19.	❹	20.	❸
21.	❶	22.	❷	23.	❸	24.	❹	25.	❶
26.	❷	27.	❶	28.	❸	29.	❹	30.	❷

WORD PROBLEMS ON SUBTRACTION

✌ INTRODUCTION :

Under this topic word problems based on subtraction are asked. After reading the question carefully select the correct answer from the given options.

Model Examples

Solve the following examples.

1. Veena had 2604 stamps of different countries. She gave 1819 to her friend. How many stamps has she now ?
   ① 685   ② 785   ③ 885   ④ 180   ❷

2. At a school function, invitation cards were sent to 2950 people only 1997 people came. How many invitation cards were not used ?
   ① 953   ② 1053   ③ 853   ④ 583   ❶

3. Each day 8050 bangles are made in a factory, out of these 1976 were found broken. How many bangles were in good condition ?
   ① 7074   ② 5074   ③ 6047   ④ 6074   ❹

4. Last year 158726 students appeared for class 10 examination. This year the number was 279615. How many more students appeared for the exam this year ?

① 120799 ② 120789 ③ 120889 ④ 121889 ❸

Explanation :

L	TTh	Th	H	T	U
		8	5	10	15
2	7	9	6	1	5
− 1	5	8	7	2	6
1	2	0	8	8	9

∴ Alternative ❸ is the correct answer.

5. In a city in Nagpur the number of men is 1847959 and the number of women is 1753989. By how many does the number of men exceed the number of women ?

① 94070 ② 93970 ③ 93980 ④ 94970 ❷

● Examples for Practice ●

1. The hospital needed 7284 bottles of medicine. The company which made medicines sent only 5798 bottles. How many more bottles does the hospital need ?

① 2486 ② 3486 ③ 1486 ④ 486

2. The circus ground can hold only 5298 people. 6900 people went into the ground. How many people were extra ?

① 1602 ② 2602 ③ 602 ④ 2061

3. At a painting competition on children's day 9765 children took part. Out of them 4897 were boys. How many were girls ?

① 4897 ② 4868 ③ 4768 ④ 4878

4. What is the difference between the numbers 28732 and 23854 ?

① 4070 ② 4870 ③ 4078 ④ 4878

5. Subtract greatest two digit number from greatest four digit number.

① 9990   ② 9999   ③ 9099   ④ 9900

6. A boy had 49673 stamps. He gave away 24724. How many stamps has he left ?

① 24949   ② 25949   ③ 34949   ④ 2994

7. There were 5000 sheets of paper. If Anil used 2150 and Ashish used 300. How many sheets were left ?

① 2550   ② 2500   ③ 2505   ④ 2005

8. Write the predecessor of the number 7325.

① 7322   ② 7324   ③ 7326   ④ 7334

9. Subtract the place value of the digit 8 from the place value of digit 6 in number 7638 and which is the even number in this difference.

① 4   ② 5   ③ 6   ④ 2

10. There were 2489 boys in a camp, 1596 went into running competition. How many were left in a camp ?

① 893   ② 839   ③ 899   ④ 833

11. Subtract the greatest six digit number from the greatest eight digit number ?

① 99000000   ② 9900000

③ 90900000   ④ 90090000

12. Write the predecessor of the number 1896949 ?

① 1896984   ② 1899648   ③ 1896948   ④ 1896950

13. In the year 2014, the population of street children in India was 45,69,897 while that in Pakistan was 36,89,898. What was the difference in the population of street children in the two countries ?

① 870999   ② 879099   ③ 897999   ④ 879999

14. In the legislative election of Maharashtra in 2013 shankarbhau got 6959869 votes and Hamidbhai at 87,689,978 votes. By how many votes did Hamidbhai win ?
    ① 1809119 ② 80730109 ③ 1819109 ④ 2809109

15. In 1991, the population in Sitapur was 3156946. In 2001, it was 4369859. By how much did the population grow ?
    ① 1212913 ② 1213913 ③ 1212113 ④ 1211913

16. A company produced 699598 cars in 2011 and 8689699 in the next. How many more cars did they produce in the next year ?
    ① 7990011 ② 8090101 ③ 79901011 ④ 7980101

17. The Forest Department of a particular state planted 49,369 trees of beheda, 65948 trees of banyan besides trees of several other kind ? If the department planted 1,25,986 trees altogether, how trees were neither behead nor banyan ?
    ① 10679 ② 10669 ③ 100669 ④ 106069

18. Rama builders spent on building a housing project was ₹ 8,69,96,850 of this amount ₹ 96,49,798 was spent on buying the land and ₹ 2,52,58,900 on the construction material and the rest on labour charges. What was the amount spent on labour charges ?
    ① ₹ 5,20,88,152   ② ₹ 5,20,98,152
    ③ ₹ 5,02,88,152   ④ ₹ 5,20,88,252

19. Pune city has a population of 1,89,74,986. If this includes 89,98,875 men and 86,89,969 women. What is the number of children in the city ?
    ① 12,85,142   ② 12,96,142
    ③ 13,86,142   ④ 12,86,142

20. Rajendra wants to buy a LED TV of 54 inches worth ₹ 6,98,545. He has ₹ 5,99,698. What is the amount he needs to be able to buy the TV ?
    ① ₹ 98,847 ② ₹ 1,08,847 ③ ₹ 99,847 ④ ₹ 96,847

Answers

1.	❸	2.	❶	3.	❷	4.	❹	5.	❹
6.	❶	7.	❶	8.	❷	9.	❹	10.	❶
11.	❶	12.	❸	13.	❹	14.	❷	15.	❶
16.	❸	17.	❷	18.	❶	19.	❹	20.	❶

2.3   MULTIPLICATION (5 DIGITS × 3 DIGITS)

✌ INTRODUCTION :

Multiplication is fundamental operation of numbers.

Product = Multiplicand × Multiplier. Zero multiplied by any number is always zero.

e.g. : 10 × 5 means 10 is added 5 times. i.e. 10 + 10 + 10 + 10 + 10 = 10 × 5 = 50

When the same number is added a given number of times then the operation is known as multiplication.

In the above example, 10 is known as the multiplicand, 5 is known as the multiplier and 50 is the product.

If a number is to be multiplied by 10 or 100 or 1000 then write that number (multiplicand) down and just add the number of zeros as there are in the multiplier to get the product.

e.g. : 59 x 100

= 5900

Here we need to learn about lattice method. What is lattice method ? It is a method where a number is written in expanded form and then multiplied to get the answer.

For example -

416 × 8 keeping in mind that 416 = 400 + 10 + 6

	400	10	6
×			
8	3200	80	48

$416 \times 8 = 3328$

3200
80
+ 48
3328

The other method is arranging the number vertically and then multiplying it.

Th	H	T	U
	1	4	
	4	1	6
	×		8
3	③3	①2	④8

For example :

1. $743 \times 5 =$ ☐

① 7615   ② 3715   ③ 3705   ④ 3725   ❷

2. $38 \times 26 =$ ☐

Lattice Method

X	30	8
20	600	160
4	120	32

```
  600
  160
+ 120
   32
  ———
  912
```

Vertical Method

H	T	U
1	3	
	3	8
	×2	4
1	5	2
+7	6	0
9	1	2

3. $37 \times 27 =$ ☐

① 890   ② 889   ③ 999   ④ 989   ❸

Model Examples

Solve the following examples.

1. $72 \times 10 =$

① 720   ② 72   ③ 7200   ④ 72000   ❶

Explanation : While multiplying 72 by 10 put one zero on 72.

∴ Alternative ❶ is the correct answer.

2. $85 \times 4 \times 0 =$
   ① 340   ② 3400   ③ 0   ④ 34000   ❸

3. 8 times 6 =
   ① 40   ② 60   ③ 80   ④ 48   ❹

4. $567 \times 10 =$
   ① 5,670 ② 56,700   ③ 567   ④ 5,67,500 ❶

Explanation : While multiplying 567 by 10, put one zero on 567. The product comes to be 5670.

∴ Alternative ❶ is the correct answer.

5. $13 \times 12 \times 0$
   ① 156   ② 13,120   ③ 0   ④ 1,312   ❸

Explanation : When any number is multiplied by zero, then the product is always zero.

∴ Alternative ❸ is the correct answer.

6. Which number should replace ☐ so that $7 \times ☐ + 5 = 5$?
   ① 1   ② 0   ③ 0.1   ④ 10   ❷

Explanation : Which number should replace ☐ so that $7 \times$ ☐ $+ 5 = 5$. Explanation is $7 \times 0 = 0$. Any number multiplied by 0 the product is 0 and $0 + 5 = 5$. ∴ $7 \times \boxed{0}$ $+ 5 = 5$. $0 + 5 = 5$. So answer is option 2.

∴ Alternative ❷ is the correct answer.

7. $4216 \times 936 =$
   ① 3945176   ② 3846176
   ③ 3946076   ④ 3946176   ❹

Explanation :

$$
\begin{array}{r}
4216 \\
\times\ 936 \\
\hline
25296 \\
+\ 12648X \\
\hline
37944XX \\
\hline
3946176 \\
\end{array}
$$

∴ Alternative ❹ is the correct answer.

8. $23,609 \times 94 =$

    ① 2128246   ② 2219246

    ③ 2218246   ④ 2129246   ❷

    Explanation :

    ```
          23609
        ×    94
    +   94436
      212481X
      2219246
    ```

    ∴ Alternative ❷ is the correct answer.

9. $53468 \times 609 =$

    ① 32045212   ② 32462012

    ③ 32562012   ④ 32561012   ❸

    Explanation :

    ```
         53468
       ×   609
       481212
    +  00000X
     320808XX
     32562012
    ```

    ∴ Alternative ❸ is the correct answer.

10. $879 \times 328 = ?$

    ① 288312   ② 278312

    ③ 278212   ④ 288212   ❶

    Explanation :

    ```
         879
       × 328
        7032
    +  1758X
     2637XX
     288312
    ```

    ∴ Alternative ❶ is the correct answer.

11. There are 1959 students in a school. If the cost of one students uniform is ₹ 378, what will be the cost of the uniform for all the students in school ?

    ① ₹ 740402   ② ₹ 730502

    ③ ₹ 749502   ④ ₹ 740502   ❹

Explanation :

$$
\begin{array}{r}
1959 \\
\times \quad 378 \\
\hline
15672 \\
+13713\text{X} \\
5877\text{X}\text{X} \\
\hline
740502
\end{array}
$$

∴ Alternative ❹ is the correct answer.

━━━━━━━━━ **Examples for Practice** ━━━━━━━━━

Solve the following examples.

1. $100 \times 0 =$

    ① 100   ② 101   ③ 10   ④ 0

2. $24 \times 3 =$

    ① 72   ② 75   ③ 82   ④ 80

3. $76 \times 6 =$

    ① 452   ② 456   ③ 5521   ④ 556

4. $88 \times 100 =$

    ① 880   ② 88000   ③ 8800   ④ 88

5. $55 \times 20 =$

    ① 1100   ② 1000   ③ 110   ④ 11000

6. $965 \times \boxed{} = 9650$

    ① 10   ② 100   ③ 1000   ④ 1

7. $85 \times 17 =$

    ① 1440   ② 1400   ③ 1445   ④ 445

8. $75 \times 25 =$

    ① 1775   ② 1875   ③ 2075   ④ 1825

9. $415 \times 28 =$

    ① 12620   ② 11600   ③ 11580   ④ 11620

10. $144 \times 15 =$

    ① 2160   ② 2150   ③ 2175   ④ 2165

11. $39 \times 30 =$

    ① 1,170   ② 117   ③ 1,107   ④ 997

12. $2 \times 9 \times 0 =$

   ① 0   ② 253   ③ 263   ④ 273

13. Which of the following multiplication is 896 ?

   ① 46×26 ② 56×16 ③ 66×6 ④ 26×26

14. The product of two numbers is 144. If the two numbers are doubled, what will be their product ?

   ① 12×12 ② 24×12 ③ 288   ④ 576

15. What is the product of 980×100 is ?

   ① 9800   ② 0   ③ 98000   ④ 980

16. $35 \; \square \; \times 16 = 5,728$, find the number which replaces the box.

   ① 2   ② 4   ③ 6   ④ 8

17. $25 \times 18 =$

   ① 460   ② 440   ③ 450   ④ 470

18. $400 \times 20 =$

   ① 800   ② 8,000   ③ 80   ④ 80,000

19. $630 \times 17 =$

   ① 10,710   ② 10,810   ③ 10,700   ④ 10,711

20. $380 \times 14 =$

   ① 5,326   ② 5,322   ③ 5,220   ④ 5,320

21. $270 \times 13 =$

   ① 3,620   ② 3,520   ③ 3,510   ④ 3,410

22. What is the product of 100×25 ?

   ① 2050   ② 250   ③ 2500   ④ 25000

23. $87 \times 92 = \square$

   ① 8000   ② 8004   ③ 8024   ④ 8804

24. $37 \times 24 = \square$

   ① 808   ② 880   ③ 888   ④ 8888

25. $70 \times 35 = \square$

   ① 2400   ② 2540   ③ 2500   ④ 2450

26. $129 \times 8 = \square$

   ① 1302   ② 1032   ③ 1230   ④ 1320

27. $28 \times 32 =$ ☐

   ① 996   ② 894   ③ 896   ④ 898

28. $224 \times 4 =$ ☐

   ① 896   ② 986   ③ 968   ④ 869

29. $225 \times 53 =$

   ① 11925   ② 11955   ③ 11825   ④ 11295

30. 334×64

   ① 11376   ② 21376   ③ 23176   ④ 2371

31. 596×53

   ① 35188   ② 35818   ③ 31588   ④ 35180

32. 447×59

   ① 23673   ② 23763   ③ 23373   ④ 26373

33. 750×38

   ① 28500   ② 25800   ③ 25080   ④ 28050

34. $496 \times 18 =$

   ① 8938   ② 8928   ③ 8828   ④ 8948

35. $299 \times 24 =$

   ① 7166   ② 7276   ③ 7176   ④ 7076

36. ……….. is the product of 180×19.

   ① 3420   ② 3220   ③ 3320   ④ 3440

37. $798 \times 29 =$ ……..

   ① 23442   ② 23042   ③ 22142   ④ 23142

38. 29970 is the product of ?

   ① 990×30 ② 999×30 ③ 999×20 ④ 989×30

39. What is 38 H and 18 T ?

   ① 3890   ② 3780   ③ 3980   ④ 3880

40. $675 \times 94 =$

   ① 63450   ② 63400   ③ 63050   ④ 63000

41. $808 \times 96 =$

   ① 76668   ② 77508   ③ 76568   ④ 77568

42. $206 \times 49 =$
    ① 9894   ② 10494   ③ 10094   ④ 9094

43. $695 \times 37 =$
    ① 24615   ② 25715   ③ 25705   ④ 24715

44. A novel costs ₹ 196 if 45 students bought this novel, what was the total amount collected?
    ① ₹ 8820   ② ₹ 8780   ③ ₹ 7720   ④ ₹7820

45. A truck carries 440 crates of apples. If each crate contains 48 apples how many apples are there in the truck?
    ① 20020   ② 21020   ③ 21120   ④ 20120

46. If one chair costs ₹ 685. What will be the cost of 18 such chairs?
    ① ₹ 12,300   ② ₹ 12,330   ③ ₹ 13,330   ④ ₹ 12,030

47. If the cost of one pair of pants is ₹790. What is the cost of 39 pair of pants?
    ① ₹ 30,800   ② ₹ 29,810   ③ ₹ 30,810   ④ ₹ 20,810

48. If a sack of wheat costs Rs 999 what will be the cost of 50 sacks?
    ① ₹ 49,950   ② ₹ 45,950   ③ ₹ 45,550   ④ ₹ 49,550

49. While planting wheat 48 rows have been planted with 389 seedlings in each row. How many seedlings have been planted in all?
    ① 18762   ② 18662   ③ 18562   ④ 18672

50. Find out the cost of 68 shirts if one shirt costs ₹ 996.
    ① ₹ 56,628   ② ₹ 67,628   ③ ₹ 67,728   ④ ₹ 66,628

51. If one sack of jowar weighs 54 kg how much would 890 sacks weigh?
    ① 48060 kg   ② 47060 kg
    ③ 47560 kg   ④ 48600 kg

52. If 720 tiles are required for one hall. How many tiles would be required for 65 such halls?
    ① 4680   ② 46800   ③ 46080   ④ 46008

53. What is the product of 980 × 43?
    ① 42100   ② 42040   ③ 41140   ④ 42140

54. A school encouraged its 1,489 students to avoid plastic bag and taught them to make paper bags. If each student made 65 paper bags. What was the total number of paper bags made ?
    ① 96885   ② 96685   ③ 96785   ④ 95785

55. Find the product of the biggest three digit number and the biggest four digit number ?
    ① 9989001   ② 99890001
    ③ 9999001   ④ 9899001

56. If Raja spent ₹ 9569 on his expedition to Sahyadris. What will be the total cost of 38 persons ?
    ① ₹ 3625522   ② ₹ 363522
    ③ ₹ 362622   ④ ₹ 363622

57. One hour has 60 minutes. How many minutes would 4785 hours have ?
    ① 1722500   ② 1722600
    ③ 1622600   ④ 1622500

58. Activa, Honda scooter costs ₹ 59480. What would be the cost of 125 such scooters ?
    ① ₹ 74,45,000   ② ₹ 73,35,000
    ③ ₹ 74,35,000   ④ ₹ 75,35,000

59. One I phone costs ₹ 65,000. What be the cost 149 such phones ?
    ① ₹ 96,85,000   ② ₹ 97,85,000
    ③ ₹ 9,60,85,000   ④ ₹ 96,80,500

60. If building one toilet block cost ₹ 69586. What would be the cost of building 65 such toilet blocks ?
    ① 4532090   ② 4522090
    ③ 4423900   ④ 4523090

═══════════ Answers ═══════════

1.	❹	2.	❶	3.	❷	4.	❸	5.	❶
6.	❶	7.	❸	8.	❷	9.	❹	10.	❶
11.	❶	12.	❶	13.	❷	14.	❹	15.	❸
16.	❹	17.	❸	18.	❷	19.	❶	20.	❹
21.	❸	22.	❸	23.	❷	24.	❸	25.	❹
26.	❷	27.	❸	28.	❶	29.	❷	30.	❷
31.	❸	32.	❹	33.	❶	34.	❷	35.	❸
36.	❶	37.	❹	38.	❷	39.	❸	40.	❶
41.	❹	42.	❸	43.	❷	44.	❶	45.	❸
46.	❷	47.	❸	48.	❶	49.	❹	50.	❸
51.	❶	52.	❷	53.	❹	54.	❸	55.	❶
56.	❹	57.	❷	58.	❸	59.	❶	60.	❹

❖ ❖ ❖

2.4   DIVISION (5 DIGITS ÷ 2 DIGITS), TABLES 2 – 30

✤ INTRODUCTION :

Multiplication and Division are the opposite operations. Dividing means making groups.

For example :

$$
\begin{array}{r}
30 \\
15\overline{)460} \\
-450 \\
\hline
\boxed{10}
\end{array}
$$

(II) ... ← ... → ... (III)
→ ... (I)
→ ... (IV)

Dividend = Divisor × Quotient + Remainder

(I) Dividend : The number which is to be divided is dividend.

(II) Divisor : The number by which dividend is divided is called divisor.

(III)   ***Quotient*** : The number which comes after division of a number by divisor is called quotient.

(IV)   ***Remainder*** : The number which remains after subtracting the dividend is called remainder.

For example :

$$2 \overline{\smash{\big)}\ \begin{aligned}7 \\ 15 \\ -14 \\ \hline 01 \end{aligned}}$$

Here, 15 is called Dividend, 2 is called Divisor, 7 is called Quotient, 1 is called Remainder.

Factor : It is a number by which the dividend is completely divided i.e. the remainder is zero.

Model Examples

Solve the following examples.

1. $658 \div 3 = \square$ Quotient $\square$ Remainder.

    ① 219, 1   ② 218, 2   ③ 209, 0   ④ 200, 1   ❶

2. $459 \div 13 = \square$ Quotient $\square$ Remainder.

    ① 4, 35   ② 13, 85   ③ 35, 4   ④ 13, 4   ❸

3. $9090 \div 45 =$

    ① 22   ② 202   ③ 20   ④ 220   ❷

4.   What is $4 \overline{\smash{\big)}\ 404}$

    ① 11   ② 100 + 4   ③ 101   ④ 100   ❸

5. $88 \div 10 = \square$ Quotient $\square$ Remainder

    ① 8, 8   ② 8, 0   ③ 88, 10   ④ 8, 10   ❶

    Explanation : When 88 is divided by 10, quotient is 8 and remainder is 8. So the answer is option ❶

    ∴ Alternative ❶ is the correct answer.

6. $97 \div 11 = \square$ Quotient $\square$ Remainder

    ① 9, 8   ② 8, 9   ③ 8, 8   ④ 97, 11   ❷

Explanation : When 97 is divided by 11, quotient is 8 and remainder is 9. So the answer is option ❷

∴ Alternative ❷ is the correct answer.

7. 825 ÷ 15 = ☐ Quotient ☐ Remainder

    ① 54, 10   ② 0, 55   ③ 55, 0   ④ 53, 12   ❸

    Explanation : When 825 is divided by 15, the quotient is 55 and remainder is 0. So the answer is option ❸

    ∴ Alternative ❸ is the correct answer.

8. 349 ÷ 13 = ☐ Quotient ☐ Remainder

    ① 26, 5   ② 11, 26   ③ 26, 11   ④ 11, 11   ❸

    Explanation : When 349 is divided by 13, the quotient is 26 and remainder is 11. So the answer is option ❸

    ∴ Alternative ❸ is the correct answer.

9. 37,110 ÷ 10 = ☐ Quotient ☐ Remainder

    ① 371; 1   ② 3,711; 0   ③ 3,711; 10   ④ 3,711; 100 ❷

    Explanation : When 37,110 is divided by 10, the quotient is 3711 and remainder is zero. So the answer is option ❷

    ∴ Alternative ❷ is the correct answer.

10. 906 ÷ 17 = ☐ Quotient ☐ Remainder

    ① 53, 29   ② 53, 15   ③ 53, 5   ④ 53, 10   ❸

    Explanation : When 906 is divided by 17, the quotient is 53 and remainder is 5. So the answer is option ❸

    ∴ Alternative ❸ is the correct answer.

11. 1,001 ÷ 20 = ☐ Quotient ☐ Remainder

    ① 50, 1   ② 100, 20   ③ 51, 1   ④ 75, 10   ❶

    Explanation : When 1001 is divided by 20, the quotient is 50 and remainder is 1. So the answer is option ❶

    ∴ Alternative ❶ is the correct answer.

12. 9,000 ÷ 30 = ☐ Quotient ☐ Remainder

    ① 30, 0   ② 3, 0   ③ 300, 0   ④ 900, 0   ❸

    Explanation : When 9000 is divided by 30, quotient is 300 and remainder is 0.   So the answer is option ❸

    ∴ Alternative❸ is the correct answer.

13. $25,320 \div 16 = \square$ Quotient $\square$ Remainder

    ① 1,582; 5   ② 1,582; 1
    ③ 1,582; 8   ④ None of these   ❸

    Explanation : When 25,320 is divided by 16, the quotient is 1582 and the remainder is 8. So the answer is option ❸

    ∴ Alternative❸ is the correct answer.

14. $1,284 \div 32 = \square$ Quotient $\square$ Remainder

    ① 40, 12   ② 40, 4   ③ 40, 8   ④ 40, 16   ❷

    Explanation : When 1284 is divided by 32, the quotient is 40 and remainder is 4. So the answer is option ❷

    ∴ Alternative ❷ is the correct answer.

15. What are the factors of 30 ?

    ①1, 2, 3, 5, 6, 15, 30   ② 30, 6, 3, 1
    ③3, 15, 5, 1, 6   ④ 6, 2, 30, 1, 3, 5   ❶

    Explanation : 1, 2, 3, 5, 6, 15, 30 are factors of 30. So the answer is option ❶

    ∴ Alternative ❶ is the correct answer.

16. Highest factor of 26 is $\square$

    ① 1   ② 2   ③ 13   ④ 26   ❹

    Explanation : Highest factor of 26 is 26 itself.

    ∴ Alternative ❹ is the correct answer.

17. Find the highest factor of 81.

    ① 1   ② 9   ③ 27   ④ 81   ❹

    Explanation : Highest factor of 81 is 81 itself.

    ∴ Alternative ❹ is the correct answer.

18. Which of the following is the factor of 144 ?

    ① 20   ② 12   ③ 28   ④ 44   ❷

    Explanation : Among the given options 12 is the factor of 144.

    ∴ Alternative ❷ is the correct answer.

19. Find the number whose smallest divisor is 5.

    ① 55   ② 45   ③ 75   ④ 70   ❶

Explanation : Among the given numbers 55 is the only number, to which 5 is the smallest divisor.

∴ Alternative ❶ is the correct answer.

20. What is serially the fourth divisor of 64 ?
    ① 16   ② 4   ③ 12   ④ 8   ❹

21. The number 79 ✪   2 is completely divisible by 9. Which of the following digit should be at ✪   ?
    ① 0   ② 3   ③ 1   ④ 6   ❶

22. If a number is divided by 9, the remainder is 7. But if it is divided by 7, the remainder is 5. What is the number ?
    ① 61   ② 63   ③ 68   ④ 70   ❶

23. There are 125 students in the second standard. If ₹ 200 were collected as the examination fees from them, how much did each student pay ?
    ① ₹ 3.20   ② ₹ 2.40   ③ ₹ 1.60   ④ ₹ 1.25   ❸

24. The number 75 ✪ 2 is completely divisible by 3 and 4. Which number should occur in the place of ✪ ?
    ① 6   ② 3   ③ 1   ④ 4   ❸

25. If in an example, the divisor, the quotient and the remainder are 14, 18, 3 in that order, what should the number be ?
    ① 255   ② 355   ③ 252   ④ 354   ❶

26. What is the sum total of all the factors of 12 ?
    ① 12   ② 24   ③ 28   ④ 15   ❸

27. 4 ✪ 4 ✪. In this number the same number is in place of ✪. If the number is divisible by 3, find the number in the place of ✪ ?
    ① 4   ② 3   ③ 2   ④ 6   ❸

28. There are 5 mangoes in one basket. How many baskets will be required to pack 535 mangoes ?
    ① 17   ② 107   ③ 104   ④ 103   ❷

29. Which of the following numbers are divisors of 15 and 30 both ?
    ① 3 and 5   ② 2 and 5
    ③ 2 and 10   ④ None of these   ❶

30. $99830 \div 32 =$
   ① Q 3118 R 22   ② Q 3119 R 22
   ③ Q 22 R 3119   ④ Q 22 R 3118   **②**

31. $58742 \div 28 =$
   ① Q = 2096, R = 26   ② Q = 2087, R = 26
   ③ Q = 2017, R = 26   ④ Q = 26, R = 2096   **③**

Explanation :

$$28)\overline{58742}(2097$$
$$-56\downarrow\downarrow$$
$$\overline{0274}$$
$$-252\downarrow$$
$$\overline{222}$$
$$-196$$
$$\overline{026}$$

∴ Alternative **③** is the correct answer.

Examples for Practice

Solve the following examples.

1. $4590 \div 42 = \square$ Quotient $\square$ Remainder
   ① 12, 109   ② 109, 12   ③ 108, 10   ④ 10, 104

2. $639 \div 7 = \square$ Quotient $\square$ Remainder
   ① 91, 2   ② 2, 91   ③ 20, 9   ④ 12, 9

3. $728 \div 7 = \square$ Quotient $\square$ Remainder
   ① 104, 1   ② 104, 10   ③ 104, 0   ④ 104, 11

4. How many notes of ₹ 5 are there in ₹ 775 ?
   ① 105   ② 200   ③ 145   ④ 155

5. The total expenditure of 201 rooms is ₹ 11055. What is the expenditure per room ?
   ① ₹ 5.5   ② ₹ 55   ③ ₹ 550   ④ ₹ 100

6. The total production in the month of June 2011 is 208020. What is the production of 1 day ?
   ① 6934   ② 6933   ③ 6834   ④ 6833

7. When 4,295 is divided by a number, the quotient is 64 and the remainder is 7. Find the number.
    ① 64   ② 67   ③ 76   ④ 46

8. A school bought 65 benches for ₹ 40,950. Find the cost of each bench.
    ① 650   ② 563   ③ 360   ④ 630

9. $818181 \div 9 =$
    ① 9090   ② 9009   ③ 90099   ④ 90909

10. How many two-rupee notes should be given to pay a bill of ₹ 70 ?
    ① 14   ② 16   ③ 35   ④ 70

11. How many fifty-rupee notes make ten thousand rupees ?
    ① 200   ② 20   ③ 2000   ④ 100

12. How many dozen mangoes do 900 mangoes make ?
    ① 750   ② 81   ③ 75   ④ 57

13. The charge for 13 railway tickets is ₹ 4,264 what is the charge per ticket ?
    ① ₹ 382   ② ₹ 302   ③ ₹ 402   ④ ₹ 328

14. There are 7575 oranges in a basket if distributed among 15 children equally. How many mangoes does one child have ?
    ① 50   ② 500   ③ 505   ④ 550

15. The greatest four digit number which can be exactly divided by 69 is ?
    ① 9999   ② 9939   ③ 9963   ④ 9936

16. When 30015 is divided by 3 what will be quotient ?
    ① 105   ② 1005   ③ 10005   ④ 10015

17. A bottle contains 11 tablets. How many bottles would be required to contain 1111 tablets ?
    ① 101   ② 91   ③ 1001   ④ 111

18. The total expenditure of 45 boys on a trip was ₹ 9090. What was the share of one boy ?
    ① 20   ② 202   ③ 200   ④ 2020

19. The cost of 30 T.V. sets is ₹ 302700. What is the cost of 1 T.V. set ?

   ① 50   ② 625   ③ 1225   ④ 10090

20. When a number is taken 75 times and added the sum is 5625. What is that number ?

   ① 65   ② 75   ③ 85   ④ 70

21. What number should replace ☐

   if ☐ $- 29 - 29 - 29 - 29 = 29$

   ① 144   ② 114   ③ 145   ④ 29

22. Amit gave the amount 16264 in form of ten-rupee notes. How much of the amount he could not pay with ten-rupee notes ?

   ① 64   ② 3   ③ 2   ④ 4

23. $4832 \div$ ☐ $= 604$

   ① 8   ② 2   ③ 4   ④ 6

24. $54000 \div 72$

   ① 720   ② 750   ③ 740   ④ 710

25. $1212 \div 4$

   ① 33   ② 300   ③ 303   ④ 330

26. $3,195 \div 45 = ?$ ☐ Quotient ☐ Remainder.

   ① 17, 0   ② 71, 0   ③ 61, 0   ④ 16, 0

27. $5,586 \div 87 =$ ☐ Quotient ☐ Remainder.

   ① 62, 20   ② 64, 21   ③ 81, 64   ④ 64, 18

28. $44,98 \div 54 =$ ☐ Quotient ☐ Remainder.

   ① 83, 29   ② 83, 16   ③ 83, 45   ④ 83, 25

29. $6,198 \div 72 =$ ☐ Quotient ☐ Remainder.

   ① 86, 8   ② 86, 10   ③ 86, 6   ④ 86, 5

30. $8,019 \div 99 =$ ☐ Quotient ☐ Remainder.

   ① 80, 19   ② 81, 19   ③ 19, 81   ④ 81, 0

31. 8,53 ÷ 89 = ☐ Quotient ☐ Remainder.

    ① 9, 58   ② 9, 52   ③ 52, 9   ④ 58, 9

32. 709 ÷ 71 = ☐ Quotient ☐ Remainder.

    ① 9, 97   ② 9, 70   ③ 70, 9   ④ 75, 9

33. How many notes of ₹ 5 are there in ₹ 825 ?

    ① 16   ② 165   ③ 825   ④ 17

34. ₹ 9,999 are distributed among 11 persons. How much each person will get ?

    ① 909   ② 9,090   ③ 90,909   ④ 90,099

35. Find the number which when divided by 65, quotient is 23 and remainder is 5.

    ① 1,495   ② 1,490   ③ 23   ④ 1500

36. How many ₹ 2 notes are there in ₹ 380 ?

    ① 190   ② 290   ③ 390   ④ 490

37. When a number is divided by 60, the quotient is 35 and remainder is 15, what will be that number ?

    ① 2,100   ② 2,115   ③ 1,521   ④ 2,160

38. Find the number when it is divided by 45, quotient is 1074 and remainder is 39 ?

    ① 48,369   ② 48,330   ③ 48,366   ④ 48,365

39. When 753 is divided by 37, what will be the remainder ?

    ① 20   ② 17   ③ 13   ④ 23

40. Which of the following is the divisor of all the numbers ?

    ① 4   ② 3   ③ 2   ④ 1

41. Divide the following 909 ÷ 9 = ☐

    ① 11   ② 110   ③ 101   ④ 100

42. 88 ÷ 10 = ☐ Quotient ☐ Remainder

    ① 8, 8   ② 8, 0   ③ 88, 1   ④ 8, 1

43. 393 ÷ 3 = ☐

    ① 121   ② 111   ③ 131   ④ 141

44. $684 \div 2 = \square$

① 434   ② 432   ③ 444   ④ 342

45. $494 \div 4 = \square$ Quotient $\square$ Remainder

① 124, 0   ② 123, 2   ③ 122, 2   ④ 123, 0

46. $700 \div 7 = \square$

① 100   ② 70   ③ 10   ④ 7

47. $800 \div 5 = \square$

① 170   ② 160   ③ 150   ④ 500

48. Divide ₹ 865 equally among 5 people.

① 175   ② 170   ③ 173   ④ 172

49. $97 \div 11 = \square$ Quotient $\square$ Remainder

① 8, 9   ② 9, 8   ③ 8, 8   ④ 9, 9

50. $728 \div 7 = \square$ Quotient $\square$ Remainder

① 104, 1   ② 104, 10   ③ 104, 0   ④ 104, 2

51. How many notes of ₹ 5 are there in ₹ 775 ?

① 105   ② 200   ③ 145   ④ 155

52. $46501 \div 306 = ?$

① Q = 295, R = 152   ② Q = 151, R = 295

③ Q = 150, R = 291   ④ Q = 295, R = 151

53. $2589 \div 724 = ?$

① Q = 52, R = 35   ② Q = 35, R = 155

③ Q = 36, R = 552   ④ Q = 35, R = 552

54. Radha needed 45 cartons to pack 2200 books. There are equal number of books in each cartoon ? How many books did she pack into each cartoon ?

① Q = 48, R = 42   ② Q = 46, R = 42

③ Q = 48, R = 40   ④ Q = 40, R = 48

55. Which number on being multiplied by 79 gives a product 20,461 ?

① 257   ② 259   ③ 258   ④ 260

56. Divide 608832 among 24 people equally ?

① 25386   ② 25367   ③ 25378   ④ 25368

57. What will you divide 6,54,430 to get 18698 as quotient ?
    ① 35   ② 34   ③ 36   ④ 37

58. What is the quotient and remainder for 36452 ÷ 333 ?
    ① Q = 109, R = 150   ② Q = 109, R = 155
    ③ Q = 155, R = 109   ④ Q = 150, R = 110

59. 18325 ÷ 143 = ?
    ① Q = 126, R = 21   ② Q = 128, R = 25
    ③ Q = 21, R = 128   ④ Q = 128, R = 21

60. A fruit seller had 78,923 apples. He packed them into boxes with each box containing 300 apples. Calculate the number of boxes required and the number of apples left after packing ?
    ① Q = 236, R = 23   ② Q = 263, R = 22
    ③ Q = 263, R = 23   ④ Q = 262, R = 23

Answers

1.	②	2.	①	3.	③	4.	④	5.	②
6.	①	7.	②	8.	④	9.	④	10.	③
11.	①	12.	③	13.	④	14.	③	15.	④
16.	③	17.	①	18.	②	19.	④	20.	②
21.	③	22.	④	23.	①	24.	②	25.	③
26.	②	27.	④	28.	②	29.	③	30.	④
31.	②	32.	②	33.	②	34.	①	35.	④
36.	①	37.	②	38.	①	39.	③	40.	④
41.	③	42.	①	43.	③	44.	④	45.	②
46.	①	47.	②	48.	③	49.	①	50.	③
51.	④	52.	④	53.	①	54.	③	55.	②
56.	④	57.	①	58.	②	59.	④	60.	③

❖ ❖ ❖

2.5

WORD PROBLEMS ON MULTIPLICATION AND DIVISION (MIXED OPERATION)

✌ INTRODUCTION :

Problems based on multiplication and division would be asked read the question carefully and then solve the given problem.

Model Examples

Solve the following example.

1. Divide 63 notebooks equally among 7 students. How many will each get ?

    ① 8   ② 9   ③ 7   ④ 10   ❷

    Explanation :

    $$7\overline{)\,63\,}\ 9$$
    $$\underline{63}$$
    $$00$$

    Here 63 notebook divided equally among 7 students. Each student will get 9 note books.

    ∴ Alternative ❷ is the correct answer.

2. There 76 marbles. How many marbles each one will get if it is divided equally among 9 children and how many will be left ?

    ① 4   ② 5   ③ 6   ④ 3   ❶

    Explanation :

    $$9\overline{)\,76\,}\ 8$$
    $$\underline{72}$$
    $$04$$

    Total 76 marbles are divided equally in 9 students each student will get 8 marbles and 4 marbles will be left.

    ∴ Alternative ❶ is the correct answer.

3. The contribution for annual day was ₹ 360 each. Altogether ₹ 17,640 was collected. How many students had paid for the annual day ?

    ① 47   ② 50   ③ 48   ④ 49   ❹

    Explanation : $360 \times 1 = 360$
                             $360 \times 2 = 720$
                             $360 \times 3 = 1080$
                             $360 \times 4 = 1440$

$$\begin{array}{r} 49 \\ 360\overline{)17640} \\ -1440\downarrow \\ \hline 03240 \\ -3240 \\ \hline 0000 \end{array}$$

$360 \times 5 = 1800$
$360 \times 6 = 2160$
$360 \times 7 = 2520$
$360 \times 8 = 2880$
$360 \times 9 = 3240$

∴ Alternative ❹ is the correct answer.

4. Which number on being multiplied by 125 gives 84,750 ?

① 687   ② 678   ③ 677   ④ 688   ❷

Explanation :

$$\begin{array}{r} 678 \\ 125\overline{)84750} \\ -750\downarrow| \\ \hline 0975| \\ -875\downarrow \\ \hline 1000 \\ -1000 \\ \hline 0000 \end{array}$$

$125 \times 1 = 125$
$125 \times 2 = 250$
$125 \times 3 = 375$
$125 \times 4 = 500$
$125 \times 5 = 625$
$125 \times 6 = 750$
$125 \times 7 = 875$
$125 \times 8 = 1000$

∴ Alternative ❷ is the correct answer.

Examples for Practice

Solve the following examples :

1. A bus covers 290 kilometres in 5 hours. What distance will it cover in 20 hours ?

① 4650 kms② 1160 kms ③ 1600 kms ④ 1260 kms

2. 275 tiles are required for a hall. How many tiles are required for 25 halls ?

① 7875   ② 6875   ③ 5875   ④ 8875

3. If 6 kilograms of rice costs ₹ 246 what is the cost of 1 kilogram of rice ?

① ₹ 61   ② ₹ 41   ③ ₹ 40   ④ ₹ 46

4. If 72 students stand in 6 equal rows for a drill, how many students will be there is each row ?

① 12   ② 14   ③ 13   ④ 11

5. If 48 litres of milk is poured into a vessel of 4 litres. How may such vessels will be required ?

① 10   ② 12   ③ 14   ④ 8

6. If 120 seeds are to planted in a garden in rows of 10 saplings each. How many such rows will be made ?
   ① 10   ② 20   ③ 12   ④ 24

7. If 81 chocolates are to be distributed equally among 27 students how many chocolate each student will get ?
   ① 3   ② 4   ③ 6   ④ 9

8. There are 72 mango trees in a farm they are planted in 8 rows. How many mango trees in each row ?
   ① 8   ② 9   ③ 6   ④ 7

9. There are 104 beads. How many necklaces with 10 beads each can be made and how many beads will be left over ?
   ① 9, 4   ② 10, 8   ③ 10, 4   ④ 10, 0

10. If the total cost of 4 compass box is ₹ 160, what is the cost of one compass box ?
    ① 30   ② 40   ③ 50   ④ 60

11. Divide 96 notebooks equally among 8 students. How many notebooks will each student get ?
    ① 12   ② 11   ③ 13   ④ 10

12. If a hostel has 144 students with 4 students in one room, in how many rooms are the students staying ?
    ① 34   ② 32   ③ 36   ④ 38

13. If 8 biscuits in one packet, how many packets can be made from 880 biscuits ?
    ① 80   ② 100   ③ 108   ④ 110

14. There are 468 flowers. How many bouquets can you make with 9 flowers in it ?
    ① 52   ② 55   ③ 53   ④ 54

15. If 273 mangoes are equally distributed among 7 families. How many mangoes will each family get ?
    ① 38   ② 37   ③ 39   ④ 36

16. Find out the total cost of 6 shirt costing 480 each ?
    ① 2800   ② 2880   ③ 2808   ④ 2088

17. If one sack of rice weighs 55 helograms, how much do 27 such sacks weigh ?
    ① 1480   ② 1455   ③ 1485   ④ 1458

18. A bus travels a distance of 9 helometers in one litre diesel. How many kilometers will it travel in 69 litres of diesel ?
    ① 611   ② 621   ③ 631   ④ 601

19. There are 45 sacks in a truck. If each sack weighs 108 kgs. What is the total weight of all sacks ?
    ① 6480   ② 4600   ③ 4680   ④ 4860

20. If the cost of one table is ₹ 850, what is the cost of 36 such tables ?
    ① 3600   ② 30600   ③ 36000   ④ 30060

21. If 495 trees are planted on 1 hectare of an orchard, how many trees can be planted on 9 hectares ?
    ① 4455   ② 4545   ③ 4554   ④ 5544

22. Raju bought 6 boxes of mangoes each costing ₹ 550 each. How much did she pay altogether ?
    ① 330   ② 3003   ③ 3030   ④ 3300

23. Radha brought 4 dresses for ₹ 950 each. How much did she pay in all ?
    ① 3060   ② 3600   ③ 3800   ④ 3080

24. If 98 sheets are required to make one notebook. How many notebooks at the most will 14510 sheets make and how many sheets will be left over ?
    ① 148, 8   ② 150, 0   ③ 6, 148   ④ 148, 6

25. What will be quotient be when the smallest five digit number is divided by the smallest three digit number ?
    ① 101   ② 100   ③ 1000   ④ 110

26. If 45 kilos of jowar costs 1260. What is the cost of 1 kilo jowar ?
    ① 28   ② 26   ③ 29   ④ 25

27. $78480 \div 48 = ?$
    ① 1630   ② 1655   ③ 1635   ④ 1645

28. Rahul bought 68 kg of sugar for ₹ 2856. What is the cost of 1 kg sugar ?
    ① 47   ② 42   ③ 41   ④ 46

29. 14994 ÷ 126 = ?
    ① 129   ② 114   ③ 118   ④ 119

30. 48 almirals were bought for 1,77,360 ? What is the cost of 1 almirals ?
    ① 3695   ② 3795   ③ 3965   ④ 3975

Answers

1.	❸	2.	❷	3.	❷	4.	❶	5.	❷
6.	❸	7.	❶	8.	❷	9.	❸	10.	❷
11.	❶	12.	❸	13.	❹	14.	❶	15.	❸
16.	❷	17.	❸	18.	❷	19.	❹	20.	❷
21.	❶	22.	❹	23.	❸	24.	❹	25.	❷
26.	❶	27.	❸	28.	❷	29.	❹	30.	❶

❖ ❖ ❖

2.6   EXPRESSION AND THE USE OF LETTERS IN PLACE OF NUMBERS

✌ INTRODUCTION :

In the given expression, if bracket is there, then that bracket should be solved first. In this expression, addition, subtraction, multiplication or division are there then the operation should be performed from left to right in the order of the terms in the expression. If more than two operations are there then they are performed serially as bracket of division, multiplication, addition and subtraction.

e.g. : $15 + 7 \times 3 - 14 \div 2 = 15 + 21 - 7 = 36 - 7 = 29$.

In some examples, both addition and subtraction are to be performed. While solving such examples, first all the numbers with positive sign are added. Then all the numbers with negative sign are added. And finally the subtraction of two numbers is performed.

For example : 180 – 65 + 59 – 82. Here 180 + 59 = 239 and 65 + 82 = 147

Finally 239 – 147 = 92. So 180 – 65 + 59 – 82 = 92

Suppose two numbers are given and we are asked to add these numbers. While adding these two numbers, if the order of the numbers are changed, even then their sum will remain unchanged. For example : 7 + 5 = 12 and 5 + 7 = 12. Suppose two numbers are given and we are asked to multiply these numbers. While performing multiplication, if the order of the numbers are changed, their product will remain unchanged.

For example : 7 × 5 = 35 and 5 × 7 = 35. When any number is multiplied by zero, the product is 0 and when any number is multiplied by 1, the product is the given number itself. For example : 39 × 0 = 0 and 39 × 1 = 39.

Remember the term BODMAS which means
- First solve the one in brackets (B)
- Then solve the division numbers (D)
- Then solve the multiplication numbers (M)
- Then solve addition (A) and finally solve subtraction (S).
  e.g. : (15 + 5) × (15 – 5)

As per rule solve brackets = 20 × 10 = 200 ***Ans.***

Model Examples

Solve the following examples.

1. 25 – 6 + 9 =

    ① 28   ② 10   ③ 34   ④ 24   ❶

    Explanation : 25 – 6 + 9 = 19 + 9 = 28, so answer is option ❶

2. 13 + (6 ÷ 3) =

    ① 15   ② 11   ③ 132   ④ 18   ❶

Explanation : $13 + (6 \div 3) = 13 + 2 = 15$, so answer is option ❶

3. $23 \times 1 \times 0 =$
    ① 23   ② 1   ③ 0   ④ 24   ❸
    Explanation : $23 \times 1 \times 0 = 23 \times 0 = 0$, so answer is option ❸

4. $25 \times 5 - 100 =$
    ① 125   ② 95   ③ 25   ④ 1   ❸
    Explanation : $25 \times 5 - 100 = 125 - 100 = 25$, so answer is option ❸

5. $48 \div 12 \times 4 =$
    ① 1   ② 16   ③ 44   ④ 12   ❷
    Explanation : $48 \div 12 \times 4 = 4 \times 4 = 16$, so answer is option ❷

6. Which of the following sets of signs should be used in the expression :
    65 □ 45 □ 91 □ 19 to make it valid ?
    ① $+ = +$ ② $+ = -$ ③ $- = +$ ④ $+ + =$ ❶

7. $(133 \div 19) \times 7 =$ How much ?
    ① 7   ② 14   ③ 49   ④ 133   ❸

8. The answer of which of the following operations is different ?
    ① $20 - 4$ ② $6 + 2 \times 5$ ③ $16 + 0$ ④ $8 \times 0 \times 2$ ❹

9. What number do you subtract from the biggest three digit even number to get 700 ?
    ① $200 \times 9 + 8$ ② $200 + 90 + 8$
    ③ $20 + 8 + 200$ ④ $9 \times 8 + 200$ ❷
    Explanation : Biggest 3 digit even number is $998 - 298 = 700$. So the answer is option ❷. $200 + 90 + 8 = 298$

10. $210 - 132 + 58 =$
    ① 190   ② 78   ③ 136   ④ 20   ❸
    Explanation : Here firstly 210 and 58 are added, and then 132 is subtracted from the answer. Thus, $210 + 58 = 268$ and $268 - 132 = 136$. So the answer is option ❸

11. 945 + 70 – 360 =
     ① 555   ② 655   ③ 775   ④ 700   ❷
     Explanation : Addition of 945 and 70 comes out to be 1015. From this 360 should be subtracted. The subtraction comes to be 655. So answer is option ❷

12. 800 – □ + 1300 = 1500
     ① 300   ② 400   ③ 500   ④ 600   ❹
     Explanation : Subtraction of 600 from 800 is 200. Addition of 200 to 1300 is 1500. So the answer is option ❹

13. 35 – 8 + 4 =
     ① 27   ② 31   ③ 43   ④ 40   ❷
     Explanation : First 35 and 4 are added and then 8 is subtracted from the answer. Thus, 35 + 4 = 39 and 39 – 8 = 31. So the answer is option ❷

14. 500 – 285 – 132 =
     ① 83   ② 115   ③ 215   ④ 230   ❶
     Explanation : 500 – 285 = 215 and 215 – 132 = 83. So the answer is option ❶

15. The sum of two numbers is 407, while their difference is 29. What is the greater number of the two ?
     ① 189   ② 378   ③ 218   ④ 220   ❸

16. If ✪ – 48 + 13 = 75, what is the value of ✪ ?
     ① 110   ② 58   ③ 148   ④ 113   ❶

17. What is the difference between the sum of all the numbers from 23 to 28 and the sum of all the numbers from 27 to 32 ?
     ① 24   ② 31   ③ 26   ④ 29.   ❶

18. The sum of ages of Rajesh and Mahesh is 38 years. IF Mahesh is 12 years younger than Rajesh, then find the age of Rajesh.
     ① 25 years ② 16 years ③ 13 years ④ 18 years ❶
     Explanation : Age of Rajesh + Mahesh is 38 years. Rajesh – Mahesh is 12 yrs.
     ∴ 25 + 13 = 38, 25 – 13 = 12 years. So Rajesh is 25 years old and Mahesh is 13 years old.

19. $18 \times 13 - 18 \times 3 =$
   ① 54   ② 180
   ③ 234   ④ None of these   ❷

   Explanation : Multiplication of $18 \times 13 = 234$ and that of 18×3 is 54. Subtract 54 from 234, it comes to be 180. So the answer is option ❷

20. $147 \times 57 - 147 \times 37 =$
   ① 294   ② 2,940
   ③ 2,646   ④ None of these   ❷

   Explanation : Multiplication of 147×57 is 8379 and that of 147×37 is 5439. The subtraction of these two products is $(8379 - 5439) = 2940$. So the ans. is option ❷

21. $13 \times 14 - 12 \times 14 =$
   ① 168   ② 182   ③ 14   ④ 196   ❸

   Explanation : Product of 13 and 14 is 182 and product of 12 and 14 is 168. The subtraction of $(182 - 168) = 014$. So the answer is option ❸

22. $56943 + 26983 - 43694 =$
   ① 40212   ② 40312   ③ 40332   ④ 40232   ❹

23. $(42 \times 2) + (16 \div 2) = ?$
   ① 50   ② 92   ③ 72   ④ 52   ❷

24. $(165 \div 5) \times (49 \times 7) = ?$
   ① 11319   ② 10319   ③ 10219   ④ 11309   ❶

25. $695684 - 568498 + 201652 = ?$
   ① 127186   ② 328838   ③ 328738   ④ 327738   ❷

26. If $n + 8 = 12$ then $n = ?$
   ① 4   ② 8   ③ 20   ④ 6   ❶

Examples for Practice

Solve the following examples.

1. $6 + 16 \div 8 =$
   ① 8   ② 6   ③ 4   ④ 1

2. $42 - 48 + 36 =$
   ① 45   ② 30   ③ 20   ④ 40

3. $12 \times \dfrac{1}{2} - 12 \times \dfrac{1}{3} =$

    ① 4   ② 6   ③ 2   ④ 1

4. $4 \times 2 \div 2 \times 1 =$

    ① 4   ② 1   ③ 2   ④ 0

5. $5 \times (7 - 3) =$

    ① 5   ② 3   ③ 125   ④ 20

6. $(10 + 8) - (10 + 3) =$

    ① 18   ② 13   ③ 5   ④ 10

7. $51 \times 50 - 50 =$

    ① 2,550   ② 2,500   ③ 2,050   ④ 2,005

8. $48 + 14 \times 15 =$

    ① 930   ② 305   ③ 258   ④ 582

9. $25 \times (20 - 4 \times 5) =$

    ① 25   ② 20   ③ 4   ④ 0

10. $35 \times (40 - 37) =$

    ① 93   ② 3   ③ 105   ④ 15,600

11. $12 \times 8 \div 2 =$

    ① 96   ② 2   ③ 32   ④ 48

12. $1 \times 135 - 1 \times 134 =$

    ① 1   ② 2   ③ 3   ④ 4

13. $29 \times 4 - 23 \times 4 =$

    ① 28   ② 23   ③ 12   ④ 24

14. $(16 + 9) \div 5 =$

    ① 25   ② 5   ③ 20   ④ 125

15. $(40 - 40) \div 9 =$

    ① 1   ② 2   ③ 0   ④ 4

16. $39 \div 13 + 2 + 0 =$

    ① 3   ② 4   ③ 5   ④ 6

17. $26 - (17 \times 0) =$

    ① 26   ② 0   ③ 17   ④ 9

18. $55 \div 11 - 3 - 2 =$

    ① 0   ② 1   ③ 2   ④ 3

19. $26 \times 0 \div 26 \times 2 =$

    ① 52   ② 26   ③ 2   ④ 0

20. $69 \times 12 - 56 + 20 =$
   ① 808   ② 792   ③ 828   ④ 772

21. $28 + 20 - 10 - 10 + 4 + 1 =$
   ① 33   ② 42   ③ 29   ④ 53

22. $6 \times 3 + 1 + 2 =$
   ① 21   ② 22   ③ 23   ④ 24

23. $(16 - 4) \times (5 \times 3) =$
   ① 27   ② 12   ③ 15   ④ 180

24. $32 + 45 \times 44 =$
   ① 1,220   ② 1,022   ③ 2,012   ④ 2,120

25. $(24 \times 28) \div (24 \times 14) =$
   ① 672   ② 366   ③ 1,008   ④ 2

26. $(10 + 2 \times 2) + (20 \times 2 + 2) + 20 =$
   ① 66   ② 76   ③ 86   ④ 96

27. $(27 + 5 \times 2 + 3) \times 0 =$
   ① 32   ② 64   ③ 67   ④ 0

28. $9 + (4 + 11) - 9 =$
   ① 24   ② 9,411   ③ 15   ④ 0

29. $55 - 47 + 32 + 10 =$
   ① 120   ② 50   ③ 44   ④ 40

30. In a class, there are 53 students. 8 new boys are admitted and 6 girls left the school. So what will be the strength of that class ?
   ① 61   ② 47   ③ 55   ④ 60

31. Sachin got ₹ 135 out of which he spend ₹ 38. His elder brother gave him   ₹ 21. So what will be the total amount Sachin has now ?
   ① 118   ② 108   ③ 99   ④ 88

32. Population of a village is 80,245. Out of which 24,813 are gents and 24,560 are ladies. Remaining are children. So what is number of children ?
   ① 55,658   ② 26,500   ③ 30,872   ④ 43,200

33. $48,277 + 33189 - 5356 =$
   ① 76,110   ② 75,110   ③ 74,110   ④ 73,110

34. $4,23,567 - 3,19,876 + 5,01,234 =$
   ① 6,04,925   ② 6,04,935   ③ 6,04,945   ④ 6,04,940

35. $91,261 + 82,375 - 1,40,189 =$
    ① 33,448   ② 33,447   ③ 33,449   ④ 33,446

36. $6,53,221 - 9,753 + 78,950 =$
    ① 7,22,318   ② 7,22,518   ③ 7,22,418   ④ 7,22,417

37. $26,003 - 13,885 + 347 =$
    ① 12,464   ② 12,466   ③ 12,375   ④ 12,465

38. $512 - 27 + 5 =$
    ① 490   ② 480   ③ 470   ④ 460

39. $50,000 - 17,000 - 3,750 - 5,000 =$
    ① 33,000   ② 24,250   ③ 45,00   ④ 25,250

40. $57 + 58 + 59 =$
    ① 154   ② 194   ③ 174   ④ 184

41. $619 + 724 + 693 =$
    ① 1,836   ② 2,036   ③ 1,936   ④ 2,139

42. $321 + 654 + 987 =$
    ① 1,383   ② 1,483   ③ 1,583   ④ 1,962

43. $908 + 708 + 909 =$
    ① 2,225   ② 2,325   ③ 2,425   ④ 2,525

44. $417 \times 88 + 417 \times 12 =$
    ① 4,170   ② 41,700   ③ 00417   ④ 0417

45. $178 \times 913 - 913 \times 178 =$
    ① 0   ② 1,62,514   ③ 1   ④ 1,62,541

46. $4,321 \times 118 - 321 \times 118 =$
    ① 5,09,878   ② 37,878   ③ 4,72,000   ④ 48,200

47. $684 \times 61 - 61 \times 684 =$
    ① 0   ② 1   ③ 41,724   ④ 41,700

48. $999 + 888 - 333 =$
    ① 1,887   ② 666   ③ 1,554   ④ 999

49. $59 \times 99 =$
    ① 5,900   ② 5,814   ③ 4,158   ④ 5,841

50. $644 \times 99 =$
    ① 6,499   ② 63,756   ③ 6,376   ④ 6,356

51. $38 \times 25 =$
    ① 95   ② 9,500   ③ 950   ④ 95,000

52. $574 \times 100 =$
    ① 574   ② 5,740   ③ 57,400   ④ 5,74,000

53. $49 \times 25 =$
    ① 225   ② 1225   ③ 825   ④ 925

54. $3,800 - 38 \times 10 =$
    ① 3,420   ② 3,663   ③ 3,66,300   ④ 34,200

55. $69 - 35 \times 1 =$
    ① 6,935   ② 34   ③ 3,435   ④ 3,534

56. Which of the following similarities is incorrect ?
    ① $28 + 25 = 25 + 28$ ② $8 \times 23 = 23 \times 8$
    ③ $19 \times 0 = 0 \times 19$ ④ $8 \div 4 = 4 \div 8$

57. $101 \times 99 =$
    ① 999   ② 9,999   ③ 99,999   ④ 9,99,999

58. $999 + 111 - 222 =$
    ① 555   ② 666   ③ 777   ④ 888

59. $916 \times 999 =$
    ① 9,16,999   ② 1,95,084   ③ 9,15,084   ④ 99,916

60. $31 \times 4 - 30 \times 2 + 603 =$
    ① 667   ② 543   ③ 607   ④ 787

61. $604 \times 90 - 726 + 94 =$
    ① 6256   ② 53734   ③ 53540   ④ 54360

62. $(798 \div 6) + 84 + (326 \times 80) =$
    ① 26164   ② 26297   ③ 26213   ④ 26917

63. $(885 \div 15) + 26 + (326 \times 80) =$
    ① 26723   ② 27055   ③ 26465   ④ 26165

64. $696 \div 12 + (56942 - 36985) =$
    ① 20015   ② 19957   ③ 19900   ④ 20641

65. $995 \times 69 + (550 \div 10) =$
    ① 67710   ② 68710   ③ 68655   ④ 122264

66. $85965 - 36786 + 46504 \div 4 =$
    ① 83380   ② 65120   ③ 49089   ④ 60805

67. $986 \times 24 - 986 + 56950 =$
    ① 74372   ② 77936   ③ 79628   ④ 73664

68. $89664 \div 16 + 696 \times 6 =$
    ① 9780   ② 5604   ③ 4176   ④ 9770

69. $69549 - 48678 + 48 \times 48 =$
    ① 50982   ② 20871   ③ 23175   ④ 18567

70. $5940 \div 12 + 6940 - 4369 =$

     ① 3660   ② 3066   ③ 7435   ④ 3606

71. $659 \times 15 - 8940 + 658 =$

     ① 1678   ② 1696   ③ 1277   ④ 1603

72. $8939 \div 7 + 694 \times 14 =$

     ① 10993   ② 10893   ③ 10983   ④ 10883

73. $36945 + 4236 - 12 \times 9 =$

     ① 41093   ② 41083   ③ 41073   ④ 41181

Answers

1.	❶	2.	❷	3.	❸	4.	❶	5.	❹
6.	❸	7.	❷	8.	❸	9.	❹	10.	❸
11.	❹	12.	❶	13.	❹	14.	❷	15.	❸
16.	❸	17.	❶	18.	❶	19.	❹	20.	❷
21.	❶	22.	❶	23.	❹	24.	❸	25.	❹
26.	❷	27.	❹	28.	❸	29.	❷	30.	❸
31.	❶	32.	❸	33.	❶	34.	❶	35.	❷
36.	❸	37.	❹	38.	❶	39.	❷	40.	❸
41.	❷	42.	❹	43.	❹	44.	❷	45.	❶
46.	❸	47.	❶	48.	❸	49.	❹	50.	❷
51.	❸	52.	❸	53.	❷	54.	❶	55.	❷
56.	❹	57.	❷	58.	❹	59.	❸	60.	❶
61.	❸	62.	❷	63.	❹	64.	❶	65.	❷
66.	❹	67.	❸	68.	❶	69.	❸	70.	❷
71.	❹	72.	❶	73.	❸					

♣ ♣ ♣

| 2.7 | TEST OF DVISIBILITY (1-10) AND FACTORS AND MULTIPLES OF NUMBERS |

(A) TEST OF DIVISIBILITY (1 to 10)

✌ INTRODUCTION :

1. **Test of Divisibility for 2** : For any number to be completely divisible by 2, the number should have the digit 2, 4, 6, 8 or 0 on its units place. e.g. 22, 34, 46, 88, 100.

2. **Test of divisibility by 3 and 9** : If the sum of the digit of given number is exactly divisible by 3 and 9.
   For e.g. 6543 = 6 + 5 + 4 + 3 = 18. Therefore, the number 6543 is divisible by 3 and 9.

3. **Test is divisibility for 4** : If the last two digits (i.e. units place and tens place) is completely divisible by 4, E-g 5476.76, the number is completely divisible by 4.

4. **Test is divisibility of 5** : Any number whose digit in the units place is 5 or 0 is divisible by 5 e.g. 10, 25, 105, 225.

5. **Test of divisibility for 7** : To find out if a number is divisible by 7 then multiply the digit in the units by 2. Then subtract the product so obtained by the remaining number. If the answer is divisible by 7 then the number is divisible by 7. e.g. 112; 2 x 2 = 4; 11 – 4 = 7 which is divided by 7. Hence, 112 is divisible by 7.

6. **Test is divisibility of 8** : If the number formed by the last three digits (i.e. units, tens and hundred) is completely divisible by 8. e.g. 27532. 352 is divisible by 8.

7. **Test is divisibility by 10** : A number is exactly divisible by 10 if the given number has the digit 0. '0' in its units place.

8. **Test of divisibility by 11:** For any given number the difference between sum total of even and odd number is 0 of multiples of 11. Then we can say the number is divisible by 11.

━━━━━━━━━━ **Model Examples** ━━━━━━━━━━

Solve the following examples.

1. In the following number 32 * 21 which digit should replace the asterisk so that the number is divisible by 9.
    ① 1   ② 3   ③ 9   ④ 6   ❶
    Explanation : The sum of the digits is completely divided by 9 :
    3 + 2 + 2 + 1 = 8 + 1 = 9.
    ∴ Alternative ❶ is the correct answer.

2. Which of the following number is exactly divisible by 3 ?
    ① 3649   ② 2333   ③ 323   ④ 2502   ❹

3. Which smallest number should be added to 91 so that the resulting number will be exactly divisible by 3 ?
    ① 0   ② 1   ③ 2   ④ 3   ❸

4. In how many ways 48 can be expressed as the product of two numbers ?
    ① 4   ② 5   ③ 6   ④ 8   ❷
    Explanation : (48, 1), (24, 2), (16, 3), (12, 4), (8, 6) are the pairs of factors of 48.
    ∴ Alternative ❷ is the correct answer.

5. Which of the following number is not divisible by 6 ?
    ① 5382   ② 9836   ③ 3582   ④ 3228   ❷

6. Which of the following number should be added to the number 9621. So that the resulting number is divisible by 6.
    ① 2   ② 3   ③ 0   ④ 4   ❸

7. Which of the following numbers is divisor of 286 ?
    ① 5   ② 13   ③ 3   ④ 9   ❷

8. Which of the following numbers is a divisor of 1001 ?
    ①17   ② 12   ③ 18   ④ 13   ❹

9. Which of the following number is divisible by 5 ?
    ① 5105   ② 5102   ③ 5114   ④ 5111   ❶

11. Common multiple of 2 and 3 are multiple of.
    ① 9   ② 6   ③ 13   ④ 7   ❷

● ═══════════ **Examples for Practice** ═══════════ ●

Solve the following examples.

1. The number 5 * 14 is divisible by 9. Which of the following digit should replace the asterisk ?
   ① 0   ② 7   ③ 3   ④ 8

2. Which of the following numbers is exactly divisible by 3 ?
   ① 3649   ② 2333   ③ 323   ④ 2502

3. Which of the following numbers is exactly divisible by 9 ?
   ① 12345   ② 12364   ③ 13284   ④ 12340

4. Which of the following numbers should be added to the number 7911. So that the resulting number is divisible by 6 ?
   ① 9   ② 1   ③ 14   ④ 18

5. 8696 * is a five digit number divisible by 6. Find the digit in the place of the asterisk mark ?
   ① 1   ② 2   ③ 4   ④ 6

6. Which of the following number is not divisible by 6 ?
   ① 3582   ② 3698   ③ 5382   ④ 8352

7. The number 9 * 57 * 5 is completely divisible by 3. Find the numbers in the place of * ?
   ① 1, 1   ② 0, 0   ③ 3, 2   ④ 8, 2

8. Which of the following exactly divisible by 4 ?
   ① 3476   ② 3478   ③ 3376   ④ 3378

9. Which of the following is exactly divisible by 11 ?
   ① 576345   ② 554376   ③ 765543   ④ 435766

10. Which of the following is not divisible by 7 ?
    ① 114   ② 1134   ③ 1142   ④ 116

● ═══════════ **Answers** ═══════════ ●

1.	❹	2.	❹	3.	❸	4.	❶	5.	❹
6.	❷	7.	❹	8.	❶	9.	❶	10.	❷

(B) FACTORS AND MULTIPLES OF NUMBERS

✤ *INTRODUCTION :*

3 × 7 = 21 or 21 can be divided by 7 exactly 21 is a multiple of 7. Of course, 21 is also a multiple of 3. So 3 and 7 are called the

factors of 21. Read the sums carefully and select the correct answer from the four alternative answers given below.

Model Examples

Solve the following example.

1. Find two factors of each of the numbers 39 =
   ① 3 and 13   ② 2 and 13
   ③ 4 and 13   ④ 5 and 13   ❶

Examples for Practice

Solve the following examples.

1. 87
   ① 5 and 29   ② 4 and 29
   ③ 2 and 29   ④ 3 and 29
2. 62
   ① 2 and 31 ② 3 and 21 ③ 4 and 21 ④ 3 and 31
3. 174
   ① 2 and 58 ② 3 and 58 ③ 4 and 58 ④ 5 and 58
4. 52
   ① 3 and 26 ② 4 and 26 ③ 2 and 26 ④ 7 and 26
5. 129
   ① 2 and 39 ② 3 and 29 ③ 3 and 43 ④ 4 and 23
6. Pairs of a number and its factor are given below. Which pair does not fit into the group ?
   ① 27, 9   ② 35, 7   ③ 31, 5   ④ 48, 8
7. Which one of the following groups of numbers show the factors of the number 15015 ?
   ① 3, 5   ② 3, 6   ③ 6, 5   ④ 4, 7
8. How many factors does the number 144 have ?
   ① 15   ② 12   ③ 10   ④ 20
9. Find the sum of all the factors of 12 ?
   ① 28   ② 6   ③ 18   ④ 38
10. Which of the following is a set of factors of the number 3040 ?
    ① 7, 5, 19 ② 2, 7, 5   ③ 2, 5, 19   ④ 3, 5, 10

11. Write three three digit numbers that are multiples of 3 ?
    ① 103, 105, 107   ② 101, 103, 105
    ③ 102, 103, 104   ④ 102, 105, 108

12. Write five three digit number that are multiples of 5 ?
    ① 100, 105, 108, 110, 115 ② 100, 105, 108, 110, 118
    ③ 105, 110, 115, 120, 125 ④ 195, 100, 105, 110, 115

13. Write 5 four digit numbers that are multiples of 4 as well as 5 ?
    ① 1205, 1210, 1220, 1230
    ② 1200, 1240, 1280, 1300, 1320
    ③ 1004, 1005, 1006, 1007, 1008
    ④ 1190, 1194, 1200, 1210, 1220

14. What are the factors of 84 ?
    ① 2, 7, 3   ② 2, 4, 3   ③ 2, 4, 7   ④ 2, 6, 7

15. Find the sum of all the factors of 36.
    ① 12   ② 18   ③ 36   ④ 10

Answers

1.	❹	2.	❶	3.	❷	4.	❸	5.	❸
6.	❸	7.	❶	8.	❶	9.	❶	10.	❸
11.	❹	12.	❸	13.	❷	14.	❶	15.	❹

✣ ✣ ✣

FRACTIONS

3.1 VULGAR FRACTIONS

❧ **Vulgar Fractions**

Vulgar fractions are a fractions expressed in the form of p/q where q ≠ 0.

For example : $\dfrac{3}{10}$, $-\dfrac{4}{5}$, $\dfrac{21}{7}$

(A) FRACTIONS

(I) Reading of Fraction

❧ **INTRODUCTION :**

A quantity that expresses a part of the whole quantity is called a fraction. The part above the horizontal line is called a numerator. The part below the horizontal line is called a denominator.

$= \dfrac{1}{2}$

Fig. 3.1

The diagram is divided into two equal parts. One part is shaded. The shaded part of the diagram is 1/2. It is read as one half.

The figure is divided into four equal parts and one part is shaded. The Shaded part of the diagram is $\dfrac{1}{4}$ and it is read as one over four. It is one fourth or a quarter.

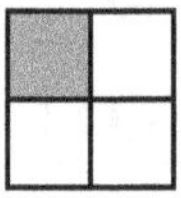

$= \dfrac{1}{4}$

Fig. 3.2

The figure is divided four equal parts and three parts are shaded. It is called (3/4) three fourth or three quarter. It is read as three over four.

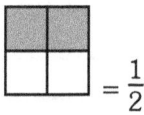

$= \dfrac{3}{4}$

Fig. 3.3

Mixed Fraction :

A fraction like $2\dfrac{1}{4}$ or $3\dfrac{1}{2}$ is called mixed fraction. For example, when we divide 4 apples equally among 3 people we can do this in two ways.

Method 1	Method 2
Divide each apple equally into 3 parts Each person gets $\frac{1}{3}$ of each apple or one part of each apple. In this way, each person gets 4 parts of $\frac{1}{3}$ of each apple. Therefore each person gets $\frac{1}{3} \times 4 = \frac{4}{3}$ apples $= 1\frac{1}{3}$	First give each person 1 whole apple. Then divide the remaining apple into three equal parts. Give each person one part of the fourth apple that is $\frac{1}{3}$ apple. Each person gets 1 whole apple and $\frac{1}{3}$ apple $= 1 + \frac{1}{3}$

A fraction like $1\frac{1}{3}$ is called a mixed fraction.

Example :

1. $2\frac{3}{4}$ is read as

   ① Two and three quarters ② Two and four quarters

   ③ Two and one quarters ④ Two and three **❶**

2. Write the fraction Ten and a half is

   ① $10\frac{1}{10}$ ② $10\frac{1}{4}$ ③ $10\frac{1}{2}$ ④ $10\frac{1}{4}$ **❸**

Model Examples

Q. Solve the following examples.

1. $\frac{5}{7}$ is read as ....

   ① seven over five ② five over seven

   ③ five and seven ④ seven and five **❷**

2. $\frac{6}{7}$ is read as ....

   ① six over seven ② seven over six

   ③ six and seven ④ seven and six **❶**

Examples for Practice

Q. Solve the following examples.

1. Write shaded portion in fraction.

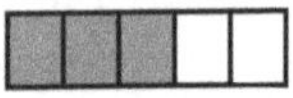

Fig. 3.4

①$\frac{5}{3}$ ②$\frac{3}{5}$ ③$\frac{4}{5}$ ④$\frac{2}{4}$

2. Read the fraction : $\frac{14}{18}$

① Fourteen over eighteenth ② Eighteen over fourteenth
③ Four over eight   ④ Eight over four

3. $\frac{4}{8}$

① Eight under four   ② Four over eight
③ Four and eight   ④ Eight over four

4. Write the fraction of the given figure.

① $\frac{2}{6}$ ② $\frac{3}{6}$

③ $\frac{4}{6}$ ④ $\frac{1}{2}$

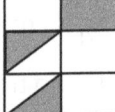

Fig. 3.5

5. $\frac{11}{19}$

① Nineteen over eleventh   ② Eleven over twentieth
③ Eleven over nineteenth   ④ One over nineteenth

6. $\frac{7}{10}$

① Seven over tenth   ② Ten over seventh
③ Seven and ten   ④ Ten and seven

7. $\frac{2}{15}$

① Fifteen over two   ② Two over fifteen
③ Two and fifteen   ④ Fifteen and two

8. $\frac{5}{12}$

① Five and twelve   ② Five over fifteenth
③ Five over twelfth   ④ Twelve and fifth

9. $\dfrac{16}{18}$

① Sixteen over eighteenth   ② Sixteen and eighteen
③ Six over eight   ④ Eighth and sixth

10. $2\dfrac{3}{4}$

① One and three quarters   ② Two and a half
③ Two and a quarter   ④ Two and a three quarters

11. $3\dfrac{1}{2}$ is read as

① Three and a quarter   ② Three and three quarters
③ Three   ④ Three and a half

12. Nine and one quarter.

① $9\dfrac{1}{2}$ ② $9\dfrac{1}{4}$ ③ $9\dfrac{3}{4}$ ④ $9\dfrac{1}{3}$

13. Eighteen and three quarters.

① $18\dfrac{1}{2}$ ② $18\dfrac{2}{3}$ ③ $18\dfrac{3}{4}$ ④ $18\dfrac{1}{4}$

14. Fifteen and three quarters.

① $15\dfrac{1}{4}$ ② $15\dfrac{3}{3}$ ③ $15\dfrac{3}{4}$ ④ $15\dfrac{1}{3}$

15. $8\dfrac{1}{2}$ is read as

① Eight and a three quarters
② Eight and one half
③ Eight and four quarters
④ Eight and two quarters

16. Seventeen and two quarters.

① $17\dfrac{1}{4}$ ② $17\dfrac{3}{4}$ ③ $17\dfrac{2}{4}$ ④ $17\dfrac{1}{2}$

17. $19\dfrac{1}{4}$ is read as

① Nineteen and one quarters
② Nineteen one four
③ Nineteen two quarters
④ Nineteen one

18. Twenty-five and three quarters is

    ① $25\dfrac{3}{3}$ ② $25\dfrac{1}{3}$ ③ $25\dfrac{2}{3}$ ④ $25\dfrac{3}{4}$

19. $29\dfrac{1}{2}$ is

    ① Twenty-nine and a half   ② Twenty-nine and one

    ③ Twenty-nine and two   ④ Twenty-nine and a quarter

20. Eleven and two quarters is

    ① $11\dfrac{2}{4}$ ② $11\dfrac{3}{4}$ ③ $11\dfrac{1}{4}$ ④ none of these

Answers

1.	❷	2.	❶	3.	❷	4.	❶	5.	❸
6.	❶	7.	❷	8.	❸	9.	❶	10.	❹
11.	❹	12.	❷	13.	❸	14.	❸	15.	❷
16.	❸	17.	❶	18.	❹	19.	❶	20.	❶

(II) Writing of The Fraction

In $\dfrac{3}{6}$, 3 is numerator and 6 is the denominator.

Diagram No.	1	2	3	4	5	6
Diagram						
Fraction of shaded part	$\dfrac{1}{2}$	$\dfrac{1}{4}$	$\dfrac{3}{4}$	$\dfrac{1}{3}$	$\dfrac{2}{3}$	$\dfrac{5}{6}$
Numerator	1	1	3	1	2	5
Denominator	2	4	4	3	3	6
Reading/ Writing	One over two $\dfrac{1}{2}$	One over four $\dfrac{1}{4}$	three over four $\dfrac{3}{4}$	One over three $\dfrac{1}{3}$	two over three $\dfrac{2}{3}$	five over six $\dfrac{5}{6}$

Model Examples

Q. Solve the following examples :

1. Three quarter is written as :

   ① $\dfrac{3}{4}$ ② $\dfrac{1}{4}$ ③ $\dfrac{3}{6}$ ④ $\dfrac{2}{6}$ ❶

2. $\dfrac{4}{8}$

   ① numerator 8 denominator 4
   ② 4 by 8
   ③ 8 divided four
   ④ numerator 4 denominator 8   ❹

3. Three over five is written as ....

   ① $\dfrac{5}{3}$ ② $\dfrac{3}{5}$ ③ $3 = 5$ ④ $5 = 3$ ❷

4. Seven over nine is written as ....

   ① $\dfrac{8}{7}$ ② $8 = 7$ ③ $\dfrac{7}{4}$ ④ $\dfrac{7}{9}$ ❹

Examples for Practice

Q. Solve the following examples :

1. Write fraction in words : $\dfrac{1}{2}$

   ① One half   ② Two divided by one
   ③ Two numerator one denominator
   ④ Two under 1

2. Write in numerical form : Numerator 8 denominator sixteen.

   ① $8 \div 16$ ② $\dfrac{8}{16}$ ③ $\dfrac{16}{8}$ ④ $\dfrac{1}{16}$

3. Numerator 4 denominator 6

   ① $\dfrac{4}{6}$ ② $4 \div 6$ ③ $\dfrac{6}{4}$ ④ $\dfrac{1}{6}$

4.

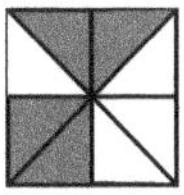

   ① $\dfrac{2}{4}$ ② $\dfrac{3}{4}$

   ③ $\dfrac{4}{4}$ ④ $\dfrac{3}{4}$

Fig. 3.6

5.

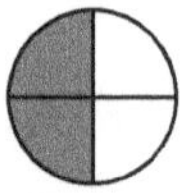

① half   ② quarter
③ three fourth
④ whole

Fig. 3.7

6. Two third :

① $\dfrac{1}{3}$ ② $\dfrac{2}{4}$ ③ $\dfrac{2}{3}$ ④ $\dfrac{3}{3}$

7. Three-eleventh :

① $\dfrac{11}{3}$ ② $\dfrac{3}{11}$ ③ $\dfrac{30}{11}$ ④ $\dfrac{11}{30}$

8. Nine-tenth :

① $\dfrac{10}{9}$ ② $\dfrac{10}{90}$ ③ $\dfrac{9}{10}$ ④ $\dfrac{90}{10}$

9. Six-thirteenth :

① $\dfrac{13}{6}$ ② $\dfrac{60}{13}$ ③ $\dfrac{13}{60}$ ④ $\dfrac{6}{13}$

10. Seven-fourteenth :

① $\dfrac{14}{7}$ ② $\dfrac{70}{13}$ ③ $\dfrac{7}{14}$ ④ $\dfrac{13}{70}$

11. How is $\dfrac{7}{10}$ written ?

① 10 on 7   ② 10 by 7   ③ 7 by 10 ④ 7 on 11.

Answers

1.	❶	2.	❷	3.	❶	4.	❶	5.	❶
6.	❸	7.	❷	8.	❸	9.	❹	10.	❸
11.	❸								

(III) Ascending & Descending order of Fractions and Comparison of Fractions

✌ INTRODUCTION :

❖ Fractions having the same denominator are called fraction with a common denominator. According to the value of the given two fractions they can be called as biggest or largest fractions and the other as the smallest. Here, we are about to study the ascending and descending order and comparison of the fraction with common denominator.

✌ LIKE FRACTION :

❖ Fractions such as $\dfrac{1}{7}, \dfrac{4}{7}, \dfrac{6}{7}$ whose denominators are equal are called 'like fractions'.

❖ Fractions such as $\dfrac{1}{3}, \dfrac{4}{8}, \dfrac{9}{11}$ which have different denominators are called 'unlike fractions'.

● Model Examples ●

Q. Solve the following examples.

1. Write in descending order and tell what fraction comes on 2nd last place ?

① $\dfrac{7}{9}$ ② $\dfrac{4}{9}$ ③ $\dfrac{5}{9}$ ④ $\dfrac{2}{9}$ ❸

2. Which of the following fraction will be in the middle, if they are arranged in the descending order ?

$\dfrac{4}{10}, \dfrac{8}{10}, \dfrac{5}{10}, \dfrac{2}{10}, \dfrac{6}{10}$

① $\dfrac{6}{10}$ ② $\dfrac{4}{10}$ ③ $\dfrac{5}{10}$ ④ $\dfrac{2}{10}$ ❸

3. Arrange the following fractions in ascending order :

$\dfrac{12}{8}, \dfrac{12}{4}, \dfrac{12}{6}, \dfrac{12}{2}, \dfrac{12}{9}, \dfrac{12}{5}$

① $\dfrac{12}{9}, \dfrac{12}{8}, \dfrac{12}{6}, \dfrac{12}{5}, \dfrac{12}{4}, \dfrac{12}{2}$ ② $\dfrac{12}{8}, \dfrac{12}{6}, \dfrac{12}{5}, \dfrac{12}{9}, \dfrac{12}{4}, \dfrac{12}{2}$

③ $\dfrac{12}{8}, \dfrac{12}{4}, \dfrac{12}{6}, \dfrac{12}{2}, \dfrac{12}{9}, \dfrac{12}{5}$ ④ $\dfrac{12}{6}, \dfrac{12}{5}, \dfrac{12}{4}, \dfrac{12}{2}, \dfrac{12}{8}, \dfrac{12}{9}$ ❶

Explanation : Arrange the denominators in descending order we get,

$9 > 8 > 6 > 5 > 4 > 2$

$\therefore \dfrac{12}{9} < \dfrac{12}{8} < \dfrac{12}{6} < \dfrac{12}{5} < \dfrac{12}{4} < \dfrac{12}{2}$

∴ Alternative ❶ is the correct answer.

4. Arrange the following fractions in descending order.

$\dfrac{23}{19}, \dfrac{23}{4}, \dfrac{23}{16}, \dfrac{23}{15}, \dfrac{23}{9}, \dfrac{23}{11}$

① $\dfrac{23}{19} > \dfrac{23}{16} > \dfrac{23}{15} > \dfrac{23}{11} > \dfrac{23}{9}$

② $\dfrac{23}{16} > \dfrac{23}{19} > \dfrac{23}{15} > \dfrac{23}{11} > \dfrac{23}{9}$

③ $\dfrac{23}{15} > \dfrac{23}{16} > \dfrac{23}{15} > \dfrac{23}{11} > \dfrac{23}{9}$

④ $\dfrac{23}{4} > \dfrac{23}{9} > \dfrac{23}{11} > \dfrac{23}{15} > \dfrac{23}{16} > \dfrac{23}{19}$

Explanation : Arrange the denominators in ascending order, we get,

$4 < 9 < 11 < 15 < 16 < 19$

$\therefore \dfrac{23}{4} > \dfrac{23}{9} > \dfrac{23}{11} > \dfrac{23}{15} > \dfrac{23}{16} > \dfrac{23}{19}$

Examples for Practice

Q. *Solve the following examples.*

Which comparing the fractions greater > smaller < and equal to = signs are used.

1. Put the proper sign.

$\dfrac{4}{7} \;\square\; \dfrac{4}{7}$

   ① >   ② <   ③ =   ④ ≥

2. $\dfrac{5}{7} \;\square\; \dfrac{3}{7}$

   ① >   ② <   ③ =   ④ ≥

3. $\dfrac{5}{8}$ ☐ $\dfrac{6}{8}$

  ① >   ② <   ③ =   ④ ≤

4. Which fraction comes in middle when arranged in ascending order ?

$$\dfrac{2}{9}, \dfrac{3}{9}, \dfrac{6}{9}, \dfrac{7}{9}, \dfrac{4}{9}$$

  ① $\dfrac{2}{9}$ ② $\dfrac{3}{9}$ ③ $\dfrac{7}{9}$ ④ $\dfrac{4}{9}$

5. Write the fraction of shaded portion.

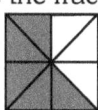

  ① $\dfrac{5}{8}$ ② $\dfrac{4}{8}$

  ③ $\dfrac{2}{8}$ ④ $\dfrac{3}{8}$

Fig. 3.8

6. Write the fraction depicting the portion in the figure.

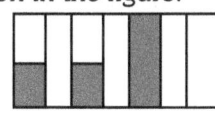

  ① $\dfrac{1}{2}$ ② $\dfrac{3}{7}$

  ③ $\dfrac{2}{7}$ ④ 0

Fig. 3.9

7. Which of the following fractions will be second, if they are arranged in ascending order ?

$$\dfrac{70}{100}, \dfrac{15}{100}, \dfrac{5}{100}, \dfrac{20}{100}, \dfrac{30}{100}$$

  ① $\dfrac{5}{100}$ ② $\dfrac{30}{100}$ ③ $\dfrac{15}{100}$ ④ $\dfrac{20}{100}$

8. Which of the following fractions will be fourth, if they are arranged in descending order ? $\dfrac{4}{9}, \dfrac{3}{9}, \dfrac{6}{9}, \dfrac{5}{9}$

  ① $\dfrac{6}{9}$ ② $\dfrac{5}{9}$ ③ $\dfrac{4}{9}$ ④ $\dfrac{3}{9}$

9. Which of the following fractions will be in the middle, if they are arranged in descending order ?

$$\dfrac{3}{12}, \dfrac{5}{12}, \dfrac{8}{12}, \dfrac{7}{12}, \dfrac{1}{12}$$

  ① $\dfrac{5}{12}$ ② $\dfrac{8}{12}$ ③ $\dfrac{1}{12}$ ④ $\dfrac{7}{12}$

Which sign will you use in the box ?

10. $\dfrac{6}{10}$ ☐ $\dfrac{3}{10}$

    ① <   ② >   ③ =   ④ +

11. $\dfrac{9}{12}$ ☐ $\dfrac{11}{12}$

    ① >   ② =   ③ <   ④ ×

12. $\dfrac{37}{69}$ ☐ $\dfrac{11}{69}$

    ① ×   ② +   ③ <   ④ >

13. $\dfrac{13}{19}$ ☐ $\dfrac{17}{19}$

    ① +   ② ×   ③ ÷   ④ <

Write the shaded part of the fraction after observing the given figures.

14.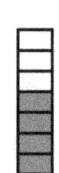

    ① $\dfrac{3}{7}$ ② $\dfrac{7}{7}$

    ③ $\dfrac{4}{7}$ ④ $\dfrac{3}{4}$

Fig. 3.10

15.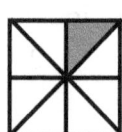

    ① $\dfrac{1}{7}$ ② $\dfrac{1}{8}$

    ③ $\dfrac{8}{1}$ ④ $\dfrac{7}{1}$

Fig. 3.11

16.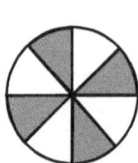

    ① $\dfrac{5}{8}$ ② $\dfrac{4}{4}$

    ③ $\dfrac{4}{8}$ ④ $\dfrac{3}{8}$

Fig. 3.12

17. Convert into like fractions : $\dfrac{3}{4}, \dfrac{5}{8}$

   ① $\dfrac{6}{8}, \dfrac{5}{8}$ ② $\dfrac{12}{16}, \dfrac{5}{8}$ ③ $\dfrac{3}{4}, \dfrac{5}{8}$ ④ $\dfrac{3}{4}, \dfrac{5}{4}$

18. Convert into like fraction : $\dfrac{5}{6}, \dfrac{4}{5}$

   ① $\dfrac{6}{5}, \dfrac{4}{5}$ ② $\dfrac{30}{36}, \dfrac{24}{30}$ ③ $\dfrac{10}{12}, \dfrac{8}{10}$ ④ $\dfrac{25}{30}, \dfrac{24}{30}$

19. $\dfrac{2}{4}, \dfrac{5}{6}$ convert into like fraction.

   ① $\dfrac{6}{12}, \dfrac{10}{12}$ ② $\dfrac{12}{24}, \dfrac{20}{24}$ ③ $\dfrac{4}{16}, \dfrac{10}{16}$ ④ $\dfrac{18}{36}, \dfrac{30}{36}$

20. $\dfrac{4}{6}, \dfrac{3}{9}$ convert into like fraction ?

   ① $\dfrac{24}{36}, \dfrac{12}{36}$ ② $\dfrac{12}{18}, \dfrac{6}{18}$ ③ $\dfrac{36}{56}, \dfrac{18}{56}$ ④ $\dfrac{24}{56}, \dfrac{18}{36}$

21. Arrange the following like fractions in ascending order.

   $\dfrac{15}{38}, \dfrac{7}{38}, \dfrac{24}{38}, \dfrac{32}{38}, \dfrac{21}{38}, \dfrac{16}{38}$

   ① $\dfrac{15}{38}, \dfrac{21}{38}, \dfrac{7}{38}, \dfrac{16}{38}, \dfrac{24}{38}, \dfrac{32}{38}$

   ② $\dfrac{7}{38}, \dfrac{15}{38}, \dfrac{16}{38}, \dfrac{21}{38}, \dfrac{24}{38}, \dfrac{32}{38}$

   ③ $\dfrac{15}{38}, \dfrac{16}{38}, \dfrac{21}{38}, \dfrac{24}{38}, \dfrac{32}{38}, \dfrac{7}{38}$

   ④ $\dfrac{16}{38}, \dfrac{15}{38}, \dfrac{21}{38}, \dfrac{24}{38}, \dfrac{32}{38}, \dfrac{7}{38}$

22. Arrange following unlike fractions in ascending.

   $\dfrac{93}{45}, \dfrac{93}{84}, \dfrac{93}{7}, \dfrac{93}{28}, \dfrac{93}{52}, \dfrac{93}{36}$

   ① $\dfrac{93}{45}, \dfrac{93}{84}, \dfrac{93}{7}, \dfrac{93}{28}, \dfrac{93}{52}, \dfrac{93}{36}$

   ② $\dfrac{93}{84}, \dfrac{93}{45}, \dfrac{93}{52}, \dfrac{93}{28}, \dfrac{93}{36}, \dfrac{93}{7}$

   ③ $\dfrac{93}{84}, \dfrac{93}{52}, \dfrac{93}{45}, \dfrac{93}{36}, \dfrac{93}{28}, \dfrac{93}{7}$

   ④ $\dfrac{93}{7}, \dfrac{93}{84}, \dfrac{93}{45}, \dfrac{93}{52}, \dfrac{93}{36}, \dfrac{93}{28}$

23. Arrange the following like fractions in descending order.

$$\frac{52}{71}, \frac{68}{71}, \frac{44}{71}, \frac{29}{71}, \frac{34}{71}, \frac{63}{71}$$

① $\frac{68}{71}, \frac{63}{71}, \frac{52}{71}, \frac{44}{71}, \frac{34}{71}, \frac{29}{71}$ ② $\frac{63}{71}, \frac{68}{71}, \frac{52}{71}, \frac{44}{71}, \frac{34}{71}, \frac{29}{71}$

③ $\frac{52}{71}, \frac{63}{71}, \frac{68}{71}, \frac{44}{71}, \frac{34}{71}, \frac{29}{71}$ ④ $\frac{44}{71}, \frac{52}{71}, \frac{63}{71}, \frac{68}{71}, \frac{34}{71}, \frac{29}{71}$

24. Arrange the following unlike fractions in descending order.

$$\frac{61}{52}, \frac{61}{43}, \frac{61}{58}, \frac{61}{29}, \frac{61}{37}, \frac{61}{40}$$

① $\frac{61}{37}, \frac{61}{29}, \frac{61}{40}, \frac{61}{43}, \frac{61}{52}, \frac{61}{58}$

② $\frac{61}{29}, \frac{61}{37}, \frac{61}{40}, \frac{61}{43}, \frac{61}{52}, \frac{61}{58}$

③ $\frac{61}{37}, \frac{61}{40}, \frac{61}{43}, \frac{61}{52}, \frac{61}{58}, \frac{61}{29}$

④ $\frac{61}{40}, \frac{61}{43}, \frac{61}{52}, \frac{61}{52}, \frac{61}{58}, \frac{61}{29}, \frac{61}{37}$

25. $\dfrac{2}{5}, \dfrac{9}{25}, \dfrac{3}{5}, \dfrac{11}{25}, \dfrac{18}{25}, \dfrac{12}{15}$

① $\dfrac{2}{5}, \dfrac{9}{25}, \dfrac{3}{5}, \dfrac{18}{25}, \dfrac{12}{15}, \dfrac{11}{25}$

② $\dfrac{12}{15}, \dfrac{2}{5}, \dfrac{9}{25}, \dfrac{3}{5}, \dfrac{11}{25}, \dfrac{12}{15}$

③ $\dfrac{12}{15}, \dfrac{18}{25}, \dfrac{3}{5}, \dfrac{11}{25}, \dfrac{2}{5}, \dfrac{9}{25}$

④ $\dfrac{12}{15}, \dfrac{18}{15}, \dfrac{11}{15}, \dfrac{9}{15}, \dfrac{3}{15}, \dfrac{2}{15}$

Answers

1.	❸	2.	❶	3.	❷	4.	❹	5.	❶
6.	❸	7.	❸	8.	❹	9.	❶	10.	❷
11.	❸	12.	❹	13.	❹	14.	❸	15.	❷
16.	❸	17.	❶	18.	❹	19.	❷	20.	❸
21.	❷	22.	❸	23.	❶	24.	❷	25.	❸

(IV) Addition & Subtractions of Fractions with Equal and Unequal Denominators

✌ INTRODUCTION :

Equal Denominators

Only the numerators of the fractions should be added. The denominator remains the same. The denominators should not be added. The subtraction should be limited to numerators only. The denominator remains the same. Subtraction should not be carried out of the denominators.

Fig. 3.13

There are two rectangular strips shown in the figure. Each strip is divided into five equal parts.

The part that is coloured in the first strip denotes the fraction $\frac{2}{5}$ and in the second strip denotes the fraction $\frac{2}{5}$. 2 parts from the first strip and 2 parts from the second strip. In all 4 parts out of 5 equal parts. So, $\frac{2}{5} + \frac{2}{5} = \frac{4}{5}$. Now if 1 uncoloured part is removed from 4 uncoloured parts. 3 parts remain the same. $\frac{4}{5} - \frac{1}{5} = \frac{3}{5}$

Unequal Denominators :

Fig. 3.14

The part that is coloured in the first strip denotes the fraction $\frac{3}{4}$ i.e. three parts from 4 and the part that is coloured in the second strip denotes the fraction $\frac{2}{5}$ i.e. 2 parts from 5.

∴ In all coloured parts are $\frac{3}{4} + \frac{2}{5}$.

Here the denominators are unequal. Now we make the denominators equal to 20. Multiply $\frac{3}{4}$ by 5 and $\frac{2}{5}$ by 4.

∴ First we find L.C.M. of denominator

$\because$ L.C.M. $= 4 \times 5 = 20$

$\therefore$ $\dfrac{3 \times 5}{4 \times 5} = \dfrac{15}{20}$

and $\dfrac{2 \times 4}{5 \times 4} = \dfrac{8}{20}$

$\therefore$ $\dfrac{15}{20} + \dfrac{8}{20} = \dfrac{15 + 8}{20} = \dfrac{23}{20}$

Model Examples

Q. Solve the following :

1. $\dfrac{1}{5} + \dfrac{2}{5} =$

   ① $\dfrac{3}{5}$ ② $\dfrac{2}{5}$ ③ $\dfrac{3}{10}$ ④ $\dfrac{1}{10}$ ❶

   Explanation : $\dfrac{1 + 2}{5} = \dfrac{3}{5}$

2. $\dfrac{4}{8} - \dfrac{2}{8} =$

   ① $\dfrac{3}{8}$ ② $\dfrac{8}{4}$ ③ $\dfrac{2}{8}$ ④ $\dfrac{1}{2}$ ❸

   Explanation : $\dfrac{4 - 2}{8} = \dfrac{2}{8}$

3. $\dfrac{3}{5} + \dfrac{1}{5} =$

   ① $\dfrac{3}{5}$ ② $\dfrac{2}{5}$ ③ $\dfrac{4}{5}$ ④ $\dfrac{1}{5}$ ❸

   Explanation : $\dfrac{3 + 1}{5} = \dfrac{4}{5}$

4. $\dfrac{5}{7} - \dfrac{4}{7} =$

   ① $\dfrac{2}{7}$ ② $\dfrac{1}{7}$ ③ $\dfrac{9}{7}$ ④ $\dfrac{3}{7}$ ❷

   Explanation : $\dfrac{5}{7} - \dfrac{4}{7}$

                 $= \dfrac{5 - 4}{7} = \dfrac{1}{7}$

5. $\dfrac{5}{2} + \dfrac{3}{4}$

  ① $\dfrac{11}{4}$ ② $\dfrac{13}{4}$ ③ $\dfrac{6}{4}$ ④ $\dfrac{14}{4}$

Explanation : Here the denominators are unequal. First we make them equal.

Multiply $\dfrac{5}{2}$ by 2

$\therefore \qquad\qquad \dfrac{5 \times 2}{2 \times 2} = \dfrac{10}{4}$

$\therefore \qquad\qquad \dfrac{10}{4} + \dfrac{3}{4} = \dfrac{10 + 3}{4} = \dfrac{13}{4}$

6. $\dfrac{8}{3} - \dfrac{2}{8}$

  ① $\dfrac{57}{24}$ ② $\dfrac{58}{24}$ ③ $\dfrac{59}{24}$ ④ $\dfrac{56}{24}$

Explanation : Here, the denominators are not equal. First we will make them equal.

Multiply $\dfrac{8}{3}$ by 8 and $\dfrac{2}{8}$ by 3.

$\therefore \qquad\qquad \dfrac{8 \times 8}{3 \times 8} = \dfrac{64}{24}$

$\therefore \qquad\qquad \dfrac{2 \times 3}{8 \times 3} = \dfrac{6}{24}$

$\therefore \qquad\qquad \dfrac{64}{24} - \dfrac{6}{24} = \dfrac{64 - 6}{24} = \dfrac{58}{24}$

Examples for Practice

Q. Solve the following examples :

1. $\dfrac{3}{8} + \dfrac{4}{8} =$

  ① $\dfrac{8}{7}$ ② $\dfrac{1}{8}$ ③ $\dfrac{7}{8}$ ④ $\dfrac{8}{1}$

2. $\dfrac{5}{7} + \dfrac{1}{7} =$

  ① $\dfrac{5}{7}$ ② $\dfrac{6}{7}$ ③ $\dfrac{4}{7}$ ④ $\dfrac{7}{6}$

3. $\dfrac{6}{9} + \dfrac{2}{9} =$

① $\dfrac{8}{9}$ ② $\dfrac{7}{9}$ ③ $\dfrac{6}{9}$ ④ $\dfrac{2}{9}$

4. $\dfrac{3}{8} + \dfrac{1}{8} =$

① $\dfrac{4}{8}$ ② $\dfrac{8}{8}$ ③ $\dfrac{3}{8}$ ④ $\dfrac{1}{8}$

5. $\dfrac{7}{8} - \dfrac{3}{8} =$

① $\dfrac{2}{8}$ ② $\dfrac{4}{16}$ ③ $\dfrac{7}{8}$ ④ $\dfrac{4}{8}$

6. $\dfrac{5}{9} - \dfrac{2}{9} =$

① $\dfrac{2}{9}$ ② $\dfrac{4}{9}$ ③ $\dfrac{3}{9}$ ④ $\dfrac{1}{9}$

7. $\dfrac{7}{8} - \dfrac{1}{8} =$

① $\dfrac{1}{8}$ ② $\dfrac{2}{8}$ ③ $\dfrac{4}{8}$ ④ $\dfrac{6}{8}$

8. $\dfrac{7}{9} - \dfrac{5}{9} =$

① $\dfrac{1}{9}$ ② $\dfrac{2}{9}$ ③ $\dfrac{3}{9}$ ④ $\dfrac{4}{9}$

9. $\dfrac{8}{15} + \dfrac{4}{15} =$

① $\dfrac{10}{15}$ ② $\dfrac{12}{30}$ ③ $\dfrac{12}{15}$ ④ $\dfrac{12}{10}$

10. $\dfrac{9}{17} - \dfrac{5}{17} =$

① $\dfrac{5}{17}$ ② $\dfrac{4}{34}$ ③ $\dfrac{9}{34}$ ④ $\dfrac{4}{17}$

11. $\dfrac{9}{16} - \dfrac{7}{16} =$

① $\dfrac{16}{16}$ ② $\dfrac{2}{16}$ ③ 1 ④ $\dfrac{16}{2}$

12. $\frac{9}{11} + \frac{1}{11} =$

① $\frac{10}{11}$ ② $\frac{8}{11}$ ③ $\frac{11}{11}$ ④ $\frac{9}{11}$

13. $\frac{1}{2} - \frac{1}{2} =$

① 0   ② 1   ③ $\frac{1}{2}$ ④ $\frac{2}{1}$

14. $\frac{7}{13} - \frac{5}{13} =$

① $\frac{12}{13}$ ② $\frac{7}{13}$ ③ $\frac{2}{13}$ ④ $\frac{1}{13}$

15. $\frac{4}{9} + \frac{2}{9} =$

① $\frac{2}{9}$ ② $\frac{4}{9}$ ③ $\frac{9}{9}$ ④ $\frac{6}{9}$

16. $\frac{3}{5} - \frac{1}{5} =$

① $\frac{1}{5}$ ② $\frac{3}{5}$ ③ $\frac{2}{5}$ ④ $\frac{4}{5}$

17. $\frac{9}{16} + \frac{5}{16} =$

① $\frac{14}{16}$ ② $\frac{15}{16}$ ③ $\frac{16}{16}$ ④ 1

18. $\frac{6}{8} + \frac{1}{8} =$

① $\frac{8}{8}$ ② 1   ③ $\frac{7}{8}$ ④ $\frac{8}{7}$

19. $\frac{6}{13} - \frac{4}{13} =$

① $\frac{6}{13}$ ② $\frac{13}{2}$ ③ $\frac{4}{13}$ ④ $\frac{2}{13}$

20. $\frac{20}{38} + \frac{8}{38} =$

① $\frac{38}{38}$ ② $\frac{28}{38}$ ③ $\frac{20}{38}$ ④ $\frac{8}{38}$

21. $\frac{3}{10} + \frac{5}{10} + \frac{1}{10} = ?$

① $\frac{10}{9}$ ② $\frac{30}{9}$ ③ $\frac{9}{30}$ ④ $\frac{9}{10}$

22. $\frac{6}{24} + \frac{8}{24} + \frac{9}{24} = ?$

① $\frac{22}{24}$ ② $\frac{23}{24}$ ③ $\frac{24}{24}$ ④ 1

23. Add $\frac{1}{8} + \frac{3}{4} = ?$

① $\frac{4}{32}$ ② $\frac{4}{12}$ ③ $\frac{7}{8}$ ④ $\frac{4}{8}$

24. $\frac{4}{5} - \frac{5}{8} = ?$

① $\frac{7}{40}$ ② $\frac{1}{8}$ ③ $\frac{1}{3}$ ④ $\frac{5}{8}$

25. $\frac{6}{14} - \frac{2}{7} = ?$

① $\frac{2}{7}$ ② $\frac{4}{14}$ ③ $\frac{4}{7}$ ④ $\frac{2}{14}$

26. $\frac{2}{21} + \frac{3}{7} = ?$

① $\frac{5}{28}$ ② $\frac{11}{21}$ ③ $\frac{5}{21}$ ④ $\frac{5}{7}$

27. $\frac{2}{3} + \frac{1}{4}$

① $\frac{10}{12}$ ② $\frac{11}{12}$ ③ $\frac{12}{11}$ ④ $\frac{15}{4}$

28. $\frac{5}{9} + \frac{3}{2}$

① $\frac{27}{18}$ ② $\frac{38}{18}$ ③ $\frac{37}{18}$ ④ $\frac{29}{18}$

29. $\frac{3}{7} + \frac{5}{11}$

① $\frac{68}{77}$ ② $\frac{68}{78}$ ③ $\frac{68}{11}$ ④ $\frac{8}{7}$

30. $\dfrac{1}{2} + \dfrac{3}{5}$

   ① $\dfrac{12}{10}$ ② $\dfrac{11}{2}$ ③ $\dfrac{11}{5}$ ④ $\dfrac{11}{10}$

31. $\dfrac{13}{20} + \dfrac{8}{15} = ?$

   ① $\dfrac{71}{60}$ ② $\dfrac{70}{60}$ ③ $\dfrac{67}{60}$ ④ $\dfrac{69}{60}$

32. $\dfrac{13}{45} - \dfrac{11}{25}$

   ① $\dfrac{63}{225}$ ② $\dfrac{43}{225}$ ③ $\dfrac{34}{225}$ ④ $\dfrac{53}{225}$

33. $6 + \dfrac{7}{9} = ?$

   ① $\dfrac{47}{9}$ ② $\dfrac{48}{9}$ ③ $\dfrac{57}{9}$ ④ $\dfrac{67}{9}$

34. $4 - \dfrac{11}{13} = ?$

   ① $\dfrac{47}{13}$ ② $\dfrac{41}{13}$ ③ $\dfrac{14}{13}$ ④ $\dfrac{42}{13}$

Answers

1.	③	2.	②	3.	①	4.	①	5.	④
6.	③	7.	④	8.	②	9.	③	10.	④
11.	②	12.	①	13.	①	14.	③	15.	④
16.	③	17.	①	18.	③	19.	④	20.	③
21.	④	22.	②	23.	③	24.	①	25.	④
26.	②	27.	②	28.	③	29.	①	30.	④
31.	①	32.	③	33.	①	34.	②		

(B) PROPER, IMPROPER AND MIXED FRACTION, THEIR CONVERSION

A mixed fraction is a whole number and a fraction combined into one mixed number.

Example : $1\dfrac{1}{2}$ is a mixed number. Mixed fraction is also known as Improper fraction. To convert a mixed fraction to an improper fraction we need to follow these steps:

1. Multiply the whole number part by the fraction's denominator.
2. Add that to the numerator.
3. Write the result on top of the denominator.

For example : Convert $\dfrac{33}{5}$ to an improper fraction.

1. Multiply the whole number by the denominator: 3×5
2. Add the numerator to that: $15 + 2 = 17$
3. Then write down above the denominator, like this : $\dfrac{17}{5}$

Examples for Practice

1. $2\dfrac{1}{7}$ is the mixed fraction of

   ① $\dfrac{15}{7}$ ② $\dfrac{22}{7}$ ③ $\dfrac{8}{7}$ ④ $\dfrac{16}{7}$

2. .... is the mixed fraction of $\dfrac{64}{12}$

   ① $6\dfrac{4}{12}$ ② $5\dfrac{4}{12}$ ③ $7\dfrac{4}{12}$ ④ $4\dfrac{4}{12}$

3. Mixed fraction of $\dfrac{108}{15}$ is ....

   ① $9\dfrac{3}{15}$ ② $7\dfrac{3}{15}$ ③ $8\dfrac{3}{15}$ ④ $6\dfrac{3}{15}$

4. .... is the mixed fraction of $\dfrac{148}{18}$.

   ① $8\dfrac{4}{18}$ ② $7\dfrac{4}{18}$ ③ $9\dfrac{4}{18}$ ④ $8\dfrac{8}{18}$

5. $6\dfrac{4}{16}$ is the mixed fraction of............

   ① $\dfrac{104}{16}$ ② $\dfrac{106}{16}$ ③ $\dfrac{100}{16}$ ④ $\dfrac{102}{16}$

6. $\dfrac{85}{9}$ =

   ① $9\dfrac{5}{9}$ ② $9\dfrac{6}{9}$ ③ $8\dfrac{4}{9}$ ④ $9\dfrac{4}{9}$

7. $6\frac{4}{11}$ =

① $\frac{72}{11}$　　② $\frac{68}{11}$　　③ $\frac{66}{11}$　　④ $\frac{70}{11}$

8. $\frac{128}{14}$ =

① $9\frac{2}{14}$　　② $9\frac{4}{14}$　　③ $9\frac{3}{14}$　　④ $9\frac{5}{14}$

9. $9\frac{8}{10}$ =

① $\frac{88}{10}$　　② $\frac{96}{10}$　　③ $\frac{98}{10}$　　④ $\frac{94}{10}$

10. $\frac{108}{13}$ =

① $9\frac{4}{13}$　　② $8\frac{4}{13}$　　③ $7\frac{8}{13}$　　④ $8\frac{6}{13}$

11. $6\frac{5}{17}$ =

① $\frac{102}{17}$　　② $\frac{100}{17}$　　③ $\frac{107}{17}$　　④ $\frac{109}{17}$

12. What is $\frac{1}{3}$ of 21 balloons ?

① 7　　② 14　　③ 3　　④ 9

13. What is $\frac{1}{5}$ of 30 km ?

① 15 km　　② 5 km　　③ 12 km　　④ 6 km

14. What is the answer $\frac{3}{8}$ of 64 ?

① 30　　② 24　　③ 48　　④ 12

15. $\frac{5}{13}$ of 65 ?

① 25　　② 26　　③ 39　　④ 30

16. $\frac{2}{3}$ of 21 ?

① 63　　② 42　　③ 14　　④ 7

17. $\frac{2}{3}$ of 30 ?

① 90　　② 60　　③ 10　　④ 20

18. $\frac{4}{5}$ of 60 ?

    ① 30   ② 48   ③ 12   ④ 36

19. $\frac{3}{5}$ of 80 ?

    ① 48   ② 16   ③ 12   ④ 60

20. $\frac{7}{11}$ of 33 ?

    ① 11   ② 14   ③ 21   ④ 22

Answers

1.	❶	2.	❷	3.	❷	4.	❶	5.	❸
6.	❹	7.	❹	8.	❶	9.	❸	10.	❷
11.	❸	12.	❶	13.	❹	14.	❷	15.	❶
16.	❸	17.	❹	18.	❷	19.	❶	20.	❸

(C) EQUIVALENT FRACTION

•❖ If one apple is divided equally between two people, each one will get half apple. The fraction is written as $\frac{1}{2}$. Here 1 is the numerator and 2 is the denominator.

Fig. 3.15

•❖ One chapatti was divided into four equal parts. Two of the parts were given away. This is shown as $\frac{2}{4}$. Here 2 is the numerator and 4 is the denominator. This also means that half of the chapatti was given.

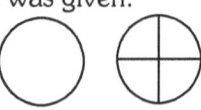

Fig. 3.16

⚫◆ Six equal parts were made of one musk melon. They were shared equally by two peoples. It means that the part that each one got was $\frac{3}{6}$. Each one got half the melon. Thus $\frac{3}{6}$ also shows the fraction 'one half'.

In the above examples, the fraction half has been shown by $\frac{1}{2}, \frac{2}{4}, \frac{3}{6}$ respectively. This means that the value of all the three fractions is the same. This is written as $\frac{1}{2} = \frac{2}{4} = \frac{3}{6}$.

Such fractions of equal value are called equivalent fractions.

⚫◆ When the numerator and denominator of a fraction are multiplied by the same number we get a fraction that is equivalent to the given fraction.

⚫◆ If the numerator and denominator have a common divisor then the fraction we get on dividing them by that divisor is equivalent to the given fraction.

────────────── **Model Examples** ──────────────

1. $\frac{1}{2} = \frac{\square}{20}$

   ① 10   ② 5   ③ 15   ④ 20   ❶

   Explanation : $\frac{1 \times 10}{2 \times 10} = \frac{10}{20}$

   ∴ Alternative ❶ is the correct answer.

2. $\frac{2}{5} = \frac{10}{\square}$

   ① 30   ② 26   ③ 25   ④ 35   ❸

   Explanation : $\frac{2 \times 5}{5 \times 5} = \frac{10}{\boxed{25}}$

   ∴ Alternative ❸ is the correct answer.

────────────── **Examples for Practice** ──────────────

1. $\frac{2}{3} = \frac{\square}{18}$

   ① 3   ② 24   ③ 6   ④ 12

2. Find two equivalent fraction for $\frac{7}{9}$.

① $\frac{14}{18}, \frac{18}{14}$ ② $\frac{14}{18}, \frac{21}{27}$ ③ $\frac{21}{27}, \frac{27}{21}$ ④ $\frac{14}{18}, \frac{21}{36}$

3. $\frac{4}{\square} = \frac{24}{42}$

① 12   ② 21   ③ 7   ④ 6

4. Find the correct pair of equivalent fraction.

① $\frac{2}{3}, \frac{7}{9}$ ② $\frac{7}{9}, \frac{15}{33}$ ③ $\frac{10}{14}, \frac{5}{8}$ ④ $\frac{2}{3}, \frac{18}{27}$

5. $\frac{24}{26} = \frac{12}{\square}$

① 11   ② 13   ③ 52   ④ 14

Answers

1.	④	2.	②	3.	③	4.	④	5.	②

❖ ❖ ❖

3.2   *DECIMAL FRACTIONS*

✌ INTRODUCTION :

A fraction whose denominator is 10, 100 or 1000 or any other ten times multiple of 10 is called decimal fraction. Both fractions and decimals are interrelated with each other. Both fractions and decimals mean a part of a whole number (quantity in general).

For example, $\frac{5}{10}, \frac{88}{100}, \frac{249}{1000}$. These fractions are written in the numerator and denominator form. It is easy to write these fractions in another way. To use this method, let us took at our usual method of writing numbers. In this method, we make new places for tens, hundreds, thousand and so on. The place value of each of these is 10 times that of the previous place. For example, one ten equals 10 units, one hundred equals 10 tens.

Decimal Point and Decimal Part : 1534.578

	Thousands	Hundreds	Tens	Ones	Tenths	Hundredth	Thousandths
Digits	1	5	3	4	5	7	8
Place value	1×1000	5×100	3×10	4×1	$5 \times \dfrac{1}{10}$	$7 \times \dfrac{1}{100}$	$8 \times \dfrac{1}{1000}$
Value	1000	500	30	4	0.5	0.07	0.008

This number 1534.578 can be written as $\dfrac{1534578}{1000}$. This means that when a number leaves a remainder on being divided, the remainder forms the decimal part.

Fractional part, which is separated from the whole number by means of a dot (known as decimal point) is known as decimal part.

A decimal point separates the whole number from a fraction that is less than 1.

Decimal part, after the decimal point is read digit-by-digit starting from the left most digit immediately after the decimal point $\dfrac{1}{10}$ is read as one tenth in fraction from.

Fractioned Number	Fraction Form	Decimal Form	Read As
1 tenth	$\dfrac{1}{10}$	0.1	Point one
9 tenth	$\dfrac{9}{10}$	0.9	Point nine
1 hundredth	$\dfrac{1}{100}$	0.01	Point zero one
8 hundredth	$\dfrac{8}{100}$	0.08	Point zero eight
1 thousandths	$\dfrac{1}{1000}$	0.001	Point zero zero one
66 thousandths	$\dfrac{66}{1000}$	0.066	Point zero six six

Study the table given below :

100 paise = 1 rupee	100 cm = 1 m
1 paise = $\frac{1}{100}$ rupee = 0.01 rupee	1 cm = $\frac{1}{100}$ m = 0.01 m
40 paise = $\frac{40}{100}$ rupee = 0.40 rupee	25 cm = $\frac{25}{100}$ m = 0.25 m
80 paise = $\frac{80}{100}$ rupee = 0.80 rupee	70 cm = $\frac{70}{100}$ m = 0.70 m = 0.7 m
1 rupee = 100 paise	1 m = 100 cm
7 rupees = 700 paise	7 m = 700 cm
0.60 rupee = 0.6 rupee = 60 paise	0.4 m = 40 cm 0.50 m = 50 cm
0.08 rupee = 8 paise	3.75 m = 3 m 75 cm
6.5 rupees = 6 rupees 50 paise	17.8 m = 17 m 80 cm
19.75 rupee = 19 rupees 75 paise	

Writing half, quarter, three quarter and one a quarter in decimal form.

Half is usually written as $\frac{1}{2}$. To convert this fraction into decimal form, the denominator of $\frac{1}{2}$ must be converted into an equivalent fraction with denominator 10. $\frac{1}{2} = \frac{1 \times 5}{2 \times 5} = \frac{5}{10}$ the decimal form of $\frac{1}{2}$ will be $\frac{5}{10}$ or 0.5.

Just as $\frac{1}{2} = \frac{1 \times 5}{2 \times 5} = \frac{5}{10} = 0.5$

Note that $\frac{1}{2} = \frac{1 \times 50}{2 \times 50} = \frac{50}{100} = 0.50$

Therefore, 'half' is written as '0.5' or '0.50'. Quarter and three quarters are written as $\frac{1}{4}$ and $\frac{3}{4}$ respectively.

Let us, convert $\frac{1}{4}$ into decimal fraction 10 is not divisible fraction

10 is not divisible by 4. Therefore, the denominators of $\frac{1}{4}$ and $\frac{3}{4}$ cannot be made into fractions with multiples of 10.

Therefore, $4 \times 25 = 100$, so the denominator can be 100.

A quarter $= \frac{1}{4} = \frac{1 \times 25}{4 \times 25} = \frac{25}{100} = 0.25$

Three quarters $= \frac{3}{4} = \frac{3 \times 25}{4 \times 25} = \frac{75}{100} = 0.75$

Model Examples

1. $3\frac{9}{10}$ is read as ………

   ① Three point nine   ② Three nine upon ten

   ③ Three point ten   ④ Three point ninety   ❶

2. $27\frac{9}{10}$ is read as   ❸

   ① Twenty seven point ten   ② Twenty seven point ninety

   ③ Twenty seven point nine ④ Twenty seven nine upon ten

Examples for Practice

1. $\frac{53}{100}$ is read as …………

   ① Fifty three upon hundred ②   zero point five two

   ③ zero point fifty three   ④   zero point zero five two

2. $\frac{78}{1000} = ?$

   ① zero point seven eight

   ② zero point zero seventy eight

   ③ zero point seventy eight

   ④ zero point zero seven eight

3. $8\dfrac{9}{1000} = ?$

    ① Eight point zero, zero nine

    ② Eight point zero nine

    ③ Eight point zero nine zero

    ④ Eighty point zero zero nine

4. 6.13 is read as

    ① six point thirteen   ② six point thirty

    ③ six point one three   ④ six hundred and thirteen

5. How many rupees and how many paise is ₹ 58.75 ?

    ① 58 point 75

    ② 58 rupees 75 paise

    ③ five thousand eight hundred and seventy five

    ④ 5 rupees and 875 paise

6. 1 m 60 cm how many metres in decimal form

    ① 1.06 m   ② 10.6 m   ③ 1.600 m   ④ 1.60 m

7. How many centimeters in decimal form is 144 mm ?

    ① 14.4 cm   ② 0.144 cm

    ③ 1.044 cm   ④ 10.44 cm

8. How many rupees in decimal form is 22 rupees 4 paise ?

    ① 22.040 rupees   ② 22.40 rupees

    ③ 2.04 rupees   ④ 22.04 rupees

9. What is one and a quarter metre and two and a half metre in decimal fraction ?

    ① $1\dfrac{3}{4} + 2\dfrac{1}{2}$ ② $2\dfrac{1}{4} + 2\dfrac{1}{2}$

    ③ $1\dfrac{1}{4} + 2\dfrac{1}{2}$ ④ $1\dfrac{1}{2} + 2\dfrac{1}{2}$

10. 35.74 + 816.6 = ?

    ① 852.34   ② 116.130   ③ 841.34   ④ 812.34

11. ₹ 5159.80 + ₹ 1562.28 = ?
    ① ₹ 6722.80   ② ₹ 6722.08
    ③ ₹ 6612.08   ④ ₹ 6712.08

12. 54.7 m + 1939.45 m =
    ① 148.645 m   ② 1993.15 m
    ③ 1994.115 m   ④ 1994.15 m

13. 64.45 – 45.8 =
    ① 18.65   ② 18.37   ③ 18.56   ④ 186.5

14. 206.36 – 168.9 =
    ① 37.27   ② 37.45   ③ 37.46   ④ 37.046

15. Raja was 1.50 m tall. After a year his height became 1.56 m. How many centimeters did his height increase in a year ?
    ① 6 m   ② 6 cm   ③ 0.6 m   ④ 0.006 m

16. Find biggest decimal number from the given alternatives ?
    ① 0.008   ② 0.0008   ③ 0.8   ④ 0.08

17. Find the smallest decimal number from the given alternatives ?
    ① 0.00005 ② 0.0002   ③ 0.0003   ④ 0.0005

18. What is the difference between the place value of digit 8 in given number 58.86 ?
    ① 0.72   ② 7.2   ③ 0.72   ④ 0.072

Answers

1.	❷	2.	❹	3.	❶	4.	❸	5.	❷
6.	❹	7.	❷	8.	❹	9.	❸	10.	❶
11.	❷	12.	❹	13.	❶	14.	❸	15.	❷
16.	❸	17.	❶	18.	❷						

❖ ❖ ❖

MEASUREMENT/ MENSURATION

LENGTH, MASS (WEIGHT), VOLUME AND CAPACITY

LENGTH

✌ *INTRODUCTION :*

Length : We write the measurement of length in millimeters, centremetres, metre, kilometre.

1 centimetres (cm)   =   10 millimetres (mm)

1 metres (m)   =   100 centimetres (cm)

∴   25 cm   =   0.25 m

1 kilometre (km)   =   1000 metres (m)

When writing metres-centimetres using a decimal point, metres are written to the left of the decimal point and centrimetres to the right. If a decimal point is used metres-centimetres get converted into metres alone.

For example, 8 m 25 cm = 8.25 m.

For example :

The timetable below lists the places between Pune and Ahmednagar and their distances in kilometers. Study it and answer the following questions.

Pune	Sanaswadi	Shikrapur	Ranjangaon	Shirur	Supa	Ahmednagar
0	30	35	40	65	97	122

1. How far is Ranjangaon from Pune ?
   ① 40   ② 35   ③ 65   ④ 30   ❶

2. What is the distance between Shirur and Supa ?
   ① 30 km   ② 32 km   ③ 35 km   ④ 37 km   ❷

3. What is the distance between Shikrapur and Supa ?
   ① 62 km   ② 65 km   ③ 97 km   ④ 35 km   ❶

━━━ **Model Examples** ━━━

Q. Solve the following examples.

1. How many kilometres are equal to 6874 metres ?

   ① 86.74 km   ② 68.74 km   ③ 6.874 km   ④ 687.4 km   ❸

   Explanation : $\dfrac{6874}{1000} = 6.874$ km

   ∴ Alternative ❸ is the correct answer.

2. How many pieces each of 2 cm can be cut out from a ribbon 1.80 metres long ?

   ① 9   ② 36   ③ 180   ④ 90   ❹

   Explanation : Convert 1.80 metres into cm

   i.e. $1.80 \times 100 = 180$ cm

   $$= \dfrac{180 \text{ cm}}{2} = 90 \text{ pieces.}$$

   ∴ Alternative ❹ is the correct answer.

3. How many kilometres are equal to 5 km and 40 metres ?

   ① 5.04 km   ② 5.40 km   ③ 15.400 km ④ 5.004 km   ❶

   Explanation :

   5 km and 40 mts. $= 5 \times 1000 + 40$ mt $= 5040$

   $$= 5.04 \text{ km.}$$

   ∴ Alternative ❶ is the correct answer.

4. If a tailor cuts 2 m and 25 cm from a piece of cloth 5 m long. How much cloth is left over ?

   ① 2 m. 25 cm   ② 2 m. 75 cm

   ③ 3.25 m   ④ 2.00 m   ❷

5. Mr. Kumar travelled 475 km by train, 56 km 975 m by car and 20 km, 720 m by scooter. What is the total distance that he covered ?

   ① 475.975   ② 531.975   ③ 552.695   ④ 695.975   ❸

6. Total length of a road is 2 kms out of which 1400 metres have been completed. How much road is left incomplete ?

   ① 800 m   ② 600 m   ③ 400 m   ④ 200 m   ❷

7. A tailor used 1.20 metre cloth and 80 cm cloth is left behind. What is the total length of the cloth ?

    ① 2 m   ② 20 m   ③ 200 m   ④ 0.2 m   ❶

8. Length of a segment is 12 cm and 5 mm. It is cut into pieces of 5 mm length. How many segments can be obtained ?

    ① 125   ② 5   ③ 20   ④ 25   ❹

9. $\frac{1}{8}$ km = How many metres ?

    ① 120 m   ② 125 m   ③ 1250 m   ④ 250 m   ❷

10. How many km of wire will be needed if a 225 m long and 150 m wide ground is to be fenced three times over ?

    ① 3 km   ② 1.8 km   ③ 2.25 km   ④ 2 km   ❸

11. The distance 40.04 km = How much ?

    ① 40 km 4 m   ② 40 km 40 m
    ③ 404 km   ④ 44 km   ❷

12. If trees have to be planted along the Pune-Nashik road at a uniform distance of 10 m, how many trees will be needed to cover a 7.5 km long road on both the sides ?

    ① 1548   ② 1401   ③ 751   ④ 1502   ❹

13. Saplings have to be planted at a uniform distance of 3 m along a 84 m row. What is the maximum number of saplings that can be planted ?

    ① 30   ② 29   ③ 28   ④ 27   ❷

14. Which of the following is the maximum distance ?

    ① Three quarters of a metre ② 0.2 decametre
    ③ 700 cm   ④ 1 m   ❸

15. Govinda walks 84 m when he walks around a rectangular field. If the length of the field is 24 m, its breadth is ......

    ① 18 m   ② 16 m   ③ 14 m   ④ 21 m   ❶

16. A field is in the form of an equilateral triangle. It requires 54 m of wire to make a three-turns fencing around its boundary. Find the length of its side.

    ① 18 m   ② 6 m   ③ 9 m   ④ 27 m   ❷

17. Saplings are planted on the one side of a road 250 m apart. Hence, the distance between the first and the twenty-fifth sapling is ......
    ① 6 km   ② 6.25 km   ③ 6,250 km   ④ 6,000 km   ❶

18. How much wire is used if 2 km 25 m wire out of 5 km wire remains unused ?
    ① 3 km 875 m   ② 2 km 975 m
    ③ 4 km 795 m   ④ 3 km 975 m   ❷

19. If a 30 m rope is cut at five places making equal parts, then what will be the length of each part ?
    ① 60 cm   ② 5 m   ③ 50 cm   ④ 600 cm   ❹

20. 3 m and 85 cm = ?
    ① 300.85 m ② 30.85 m   ③ 3.85 m   ④ 0.385 m   ❸

21. 13 metres and 75 cm = ? metres
    ① 13.75   ② 137.5   ③ 1.375   ④ 0.1375   ❶

22. 4 metres 5 cm + 1.35 metres = ?
    ① 5.4 metres   ② 0.54 metres
    ③ 0.054 metres   ④ 0.0054 metres   ❶

23. How many metres are there in 1002 cm ?
    ① 100.2 metres   ② 10.02 metres
    ③ 1.002 metres   ④ 100.002 metres   ❷

24. How many metres are equal to 4903 cms ?
    ① 4.903 metres   ② 490.3 metres
    ③ 49.03 metres   ④ 0.4903 metre   ❸

25. 89 km. and 92 metres = How many metres ?
    ① 89.092 metres   ② 89,092 metres
    ③ 8.992 metres   ④ 899.2 metres   ❷

26. How many cms make one and a quarter metre ?
    ① 175   ② 150   ③ 125   ④ 225   ❸

27. Which of the following is the least distance ?
    ① Half and a quarter metre   ② 72 cm
    ③ 0.8 m   ④ 730 mm   ❷

Examples for Practice

Q. *Solve the following examples.*

1. The station was 10 km. from Hari's house. He walked 7 km. 985 m. and sat down. How much distance remained to be covered ?
   ① 2 km. 15 m　　　　② 3 km. 85 m
   ③ 2 km. 85 m　　　　④ 1 km. 15 m

2. How many pieces each of length 5 cm. long can be cut from a bundle of ribbon having length 1.35 metres ?
   ① 37　　　② 27　　　③ 270　　　④ 180

3. In which of the following pairs is one unit $\dfrac{1}{1000}$ times the other.
   ① Metre-Kilometer　　　② Gram - Hectogram
   ③ Gram - Decigram　　　④ Gram - Decagram

4. Trees are to be planted on the border of a square ground having perimeter 4000 metres. Distance between two trees is 40 metre. How many trees can be planted ?
   ① 99　　　② 400　　　③ 100　　　④ 1000

5. Trees are to be planted on both sides of the road 7.5 km. in length. Distance between two plants is 150 metres. How many trees can be planted ?
   ① 100　　　② 102　　　③ 50　　　④ 200

6. 1 cm. = how many metres ?
   ① 0.1 m　　② 0.01 m　　③ 0.001 m　　④ 0.0001 m

7. The depth of a tank is 88 cm. There is water in the tank upto 3/8 of the depth of the tank. Find the depth of water in the tank in centimeters ?
   ① 60　　　② 88　　　③ 55　　　④ 33

8. If trees are to be planted at a distance of every 30 metres on both sides of the road. What will be the total number of trees required for the road 3 kms long ?
   ① 101　　　② 100　　　③ 200　　　④ 202

9. How many metres are there in 20 km and 85 m ?
   ① 285   ② 2,850   ③ 20,085   ④ 28,500

10. How many metres are there in 7 km and 200 m ?
   ① 72   ② 720   ③ 7,200   ④ 72,000

11. How many centimetres are there in 2 metre and 25 cm ?
   ① 2.25   ② 225   ③ 2,250   ④ 22,500

12. 805 cm means how many metres ?
   ① 8.5   ② 0.85   ③ 850   ④ 8.05

13. How many metres are there in 405 cm ?
   ① 45   ② 4.5   ③ 4.05   ④ 40.5

14. How many km are there in 9275 m. ?
   ① 927.5   ② 92.75   ③ 9.275   ④ 90.275

15. 5 metres make ……… cm.
   ① 50 cm   ② 5000 cm   ③ 500 cm   ④ 5 cm

16. 2 km. 300 m. = ……… m.
   ① 2,300 m   ② 20,300 m   ③ 230 m   ④ 23,000 m

17. 8560 m. = ……… km. ……… m.
   ① 85 km. 60 m   ② 80 km. 560 m
   ③ 8 km. 560 m   ④ 8 km. 5,600 m

18. 29 m. 45 cm. = ……… cm.
   ① 2,945 cm.   ② 29,0045 cm.
   ③ 29,450 cm.   ④ 29,045 cm.

19. A 60 cm long string is cut into 6 equal parts. What is the length of each part ?
   ① 16 cm   ② 6 cm   ③ 54 cm   ④ 10 cm

20. What is the cost of 40 metres long wire at the rate of ₹ 7 per metre ?
   ① ₹ 140   ② ₹ 280   ③ ₹ 47   ④ ₹ 74

21. 3 metres 25 centimeters = ?
   ① 325 centimetres   ② 3025 centimetres
   ③ 55 centimetres   ④ 3250 centimetres

22. 8 metres = ……………… cm
   ① 80   ② 8000   ③ 800   ④ 8

23. 9 cm = ... mm
    ① 900   ② 9   ③ 9000   ④ 90

24. $5\frac{1}{2}$ metres = ... cm

    ① 500 cm   ② 550 cm   ③ 575 cm   ④ 525 cm

25. 845 cm = ☐ m ☐ cm
    ① 8, 45   ② 84, 5   ③ 845, 0   ④ 8, 450

26. 11 km = ... m
    ① 1000   ② 1100   ③ 11000   ④ 110000

27. 5060 metres = ☐ km ☐ metres
    ① 5, 6   ② 50, 60   ③ 5,600   ④ 5, 60

28. 9 metre = ... mm
    ① 900   ② 9000   ③ 90   ④ 90000

29. 3675 metres = ☐ km ☐ metres
    ① 3, 675   ② 36, 75   ③ 367, 5   ④ 3, 67

30. Convert two and a quarter metres into centimeters.
    ① 225 cm   ② 250 cm   ③ 275 cm   ④ 200 cm

31. Convert 6 centimetres into millimetres.
    ① 6 mm   ② 600 mm   ③ 60 mm   ④ 6000 mm

32. Half of 3 metre is .... cm
    ① 125 cm   ② 175 cm   ③ 250 cm   ④ 150 cm

33. There quarters of 300 cm is .... cm
    ① 225 cm   ② 150 cm   ③ 175 cm   ④ 125 cm

34. Half a kilometre = ...
    ① 5000 m   ② 500 m   ③ 50 m   ④ 1000 m

35. Three quarters of a kilometre
    ① 500 m   ② 750 m   ③ 250 m   ④ 125 m

36. 5 cm = ... mm
    ① 500   ② 5000   ③ 50   ④ 5

37. 7 cm 8 mm + 9 cm 4 mm = ☐
    ① 17 cm 2 mm   ② 16 cm 12 mm
    ③ 16 cm 2 mm   ④ 17 cm 2 mm

38. 50 km 255 m – 16 km 960 m =
    ① 43 km 295 m   ② 34 km 295 m
    ③ 46 km 715 m   ④ 33 km 295 m

39. 38 km 450 m + 16 km 940 m = ?
    ① 53 km 390 m   ② 55 km 390 m
    ③ 54 km 390 m   ④ 44 km 390 m

40. 35 cm 4 mm – 4 cm 8 mm = ?
    ① 30 cm 4 mm   ② 31 cm 6 mm
    ③ 30 cm 6 mm   ④ 31 cm 4 mm

41. At a speed of 80 km per hour, what distance will a car cover in three and a half hour ?
    ① 280 kms   ② 240 km
    ③ 320 km   ④ 260 km

42. If one dress requires 4 m 50 cm of cloths how much do 8 dresses need ?
    ① 32 m 40 cm   ② 36 m
    ③ 32 m 20 cm   ④ 36 m 40 cm

43. If a wire that is 8 m 40 cm long is cut into pieces of 5 cm each, how many pieces will be made ?
    ① 164 pieces   ② 165 pieces
    ③ 158 pieces   ④ 168 pieces

44. If a trains travel 90 km in an hour, how far will it travel in 2 and a half hours ?
    ① 230 km   ② 270 km   ③ 225 km   ④ 200 km

45. If the speed of a scooter is 40 km, per hour, how far will it travel in two and a quarter ?
    ① 90 km   ② 100 km
    ③ 110 km   ④ 80 km

46. Convert 9 m 10 cms in cms.
    ① 9010 cm   ② 9100 cm   ③ 910 cm   ④ 90100 cm

47. Convert 875 cm into m.
    ① 8750 m   ② 8.75 m   ③ 87.50 m   ④ 8.750 m

48. 12 cm. + 59 cm. = ? metre
 ① 0.71   ② 71   ③ 7.1   ④ 47

49. 156 cm means how many metres ?
 ① 15.6   ② 150   ③ 0.156   ④ 1.56

50. 305 cm = ... metres.
 ① 305   ② 30.5   ③ 3.05   ④ 30.05

Answers

1.	❶	2.	❷	3.	❶	4.	❸	5.	❷
6.	❷	7.	❹	8.	❹	9.	❸	10.	❸
11.	❷	12.	❹	13.	❸	14.	❸	15.	❸
16.	❶	17.	❸	18.	❶	19.	❹	20.	❷
21.	❶	22.	❸	23.	❹	24.	❷	25.	❶
26.	❸	27.	❹	28.	❷	29.	❶	30.	❶
31.	❸	32.	❹	33.	❶	34.	❷	35.	❷
36.	❸	37.	❶	38.	❹	39.	❷	40.	❸
41.	❶	42.	❷	43.	❹	44.	❸	45.	❶
46.	❸	47.	❷	48.	❶	49.	❹	50.	❸

❖ ❖ ❖

MASS (WEIGHT)

✌ INTRODUCTION :

Mass or weight is measured in grams, kilograms, tons etc. Grains, metals, vegetables are measured in grams and helograms.

We are going to learn about the below mentioned units to measure weight.

1 centregram = 10 milligrams

1 gram = 100 centigrams

1 kilogram = 1000 grams.

For example :

1. What is a quarter kilogram ?

 1 kilogram is 1000 gram.

$\frac{1}{2}$ kilogram will be 500 gm and $\frac{1}{4}$ kilogram will be $\frac{1}{2}$ of $\frac{1}{2}$ kilogram i.e. 250 gm.

So the answer, is 250 gms.

2. How many grams are 5 kilograms ?

$$1 \text{ kilogram} = 1000 \text{ grams}$$
$$\therefore \quad 5 \text{ kilograms} = 1000 \times 5$$
$$= 5000 \text{ gms}$$

3. Convert 6500 gms into kilograms and grams ?

6500 gm = 6 kg 500 gm

4. Convert 9 kg 400 gms into grams ?

9 kg 400 gm = 9400 gms

5. How many gram is one and a quarter kelogram ?

One and a quarter kilograms means

1000 grams + 250 gram = 1250 grams.

Therefore one and a quarter kilogram are 1250 gms.

Units to measure weight :

10 milligram : 1 centigram.

10 centigram : 1 decigram.

10 decigram : 1 gram.

10 grams : 1 decagram.

10 decagram : 1 hectogram.

10 hectograms : 1 kilogram.

But we are going to study only the below mentioned topics.

1 Quantal = 100 kg

1 kilogram : 1000 grams.

1 gram : 100 centigrams.

1 centigrams : 10 milligrams.

Model Examples

Solve the following examples.

1. 17285 gm = ? kg

① 17.285   ② 1.7285   ③ 172.85   ④ 1728.5   ❶

2. In a truck there are 25 sacks of sugar each of 100 kg. What is the weight of sugar in a truck ?
   ① 2500 kg   ② 25000 kg   ③ 250 kg   ④ 2.50 kg   ❶

3. From 3 kg sugar, 2.200 kg sugar has been used. How much sugar is left ?
   ① 8 gm   ② 80 gm   ③ 800 gm   ④ 8000 gm   ❸
   Explanation : 3 kg = 3000 gm and 2.200 kg = 2200 gm.
   Now, 3000 gm – 2200 gm = 800 gm sugar is left.
   ∴ Alternative ❸ is the correct answer.

4. Ramesh weights 38 kg. The weight of Mahesh is 20 kg 500 gm less than that of Ramesh. What is the weight of Mahesh ?
   ① 21 kg 500 gm   ② 22 kg 500 gm
   ③ 17 kg 500 gm   ④ 18 kg 500 gm   ❸

5. 9321 mg = ... ?
   ① 93 centigrams, 21 milligrams
   ② 932 centigrams, 1 milligram
   ③ 931 centigrams, 2 milligrams
   ④ 9321 centigrams, 0 milligram   ❷

6. Two different bags hold 15 kg, 750 gm and 12 kg 500 gm of pulses respectively. Then how much is the total weight of pulses in kilograms ?
   ① 27.250 kg   ② 27.205 kg   ③ 28.250 kg   ④ 28.750 kg   ❸

Examples for Practice

Q. Solve the following examples.

1. A pocket contains 250 gms of salt. How many packets can be filled with 11 and 3 quarters kilogram of salt ?
   ① 47 packets   ② 56 packets
   ③ 407 packets   ④ 37 packets

2. A family requires 12 kg wheat and 5 kg sugar per month. How many quintals of sugar and wheat is required for the full year ?
   ① 1.44 gm wheat and 60 gms sugar
   ② 1.44 quintal wheat and 0.6 quintal sugar
   ③ 1.44 quintal sugar and 6 quintal wheat
   ④ 1.44 quintal wheat and 6 quintal sugar

3. The price of 10 kg of oil is ₹ 250. What is the price of one and half kilogram of oil ?
    ① ₹ 65.50   ② ₹ 25   ③ ₹ 50   ④ ₹ 37.50

4. 8.05 kilogram = ?
    ① 8 kg 5 gm   ② 8 kg 50 gm
    ③ 8 kg 500 gm   ④ All correct

5. A can contains 16 kg. of oil. How much oil will there in 25 such cans ?
    ① 250 kg   ② 160 kg   ③ 2500 kg   ④ 400 kg

6. There are 8100 kg. grain. It packed 810 kg. per sack. How many sacks will be required ?
    ① 10   ② 11   ③ 50   ④ 100

7. How many gms are there in 7 kg ?
    ① 7   ② 70   ③ 700   ④ 7000

8. How many gms are there in 8.5 kg ?
    ① 8050   ② 850   ③ 85   ④ 8500

9. Raghav had 310 kg 600 gm of rice in his shop. He bought 400 kg 900 gm more. What is the quantity of rice he has now ?
    ① 711 kg 500 gm   ② 710 kg 150 gm
    ③ 711 kg 15 gm   ④ 710 kg 105 gm

10. There is 25 kg 600 gm of wheat in one bag and 13 kg 200 gm in the other. How much more wheat is there in the first bag ?
    ① 38 kg 800 gm   ② 12 kg 800 gm
    ③ 12 kg 400 gm   ④ 13 kg 400 gm

11. If one can contains 18 kg of oil, how much oil will there be in 30 such cans ?
    ① 48 kg   ② 540 kg   ③ 54 kg   ④ 5400 kg

12. 10 kg 500 gm of rice was distributed equally among 5 persons. How much does each get ?
    ① 1 kg 100 gm   ② 2 kg 100 gm
    ③ 105 gm   ④ 210 gm

13. 2 kg 500 grams means how many grams ?
    ① 25   ② 250   ③ 2500   ④ 205

14. 1 kg 500 gram sugar was bought. From it 400 grams sugar was used. How many grams sugar was left ?
    ① 1100 grams ② 1010 grams ③ 1900 grams ④ 1001 grams

15. There are 7 sacks each containing 80 kg grain. This grain was put into cans. If each can is of 16 kg, how many such cans will be needed ?
    ① 35   ② 70   ③ 56   ④ 80

16. 5 kg = ... gms
    ① 50 gm   ② 500 gm   ③ 50000 gm ④ 5000 gm

17. How many grams is 3 and a quarter kilogram ?
    ① 3750 gm   ② 3250 gm   ③ 3125 gm   ④ 3500 gm

18. How many kiolograms and grams does 7425 gms make ?
    ① 7 kg 425 gm   ② 74 kg 25 gm
    ③ 7 kg 400 gm   ④ 7425 kg

19. 9 kg means .... centigrams.
    ① 900000 centigrams   ② 90000 centigrams
    ③ 9000 centigrams   ④ 900 centigrams

20. What is quarter kilogram + three quarters kilogram and half kilogram equal to ?
    ① 1 kg 500 gm   ② 1 kg 750 gms
    ③ 1 kg 250 gm   ④ 1 kg

21. ☐ weight of 100 gms is 2000 gms.
    ① 10   ② 20   ③ 5   ④ 30

22. ☐ weight of 500 gms is 3000 gms.
    ① 5   ② 7   ③ 6   ④ 8

23. ☐ weight of 200 gms is 4000 gms.
    ① 20   ② 40   ③ 10   ④ 200

24. 3000 gm – 1500 grms = ...
    ① 1500 gm   ② 2500 gm
    ③ 500 gm   ④ 15000 gms

25. 7800 gm + 400 gms = ...
    ① 7012 gms ② 8200 gm   ③ 7200 gm   ④ 82000 gms

26. 38022g = ... kg .... g
    ① 38 kg 220 g   ② 3 kg 802 g
    ③ 380 kg 22 g   ④ 38 kg 22 g

27. 57154 g = ... kg .... g
    ① 57 kg 154 kg   ② 571 kg 54 g
    ③ 5 kg 7154 g   ④ 57 kg 1540 g

28. 15 kg 53 g = ... g.
    ① 150530 g ② 150053 g   ③ 15053 g   ④ 1553 g

29. What is a quarter kilogram + one kilogram and half kilogram + three quarter of kilogram equal to ? ....
    ① 2 kg 750 kg   ② 2 kg 500 g
    ③ 2 kg   ④ 1 kg 500 g

30. Suresh bought 84 kg 600 g of jowar from one shop and 28 kg 500 g of jowar from another shop. How much jowar and he buy in all ?
    ① 112 kg 100 g   ② 113 kg 200 g
    ③ 112 kg 200 g   ④ 113 kg 100 g

31. A sack had 45 kg 300 g of vegetables. There were 18 kg 800 g onion, 13 kg 500 g cabbage and the rest were potatoes. What was the weight of the potatoes ?
    ① 13 kg   ② 13 kg 200g
    ③ 13 kg 100 g   ④ 12 kg

32. If one gold bangle is made from 15 gms 500 milligrams of gold, how much gold will be needed to make 9 such bangles ?
    ① 13 gms 9500 milligrams
    ② 13 kilogram 9 grams 500 milligrams
    ③ 139 gms 500 milligrams
    ④ 1 kilogram 395 grams

33. Radha bought 4 kg 500 g of onions, 2 kg 750 gm of potatoes, 750 g of cauliflower, 500 g of bitter gourd and 1 kg 250 g of tomatoes. How much was the total weight of the vegetables he bought.
    ① 8 kg 750 g   ② 9 kg 750 g
    ③ 9 kg 500 g   ④ 9 kg 250 g

34. Mother asked Rahul to buy 2 kg of rice, 3 kg of wheat, half a kg of sugar, a quarter kg of groundnut, 750 g of poha and 200 g of chillie. What is the total weight that Rahul needs to carry home ?

① 6 kg 250 g   ② 7 kg
③ 6 kg 500 gm   ④ 6 kg 700 g

Answers

1.	❶	2.	❶	3.	❹	4.	❷	5.	❹
6.	❶	7.	❹	8.	❹	9.	❶	10.	❸
11.	❷	12.	❷	13.	❸	14.	❶	15.	❶
16.	❹	17.	❷	18.	❷	19.	❶	20.	❶
21.	❷	22.	❸	23.	❶	24.	❶	25.	❷
26.	❹	27.	❶	28.	❸	29.	❷	30.	❹
31.	❶	32.	❸	33.	❷	34.	❹		

✤ ✤ ✤

VOLUME AND CAPACITY

❧ INTRODUCTION :

Kilolitre, Hectolitre, Decalitre, Litre, Decilitre, Centilitre, Millilitre are the units of capacity. As we go from the smaller unit to the larger unit, every unit is 10 times larger than the preceding unit.

10 millilitres = 1 centilitre

10 centilitre = 1 decilitre

10 decilitres = 1 litre

10 litres = 1 decalitre

10 decalitres = 1 hectolitre

10 hectolitres = 1 kilolitre

The units of capacity given below are to be learnt.

1 kilolitre = 1,000 litres

1 litre = 100 centilitre

1 centilitre = 10 millilitres

1000 ml = 1 litre

We use litre and milliliters to measure liquids like milk, oil, diesel and petrol. Litre is written as '*l*' and milliliter is written as 'ml'.

1 litre *(l)* = 1000 millilitre (ml)

For example :

1. 4 litres = ... millilitre

    ① 400 ml   ② 40000 ml   ③ 4000 ml   ④ 49 ml   ❸

2. How many ml is 1.25 *l* ?

    ① 125 ml   ② 12500 ml   ③ 1250 ml   ④ 1205 ml   ❸

Model Examples

Q. Solve the following examples.

1. Liquid ink is sold in bottles each of capacity 125 ml. How many bottles will be required to fill 3 litres of ink ?

    ① 16   ② 8   ③ 32   ④ 24   ❹

    Explanation : $3 = 3000$ ml, $\dfrac{3000}{125} = 24$

    ∴ Alternative ❹ is the correct answer.

2. 2 kilolitre = litres.

    ① 200 litres   ② 100 litres   ③ 2000 litres   ④ 20000 litres   ❸

3. A bottle contains 1 litre and 750 ml of water out of which 0.25 litres water is spoiled. How much water remained ?

    ① 1.5 litre   ② 1.25 litre   ③ 1.75 litre   ④ 1.0 litre   ❶

    Explanation : 1 litre and 750 ml = 1,000 ml + 750 ml = 1750 ml.

    0.25 litres water is spoiled, it means that $0.25 \times 1,000 = 250$ ml. water is spoiled.

    ∴   Water remained =   1750 – 250

    $$= \ 1{,}500 \text{ ml} = \frac{1{,}500}{1{,}000} = 1.5 \text{ litre.}$$

    ∴ Alternative ❶ is the correct answer.

4. A tank can hold 10 litres of water. If it is filled with 4 litres of water, how much portion of the tank will be filled ?

    ① $\dfrac{2}{5}$ ② $\dfrac{5}{2}$ ③ $\dfrac{2}{3}$ ④ $\dfrac{2}{4}$ ❶

5. Two and half litres + Two and a quarter litres means how many millilitres ?

① 675   ② 4,750   ③ 4,500   ④ 475   ❷

6. A jar has a capacity for 8 litres of milk. How many 200 ml measures will be needed to fill it ?

① 40   ② 20   ③ 4   ④ 16.   ❶

Examples for Practice

Q. Solve the following examples.

1. Coconut oil is to be packed in plastic bottles each of capacity 50 ml. How many bottles will be required to fill 30 litres of coconut oil ?

① 1 bottle   ② 1000 bottles
③ 100 bottles   ④ 10 bottles

2. 1300 ml = ? litres

① 1.3   ② 0.13   ③ 13   ④ 0.013

3. How many bottles of capacity 125 ml. will be required to contain one and half litres of soda ?

① 8   ② 10   ③ 12   ④ 14

4. Each students is given 125 ml of milk. What is the quantity of milk in litres required for 30 boys ?

① 3.750 litres   ② 37.50 litres
③ 0.375 litres   ④ 37.00 litres

5. My father has 20 litres 500 ml. of petrol put in his car. If he puts 4 liters 500 ml. more the indicator in the car would read 'full'. How much petrol can be put in the car ?

① 30 *l*   ② 29.500 *l*   ③ 24 *l*   ④ 25 *l*

6. In school 250 students are given milk. Each child was given 140 ml. milk. How much litre milk required ?

① 32 *l*   ② 34 *l*   ③ 35 *l*   ④ 36 *l*

7. The water tank contains 250 litres of water. 199 *l* and 500 ml. water was pumped out. How much water remained in water tank ?

① 5 *l*. 500 ml   ② 10 *l*. 500 ml   ③ 50 *l*. 500 ml   ④ 50 *l*

8. 17 litre and 125 ml is equal to how many millilitres ?
    ① 17.125   ② 17125   ③ 171.25   ④ 1.7125

9. How many millilitres are there in 4 litre and 9 ml ?
    ① 13   ② 49   ③ 4.9   ④ 4009

10. If there is 600 litre 400 ml. of water in one barrel, 300 litre 460 ml. of water in the second barrel and 400 litre 340 ml. in the third barrel what is the total quantity of water ?
    ① 1301 litre 120 ml   ② 1301 litre 200 ml
    ③ 1301 litre 100 ml   ④ 1201 litre 200 ml

11. One container holds 18 litre of milk and the other, 11 *l* 300 ml milk. How much more milk does the first container hold ?
    ① 29 litre 300 ml   ② 7 litre 300 ml
    ③ 6 litre 700 ml   ④ 6 litre 600 ml

12. 567 ml. of medicine is filled in 7 bottles. How much medicine will there be in every bottle ?
    ① 80 ml   ② 801 ml   ③ 800 ml   ④ 81 ml

13. If a family uses 750 ml milk everyday how much milk will they need for the month of June ?
    ① 22 litre 500 ml   ② 2,250 ml
    ③ 2,20,500 ml   ④ 2,205 ml

14. 25 litres = ... ml
    ① 2500 ml   ② 20500 ml
    ③ 250000 ml   ④ 25000 ml

15. 2205 ml = ... kg .... ml
    ① 2, 250   ② 2, 205   ③ 2, 255   ④ 2, 200

16. How many milliliters are there is one and a quarter litre ?
    ① 1500   ② 1250   ③ 1750   ④ 1125

17. 19 *l* = ... ml.
    ① 1900   ② 190   ③ 19000   ④ 190000

18. Which measure will you use to pour three and half litre of oil and how many times will they be used ?
    ① 500, 6   ② 500, 7   ③ 6, 500   ④ 7, 500

19. How many milliliters are there in two and a three quarter litre ?

    ① 2125   ② 2250   ③ 2500   ④ 2750

20. How many milliliter are there in 6 litres and 6 ml ?

    ① 606   ② 6006   ③ 6060   ④ 60006

21. Four and half litres + two and a three quarter litre means how many milliliters ?

    ① 7125 ml ② 7250 ml ③ 6750 ml ④ 7750 ml

22. How many measures of 200 ml will be used for 6 litres of oil ?

    ① 30   ② 12   ③ 20   ④ 25

23. How many measures of 50 ml will be used in 800 ml of oil ?

    ① 15   ② 17   ③ 16   ④ 20

24. How many measures of 500 ml will be used in 13 litres of milk ?

    ① 20   ② 24   ③ 28   ④ 26

25. How many measure of 100 ml will you use in 4 litres of milk ?

    ① 400   ② 40   ③ 4   ④ 4000

26. If a half litre of milk cost 28 rupees, then how much will 9 and a half litre cost ?

    ① ₹ 266   ② ₹ 267   ③ ₹ 26.60 ④ ₹ 2660

27. A water tank in Navyug society holds 1000 *l* of water. If 675 *l* 450 ml is used, how many litres of water remains in the tank ?

    ① 335 *l* 550 ml   ② 325 *l* 550 ml
    ③ 324 *l* 550 ml   ④ 324 *l* 450 ml

28. A can of milk has 25 *l* 650 ml of milk. Another can has 24 *l* 900 ml of milk. How much milk is there in the two cans altogether ?

    ① 50 *l* 500 ml   ② 49 *l* 350 ml
    ③ 750 ml   ④ 50 *l* 550 ml

29. What is 59 *l* 200 ml – 39 *l* 750 ml ?

    ① 19 *l* 550 ml   ② 19 *l* 450 ml
    ③ 98 *l* 950 ml   ④ 20 *l* 550 ml

30. 29 *l* 900 ml + 25 *l* 650 ml = ?

　　① 55 *l* 550 ml　　　　　② 54 *l* 550 ml

　　③ 4 *l* 350 ml　　　　　④ 4 *l* 250 ml

1.	❷	2.	❶	3.	❸	4.	❶	5.	❹
6.	❸	7.	❸	8.	❷	9.	❹	10.	❷
11.	❸	12.	❹	13.	❶	14.	❹	15.	❷
16.	❷	17.	❸	18.	❷	19.	❹	20.	❷
21.	❷	22.	❶	23.	❸	24.	❹	25.	❷
26.	❶	27.	❸	28.	❹	29.	❷	30.	❶

❖ ❖ ❖

4.2 　 *MEASUREMENT OF TIME*

✌ *INTRODUCTION :*

1 day : 24 hours.

1 hour : 60 minutes.

1 minute : 60 seconds

∴ 1 hour : 60×60 seconds = 3600 seconds

We measure time in two ways i.e. (1) 12 hour clock with a.m. and p.m. (2) 24 hour clock where after 12 noon instead of using 1 pm it is called as 13, 14, 15, 16, ...24 hour. 5 p.m. is called as 17 hours. i.e. 12 + 5 = 17 hours. 24 hour clock is used in government office, railway and bus time table, police and registration in government office also.

Model Examples

Q. Solve the following examples :

1. I go to school at 8.00 a.m. and come back at 12.30 p.m. How much time do I spend in school ?

　　① 3.30 hr.　　　　　② 4 hr. 30 min.

　　③ 2 hr. 30 min.　　　　④ 3 hr. 35 min.

2. 2 hour 36 minutes 24 seconds. How many seconds ?
   ① 9360   ② 156   ③ 9384   ④ 9380   ❸

3. A holiday class begins at 8 : 10 in the morning and closes at quarter past eleven before noon. For how much time does the class meet on that day ?
   ① 4 hours 25 minutes   ② 3 hours 5 minutes
   ③ 3 hours 55 minutes   ④ 3 hours 10 minutes   ❷

4. A journey by train from Pune to Kolkatta requires one day and 20 hours. How many hours does the journey take ?
   ① 24   ② 34   ③ 44   ④ 42   ❸

Examples for Practice

Q. Solve the following examples :

1. A quarter to 7 means ....
   ① 7 hr. 45 min.   ② 6 hr. 45 min.
   ③ 7 hr. 15 min.   ④ 6 hr. 15 min.

2. The cricket match began at 9.00 am and finished at 5.30 p.m. How long did the match last ?
   ① 7 hr. 30 min.   ② 6 hr. 30 min.
   ③ 8 hr. 30 min.   ④ 9 hr. 30 min

3. Ten minutes to 4 means .... hr. .... min.
   ① 4 hr. 50 min.   ② 4 hr. 10 min.
   ③ 3 hr. 50 min.   ④ 3 hr. 10 min.

4. Radha travelled to her native place by train for 6 hours 25 minutes and by car for 3 hours 35 minutes. How long was Radha travelling ?
   ① 9 h 50 min   ② 10 hours
   ③ 9 h 55 mins   ④ 9 hours

5. 7 hours = ☐ minutes.
   ① 140   ② 420   ③ 460   ④ 500

6. 200 minutes = ... hr. .... minutes.
   ① 3 hr. 20 min.   ② 6 hr.
   ③ 4 hrs. 10 min.   ④ 2 hr. 30 min

7. What is 23 hours ?
   ① 12 O'clock   ② 11.00 p.m.
   ③ 10.00 a.m.   ④ 11.00 a.m.

8. Convert 15 hours into 12 hour clock.
   ① 1 p.m.   ② 2 p.m.   ③ 3 p.m.   ④ 3 a.m.

9. Ram was expected to reach railway station at 19 hours and 20 min. ? Choose the correct option of 12 hour clock ?
   ① 7.20 p.m.   ② 7.20 a.m.
   ③ 6.20 p.m.   ④ 6.20 a.m.

10. Radha reached home at 21 hours 30 minutes that means she reached at .... p.m.
    ① 8.30 p.m.   ② 7.30 p.m.   ③ 9.30 p.m.   ④ 10.30 p.m.

11. Sham worked from 8.00 a.m. to 12.00 p.m. How many hours he worked in all ?
    ① 4 hrs.   ② 2 hrs.   ③ 8 hrs.   ④ 10 hrs.

12. 9 O' clock in the morning means ....
    ① 9 p.m.   ② 9 a.m.   ③ 9 noon   ④ None of these

13. A movie was to start at one forty five in the afternoon was delayed by a quarter of an hour because of power cut. What time did the movie start ?
    ① 2.30 p.m.   ② 1.45 p.m.   ③ 2.15 p.m.   ④ 2 p.m.

14. If train leave Pune junction at four forty five in the evening and reaches Agra at three forty the next afternoon, how long does the journey takes ?
    ① 23 h 5 min   ② 22 h 5 min
    ③ 22 h 20 min   ④ 23 h

15. Mrs. John taught in Class V for 2 hours and 30 mins in the morning and class IV 1 hour and 35 mins in the afternoon. How long was she teaching in all ?
    ① 4 h 5 min   ② 3 h 5 min
    ③ 4 h 60 min   ④ 3 hours 55 min

16. A certain school starts at 7.15 in the morning and gets over at 2.05 in the afternoon. How long does the school work ?
    ① 7 hrs 5 min   ② 6 h 55 min
    ③ 6 h 50 min   ④ 7 hrs

1.	❷	2.	❸	3.	❸	4.	❷	5.	❷
6.	❶	7.	❷	8.	❸	9.	❶	10.	❸
11.	❹	12.	❷	13.	❹	14.	❷	15.	❶
16.	❸								

✤ ✤ ✤

4.3   THE CALENDAR

✌ INTRODUCTION :

7 days : 1 week.   4 weeks : 1 month : 30 days or 31 days.

52 weeks : 12 months : 1 year.

365/366 days make a year : In a year 7 months i.e. January, March, May, July, August, October and December have 31 days. 4 months i.e. April, June, September, November have 30 days. February has 28 days and 29 days in leap year.

July and August are the two successive months having 31 days. If Monday fall on 5th day of the month, then the next Monday will fall on 12th day of that month. Thus, the difference between the two consecutive Mondays is of 7 days. Similar thing happens in case of Tuesday, Wednesday, Thursday, Friday, Saturday and Sunday.

In the year there are 12 months and 365 days. In leap year there are 366 days and February is of 29 days.

What is a leap year ? : If the number of a year is completely divided by four, it is a leap year. How to find out a leap year ?

For Example. : Find out whether 1996 is a leap year or not ?

Answer : 1996 is a leap year because it is completely divisible by 4.

$$
\begin{array}{r|r|l}
4 & 1996 & \underline{\,499\,} \\
& -16\!\downarrow & \\
\hline
& 39\,\big\downarrow & \\
& -36 & \\
\hline
& 36 & \\
& -36 & \\
\hline
& 00 &
\end{array}
$$

A centenary year whose number is not divisible by 4 is not a leap year.

For example : 1900 year was not a leap year but 2000 is a leap year.

Model Examples

Q. Solve the following examples :

1. If Sunday falls on 7th. On what date next Sunday comes ?
   ① 14   ② 15   ③ 13   ④ 12   ❶

2. Put odd month out.
   ① April   ② June   ③ August   ④ September ❸

3. Diwali vacation of a certain school starts on 24 October and it reopens after 14 days of vacation, on.
   ① 5 November   ② 2 November
   ③ 6 November   ④ 7 November   ❹

4. If Tuesday falls on 7th, on what date Saturday will fall ?
   ① 11   ② 12   ③ 13   ④ 14   ❶
   Explanation : Tuesday falls on 7th. After 4 days Saturday will fall. So Saturday will fall on 11th.
   ∴ Alternative ❶ is the correct answer.

5. Which of the following dates is incorrect ?
   ① 30/9/1995   ② 29/2/1995
   ③ 31/7/1995   ④ 31/8/1995   ❷
   Explanation : Here, 1995 is not a leap year. So in that year February will not have 29 days. Thus, 29/2/1995 is an incorrect date.
   ∴ Alternative ❷ is the correct answer.

6. If 2nd August, falls on first Thursday then 22nd August will fall on which day ?
   ① Tuesday   ② Wednesday ③ Thursday ④ Friday   ❷
   Explanation : 2, 9, 16, 23 will Thursday. So 22nd August will be Wednesday.
   ∴ Alternative ❷ is the correct answer.

7. In which of the following months 3 days fall 5 times ?
    ① April   ② June
    ③ November   ④ December   ❹

8. Which of the following months cannot be a part of the set ?
    ① April   ② July
    ③ September   ④ November.   ❷

9. If 11th September 1995 was a Monday, what day will it be on the 11th September 1996 ?
    ① Tuesday   ② Sunday
    ③ Thursday   ④ Wednesday   ❹

10. If it was Monday on 1st August, on which day of the same year, will the children's day be celebrated ?
    ① Tuesday   ② Thursday
    ③ Friday   ④ Monday   ❹

11. 12th May 1996 falls on Friday. Which day in that month occurred five times ?
    ① Saturday   ② Friday
    ③ Thursday   ④ Wednesday   ❹

12. Study the following portion of a diary and answer the question that follows :

    ### March 1995

Monday	Tuesday	Wednesday	Thursday	Friday	Saturday	Sunday
5	6	7	8	9	10	11

    Which day was 8th April 1995 ?
    ① Sunday   ② Saturday
    ③ Monday   ④ Tuesday   ❶

13. The summer vacation of a certain school starts on May 11. It reopens after 27 days of vacation on .....
    ① 5 June   ② 2 June   ③ 7 June   ④ 8 June.   ❸

14. 12th of October, 1998 is Monday, then which of the following days will come for 5 times in the same month ?
    ① Thursday, Friday, Saturday.
    ② Tuesday, Wednesday, Thursday.
    ③ Monday, Tuesday, Wednesday.
    ④ Wednesday, Thursday, Friday.   ❶

15. There are .... weeks in a year.

    ① 53   ② 52   ③ 54   ④ 51   ❷

16. .... has 29 days in a leap year.

    ① March   ② April   ③ January   ④ February   ❹

17. How many years and months make 3.25 years ?

    ① 3 years and 9 months   ② 3 years and 6 months

    ③ 3 years and 3 months   ④ 3 years and 10 months   ❸

Examples for Practice

Q. Solve the following examples :

1. Independence day falls on Friday. Which day comes on Teacher's Day ?

    ① Thursday ② Friday   ③ Saturday ④ Sunday

2. Which is the shortest month of the year ?

    ① January   ② March

    ③ February   ④ June

3. How many days are in February 2004 ?

    ① 29   ② 28   ③ 30   ④ 31

4. Which of the following dates fall on the same day ?

    ① 3, 10, 16, 24   ② 7, 15, 20, 27

    ③ 2, 8, 15, 21   ④ 3, 10, 17, 24

5. 3rd March, 2002 falls on Sunday. Which day in that month occurred five times ?

    ① Sunday   ② Monday   ③ Tuesday   ④ Wednesday

6. Sunil will go on 6 days trip after 7th. On which date will he come back from the trip ?

    ① 11th ② 13th ③ 14th ④ 15th

7. Which of the following dates is incorrect ?

    ① 31.2.2002 ② 31.3.2002 ③ 30.6.2002 ④ 30.4.2002

8. Which year is a leap year ?

    ① 1998   ② 1999   ③ 2000   ④ 2001

9. How many days are there in 2008 ?
   ① 366   ② 365   ③ 30   ④ 31

10. Which of the month has 31 days ?
    ① April   ② June   ③ August   ④ November

11. Three week means .... days.
    ① 30   ② 25   ③ 18   ④ 21

12. Independence day falls on Thursday in the year 1996. On what day will Gandhi Jayanti fall on ?
    ① Thursday   ② Friday   ③ Monday   ④ Wednesday

13. If 14th February 1984 was Tuesday. What was the day on 13th February, 1985 ?
    ① Tuesday   ② Wednesday
    ③ Thursday   ④ Sunday

14. In which of the following months 3 days fall for five times ?
    ① November   ② June
    ③ February   ④ August

15. If Republic day falls on Monday then on which day will 1 February be ?
    ① Sunday   ② Tuesday
    ③ Wednesday   ④ Thursday

16. If January 1st, 1991 falls on Thursday, then on which day 31st December, 1991 will fall ?
    ① Thursday   ② Tuesday
    ③ Wednesday   ④ Friday

17. When is Children's day celebrated ?
    ① 1st May   ② 15th August
    ③ 5th September   ④ 14th November

18. When is Teacher's day celebrated ?
    ① 1st May   ② 15th August
    ③ 5th September   ④ 14th November

19. If Monday is on 10th, then on which day does 2nd fall ?
    ① Sunday   ② Monday   ③ Tuesday   ④ Wednesday

20. Which among the following is a leap year ?
    ① 1993   ② 1994   ③ 1995   ④ 1996

21. Which of the following month has 31 days ?
    ① February   ② March   ③ April   ④ June

22. Which of the following months is of 30 days ?
    ① January   ② February   ③ March   ④ April

23. Same day repeats after how many days ?
    ① 5   ② 6   ③ 7   ④ 8

24. Which of the following dates fall on the same day ?
    ① 4, 11, 18, 24   ② 2, 9, 16, 23
    ③ 3, 11, 19, 27   ④ 4, 12, 19, 26

25. Which of the following date is correct ?
    ① 31st April   ② 31st May   ③ 31st June   ④ 31st September

26. One week means .... days.
    ① 6   ② 30   ③ 8   ④ 7

27. October 2 was a Wednesday. What day will October 17 be ?
    ① Thursday   ② Wednesday
    ③ Tuesday   ④ Sunday

28. Is 2000 is leap year ?
    ① Yes   ② No   ③ Can't say   ④ None of these

29. How many months make two years ?
    ① 36 months   ② 12 months
    ③ 24 months   ④ None of these

30. We went to Punjab on 26th of December and returned on 10th of next month. Name the month in which we   returned ?
    ① February   ② January
    ③ December   ④ November

31. If Ram worked from 6th January 1992 to 3rd February 1992 (both days inclusive). What is the total number of days he worked ?
    ① 29 days   ② 28 days   ③ 30 days   ④ 27 days

32. Mother bought newspaper from 25th July to 25th August (both days inclusive). For how many days did she buy the newspaper ?
    ① 31 days   ② 30 days   ③ 32 days   ④ 33 days

33. How many years will 1095 days make ?
    ① 2 years   ② 3 years
    ③ 2 $\frac{1}{2}$ years   ④ 3 $\frac{1}{2}$ years

34. I start for picnic on Monday morning and reach the spot on Saturday morning. How many days did I require to reach ?
    ① 6 days   ② 4 days   ③ 5 days   ④ 7 days

35. Find the pair of months whose sum is 62 days ?
    ① January – February   ② April – May
    ③ July – August   ④ October – November

36. The school closed for Diwali vacation on 23rd Oct. and reopened on 14th Nov. ? How many days holiday were there?
    ① 21 days   ② 20 days   ③ 22 days   ④ 23 days

37. How many weeks will 63 days make ?
    ① 7   ② 9   ③ 8   ④ 6

38. How many months of 30 days do 720 days make ?
    ① 20   ② 30   ③ 22   ④ 24

39. There are ……… days in a fortnight ?
    ① 7 days   ② 14 days   ③ 15 days   ④ 16 days

40. Teacher's day is in the month of …………
    ① February   ② September   ③ January   ④ October

41. Which is the month between March and May ?
    ① July   ② February   ③ April   ④ June

42. How many hours make a week ?
    ① 192   ② 168   ③ 96   ④ 14

Answers

1.	❷	2.	❸	3.	❶	4.	❹	5.	❶
6.	❷	7.	❶	8.	❸	9.	❶	10.	❸

11.	❹	12.	❹	13.	❷	14.	❹	15.	❶
16.	❶	17.	❹	18.	❸	19.	❶	20.	❹
21.	❷	22.	❹	23.	❸	24.	❷	25.	❷
26.	❹	27.	❶	28.	❶	29.	❸	30.	❷
31.	❶	32.	❸	33.	❷	34.	❸	35.	❸
36.	❹	37.	❷	38.	❹	39.	❷	40.	❷
41.	❸	42.	❷						

❖ ❖ ❖

4.4 PAPER MEASUREMENT (RIM, DASTA, GROSS)

✌ INTRODUCTION :

Dozen - A bunch of 12 papers is called as 1 Dozen.

Dasta - A bunch of 24 papers is called as a Dasta.

Gross - A Group of 12 dozen papers is called as Gross.

Rim - A bunch of 20 dasta or group of 480 papers is called as Rim.

$$1 \text{ Dozen} = 12 \text{ Papers}$$
$$1 \text{ Dasta} = 24 \text{ Papers} = 2 \text{ dozen}$$
$$1 \text{ Gross} = 144 \text{ Papers} = 12 \text{ dozen}$$
$$1 \text{ Rim} = 480 \text{ Papers} = 20 \text{ Dasta's}$$

 Model Examples

Q. Solve the following examples :

1. 4 Gross = ...

   ① 566 Papers   ② 586 Papers

   ③ 576 Papers   ④ 590 Papers   ❸

   Explanation : 1 Gross = 144 Papers

   ∴ 4 Gross = $144 \times 4 = 576$ Papers

   ∴ Alternative ❸ is the correct answer.

2. 2 Rim, 2 Gross is equal to how many papers ?
    ① 960 Papers   ② 1, 488 Papers
    ③ 288 Papers   ④ 1, 248 Papers   ❹

    Explanation : 1 Rim   = 480 Papers

    ∴ 2 Rim   = 480 × 2

    = 960 Papers   ------ (i)

    1 Grose   = 12 dozen Papers

    = 144 Papers

    2 Grose   = 480 × 2

    = 288 Papers   ------ (ii)

    ∴ From equation (i) and (ii)

    $$\begin{array}{r} 960 \\ + \ 288 \\ \hline 1248 \text{ Papers} \end{array}$$

    ∴ Alternative ❹ is the correct answer.

3. If cost of one paper is ₹ 3, then find the cost of 3 gross ?
    ① 1269   ② 1196
    ③ 1369   ④ 1296   ❹

    Explanation : Cost of one paper = ₹ 3. We want to find the cost of 3 gross i.e.

    3 gross = 144 × 3

    = 432 Papers

    Cost of 1 paper = ₹ 3

    ∴   Cost of 1 gross = 432 × 3

    = ₹ 1296

    ∴   Alternative ❹ is the correct asnwer.

4. 3600 Papers = ------------------ Dasta's

    ① 180 Dasta's   ② 150 Dasta's

    ③ 300 Dasta's   ④ 240 Dasta's

    Explanation :

    1 Dasta = 2 Dozen Papers = 24 Papers

∴   24 Papers = 1 Dasta

∴   Dasta = $\dfrac{\text{Total No. of Paper}}{24}$

                    = $\dfrac{3600}{24}$ = 150

∴   3600 Papers = 150 Dasta

∴   Alternative ❷ is the correct answer.

Examples for Practice

1. Fill in the blank.

    10 Gross ☐ 5 Rim

    ① >   ② <   ③ =   ④ ∨

2. Arrange the following units in assending order and write the unit which is at the middle of the order.

    1 Rim, 1 Paper, 1 Dasta, 1 Gross, 1 Dozen

    ① 1 Gross   ② 1 Dozen
    ③ 1 Dasta   ④ 1 Rim

3. 40 Dasta = ------- Rim.

    ① 2   ② 8   ③ 48   ④ 12

4. 8 Rim = ---------- Dasta.

    ① 160   ② 40   ③ 80   ④ 100

5. Fill in the blank.

    25 Dozen ☐ 25 Dasta.

    ① >   ② <   ③ ∨   ④ =

6. 9 Rim 10 Dozen = --------- Dasta

    ① 180   ② 185   ③ 190   ④ 175

7. 2 Dozen = ----------- Dasta.

    ① 1   ② 2   ③ 4   ④ $\dfrac{1}{2}$

8. 504 Papers = -----------

    ① 1 Rim 1 Dasta   ② 1 Rim 1 Dozen
    ③ 1 Gross 1 Dasta   ④ 1 Gross 1 Dozen

9. 4 Dasta = ----------- Papers.
   ① 576   ② 566   ③ 96   ④ 48

10. 10 Rim = ----------- Papers
    ① 1440   ② 480   ③ 4800   ④ 240

11. Choose the correct alternative :

    ① 14 Dasta = 8 Dozen   ② $\frac{1}{2}$ Rim = 10 Dasta

    ③ $\frac{1}{2}$ Rim = 20 Dozen   ④ $\frac{1}{2}$ Rim = 40 Dozen

12. Four Dasta = ----------- Dozen.
    ① 24   ② 8   ③ 48   ④ 12

13. $\frac{1}{4}$ Rim = ----------- Papers

    ① 120 Papers   ② 240 Papers
    ③ 480 Papers   ④ 160 Papers

Answers

1.	❷	2.	❸	3.	❶	4.	❶	5.	❷
6.	❷	7.	❶	8.	❶	9.	❸	10.	❸
11.	❹	12.	❷	13.	❶				

❖ ❖ ❖

4.5   COINS AND CURRENCY-RUPEES, PAISA CONVERSION

✌ INTRODUCTION :

We make use of a dot (.) to separate rupees and paise. The figures on the left of the dot (.) denote the number of rupees and the two figures on the right of the dot (.) denote the number of paise.

For example 40 rupees 5 paise are written in short form as ₹ 40.05 (not ₹ 40.5).

We write paise as a 2 digit number. If a decimal point is used Rupees-paise get converted into rupees alone. If the decimal point is deleted. It gets converted into rupees-paise.

$$₹ 1 \ = \ 100 \text{ paise.}$$

Model Examples

Q. Solve the following examples :

1. Rupees 356 and 50 paise. How many rupees ?
    ① ₹ 356.50   ② ₹ 35.650   ③ ₹ 356.05   ④ ₹ 36.505   ❶

2. ₹ 4 Paise 60 + 6.10 = ?
    ① ₹ 5.70   ② ₹ 10.70   ③ 100.70   ④ 40.70   ❷

3. ₹ 8 and paise 5 means how many rupees ?
    ① ₹ 8.50   ② ₹ 0.85   ③ ₹ 8.05   ④ ₹ 8.50   ❸

4. ₹ 6 and paise 75 + ₹ 5.50 = ?
    ① ₹ 12.25   ② ₹ 1.25   ③ ₹ 125   ④ ₹ 12.5   ❶

5. What equal number of coins of 25 paise, 50 paise and ₹ 1 each can you get in five rupees and a quarter ?
    ① 5   ② 3   ③ 9   ④ 15   ❷

6. How many 20 paise coins will make ₹ 10 ?
    ① 200   ② 50   ③ 100   ④ 250   ❷

7. Taking an equal number of notes of ₹ 2, 5, 10 and 20 each, if you collect ₹ 555, how many notes of ₹ 5 will you get there in ?
    ① 15   ② 37   ③ 111   ④ 100   ❶

8. Sarfaraz has withdrawn ₹ 195 from the bank. Out of the total notes some are of ₹ 5 and the remaining are of ₹ 10. Then find the number of notes of ₹ 5.
    ① 20   ② 24   ③ 41   ④ 33   ❹

9. If ₹ 18.87 is subtracted from ₹ 20.15, how do you write the answer dropping the decimal point ?
    ① 2 ₹ 18 paise   ② 2 ₹ 28 paise
    ③ 1 ₹ 28 paise   ④ 3 ₹ 28 paise   ❸

10. Out of ₹ 5,248, there are 48 notes of Re. 1 and the remaining are notes of ₹ 100. Find the total number of ₹ 100 notes.
   ① 25   ② 50   ③ 52   ④ 24   ❸

11. An amount of rupees hundred and seventy five is in the form of 10 rupee notes and 5 rupee notes. Then the number of notes of rupee 5 can be ....
   ① 37   ② 12   ③ 20   ④ 23   ❹

12. Deepak has ₹ 153 in the form of ₹ 2, ₹ 5 and ₹ 10 notes. If the notes of each denomination are equal in number, the total number of notes he has is ....
   ① 9   ② 27   ③ 18   ④ 51   ❷

13. ₹ 0.9 + ₹ 0.5 + ₹ 0.05 = ...
   ① ₹ 1.9   ② ₹ 0.19   ③ ₹ 14.5   ④ ₹ 1.45   ❹

14. ₹ 5,972 are in the form of 7 notes of ₹ 10, 2 notes of ₹ 1 and x notes of ₹ 100. $\therefore$ x = ...
   ① 597   ② 59   ③ 972   ④ 5972   ❷

15. How many equal numbers of 10 rupees, 5 rupees, 2 rupees and 1 rupee notes will be there in 360 rupees ?
   ① 36   ② 18   ③ 20   ④ 24   ❸

16. A ball pen costs three and a half rupees. Genu bought two such ball pens. What amount should he pay to the shopkeeper ?
   ① 6   ② 7   ③ 8   ④ 3   ❷

Examples for Practice

Q. Solve the following examples :

1. 740 paise = ... ₹
   ① 740   ② 7.40   ③ 74.00   ④ 7400

2. 400 paise = ... ₹
   ① 4.00   ② 40.00   ③ 400.00   ④ 0.4

3. Add ₹ 40.00, ₹ 87.00 and 78.00 = ?
   ① ₹ 127.00   ② ₹ 205.00   ③ ₹ 85.00   ④ ₹ 118.00

4. Subtract 92 paise from 20 rupees = ?
   ① ₹ 72   ② ₹ 27   ③ ₹ 19.08   ④ ₹ 29.08

5. Smit bought a shirt for ₹ 164.50 and shorts for ₹ 72.75. How much money in all did he spend ?
    ① ₹ 164.50   ② ₹ 238.25   ③ ₹ 237.25   ④ ₹ 40.75

6. I have ₹ 95.40 with me. How much short of ₹ 100 is this money ?
    ① ₹ 6.40   ② ₹ 4.60   ③ ₹ 5.40   ④ ₹ 5.60

7. Riya bought a colour box for ₹ 63.25. She gave the salesman seven 10 rupee notes. How much money did she get back ?
    ① ₹ 6.75   ② ₹ 7.25   ③ ₹ 8.50   ④ ₹ 6.25

8. Eight boys went on a picnic. They equally spent ₹ 82.00. How much did each one spend ?
    ① ₹ 8   ② ₹ 7   ③ ₹ 9.20   ④ ₹ 10.25

9. Yash had ₹ 75.00 in his piggy bank. On his tenth birthday he got ₹ 50.00 from his parents and ₹ 30.00 from his uncle. How much money is there in his piggy bank now ?
    ① ₹ 135   ② ₹ 125   ③ ₹ 80   ④ ₹ 155

10. My father gave me ₹ 40.00 to buy a geometry box. Its price was ₹ 27.50. How much money should I return to my father ?
    ① ₹ 12.50   ② ₹ 10.50   ③ ₹ 2.50   ④ ₹ 5.50

11. Paise 65 + Paise 20 = ? ₹
    ① ₹ 85   ② ₹ 0.85   ③ ₹ 8.5   ④ ₹ 8.05

12. ₹ 20 and Paise 20 = ? ₹
    ① 20.2   ② 0.20   ③ 0.202   ④ 0.22

13. ₹ 6.45 – ₹ 4.40 = ?
    ① ₹ 2.25   ② ₹ 2.20   ③ ₹ 2.10   ④ ₹ 2.05

14. ₹ 5.5 – ₹ 4.5 = ?
    ① ₹ 17.5   ② Re. 1   ③ ₹ 7.5   ④ ₹ 175

15. 750 paise means how many rupees ?
    ① 750   ② 75   ③ 7.5   ④ 0.75

16. Radha brought two books for ₹ 10 and a pen for ₹ 8. She gave the shopkeeper a ₹ 50 note. What amount should the shopkeeper return ?
    ① ₹ 22   ② ₹ 32   ③ ₹ 12   ④ ₹ 34

17. I brought 2 roses for 75 paise each and 1 aster for 25 paise. How much I need to pay ?
    ① ₹ 7.00   ② ₹ 2.15   ③ ₹ 1.75   ④ ₹ 1.50

18. Chetan bought a top for six and a half rupees, a towel for nine and a three quarter rupees and a water pistol for three and a quarter rupees. What is the total cost of all things ?
    ① ₹ 20.00   ② ₹ 19.50   ③ ₹ 19.00   ④ ₹ 19.25

19. John brought a silk handkerchief for ₹ 24.25 and socks for ₹ 12.50. He gave the shopkeeper a fifty rupee note. What amount should the shopkeeper return ?
    ① ₹ 12.75   ② ₹ 13.25   ③ ₹ 13.05   ④ ₹ 13.75

20. Mira purchased wheat for ₹ 19.75, rice for ₹ 17.95 and sugar for ₹ 18.70. What was the total amount she spent ?
    ① ₹ 56.40   ② ₹ 50.75   ③ ₹ 50.40   ④ ₹ 50.95

21. If a pen costs ₹ 7 and a notebook ₹ 13. What is the total cost ?
    ① ₹ 25   ② ₹ 30   ③ ₹ 20   ④ ₹ 15.

22. How many handkerchiefs can be brought for ₹ 56 if each costs ₹ 7 ?
    ① 8   ② 9   ③ 4   ④ 10

23. If the daily wages is ₹ 70, what is the total wages for 12 days ?
    ① ₹ 89   ② ₹ 840   ③ ₹ 88   ④ ₹ 80

24. Siraj has ₹ 260 and Raju has ₹ 251. How many more rupees does Siraj have ?
    ① ₹ 9   ② ₹ 10   ③ ₹ 11   ④ ₹ 13

25. If a shirt costs ₹ 100. What is the cost of 8 such shirts ?
    ① ₹ 800   ② ₹ 700   ③ ₹ 900   ④ ₹ 500

26. Rupees 5 = ? paise.
    ① 5   ② 50   ③ 5000   ④ 500

27. Madan bought a compass-box for ₹ 30, a note-book for ₹ 12.50 and a ruler for ₹ 4.50. If he gives the shopkeeper a note of ₹ 100, how many rupees will he get back ?
    ① ₹ 47   ② ₹ 53   ③ ₹ 42   ④ ₹ 58

28. Multiply ₹ 5.33 by 6.
    ① ₹ 31.98   ② ₹ 30.98   ③ ₹ 309.8   ④ ₹ 36.98

29. ₹ 8 consists of how many paise ?
    ① 80 p   ② 8 p   ③ 8000 p   ④ 800 p

30. Ramlal's milk expenses is ₹ 32 for daily. What is his total milk expenses in month of July ?
    ① ₹ 932   ② ₹ 960   ③ ₹ 992   ④ ₹ 994

Answers

1.	❷	2.	❶	3.	❷	4.	❸	5.	❸
6.	❷	7.	❶	8.	❹	9.	❹	10.	❶
11.	❷	12.	❶	13.	❹	14.	❷	15.	❸
16.	❷	17.	❸	18.	❷	19.	❷	20.	❶
21.	❸	22.	❶	23.	❷	24.	❶	25.	❶
26.	❹	27.	❷	28.	❶	29.	❹	30.	❸

❖ ❖ ❖

4.6 BASIC CONCEPTS OF SELLING AND PURCHASING OF ARTICLES

❦ INTRODUCTION :

In this topic your basic skill of selling and purchasing of articles will be assessed. You should be aware of buying things or articles as you may be shopping for your mother. You may be visiting shops for smaller purchases and are able to count and do total while paying the shopkeeper.

Model Examples

1. Raj bought a litre of milk for ₹ 46, bread for ₹ 24 and cake for ₹ 27. How much did he pay to the shopkeeper?
   ① ₹ 97   ② ₹ 87   ③ ₹ 107   ④ ₹ 117   ❶

2. Raghav had ₹ 100 with him, he bought a dozen of bananas for ₹ 25, $\frac{1}{2}$ kg of apples for ₹ 45 and 6 oranges for ₹ 20.
   How many rupees will remain with him?
   ① ₹ 15   ② ₹ 20   ③ ₹ 10   ④ ₹ 25   ❸

Examples for Practice

1. Ram had 5 dozens of alphonso (mangoes). He was selling it at the rate of ₹ 350 per dozen. If he sold $3\frac{1}{2}$ dozen how much did he earn?

   ① ₹ 1225   ② ₹ 1125   ③ ₹ 1325   ④ ₹ 1250

2. Gopal got his Diwali bonus of ₹ 28650. He decided to buy a microwave oven for ₹ 7980, a toaster for ₹ 1200 and a cooler for ₹ 13690. How much did he spend?

   ① ₹ 22890   ② ₹ 22870   ③ ₹ 21880   ④ ₹ 22980

3. Mrs Rao wanted to purchase dresses for Diwali. She spent ₹ 850 for Chinu's dress, ₹ 960 for Manu's dress and ₹ 1000 on saree. How much did she spend in all?

   ① ₹ 2910   ② ₹ 2800   ③ ₹ 2810   ④ ₹ 2710

4. Shyama had 8 dresses she sold each dress for ₹ 850 each. How much did she earn?

   ① ₹ 6800   ② ₹ 6400   ③ ₹ 6840   ④ ₹ 6480

5. Shankar's mother gave him the grocery list and asked him to purchase 1 kg of groundnut at ₹ 74, 1 kg of rice at ₹ 65, 1 kg of dal at ₹ 85, 1 kg of sugar for ₹ 40, salt for ₹ 18 and 1 kg of wheat flour for ₹ 35. What was the total amount he had to pay the grocer?

   ① ₹ 307   ② ₹ 327   ③ ₹ 316   ④ ₹ 317

6. Govind paid ₹ 9650 for deep freezer and ₹ 8750 for electric oven. What was the total amount he spent?

   ① ₹ 18500   ② ₹ 18400   ③ ₹ 18300   ④ ₹ 18450

7. Raghu sold crackers worth ₹ 1800, lantern for ₹ 350 and diyas for ₹ 250. How much did he earn in all?

   ① ₹ 2100   ② ₹ 2300   ③ ₹ 2500   ④ ₹ 2400

8. Rosy and Daniel went for Christmas shopping. They bought a Christmas tree for ₹ 1200, cake for ₹ 750 and some decorations for ₹ 550. What is the total amount spent by them?

   ① ₹ 2450   ② ₹ 2550   ③ ₹ 2500   ④ ₹ 2400

9. Raja had 35 school bags. He sold each school bag for ₹ 950. How much did he earn?
   ① ₹ 33250   ② ₹ 32250   ③ ₹ 23250   ④ ₹ 33050

10. A fruit seller sold 25 dozens of apples at ₹ 85 per dozen. What is the amount he earned?
    ① ₹ 2105   ② ₹ 2125   ③ ₹ 2205   ④ ₹ 2115

11. Ram purchased 2 kg sugar for ₹ 32 per kg, 3 kg price for ₹ 35 per kg, 1.5 kg toor dal for ₹ 70 per kg. How many rupees did Ram give the shop keeper ?
    ① ₹ 284   ② ₹ 254   ③ ₹ 137   ④ ₹ 274

12. Mrs. Rao had 99 sweaters. She sold each sweater for ₹ 475. How much did she earn ?
    ① ₹ 46925   ② ₹ 47025   ③ ₹ 47205   ④ ₹ 47250

13. Rajesh had a stock of 45 sewing machine. Each machine costs ₹ 3765. What is the total cost of sewing machines ?
    ① ₹ 1,69,425 ② ₹ 1,68,425   ③ ₹ 169405   ④ ₹ 169452

14. A vegetable vendor sold 45 kg of potatoes at ₹ 16 per kg and 55 kg of onions at ₹ 18 per kg What was total amount he learned ?
    ① ₹ 1700   ② ₹ 1610   ③ ₹ 1710   ④ ₹ 990

15. A fast food stall earned ₹ 18460 on Monday, ₹ 17580 on Tuesday and ₹ 19690 on Wednesday. How much did he earn altogether ?
    ① ₹ 55720   ② ₹ 45730   ③ ₹ 55630   ④ ₹ 55730

16. 5 kg potatoes were bought at the rate of ₹ 8 per kg. The shopkeeper was given a note of ₹ 50. How many rupees will the shopkeeper return ?
    ① ₹ 40   ② ₹ 10   ③ ₹ 55   ④ ₹ 45

Answers

1.	❷	2.	❷	3.	❸	4.	❶	5.	❹
6.	❷	7.	❹	8.	❸	9.	❶	10.	❷
11.	❹	12.	❷	13.	❶	14.	❸	15.	❹
16.	❷								

UNIT 5

MATHEMATICS IN DAILY LIFE

5.1   PROFIT AND LOSS

➤ When a person purchases things for a lower amount and sells it at a higher rate it is called profit.

For example : Radha bought a story book for ₹ 50 and sold it for ₹ 60. What is the profit that she made ?

    Selling Price – Cost price = Profit

∴   60 – 50 = 10

Radha made a profit of ₹ 10.

➤ When a person purchases for more price and sells for less price it is called loss.

For example : Akshay purchased a geometry box for ₹ 75 and sold it for ₹ 55. How much less amount did Akshay get or what was the loss that Akshay incurred ?

    Cost price – Selling price = Loss

∴   75 – 55 = 20

Akshay incurred a loss of ₹ 20.

The formula can be written as

$$S.P. - C.P. = Profit$$
$$C.P. - S.P. = Loss$$

Model Examples

1. If cost price of a scooter is ₹ 49650 and the selling price is ₹ 39780. What is the loss incurred ?

  ① ₹ 9870   ② ₹ 9840   ③ ₹ 90870 ④ ₹ 10880   ❶

  Explanation :   C.P. – S.P. = Loss

    i.e.   49650 – 39780 = ₹ 9870

2. Ram purchased a flat for ₹ 7,96,900 and sold it for ₹ 9,49,800 ? What was profit gained by Ram ?

① ₹ 1,52,090   ② ₹ 1,53,900

③ ₹ 1,52,900   ④ ₹ 2,52,900   ❸

Explanation :   S.P. – C.P. = Profit

∴   949800 – 796900 = ₹ 1,52,900

Examples for Practice

1. Usha sewing factory had 75 sewing machines costing ₹ 5984 per machine. If they sold all machines with a profit of ₹ 800 per machine what was the total profit earned ?

① 45,000   ② 55,000   ③ 60,000   ④ 65,000

2. Shyam had a bullet which he bought for ₹ 90,000. He sold it for ₹ 75,000. What was the loss he incurred ?

① 82,000   ② 15,000   ③ 130,00   ④ 65,000

3. Rajesh had 75 bags of rice in godown costing ₹ 785 each. He sold each bag for ₹ 1085. What was his profit per bag.

① 300   ② 200   ③ 400   ④ 100

4. Rashmi bought five dress for ₹ 2100 each and sold it for ₹ 2815 each ? What was the total amount of profit she earned ?

① 3,500   ② 3,485   ③ 3,565   ④ 3,575

5. Santosh had 9 buffaloes. The cost price of each buffalo was ₹ 45000/-. He sold each for ₹ 59000/-. What is the profit he earned ?

① 1,25000   ② 1,26,000   ③ 1,24,000   ④ 1,28,000

6. Hamid bought a pair of bullocks for ₹ 18000/- and he sold them for ₹ 15,800/- ? What was the loss incurred by him ?

① 2200   ② 2300   ③ 2100   ④ 2250

7. Ruksana bought vespa scooter for ₹ 69800/- in 2014. She sold it for ₹ 48,000 in 2016. What was the loss incurred by her ?

① 21,500   ② 21,600   ③ 21,800   ④ 21,900

8. Shekhar bought a plot of one acre for ₹ 5,49,800. He sold the same plot and made a profit of ₹ 2,50,000. What was the total amount he got ?

① 7,99,000   ② 799800

③ 8,00,000   ④ 8,99,800

9. Raghu's toy shop had remote control car worth ₹ 3650/-. He sold the car and made a profit of ₹ 375 – For how much did he sell the car ?

① 4025   ② 4020   ③ 4015   ④ 4010

10. Rajan bought a second hand tractor for ₹ 2,75,000/- and sold it after few months for ₹ 2,60,000/-. How much loss did he incur ?

① 10,000   ② 12,000   ③ 14,000   ④ 15,000

11. Adbul's shop had 10 school bags worth ₹ 4000/- each for sale and he sold each for ₹ 6890/-. What was the profit he earned ?

① 28,600   ② 28,200   ③ 28,900   ④ 28,700

12. A vendor bought toffees at 6 for a rupee. How many for a rupee must he sell to gain 20%?

① 6   ② 3   ③ 4   ④ 5

13. A man buys an article for ₹ 27.50 and sells it for ₹ 28.60. Find his gain percent.

① 1%   ② 2%   ③ 3%   ④ 4%

14. If a handbag is sold of ₹ 2000, at gain of 20% on cost price then cost price is

① ₹ 2,400   ② ₹ 2,666   ③ ₹ 2,666   ④ ₹ 2,850

15. A TV is purchased at ₹ 5000 and sold at ₹ 4000, find the lost percent.

① 10%   ② 20%   ③ 25%   ④ 28%

16. A shopkeeper expects a gain of 22.5% on his cost price. If in a week, his sale was of ₹ 392, what was his profit?

① ₹ 72   ② ₹ 70   ③ ₹88.25   ④ ₹18.20

17. In terms of percentage profit, which among following the best transaction.
    ① C.P. 36, Profit 17   ② C.P. 50, Profit 24
    ③ C.P. 40, Profit 19   ④ C.P. 60, Profit 29

18. A person incurs a loss of 5% be selling a watch for ₹ 1140. At what price should the watch be sold to earn 5% profit.
    ① ₹1200   ② ₹ 1230   ③ ₹1260   ④ ₹1290

19. A book was sold for ₹ 27.50 with a profit of 10%. If it were sold for ₹ 25.75, then would have been percentage of profit and loss ?
    ① 2% Profit ② 3% Profit ③ 2% Loss ④ 3% Loss

20. If the cost price is 25% of selling price. Then what is the profit percent.
    ① 150%   ② 200%   ③ 300%   ④ 350%

21. If Ana sells her house at loss of 10% on cost and paid ₹ 125000 for it then its selling price is
    ① ₹ 1,17,500   ② ₹ 1,24,500
    ③ ₹ 1,12,500   ④ ₹ 1,22,500

22. If antique piece is sold for ₹ 1200 at gain of 30% on sale price then profit is
    ① ₹ 360   ② ₹ 923   ③ ₹ 823   ④ ₹ 723

23. Harry bought 50kg of potatoes for resale on his retailer store whereas he paid ₹ 2/kg. he expects that 5% potatoes will be rotten. If 95% profit on cost is to be obtained then selling price is
    ① ₹ 4.10   ② ₹ 6.20   ③ ₹ 5.80   ④ ₹ 7.30

24. If a book is sold for ₹ 250 at 15% loss on cost then cost price of book is
    ① ₹ 350   ② ₹ 300   ③ ₹ 365   ④ ₹ 210

Answers

1.	❸	2.	❷	3.	❶	4.	❹	5.	❷
6.	❶	7.	❸	8.	❷	9.	❶	10.	❹

11.	❸	12.	❹	13.	❹	14.	❶	15.	❷
16.	❶	17.	❹	18.	❸	19.	❷	20.	❸
21.	❸	22.	❶	23.	❶	24.	❹		

5.2   SIMPLE INTEREST

✵ INTRODUCTION :

Simple interest is the interest calculated only on the principal regardless of the interest earned so far. Simple interest is the interest calculated only on the initial amount that you have invested.

The formula for simple interest is

$$I = \frac{P \times R \times T}{100}$$

I = Interest

P = Principal

R = Rate

T is the period of time.

Model Examples

Q. Solve the following examples.

1. How much will Radha get by investing ₹ 1000 for 1 year with a bank that pays 5% p.a. simple interest ?

   ① ₹ 55   ② ₹ 500   ③ ₹ 45   ④ ₹ 50   ❹

   Explanation :   Interest R $= 1000 \times \dfrac{5}{100}$

                             $= 1000 \times 0.05$

                 R $= 50$

2. Rajesh invested ₹ 4000 for 2 years with a bank that pays 4.5 % p.a. simple interest ? What is the amount that he will get after 2 years ?

   ① ₹ 4400   ② ₹ 4360   ③ ₹ 360   ④ ₹ 400   ❷

Explanation :   Interest $= \dfrac{P \times R \times T}{100}$

$$= \dfrac{4000 \times 4.5 \times 2}{100}$$

$$= 360$$

The amount what he will get after 2 years is

$4000 + 360 = ₹ 4360$.

Examples for Practice

Q. Solve the following examples.

1. Rajan kept ₹ 6000 for 3 years in a bank that pays 5% p.a. simple interest ? What is the interest that he will get ?
   ① ₹ 900   ② ₹ 6900   ③ ₹ 300   ④ ₹ 600

2. Rashid kept ₹ 35000 in Gomantak bank for 2 years at a rate of 4.5% p.a. simple interest. What is the total amount that he will get after 2 years ?
   ① ₹ 37,150   ② ₹ 3150   ③ ₹ 38,150   ④ ₹ 3815

3. Rahul invested ₹ 4500 for 2 years in a bank that pays 6% interest p.a. What is the interest that he will get ?
   ① ₹ 810   ② ₹ 5040   ③ ₹ 270   ④ ₹ 540

4. Mr. Iyer deposited ₹ 40,000 in a bank for 4 years at a rate of 5% p.a. simple interest. What is the total amount that he will get after 4 years ?
   ① ₹ 45,000   ② ₹ 48,000   ③ ₹ 42,666   ④ 47,200

5. Hamidabanu kept ₹ 19000 in a bank for a year at the interest of 4.5% p.a. What is the interest that she will get ?
   ① ₹ 855   ② ₹ 19855   ③ ₹ 860   ④ ₹ 800

6. Raghu deposited ₹ 85,000/- in a bank for 2 years at the interest of 3.5 % p.a. What is the amount Raghav will get after 2 years ?
   ① ₹ 93,925   ② ₹ 5,950   ③ ₹ 89,950   ④ ₹ 90,950

7. Mrs. Shinde got an interest of ₹ 525 for the ₹ 15,000 that she had deposited in the bank for a year ? What is the rate of interest ?

① 4.5%   ② 3.5%   ③ 4%   ④ 3%

8. Mr. Shaikh got an interest of 3510 for ₹ 26,000 that he deposited in the bank for three years. What is the rate of interest ?

① 5%   ② 3.5%   ③ 4.5%   ④ 4%

9. Roshan deposited ₹ 50,000 for a period of 5 years at 4.5% p.a. interest. What is the amount he will get after 5 years ?

① ₹ 53,750 ② ₹ 52,812 ③ ₹ 11,250 ④ ₹ 61,250

10. What will be the interest if ₹ 45,000/- is deposited in a bank for 7 years at 4.5% p.a. ?

① ₹ 14,175 ② ₹ 59,175 ③ ₹ 50,000 ④ ₹ 55,125

Answers

1.	❶	2.	❸	3.	❹	4.	❷	5.	❶
6.	❹	7.	❷	8.	❸	9.	❹	10.	❶

❖ ❖ ❖

6 UNIT

GEOMETRY

6.1   ANGLES

✌ INTRODUCTION :

When two rays have a common endpoint they form an angle. An angle has two arms formed by rays with a common endpoint. This common endpoint is called a vertex. These rays hold an angle enclosed between them.

AB and BC are known as arms of the angle. The angle enclosed within these arms is known as ∠ABC or ∠CBA. The middle letter is the vertex of the angle.

The plural of vertex is vertices.

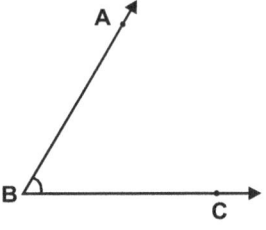

Fig. : 6.1

✌ TYPES OF ANGLES :

•◆ Acute angle less than 90°.

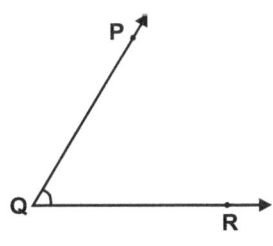

Fig. : 6.2 (a)

•◆ Right angle is equal to 90°.

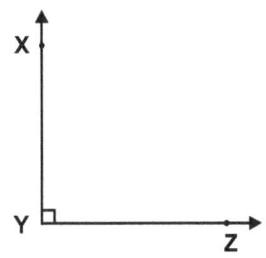

Fig. : 6.2 (b)

•◦ Obtuse angle between 90° to 180°

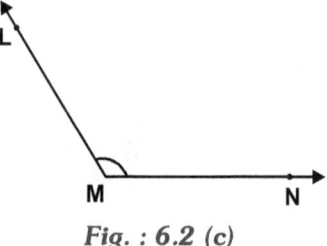

Fig. : 6.2 (c)

•◦ A protractor is used to measure an angle and also to draw an angle according to a given measure.

✌ *TYPES OF PAIR OF ANGLES* :

We can classify pair of angles as :

•◦ ***Adjacent Angles*** *:* Adjacent angles are side-by-side and share a common ray.

For example,

(1)   (2)

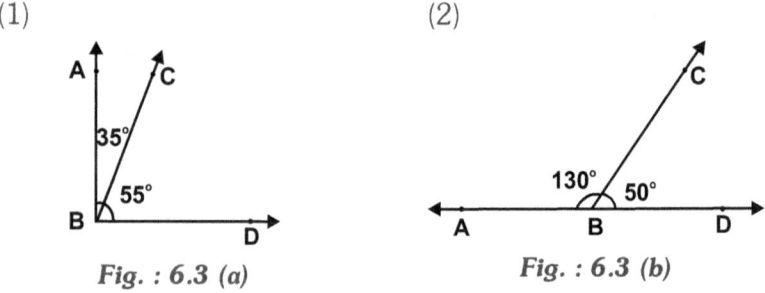

Fig. : 6.3 (a)   *Fig. : 6.3 (b)*

•◦ ***Vertically Opposite Angles or Vertical Angles :***

When 2 lines intersect they make vertical angles. Vertical angles are opposite to one another.

For example, Vertical angles are congruent (equal).

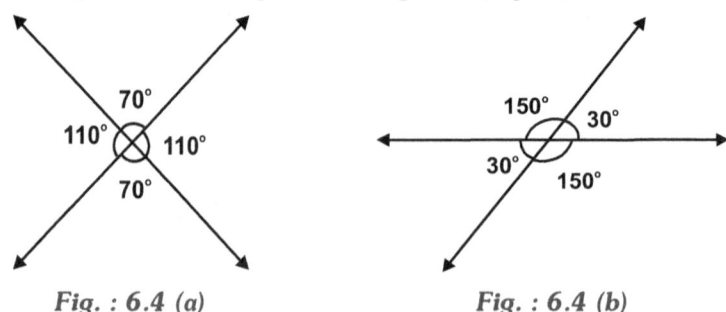

Fig. : 6.4 (a)   *Fig. : 6.4 (b)*

❖ *Supplementary Angles :*

Supplementary angles add up to 180° Adjacent and supplementary angles.

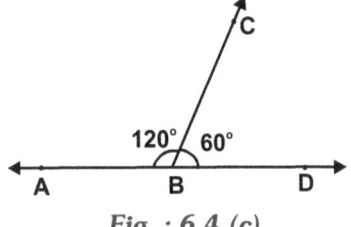

Fig. : 6.4 (c)

❖ *Complementary Angles :*

Complementary angles add upto 90°. Complementary and adjacent angles.

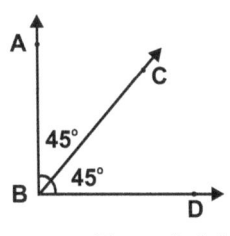

Fig. : 6.4 (d)

Model Examples

1. ∠ABC is ....
   ① Obtuse angle
   ② Acute angle
   ③ Right angle
   ④ Adjacent angle ❷

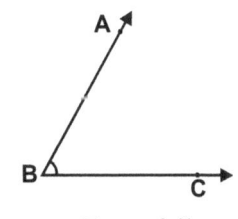

Fig. : 6.5

Explanation : ∠ABC is less than 90° so it is Acute angle.
∴ Alterative ❷ is the Correct Answer

2. ∠PQR is ....
   ① Acute angle
   ② Complementary angle
   ③ Right angle ❸
   ④ Obtuse angle

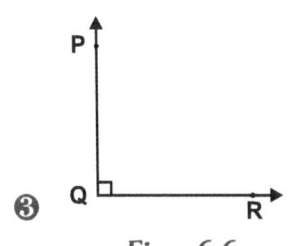

Fig. : 6.6

Explanation : ∠PQR is equal 90° so it is right angle

Examples for Practice

1. ∠LMN is ....
   ① Right angle
   ② Acute angle
   ③ Obtuse angle
   ④ Complementary angle

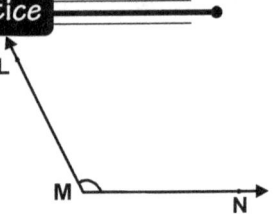

Fig. : 6.7

2. ∠PQR is ....
   ① Straight angle
   ② Obtuse angle
   ③ Right angle
   ④ Acute angle

Fig. : 6.8

3. ∠PQR and ∠ RQS are ......
   ① Right angle
   ② Adjacent angle
   ③ Obtuse angle
   ④ Vertically opposite angle

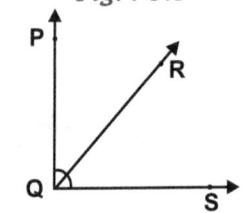

Fig. : 6.9

4. ∠ABC and ∠ CBD are ......
   ① Supplementary angle
   ② Vertically opposite angle
   ③ Obtuse angle
   ④ Right angle

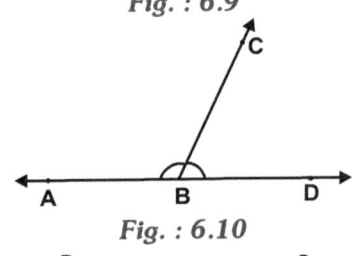

Fig. : 6.10

5. ∠PTS and ∠ QTR are ......
   ① Supplementary angle
   ② Adjacent angle
   ③ Vertically opposite angle
   ④ Complementary angle

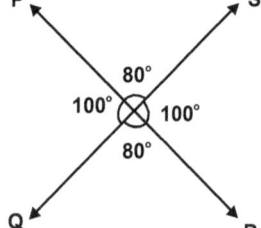

Fig. : 6.11

6. ∠LMN is ......
   ① Acute angle
   ② Obtuse angle
   ③ Right angle
   ④ Adjacent angle

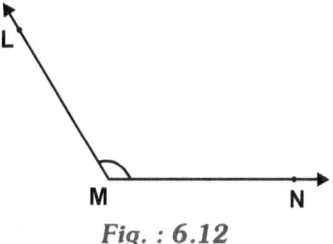

Fig. : **6.12**

7. ∠MNO is ......
   ① Acute angle
   ② Obtuse angle
   ③ Supplementary angle
   ④ Right angle

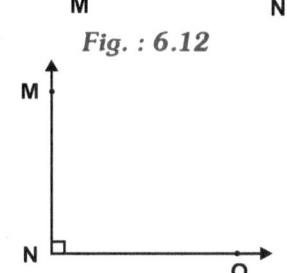

Fig. : **6.13**

8. ∠ABC and ∠ PQR are ......
   but not ....
   ① Complementary, adjacent
   ② Obtuse, acute
   ③ Supplementary, adjacent
   ④ Vertically, Opposite, Complementary

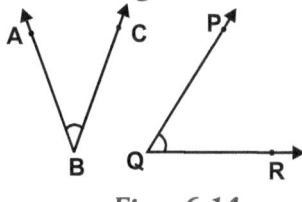

Fig. : **6.14**

9. What is the measure of
   ∠DBE is ?
   ① 145°
   ② 50°
   ③ 115°
   ④ 35°

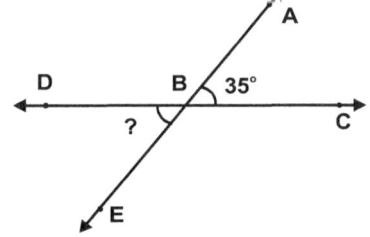

Fig. : **6.15**

10. ∠ABC = ?
    ① 115°
    ② 25°
    ③ 35°
    ④ 40°

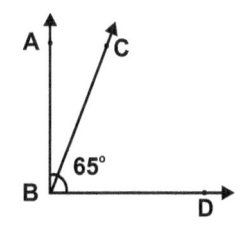

Fig. : **6.16**

Answers

1.	❸	2.	❹	3.	❷	4.	❶	5.	❸
6.	❷	7.	❹	8.	❶	9.	❹	10.	❷

❖ ❖ ❖

6.2   PARALLEL AND PERPENDICULAR LINES

Parallel Lines : Lines in the same plane which do not intersect each other are called parallel lines.

Fig. : 6.17

Perpendicular lines : When the angle between any two lines is 90°, they are called perpendicular lines.

Two show two lines are perpendicular we always use symbol of right angle.

Example : A vertical pole and its shadow on the road.

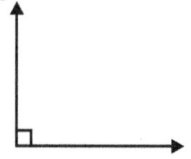

Fig. : 6.18

Model Examples

1. From the following figures find out the pair of lines which are not parallel.

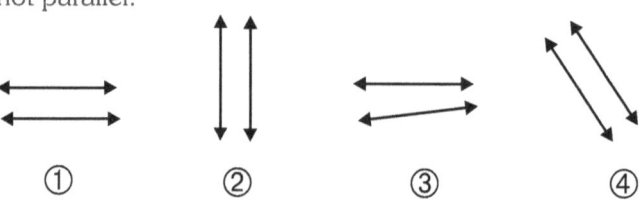

①   ②   ③   ④

Fig. : 6.19

Explanation : We want to find out from the above alternatives pair of lines which are not parallel.

Parallel Lines : Two lines extended in any direction when they do not intersect each other anywhere in the space. They are called as parallel lines.

In the above alternatives, in option 1, 2 and 4 if lines are extended they do not intersect each other. But the lines in option 3 if we extend them they intersect each other. So, they are not parallel lines.

∴ Alternative ❸ is the correct answer.

2. What is the angle between any two perpendicular lines ?
   ① 60°   ② 180°   ③ 45°   ④ 90°   ❹

Explanation : When two lines intersect each other in 90°, they are called as perpendicular lines.

∴ Alternative ❹ is the correct answer.

3. Which is the correct alternative of parallel lines from the figure along side ?

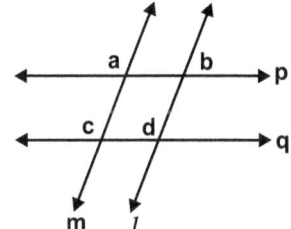

Fig. : 6.20

① line p and parallel line l   ② line q parallel line p
③ line m parallel line p   ④ line l parallel line p   ❷

Explanation : In the above example line l and line m are parallel to each other. And line p and line q parallel to each other.

∴ Alternative ❷ is the correct answer.

4. Opposite sides of rectangle are ....
   ① Perpendicular   ② Parallel
   ③ Alternative (1) and (2)   ④ None of these   ❷

Explanation : Opposite sides of rectangle are parallel.

∴ Alternative ➋ is the correct answer.

5. ΔPQR is a right angle triangle. Choose the correct alternative which show the perpendicular sides of right angle triangle ?

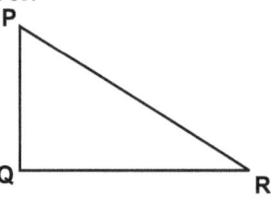

Fig. : 6.21

① Side PR || Side PQ   ② Side PR ⊥ Side QR

③ Side PQ ⊥ side QR   ④ No one of the above.   ➌

Explanation : Δ PQR is a right angled triangle. In right angle triangle two sides are perpendicular to each other. ∵ From above figure it is dear that side PQ is perpendicular to side QR.

∴ Alternative ➌ is the correct answer.

═══════ **Examples for Practice** ═══════

1. Which type of lines do not intersect to each other ?

① Parallel lines   ② Non-parallel lines

③ Perpendicular lines   ④ All of the above.

2. Which pair of lines from the following are parallel lines ?

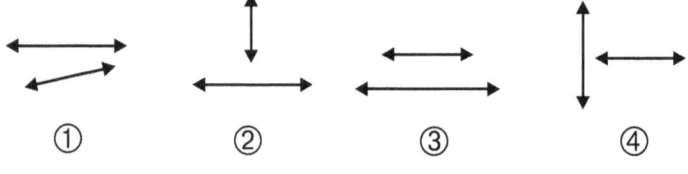

①   ②   ③   ④

Fig. : 6.22

3. Opposite sides of the square are ………..

① Parallel   ② Non-parallel

③ Perpendicular   ④ None of these.

4. Adjacent sides of the rectangle are ……… to each other.

① Parallel   ② Perpendicular

③ (1) and (2)   ④ None of these.

5. Write down the pair of parallel lines from the above figure.

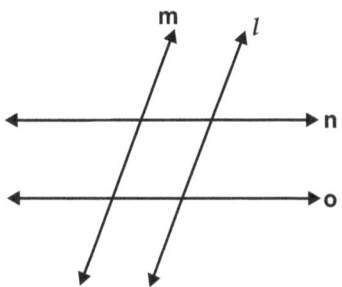

Fig. : 6.23

① line *l* || line m   ② line n || line *l*

   line n || line *l*   line o line m

③ line m || line o   ④ line *l* || line m

   line *l* || line n   line o || line n

Answers

1.	❶	2.	❸	3.	❶	4.	❷
5.	❹						

❖ ❖ ❖

6.3   *TRIANGLES, SQUARE, RECTANGLE, VERTICES & SIDES*

(A) TRIANGLES

✌ **INTRODUCTION :**

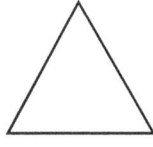

A triangle has 3 vertices, 3 sides and 3 angles.

Fig. : 6.24

Types of triangles :

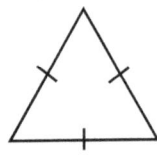

Fig. : 6.25

Equilateral triangle : All the sides and the three angles of the triangle are equal in length. Such a triangle is called an equilateral triangle.

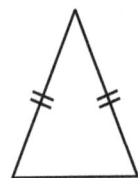

Fig. : 6.26

Isosceles triangle : Two adjacent sides of the triangle are of equal length and their opposite angles are equal. Such a triangle is called an isosceles triangle.

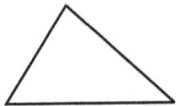

Fig. : 6.27

Scalene triangle : All the sides are of unequal lengths and three angles of the triangle are unequal. Such a triangle is called a scalene triangle.

Model Examples

1. Which is the equilateral triangle ?

① 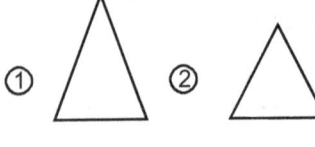 ② ③ 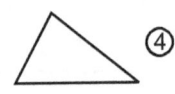 ④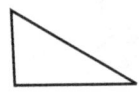

Fig. : 6.28

Examples for Practice

1. A triangle has .... vertices.

   ① 2   ② 3   ③ 4   ④ 1

2. All the three sides and three angles are equal. I am ....
   triangle.

   ① isosceles   ② scalene   ③ equilateral   ④ triangle

3. Two sides and their opposite angles are equal. I am ......
   triangle.
   ① scalene   ② equilateral
   ③ triangle   ④ isosceles

4. All the three sides and three angles are unequal. I am ......
   triangle.
   ① scalene   ② isosceles
   ③ equal   ④ equilateral

5. A triangle has .... angles.
   ① 1   ② 3   ③ 4   ④ 2

6. Which is the isosceles triangle of the following different
   figures ?

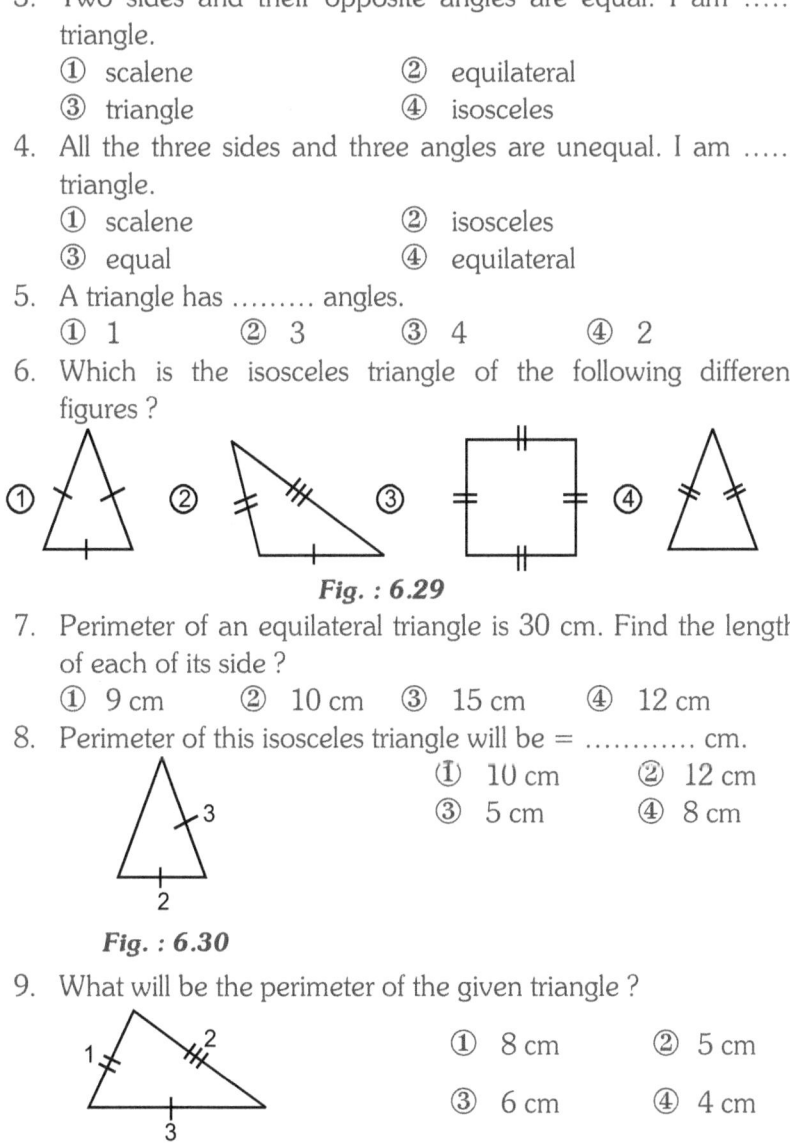

Fig. : 6.29

7. Perimeter of an equilateral triangle is 30 cm. Find the length
   of each of its side ?
   ① 9 cm   ② 10 cm   ③ 15 cm   ④ 12 cm

8. Perimeter of this isosceles triangle will be = ... cm.

   ① 10 cm   ② 12 cm
   ③ 5 cm   ④ 8 cm

Fig. : 6.30

9. What will be the perimeter of the given triangle ?

   ① 8 cm   ② 5 cm
   ③ 6 cm   ④ 4 cm

Fig. : 6.31

10. If the perimeter of an equilateral triangle is 18 cm, what is the
    length of one of its sides ?
    ① 5 cm   ② 8 cm   ③ 4 cm   ④ 6 cm

1.	❷	2.	❸	3.	❹	4.	❶	5.	❷
6.	❹	7.	❷	8.	❹	9.	❸	10.	❹

✤ ✤ ✤

(B) SQUARES AND RECTANGLES

✌ INTRODUCTION :

1. **Quadrilateral :** A closed figure having four sides is called a quadrilateral.

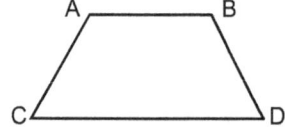

Fig. : 6.32

2. **Square :** A square is quadrilateral having all its sides of equal length and are at right angle to each other. All the angles of square are at a right angle.

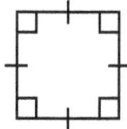

Fig. : 6.33

3. **Rectangle :** A rectangle is a quadrilateral having its opposite sides of equal lengths and all sides are at right angle to each other.

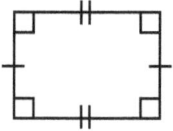

Fig. : 6.34

4. **Rhombus :** All the sides of a rhombus are equal in length but its angles are not right angles.

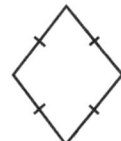

Fig. : 6.35

5. Kite : A kite has two smaller sides which are equal in length and two longer sides that are also equal in length.

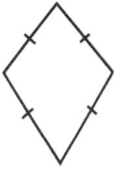

Fig. : 6.36

Model Examples

Solve the following :

1. Which of the following figure is a rectangle ?   ❸

    ①   ②   ③   ④

Fig. : 6.37

Examples for Practice

Q. Solve the following examples :

1. A square has .... sides and .... corners.

    ① equal, four   ② three, four

    ③ four, three   ④ two, four

2. .... opposite sides are of the same length.

    ① Square   ② Kite   ③ Rectangle ④ Rhombus

3. Triangle has .... vertices.

    ① four   ② three   ③ two   ④ one

4. How many triangles does the accompanying figure contain ?

    ① 3   ② 4

    ③ 6   ④ 5

Fig. : 6.38

5. How many rectangles does the following figure have ?

   ① 6   ② 4
   ③ 5   ④ 3

Fig. : 6.39

6. How many square does the following figure have ?

   ① 9   ② 8
   ③ 10   ④ 7

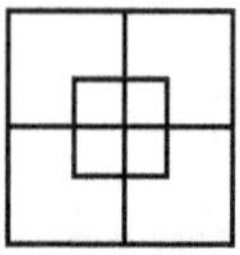

Fig. : 6.40

7. Which of the following is a kite ?

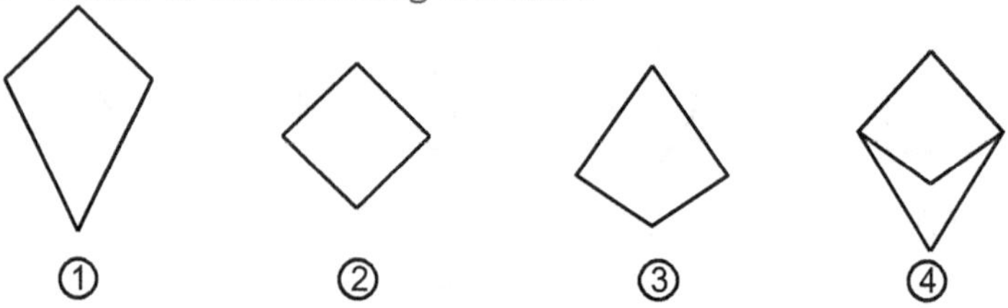

   ①   ②   ③   ④

Fig. : 6.41

8. Which figure is not a rectangle ?

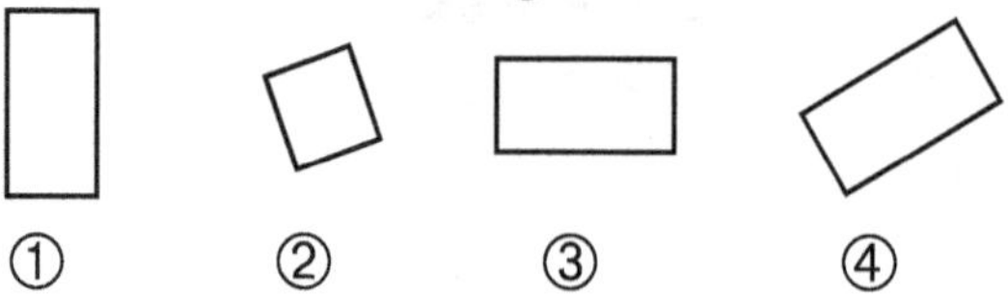

   ①   ②   ③   ④

Fig. : 6.42

9. All four sides of ...... are equal, but its angles are not right angles.

   ① square   ② rectangle ③ rhombus   ④ kite

10. A figure with four sides is called a ....
    ① triangle   ② circle   ③ angle   ④ quadrilateral

11. Perimeter of a rectangle is .... cm.

    ① 5 cm   ② 6 cm
    ③ 10 cm   ④ 8 cm

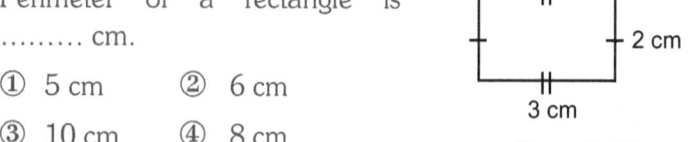
3 cm
2 cm

Fig. : 6.43

12. Perimeter of a quadrilateral is
.... cm.

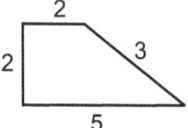

Fig. : 6.44

① 10 cm   ② 12 cm

③ 8 cm   ④ 20 cm

13. The length and breadth of a rectangular ground is 60 m and 30 m respectively. Find its perimeter.

① 90 m   ② 150 m   ③ 120 m   ④ 180 m

14. How many rectangles are there in the adjoining figure ?

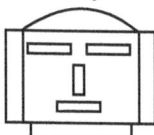

Fig. : 6.45

① 9   ② 11

③ 10   ④ 8

15. Join the dots and state which figure do you get ?

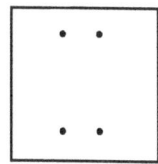

Fig. : 6.46

① Square ② Triangle

③ Kite④Rectangle

16. Name the shaded figure.

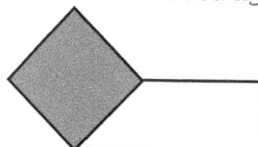

Fig. : 6.47

① Circle

② Rhombus

③ Triangle

④ Rectangle

17. What is the number of shaded square ?

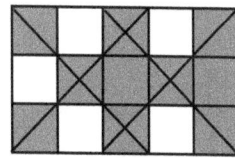

Fig. : 6.48

① 10   ② 5

③ 6   ④ 2

18. In figure how many quadrilaterals can you get ?

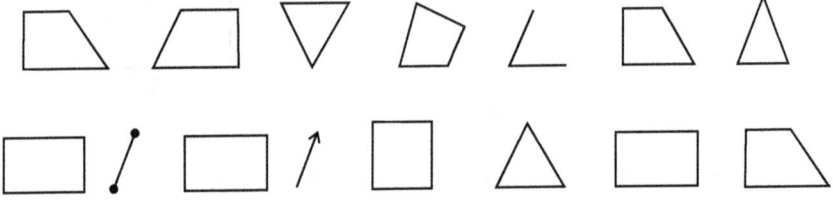

Fig. : 6.49

① 9   ② 15   ③ 12   ④ 10

19. Which of the following figure is a square ?

Fig. : 6.50

20. Which of the following is not a kite ?

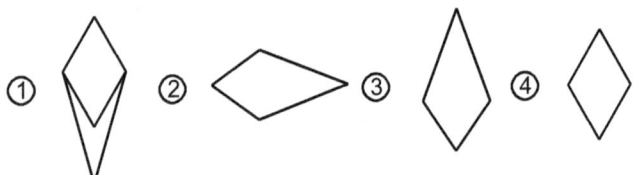

Fig. : 6.51

21. What is the figure given below called ?

Fig. : 6.52

① Square

② Rhombus

③ Triangle

④ Quadrilateral

22. Which of the following is not a rectangle ?

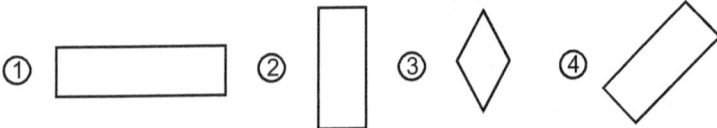

Fig. : 6.53

23. What is the figure inside the circle called ?

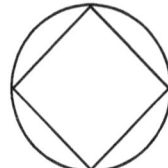

Fig. : 6.54

① Kite

② Square

③ Rectangle

④ Rhombus

24. How many sides does a rectangle have ?

① 2   ② 3   ③ 4   ④ 5

25. Which of these figures is a 'Square' ?

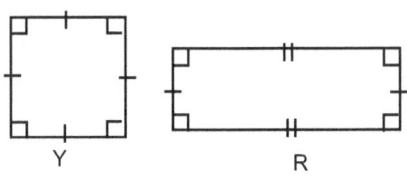 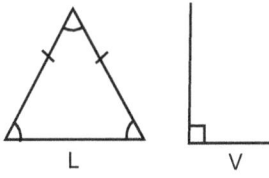

Fig. : 6.55

① Y   ② R   ③ L   ④ V

Answers

1.	❶	2.	❸	3.	❷	4.	❹	5.	❶
6.	❸	7.	❶	8.	❷	9.	❸	10.	❹
11.	❸	12.	❷	13.	❹	14.	❷	15.	❹
16.	❷	17.	❶	18.	❶	19.	❸	20	❹
21.	❷	22.	❸	23.	❷	24	❸	25.	❶

❖ ❖ ❖

6.4	*CIRCLE – RADIUS, DIAMETER, CENTRE, CHORD*

✌ INTRODUCTION :

1. **Centre :** 'C' is called centre of circle.

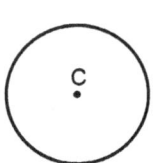

Fig. : 6.56

2. **Radius :** Segment AB is called as radius of circle.

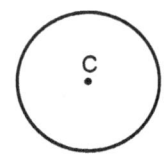

Fig. : 6.57

3. **Diameter :** Any line that joins two points on the circle and passes through the centre of the circle is called as a diameter.

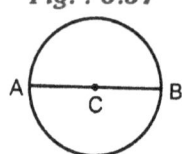

Fig. : 6.58

4. **Chord :** Any segment that joins two points on a circle is called a chord. Also, the diameter is the greatest chord.

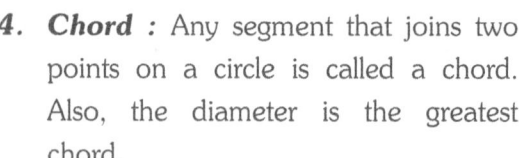

Fig. : 6.59

5. **Arc :** On the given circle, there are points PQ and AB. These points have divided the circle into four parts. Each of these parts is an arc of the circle. P and Q have created two arcs, P and Q are the end points. A and B have created two arcs, A and B are the end points.

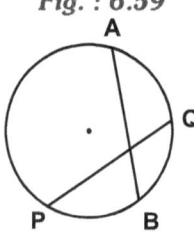

Fig. : 6.60

6. Circumference of the circle : The circumference of the circle is the distance around it.

We measure circumference - $\pi \times$ diameter $= 2 \times \pi \times r$. The circumference is the length of the edge around a circle. For any circle the circumference is 3.14 or $\frac{22}{7}$.

7. Interior and exterior of circle : Points R, C, P, Q are points in the interior of the circle.

Points K, L, D are points in the exterior of the circle.

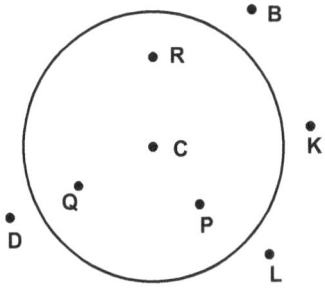

Fig. : 6.61

Model Examples

Q. Solve the following :

1. In following Fig. C is centre of circle. Then CD is which part of the circle ?
    ① Chord   ② Diameter
    ③ Perimeter   ④ Radius   ❹

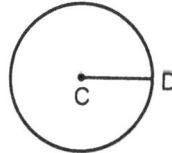

Fig. : 6.62

2. Which is the greatest chord of circle ?
    ① Radius   ② Diameter
    ③ Perimeter   ④ Ray   ❷

Examples for Practice

Q. Solve the following examples :

1. How many centres can be found in a circle ?
    ① One   ② Many   ③ Multiple   ④ Two

Read the given figure and give the answer of following
questions :

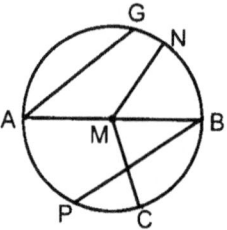

Fig. : 6.63

2. Which is the centre of circle ?

   ① Point B   ② Point M ③ Point G   ④ Point A

3. Which is the chord of the circle ?

   ① Seg AG   ② Seg PB ③ Seg AB   ④ All of these

4. From the following options write that which seg is the radius
   of circle ?

   ① Seg AG   ② Seg PB ③ Seg AB   ④ Seg MB

5. In the above figure which is the largest chord of a circle ?

   ① Seg AB   ② Seg AG ③ Seg PB   ④ Seg MC

6. How many radii can be drawn in a circle ?

   ① 1   ② 2   ③ Many   ④ 10

7. AB is an ....

   ① radius   ② diameter

   ③ arc   ④ circumference

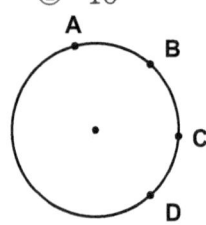

Fig. : 6.64

8. The .... of the circle is the distance around it.

   ① circumference   ② radius

   ③ arc   ④ diameter

9. ...... is the centre of the given circle.
   - ① R
   - ② Q
   - ③ S
   - ④ P

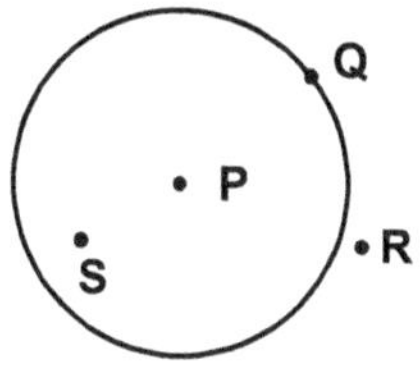

Fig. : 6.65

10. If AB is 4 cm then CD is ....
    - ① 4 cm
    - ② 8 cm
    - ③ 16 cm
    - ④ 12 cm

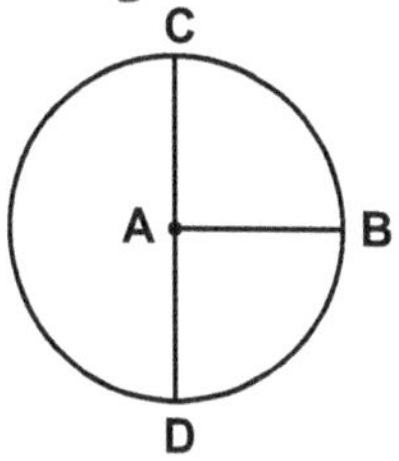

Fig. : 6.66

11. The .... of a circle is twice the length of its ....
    - ① diameter, radius
    - ② radius, diameter
    - ③ diameter, arc
    - ④ diameter, circumference

12. All the .... of the circle are of the same length.
    - ① arc
    - ② circumference
    - ③ diameters
    - ④ point

13. A segment joining any two points on a circle is called a ......
    - ① chord
    - ② arc
    - ③ radius
    - ④ diameter

14. We use a .... to draw a circle.
    - ① scale
    - ② protector
    - ③ pencil
    - ④ compass

15. If the radius of the circle is 7 cm, what will be its diameter ?
    - ① 21 cm
    - ② 14 cm
    - ③ 7 cm
    - ④ 28 cm

16. .... point is on the circle.
    - ① A
    - ② B
    - ③ D
    - ④ C

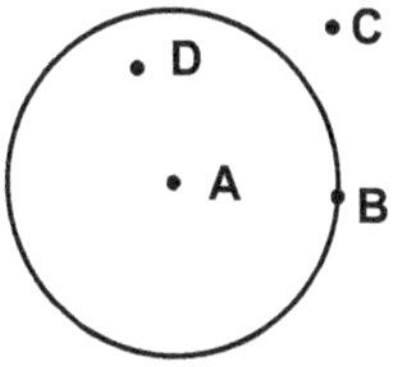

Fig. : 6.67

17. .... point is in the exterior of the circle.
① S
② R
③ P
④ Q

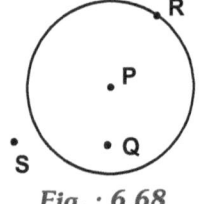

Fig. : 6.68

18. .... Is the chord of the circle.
① BA
② DC
③ AB
④ PQ

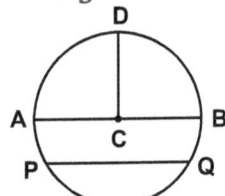

Fig. : 6.69

Answers

1.	❶	2.	❷	3.	❹	4.	❹	5.	❶
6.	❸	7.	❸	8.	❶	9.	❹	10.	❷
11.	❶	12.	❶	13.	❶	14.	❹	15.	❷
16.	❸	17.	❶	18.	❹				

❖ ❖ ❖

6.5   *PERIMETER*

INTRODUCTION :

The perimeter of any closed figure is the sum of the lengths of all its sides.

Perimeter of a triangle = Sum of all three sides.

Perimeter of a square = 4 × side.

Perimeter of a rectangle = 2 (length + breadth).

Model Examples

Solve the following :

1. A garden is 20 m. in breadth and 25 m. in length. What is its perimeter ?
① 45 m
② 90 m
③ 50 m
④ 40 m   ❷

Explanation :

Perimeter of rectangle = 2 (length + breadth)

$$= 2 (20 + 25) = 2 \times 45 = 90 \text{ m}$$

2. The square perimeter of a square is 32 m. Find its side.

① 8 m   ② 16 m   ③ 10 m   ④ 4 m

Explanation :

Perimeter of square = 4 × side

$$32 = 4 \times \text{side}$$

$$\frac{32}{4} = \text{side}$$

$$8 \text{ m} = \text{side}$$

Examples for Practice

Solve the following examples :

1. The length of a side of a square is 26 cm. What will be its perimeter ?

   ① 52 cm   ② 104 cm   ③ 100 cm   ④ 75 cm

2. How many kilometers of wire will be required to fence a field 250 m long and 150 m wide. Five times over.

   ① 4 km   ② 400 km   ③ 500 m   ④ 3 km

3. Find the perimeter of the figure ?

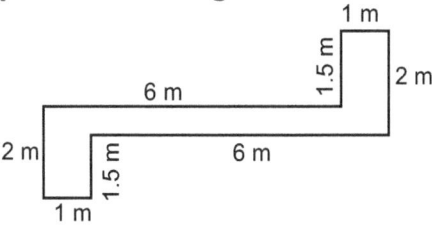

Fig. : 6.70

   ① 20 m   ② 12 m   ③ 21 m   ④ 22 m

4. The sides of the triangle measure 4x cm, 2x cm and 3x cm. What is the perimeter ?

   ① 9x cm   ② 3x cm   ③ $6x^2$ cm   ④ 4x cm

5. The perimeter of an equilateral triangle is 21 cm. What is the measure of one of its side ?

    ① 6 cm   ② 9 cm   ③ 7 cm   ④ 4 cm

6. What is the perimeter of square whose side is 9 cm ?

    ① 81 cm   ② 18 cm   ③ 36 cm   ④ 18 cm

7. A square field whose side measures 20 m. is to be fenced 4 times over. How many m wire will be   required ?

    ① 320 m   ② 420 m   ③ 80 m   ④ 200 m

8. What is the perimeter and area of the given figure ?

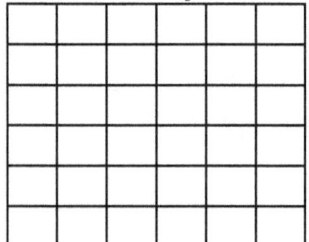

    ① 36 sq. cm

    ② 30 sq. cm

    ③ 36 sq. mt

    ④ 24 sq. cm

9. What is the perimeter of ⊏ABCD ?

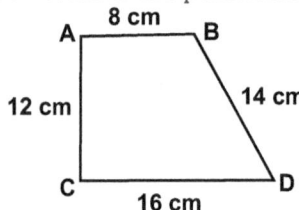

    ① 100 cm

    ② 24 cm

    ③ 26 cm

    ④ 50 cm

    Fig. : 6.71

10. The perimeter of the given figure is ....

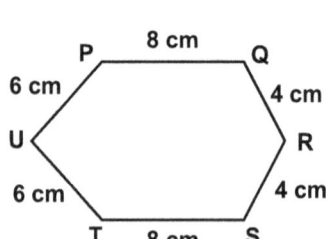

    ① 72 cm

    ② 36 cm

    ③ 40 cm

    ④ 28 cm

    Fig. : 6.72

11. Perimeter of ∈ABCD is ....

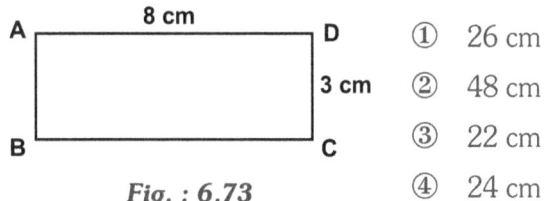

Fig. : 6.73

① 26 cm

② 48 cm

③ 22 cm

④ 24 cm

12. The length of one side of a a square is 4 cm. Then its perimeter would be ....

Fig. : 6.74

① 16 cm

② 32 cm

③ 64 cm

④ 8 cm

13. If the length of a rectangle is 24 m and its width is 18 m. What is its perimeter ?

① 48 cm   ② 54 cm   ③ 42 cm   ④ 84 cm

14. If the sides of a triangle are 26 cm, 23.4 cm and 12.6 cm respectively. What is the perimeter of the triangle ?

① 61.4 cm   ② 62 cm   ③ 61 cm   ④ 61.6 cm

15. The length of a square plot of land is 60 m. A double fence is put along its edges. If the wire costs 75 rupees per meter. What will the total cost of the wire needed for the fence ?

① ₹ 1,800   ② ₹ 18,000   ③ ₹ 36,000   ④ ₹ 3600

Answers

1.	❷	2.	❶	3.	❸	4.	❶	5.	❸
6.	❸	7.	❶	8.	❶	9.	❹	10.	❷
11.	❸	12.	❶	13.	❹	14.	❷	15.	❸

♣ ♣ ♣

6.6   AREA

✌ INTRODUCTION :

Area means on any surface, the measure of the place occupied by a figure is the area of that figure.

For example,

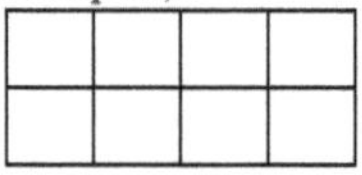

Fig. : 6.75

The measure of a figure remains the same no matter who measures it so we use a square of side 1 cm is used as the standard unit of measurement of area.

The area of a figure is given in square centimeters (sq. cm).

To find out the area of the rectangle given above let us count the number of squares with sides of 1 cm on the papers.

Fig. : 6.76

There are 8 such squares in the above figure. Therefore, the area of the figure is 8 sq cm.

What is the area of the given figure ?

Let us count the squares with sides 1 cm in it.

$$\text{Area of the shape} = \text{number of squares}$$
$$= 16$$

Therefore, area of the figure = 16 sq cm.

Example,

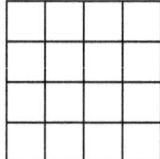

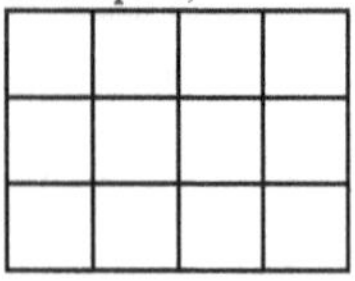

Fig. : 6.77

Find out the area and perimeter of the given figure.

Area : Number of squares = 12

Therefore area of the figure = 12 sq cm

$$\text{Perimeter} = \text{Perimeter of the surface}$$
$$= \text{Sum of the length of all four sides of the surface}$$
$$= 3 + 4 + 3 + 4 = 14 \text{ sq cm.}$$

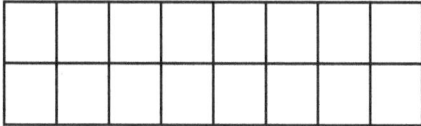

Model Examples

Solve the following :

1. Area of the above figure is ....

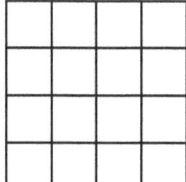

Fig. : 6.78

  ①   16 sq. cm   ②   20 sq. cm
  ③   18 sq. cm   ④   14 sq. cm   ❶

2. What is the perimeter and area of the given figure ?

                      ①   16 sq. cm   ②   18 sq. cm
                      ③   12 sq. cm   ④   20 sq. cm
                                            ❶

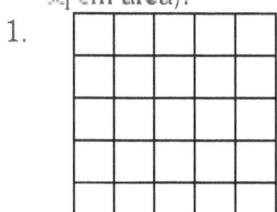

Fig. : 6.79

Examples for Practice

Solve the following examples :

Find the area of the following figure (all small squares are of 1 sq cm area).

1.

                          ①   20 sq. cm
                          ②   25 sq. cm
                          ③   30 sq. cm
                          ④   30 sq. mt

Fig. : 6.80

2. Area of the given figure is ....

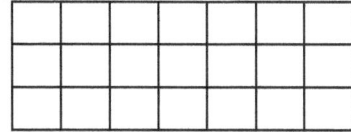

Fig. : 6.81

  ①   20 sq. cm   ②   21 sq. cm ③   21 sq. mt   ④   20 sq. mt   ❷

3. What is the area of the given figure ....

   ① 9 sq. cm   ② 12 sq. cm

   ③ 9 sq. mt   ④ 12 sq. mt

Fig. : 6.82

4. Area of given rectangle is ....

   ① 20 sq. cm

   ② 18 sq. cm

   ③ 24 sq. cm

   ④ 24 sq. mt

Fig. : 6.83

5. What is the area of the given figure ?

Fig. : 6.84

① 9 sq. cm   ② 9 sq. mt   ③ 10 sq. cm   ④ 10 sq. mt

6. Area of the given figure is ....

   ① 18 sq. cm

   ② 18 sq. mt

   ③ 20 sq. cm

   ④ 20 sq. mt

Fig. : 6.85

7. What is the area of the given figure ?

   ① 4 sq. cm   ② 1 sq. cm

   ③ 4 sq. mt   ④ 1 sq. mt

Fig. : 6.86

8. The side of the square is 8 cm. Find its area of ....

   ① 640 cm   ② 32 cm   ③ 16 cm   ④ 64 cm

9. What will be the cost of laying the floor in a house that is 18 m long and 14 m wide if the cost of laying 1 sq. m is 90 rupees ?

   ① ₹ 2268   ② ₹ 22680   ③ ₹ 22860   ④ ₹ 252

10. If the cost of 1 sq m of a plot of land is 1200 rupees, find the total cost of a plot of a land that is 28 m long and 23 m broad.
    ① ₹ 772800 ② ₹ 7728 ③ ₹ 77280 ④ ₹ 772008

11. What is the area of a rectangle of length 25 cm and breadth 19 cm ?
    ① 480 cm ② 225 cm ③ 475 cm ④ 485 cm

12. A wall that is 9 m long and 8 m wide has to be white washed. If the labour charges as ₹ 45 per sq. m. What is the cost of labour for painting this wall ?
    ① ₹ 3204 ② ₹ 324 ③ ₹ 72 ④ ₹ 3240

13. The length of the side of square is 16 cm. Find its area.
    ① 246 cm ② 256 cm ③ 156 cm ④ 250 cm

14. How many more squares with the same measure will fit in the empty space in the figure ?

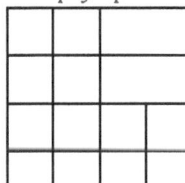

    ① 4   ② 2
    ③ 6   ④ 8

Fig. : 6.87

15. What is the area of a rectangle of length 32 cm and width 26 cm ?
    ① 723 cm ② 823 cm ③ 832 cm ④ 732 cm

Answers

1.	❷	2.	❷	3.	❶	4.	❸	5.	❶
6.	❸	7.	❶	8.	❹	9.	❷	10.	❶
11.	❸	12.	❹	13.	❷	14.	❶	15.	❸

❖ ❖ ❖

| 6.7 | THREE DIMENSIONAL OBJECTS AND NETS |

❦ INTRODUCTION :

Under this topic you have to understand the 3D shapes and answer the question asked. The figures are mostly cuboids. If you cut the figure and make a cube you get the correct answer.

Model Examples

1.

		a	
b	c	d	e
	f		

In the given figure when a box is formed by folding it as shown in figure which alphabet is seen on the surface opposite 'f'?

① a   ② d   ③ e   ④ b   ❶

2.

		5	
6	7	8	9
	10		

In the given figure when a box is formed by folding it as shown in figure which number is seen on the surface opposite '5'?

① 6   ② 7   ③ 9   ④ 10   ❹

Examples for Practice

1. In the given figure when a box is formed by folding it as shown in figure which number is seen on the surface opposite '2'?

		6	
2	3	4	5
	1		

① 3   ② 4   ③ 5   ④ 1

2. In the given figure when a box is formed by folding it as shown in alphabet which number is seen on the surface opposite 'l'?

		j	
k	l	m	n
	o		

① j   ② o   ③ n   ④ k

3. In the given figure when a box is formed by folding it as shown in figure which number is seen on the surface opposite '8'?

		3	
4	5	6	7
	8		

① 4   ② 5   ③ 6   ④ 3

4. In the given figure when a box is formed by folding it as shown in alphabet which number is seen on the surface opposite 'v'?

		u	
v	w	x	Y
	z		

① x   ② y   ③ u   ④ z

5. In the given figure when a box is formed by folding it as shown in figure which number is seen on the surface opposite '12'?

		6	
2	3	4	5
	1		

① 6   ② 2   ③ 10   ④ 4

6. In the given figure when a box is formed by folding it as shown in alphabet which number is seen on the surface opposite 'e'?

		a	
b	c	d	e
	f		

① b   ② f   ③ c   ④ a

7. In the given figure when a box is formed by folding it as shown in figure which number is seen on the surface opposite '9' ?

		25	
3	4	9	16
	5		

① 3   ② 4   ③ 25   ④ 5

8. In the given figure when a box is formed by folding it as shown in alphabet which number is seen on the surface opposite 'e'?

		a	
c	e	g	I
	k		

① g   ② a   ③ k   ④ I

Answers

1.	②	2.	❸	3.	❹	4.	❶	5.	②
6.	❸	7.	❶	8.	❹				

❖ ❖ ❖

6.8   *FIGURE PATTERN*

✤ *INTRODUCTION :*

Under this topic you are expected to observe the given figures and diagrams and write the correct answer. It includes geometrical figures and designs, all kinds of symbols, pictures, designs, letters, digits and drawings.

Model Examples

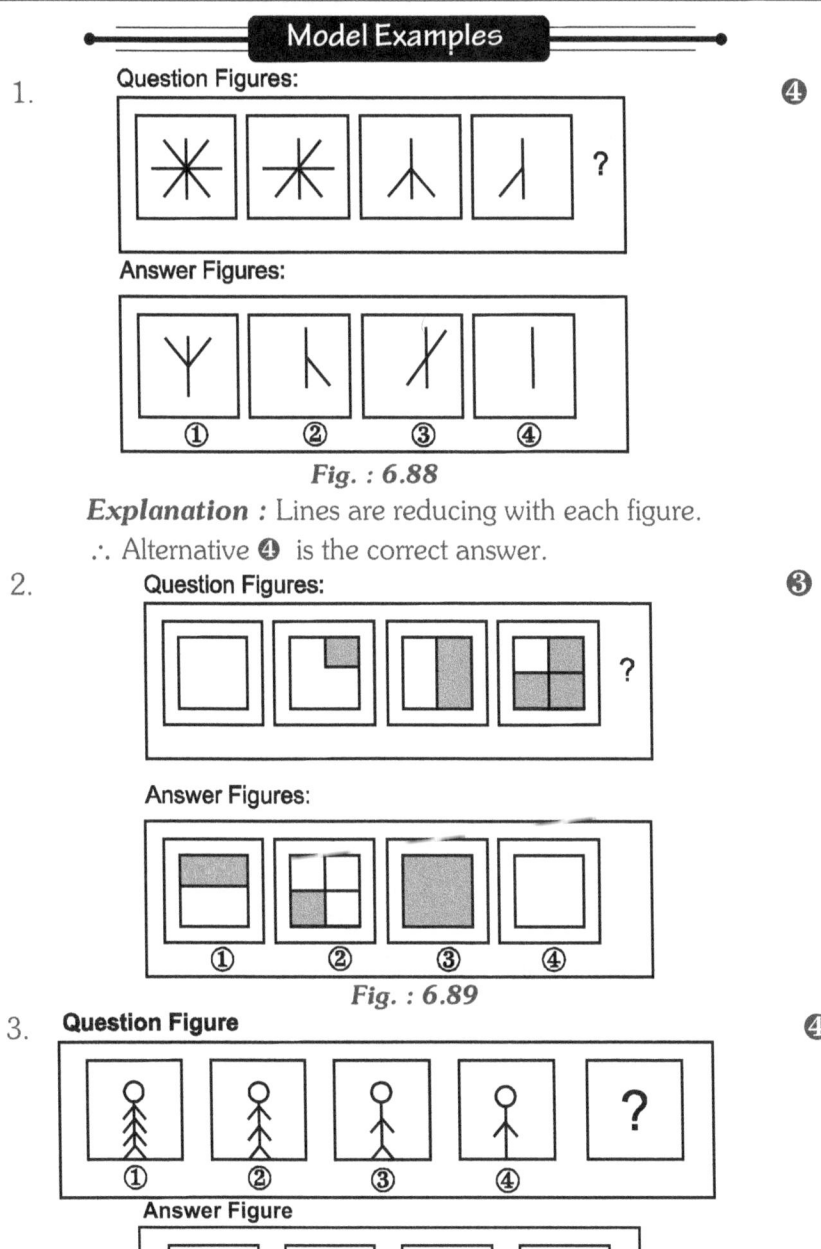

1. **Question Figures:**   ❹

   Answer Figures:

   ①   ②   ③   ④

   Fig. : 6.88

   Explanation : Lines are reducing with each figure.

   ∴ Alternative ❹ is the correct answer.

2. **Question Figures:**   ❸

   Answer Figures:

   ①   ②   ③   ④

   Fig. : 6.89

3. **Question Figure**   ❹

   ①   ②   ③   ④   ?

   Answer Figure

   ①   ②   ③   ④

   Fig. : 6.90

Explanation : Pair of lines are reducing by one with each figure. ∴ Alternative ❹ is the correct answer.

4.   ❶

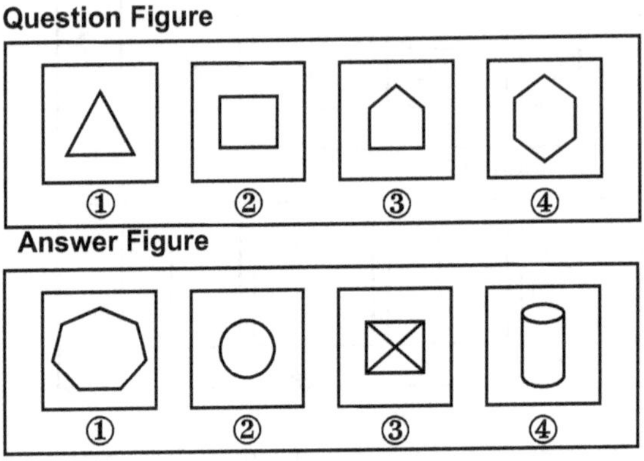

Question Figure

Answer Figure

Fig. : 6.91

Explanation : If you observe carefully, the first figure have three sides, next figure have four sides I. In this way, in each next figure there is increase of by one side.

∴ Alternative ❶ is the correct answer.

5.

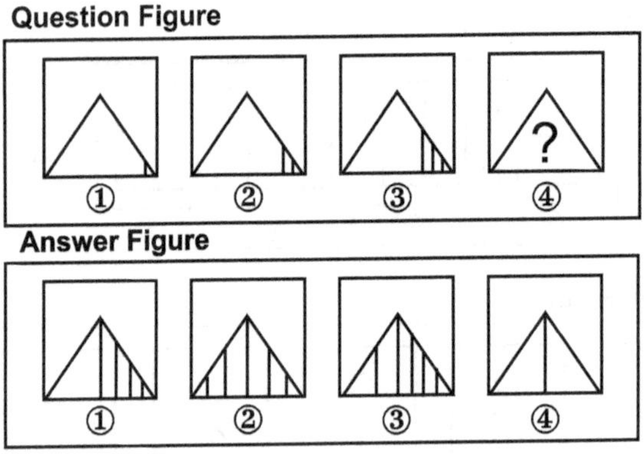

Question Figure

Answer Figure

Fig. : 6.92

Explanation : If you observe carefully, the number of vertical lines in triangle is in increasing pattern i.e. 1, 2, 3, 4.

∴ In place of question mark the triangle with 4 lines will appear.

∴ Alternative ❶ is the correct answer.

Examples for Practice

Q. Find the exact term in place of question mark.

1.

Question Figures:

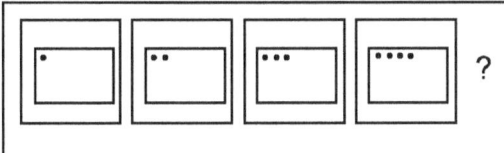

Answer Figures:

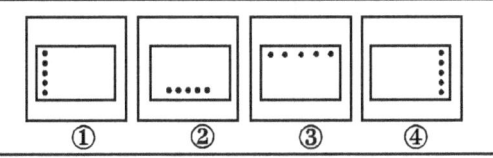

Fig. : 6.93

2. Question Figures:

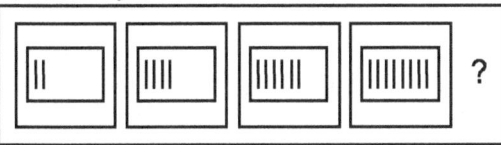

Answer Figures:

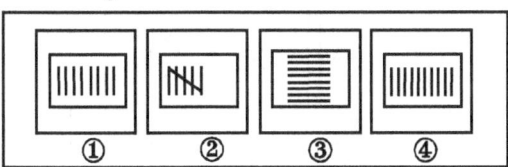

Fig. : 6.94

3. Question Figures:

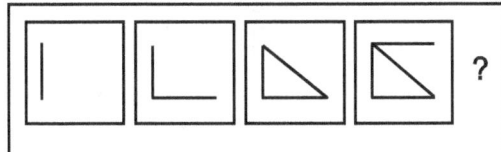

Answer Figures:

Fig. : 6.95

4.

Question Fig.

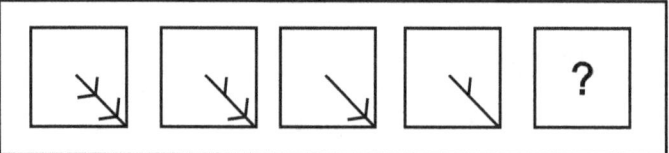

Answer Figure

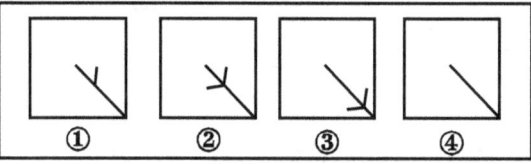

Fig. : 6.96

5.

Question Figures:

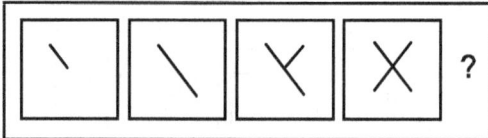

Answer Figures:

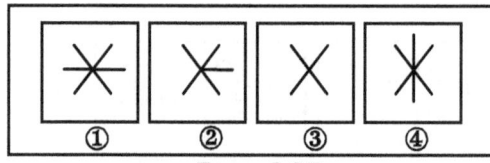

Fig. : 6.97

6.

Question Figures:

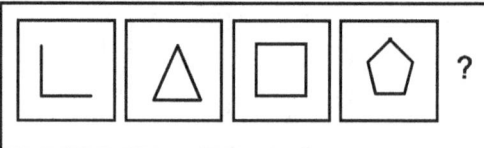

Answer Figures:

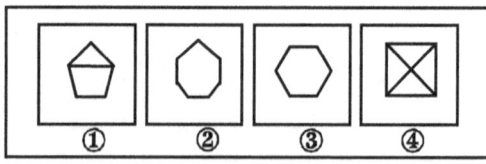

Fig. : 6.98

7.

Question Figures:

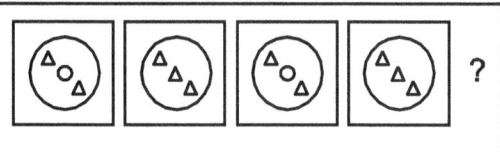

Answer Figures:

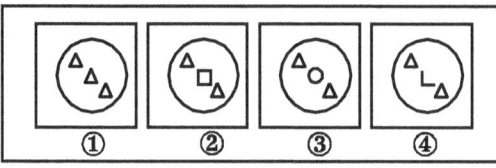

Fig. : 6.99

8.

Question Figures:

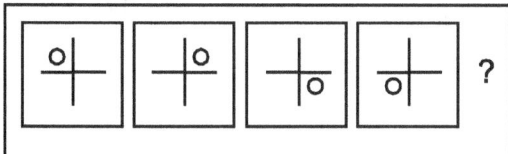

Answer Figures:

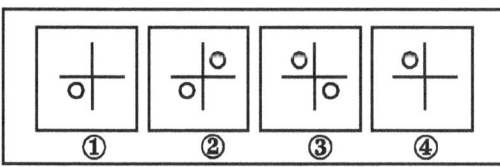

Fig. : 6.100

9.

Question Figures:

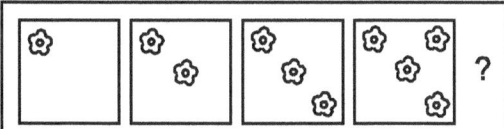

Answer Figures:

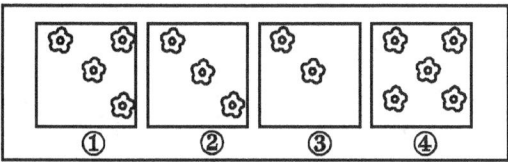

Fig. : 6.101

10.   Question Figures:

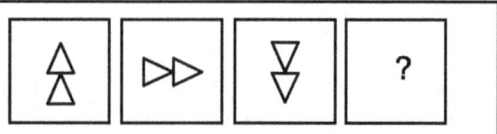

Answer Figures:

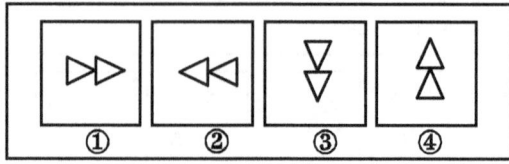

Fig. : 6.102

11.   Question Figures:

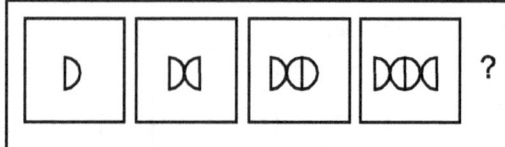

Answer Figures:

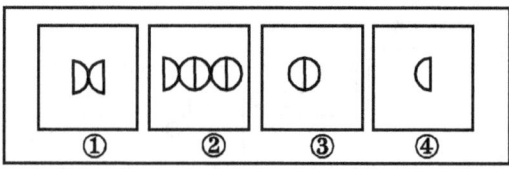

Fig. : 6.103

12.   Question Figures:

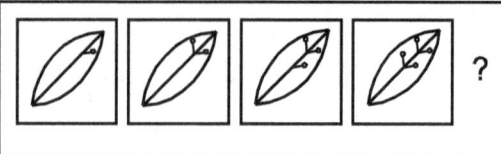

Answer Figures:

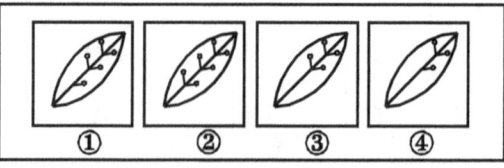

Fig. : 6.104

13.

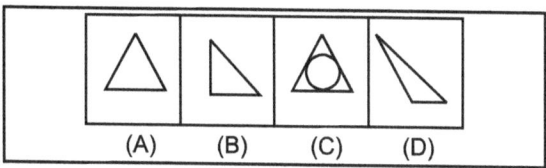

Fig. : 6.105

Which of the given figures is the odd man out ?

① D   ② A

③ C   ④ B

14.

Question Figure

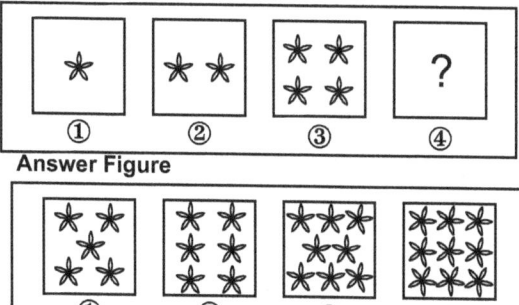

Answer Figure

Fig. : 6.106

15.

Question Figure

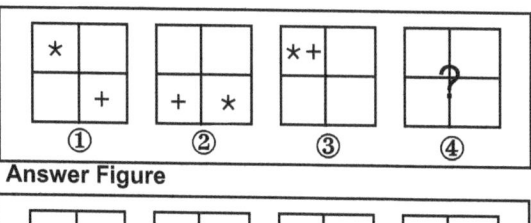

Answer Figure

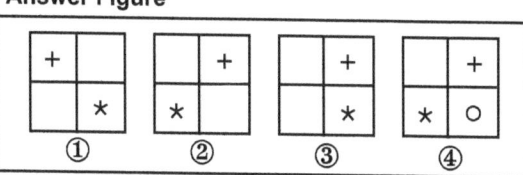

Fig. : 6.107

16. **Question Figure**

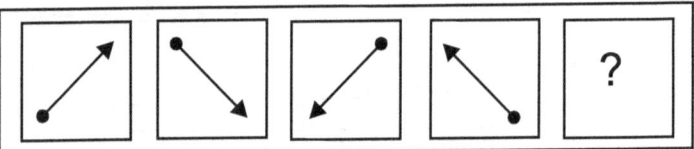

Answer Figure

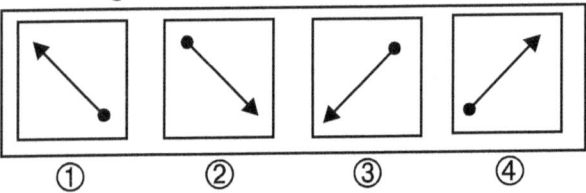

Fig. : 6.108

17. **Question Figure**

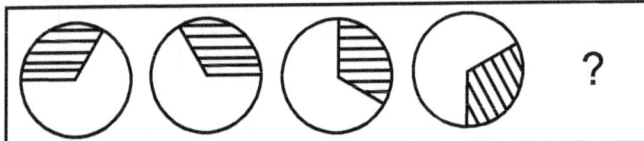

Answer Figure

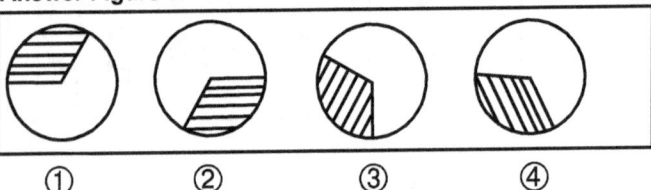

Fig. : 6.109

18. **Question Figure**

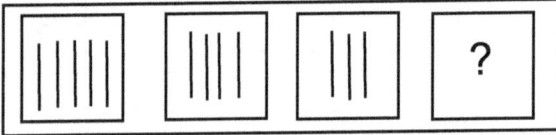

Answer Figure

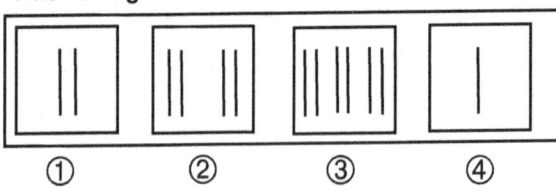

Fig. : 6.110

19.

Question Figure

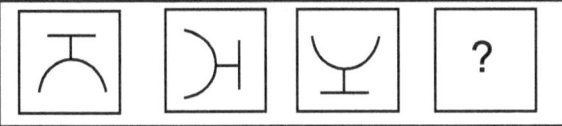

Answer Figure

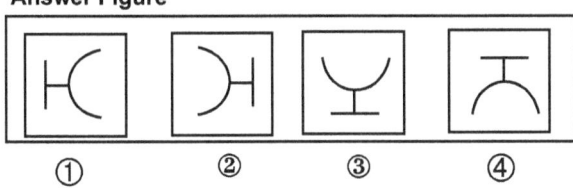

Fig. : 6.111

20.

Question Figure

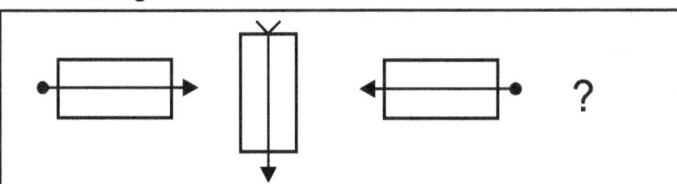

Answer Figure

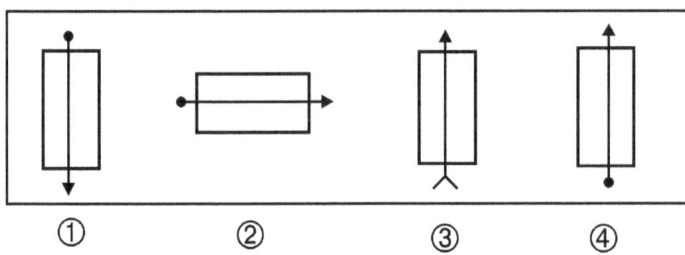

Fig. : 6.112

21.

Question Figure

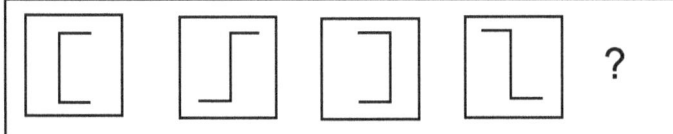

Answer Figure

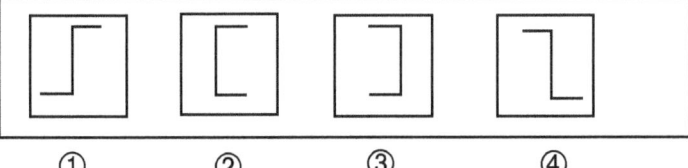

Fig. : 6.113

1.	❸	2.	❹	3.	❹	4.	❹
5.	❷	6.	❸	7.	❸	8.	❹
9.	❹	10.	❷	11.	❷	12.	❶
13.	❸	14.	❸	15.	❸	16.	❹
17.	❸	18.	❷	19.	❹	20.	❷
21.	❶						

❖ ❖ ❖

6.9   *CUBE AND CUBOID (EDGES AND VERTICES AND FACES)*

✌ CUBE :

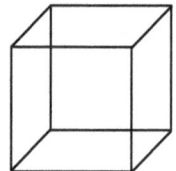

Fig. : 6.114

A cube is a three-dimensional solid object bounded by six square faces, with three meeting at each vertex. The cube is the only regular hexahedron and is one of the five Platonic solids. It has 12 edges, 6 faces and 8 vertices.

✌ CUBOIDE

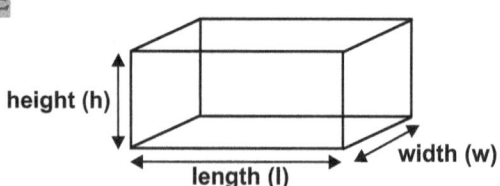

Fig. : 6.115

A cuboid is a 3D shape. Cuboids have six faces, which form a convex polyhedron. Simply speaking, cuboids are made from 6 rectangles, which are placed at right angles. A cuboid that uses square faces is a cube, if the faces are rectangles, other than cubes, it looks like a shoe box.

Properties of a Cuboid are:

- It has 12 edges
- It has 8 corners or vertices
- It has 6 faces.

Formula volume = length × width × height or simpler notations, or $v = l \times w \times h$.

Its surface area is given as

$a = 2wl + 2lh + 2hw$,

where "a" denotes the surface area.

designs, letters, digits and drawings.

Model Examples

1. What is the shape of faces of cube ?

    ① Coboid ② Square ③ Rectangle ④ Triangle   ❹

    Explanation :

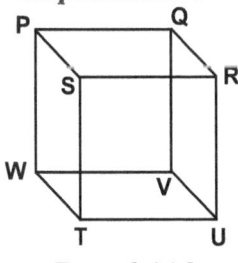

Fig. : **6.116**

The Fig. along side is a fig. of cube.

From it, it is clear that the faces of cube are of square shape.

∴ Alternative ❷ is the correct answer.

2. The vertices of cuboid = ----------

    ① 4   ② 8   ③ 12   ④ 10   ❷

    Explanation :

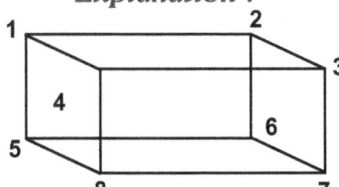

Fig. : **6.117**

Cuboid have 8 vertices.

∴ Alternative ❷ is the correct answer.

3. From the following Fig. Find out the correct Fig. of cube?

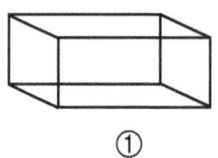 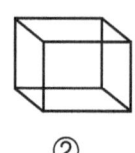  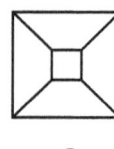

①   ②   ③   ④

Fig. : 6.118

Explanation : The length, breadth and height of cube are equal in Fig. 2 the length, breadth and height are equal

∴ Alternative ❷ is the correct answer

Examples for Practice

Q. Find the exact term in place of question mark.

1. How many edges does a cuboid have ------
    ① 12   ② 13   ③ 10   ④ 8

2. What is a three-dimensional rectangle called ?
    ① Square   ② Rectangle
    ③ Cuboids   ④ None of these

3. How many faces of cube are equal length ?
    ① 6   ② 4   ③ 3   ④ 2

4. Number of Vertices of cube = -------
    ① 6   ② 8   ③ 10   ④ 12

5. Number of Vertices of cuboids =
    ① 8   ② 10   ③ 12   ④ 6

6. How many faces of cuboide have equal area ?
    ① 6   ② Two groups of 3 faces
    ③ Three groups of 2 faces ④ 4

Answers

1.	❶	2.	❸	3.	❶	4.	❷
5.	❶	6.	❸				

DATA HANDLING

| 7.1 | COMPREHENSION ON PICTORIAL INFORMATION |

✌ INTRODUCTION :

In pictorial information, we have to read the given information and answer the questions based on it.

Example 1 :

Types of Shop	Number of Shops
Food Items	⌂ ⌂ ⌂ ⌂ ⌂
Toys	⌂ ⌂ ⌂ ⌂
Clothes	⌂ ⌂ ⌂
Other	⌂ ⌂ ⌂ ⌂ ⌂ ⌂

Fig. : 7.1

Radha : What do the pictures mean ?

Rahul : One picture stands for one shop.

There are three clothes shop so there are three pictures.

Sarita : Suppose there are lots of sops, will you draw as many pictures ?

Sunita: No it is not possible to draw so many pictures every time. We pack the things in a bundles of 12 and we count each bundle and from there we come to know the number of things packed. We can do this with pictures.

Example 2 :

Raja : I will explain in the park in front of my house there are 50 mogra bushes, 40 rose buses, 30 dahlia shrubs. I will make a table to show this using pictures.

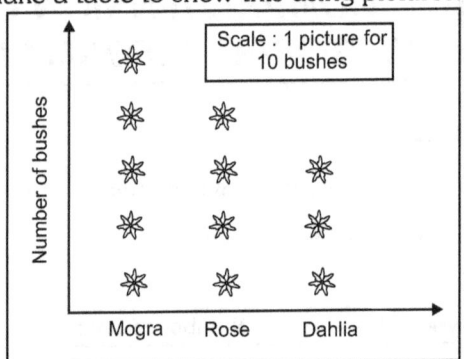

Fig. : 7.2

1. Which bushes are more ?

   ① Mogra　　② Rose　　③ Dahli　　④ None of these ❶

2. How many rose shrubs are there ?

   ① 30　　② 40　　③ 4　　④ 20　　❷

3. How many more Mogra Shurbs than Dahlia ?

   ① 20　　② 2　　③ 5　　④ 200　　❷

Example 3 :

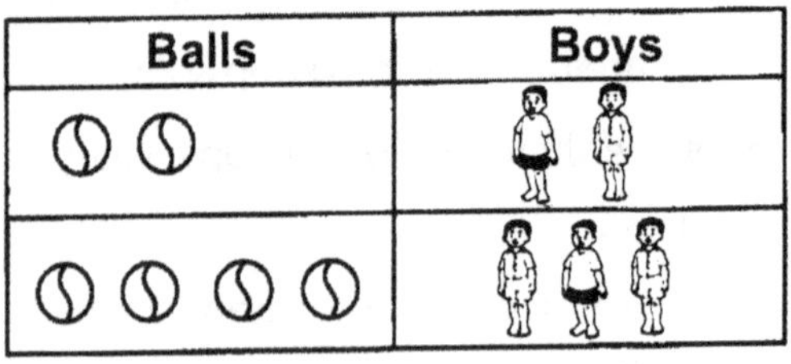

Balls	Boys
Ⓞ Ⓞ	🧍 🧍
Ⓞ Ⓞ Ⓞ Ⓞ	🧍 🧍 🧍

Fig. : 7.3

1. How many boys have two balls ?

   ① Two　　② three　　③ one　　④ None of these ❶

2. Total number of boys which have ball ?

   ① Four　　② Five　　③ three　　④ None of these ❷

Model Examples

Write the correct answer for the given pictorial information.

(I)

Flowers	Number of seedlings
 Shoe flower	 ⚘ ⚘ ⚘ ⚘ ⚘ ⚘
 Rose	 ⚘ ⚘ ⚘ ⚘ ⚘ ⚘ ⚘ ⚘ ⚘
 Periwinkle	 ⚘ ⚘ ⚘ ⚘

Fig. : 7.4

1. What is the total number of seedlings ?

    ① 2   ② 19   ③ 20   ④ 5   ❷

2. Which flower requires the most number of seedlings ?

    ① Rose   ② Shoe flower

    ③ Periwinkle   ④ None of these   ❶

3. Which flower has six seedlings ?

    ① Rose   ② Shoe flower

    ③ Periwinkle   ④ None of these   ❷

4. Which flower has the least number of seedlings ?

    ① Rose   ② Shoe flower

    ③ Periwinkle   ④ None of these   ❸

5. By how many are Rose seedlings more than the seedlings of shoe flower ?

    ① 1   ② 3   ③ 2   ④ 5   ❷

(II)

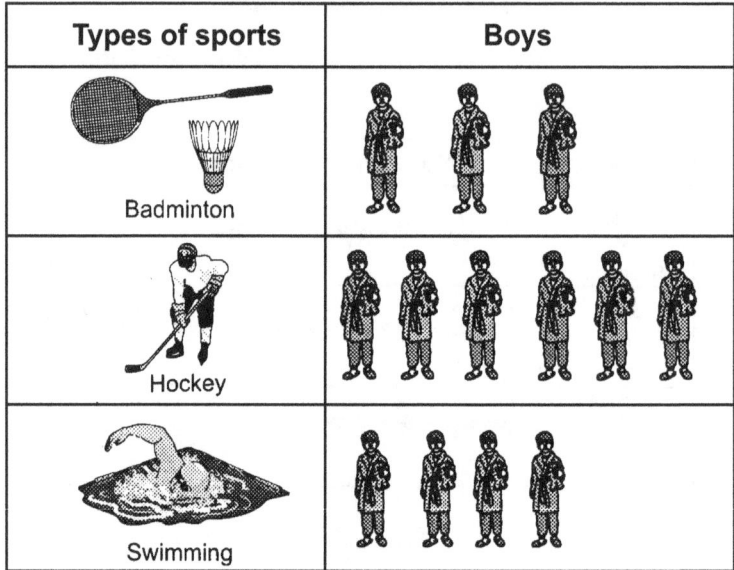

Types of sports	Boys
Badminton	
Hockey	
Swimming	

Fig. : 7.5

1. How many boys play hockey ?

   ① 2   ② 4   ③ 6   ④ 10   ❸

2. Which sport is used by three boys ?

   ① Badminton   ② hockey

   ③ swimming   ④ None of these   ❶

3. How many boys take part in swimming ?

   ① 2   ② 3   ③ 4   ④ 6   ❸

4. By how many are hockey boys more than the boys of swimming ?

   ① 1   ② 2   ③ 4   ④ 3   ❷

5. What is the total number of boys which take part in sport ?

   ① 10   ② 13   ③ 12   ④ 14   ❷

===● Examples for Practice ●===

Write the correct answer for the given pictorial information.

(I)

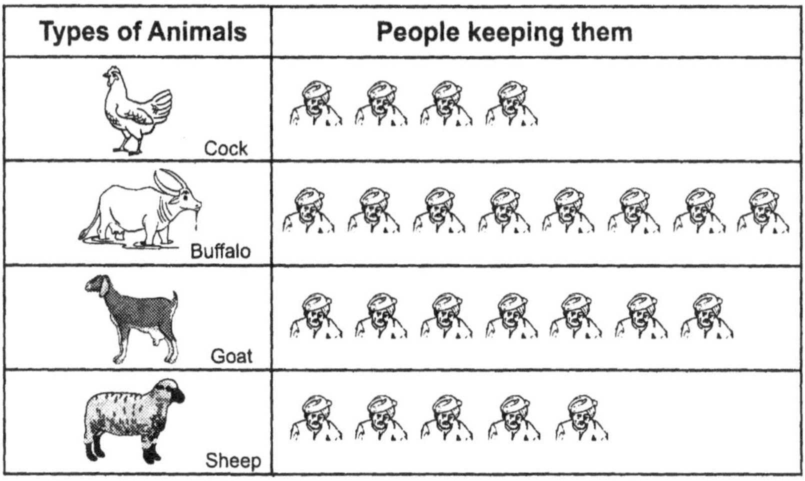

Types of Animals	People keeping them
Cock	
Buffalo	
Goat	
Sheep	

Fig. : 7.6

1. How many people used to keep domestic animals ?

    ① 24   ② 8   ③ 4   ④ 7

2. How many people keep sheep ?

    ① 8   ② 5   ③ 4   ④ 7

3. How many people altogether keep cock and goat ?

    ① 4   ② 8   ③ 11   ④ 7

4. How many people keep buffalo ?

    ① 8   ② 7   ③ 4   ④ 5

5. By how many are the people keeping goats more than those keeping sheep ?

    ① 1   ② 2   ③ 4   ④ 5

(II)

Objects	Girls
School bag	
Tiffin box	
Water bag	

Fig. : 7.7

1. How many girls have waterbags ?

   ① 5   ② 8   ③ 7   ④ 6

2. How many girls use tiffin boxes ?

   ① 6   ② 8   ③ 7   ④ 5

3. How many girls altogether have school bag and waterbag ?

   ① 10   ② 12   ③ 11   ④ 8

4. Which object is used by six girls ?

   ①   School bag   ②   Tiffin

   ③   Water bag   ④   None of these

5. By how many are the girls having tiffin box more than the girls having waterbag?

   ① 5   ② 8   ③ 7   ④ 3

(III)

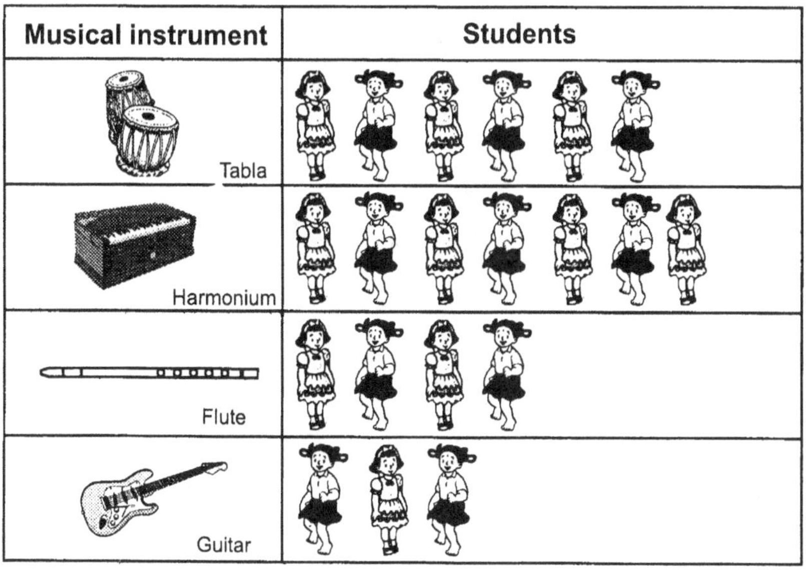

Musical instrument	Students
Tabla	
Harmonium	
Flute	
Guitar	

Fig. : 7.8

1. How many students are learning to play the guitar ?

   ① 3   ② 4   ③ 7   ④ 5

2. Which is the instrument that four students are learning to play ?

   ① Tabla   ② Guitar

   ③ Harmonium   ④ Flute

3. How many students are learning to play the tabla ?

   ① 3   ② 5   ③ 4   ④ 6

4. Which is the instrument that maximum number of children are learning to play ?

   ① Tabla   ② Guitar

   ③ Harmonium   ④ Flute

5. What is the total number of students which play different types of instruments ?

   ① 13   ② 20   ③ 17   ④ 15

(IV)

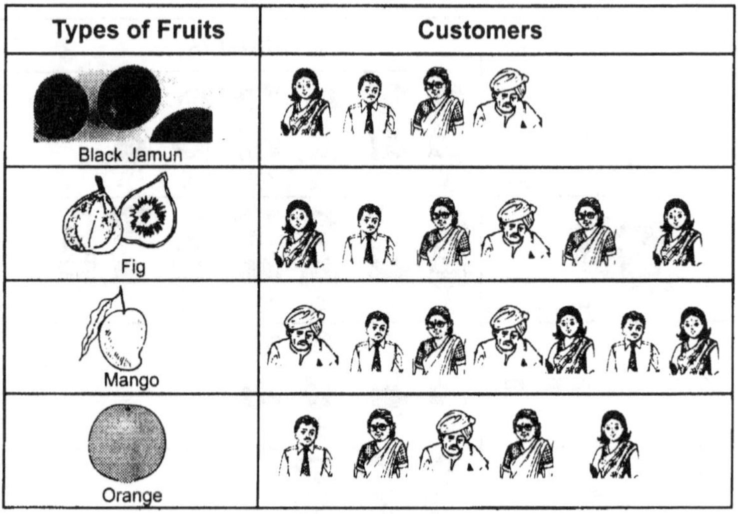

Types of Fruits	Customers
Black Jamun	
Fig	
Mango	
Orange	

Fig. : 7.9

1. How many customers had mangoes ?

    ① 7   ② 5   ③ 4   ④ 6

2. Which is the fruit that five customers had ?

    ① Jamun   ② Orange

    ③ Mango   ④ Fig

3. Which was the fruit that four customers had ?

    ① Mango   ② Orange

    ③ Fig   ④ Jamun

4. Which fruit did the most customers have ?

    ① Jamun   ② Orange

    ③ Mango   ④ Fig

5. Which was the fruit which was consumed by the least number

    of people ?

    ① Jamun   ② Fig

    ③ Mango   ④ Orange

(V)

Types of Vehicles	Passengers
 Bus	
 Train	
 Aeroplane	
 Car	

Fig. : 7.10

1. Which vehicle is used by six people ?

   ① Aeroplane   ② Train

   ③ Car   ④ ST

2. How many people travel by car ?

   ① 6   ② 4   ③ 21   ④ 9

3. By which vehicle do the least number of people travel ?

   ① Aeroplane ② Car   ③ ST   ④ Train

4. By how many are train passengers less than ST passengers.

   ① 6   ② 4   ③ 3   ④ 9

5. What is the total number of passengers ?

   ① 6   ② 20   ③ 22   ④ 21

(VI) *People in town collected aid for Uttarakhand relief fund. This is its pictorial representation.*

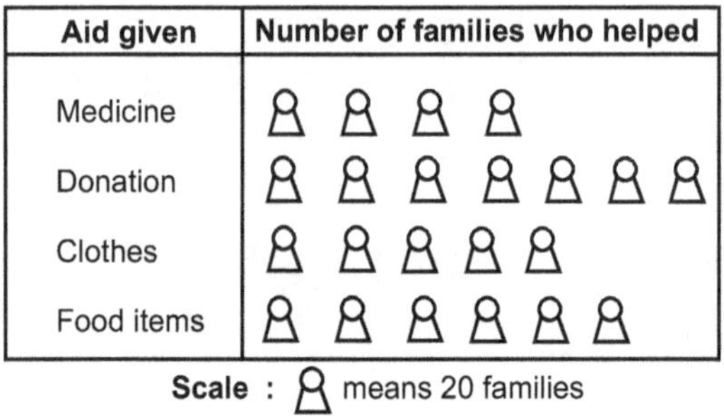

Aid given	Number of families who helped
Medicine	𝔸 𝔸 𝔸 𝔸
Donation	𝔸 𝔸 𝔸 𝔸 𝔸 𝔸 𝔸
Clothes	𝔸 𝔸 𝔸 𝔸 𝔸
Food items	𝔸 𝔸 𝔸 𝔸 𝔸 𝔸

Scale : 𝔸 means 20 families

Fig.: 7.11

1. In all how many families help ?

   ① 22   ② 440   ③ 40   ④ 220

2. What was the form of help given by the largest number of families ?

   ① Medicine ② Donation ③ Clothes ④ Food items

3. What form of aid was given by the least number of families ?

   ① Medicine ② Donation ③ Clothes ④ Food items

(VII) *This is a chart showing what fund of fuel is used in the kitchen in 200 houses of Rampur ?*

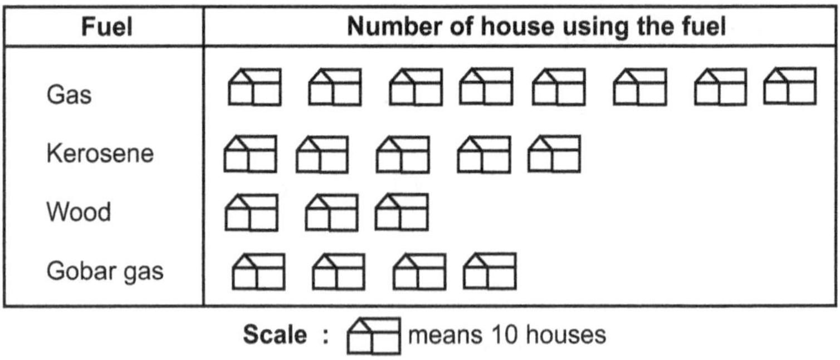

Fuel	Number of house using the fuel
Gas	⌂ ⌂ ⌂ ⌂ ⌂ ⌂ ⌂ ⌂
Kerosene	⌂ ⌂ ⌂ ⌂ ⌂
Wood	⌂ ⌂ ⌂
Gobar gas	⌂ ⌂ ⌂ ⌂

Scale : ⌂ means 10 houses

Fig. : 7.12

1. What kind of fuel is used in most houses ?

   ① Gobar gas   ② wood

   ③ Gas   ④ Kerosene

2. How many houses use wood as fuel ?

    ① 40   ② 50   ③ 80   ④ 30

3. How many houses use Kerosene as fuel ?

    ① 80   ② 50   ③ 30   ④ 40

(VIII) *A chart showing the crop grown by the farmers in a village ?*

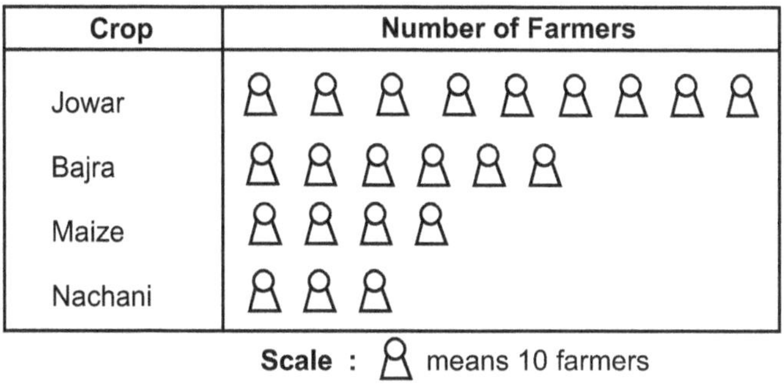

Crop	Number of Farmers
Jowar	𝗔 𝗔 𝗔 𝗔 𝗔 𝗔 𝗔 𝗔 𝗔
Bajra	𝗔 𝗔 𝗔 𝗔 𝗔 𝗔
Maize	𝗔 𝗔 𝗔 𝗔
Nachani	𝗔 𝗔 𝗔

Scale : 𝗔 means 10 farmers

Fig. : 7.13

1. About how many farmers does the chart tell us ?

    ① 220   ② 22   ③ 2200   ④ 202

2. Which crop is grown by the least number of farmers ?

    ① Jowar   ② Bajra   ③ Nachani ④ Maize

3. How many more farmers grow Jowar than Maize ?

    ① 50   ② 500   ③ 5   ④ 5000

(IX) *A chart showing what snacks Pre-Primary students of Rainbow School brought ?*

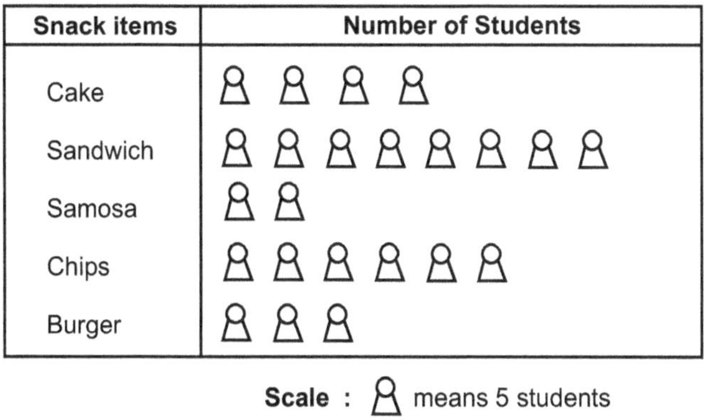

Snack items	Number of Students
Cake	𝗔 𝗔 𝗔 𝗔
Sandwich	𝗔 𝗔 𝗔 𝗔 𝗔 𝗔 𝗔 𝗔
Samosa	𝗔 𝗔
Chips	𝗔 𝗔 𝗔 𝗔 𝗔 𝗔
Burger	𝗔 𝗔 𝗔

Scale : 𝗔 means 5 students

Fig. : 7.14

1. What is the total number of students in Rainbow Pre-Primary School ?

    ① 115   ② 105   ③ 151   ④ 511

2. How many students brought chips ?

    ① 6   ② 60   ③ 30   ④ 36

3. Which snack was brought by least number of students ?

    ① Cake   ② Burger   ③ Chips   ④ Samosa

(X) *On a the last day of school students were civil dress of to school. A chart showing what colours was worn by children is given below.*

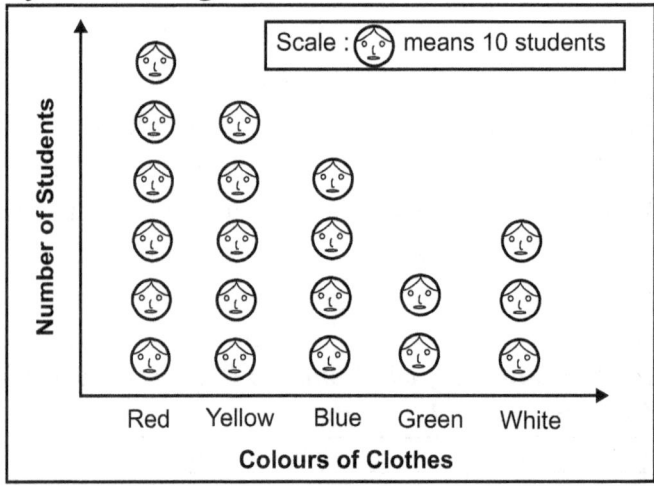

Fig. : 7.15

1. How many students are there in all ?

    ① 20   ② 200   ③ 2000   ④ 2

2. How many students were white clothes ?

    ① 3   ② 15   ③ 30   ④ 300

3. What colour did the greatest number of students wear ?

    ① Yellow   ② Blue   ③ green   ④ Red

(XI) *In a vegetables shop the number of vegetables are shown in pictograph :*

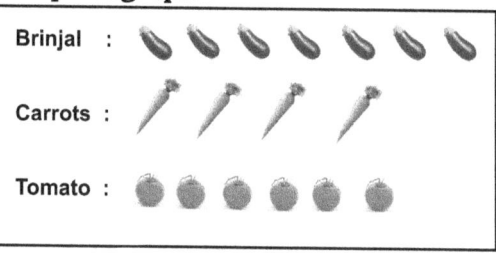

Brinjal :

Carrots :

Tomato :

Fig. : 7.16

1. By how many are tomatoes less than that the sum of carrots and brinjals ?
   ① 5   ② 2   ③ 1   ④ 6

2. How many vegetables are there in all ?
   ① 17   ② 5   ③ 9   ④ 16

3. How many tomatoes are shown there ?
   ① 7   ② 4   ③ 6   ④ 3

4. How many carrots are there ?
   ① 4   ② 2   ③ 6   ④ 8

(XII) *In Timex Watch Company the number of clocks sold in a week is represented in a pictograph. Solve the questions (1 clock = 200)*

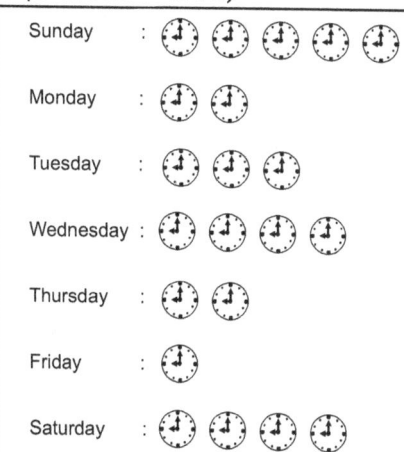

Sunday :

Monday :

Tuesday :

Wednesday :

Thursday :

Friday :

Saturday :

Fig. : 7.17

1. Two clocks = ……. Clocks.
   ① 400   ② 600   ③ 200   ④ 100

2. On which day minimum clocks were sold ?
   ① Friday   ② Sunday   ③ Tuesday ④ Wednesday

3. How many clocks are sold on Thursday ?
   ① 400   ② 200   ③ 800   ④ 100

4. The maximum number of clocks were sold on which day ?
   ① Sunday   ② Monday   ③ Tuesday ④ Friday

Answers

(I)	1.	❶	2.	❷	3.	❸	4.	❶	5.	❷
(II)	1.	❶	2.	❷	3.	❸	4.	❶	5.	❹
(III)	1.	❶	2.	❹	3.	❹	4.	❸	5.	❷
(IV)	1.	❶	2.	❷	3.	❹	4.	❸	5.	❶
(V)	1.	❷	2.	❷	3.	❶	4.	❸	5.	❹
(VI)	1.	❷	2.	❷	3.	❶				
(VII)	1.	❸	2.	❹	3.	❷				
(VIII)	1.	❶	2.	❸	3.	❷				
(IX)	1.	❶	2.	❸	3.	❹				
(X)	1.	❷	2.	❸	3.	❹				
(XI)	1.	❶	2.	❶	3.	❸	4.	❶		
(XII)	1.	❶	2.	❶	3.	❶	4.	❶		

❖ ❖ ❖

7.2	PATTERNS IN NUMBER AND SHAPES

✌ INTRODUCTION :

We generally observe various patterns in our daily life. We use them and many time place them according to our requirement. Here you are supposed to observe pattern and answer the question.

Model Examples

Observe the pattern and answer the questions given below.

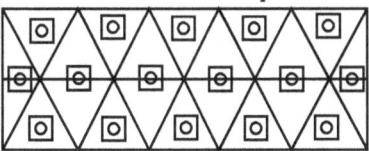

Fig. : 7.18

1. How many geometrical shapes are there in the above figure.

   ① 4   ② 5   ③ 6   ④ 7   ❷

2. What is the pattern followed in a times table.

   ① Number in the units place are in decreasing value

   ② Number in the tens place are in decreasing value

   ③ Number in the units place are in increasing value

   ④ Numbers in the tens place are in increasing value.

Examples for Practice

1. What is the pattern in the units place in 5 time table ?

   ① 5, 0   ② 0, 5   ③ 5, 5   ④ 0, 0

2. What is the pattern in tens place in 11 times table ?

   ① 1, 2, 3   ② 9, 8, 7   ③ 5, 4, 3   ④ 6, 5, 4

3. Multiply 12 by 3, 6, 9, 12 and observe the pattern ?

   ① difference of 36   ② No pattern

   ③ Addition of all the digit is 9

   ④ Addition of all digits is 8

4. What is the pattern in units place in 2 times table ?

    ① 2, 4, 6, 8, 0   ② 0, 8, 6, 4, 2
    ③ No Pattern   ④ 1, 2, 3, 4

5. Complete the pattern given below :

    (i)

    (ii)

       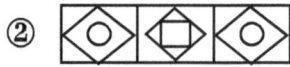

    ④   None of these

Fig. : 7.19

6. How many geometric shapes in the pattern given below :

    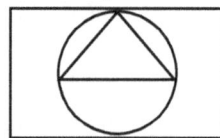

Fig. : 7.20

    ① 2   ② 4   ③ 3 ④   5

7. Complete the pattern given below :

    ①    ②   ③   ④

Fig. : 7.21

8.

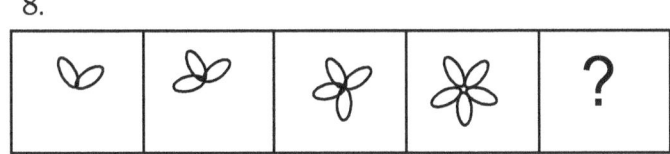

①   ②   ③   ④ None of these

Fig. : 7.22

9.

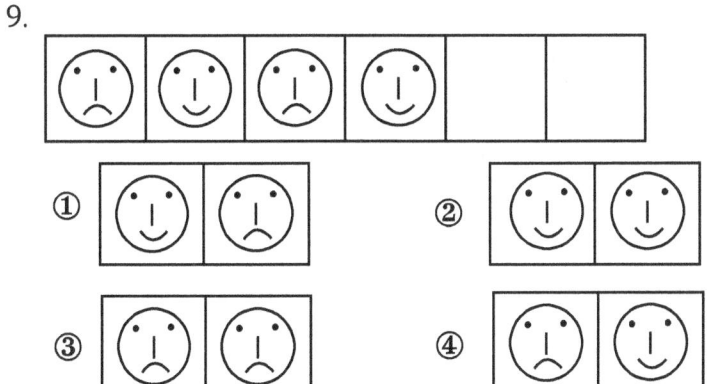

①   ②   ③   ④

Fig. : 7.23

10.

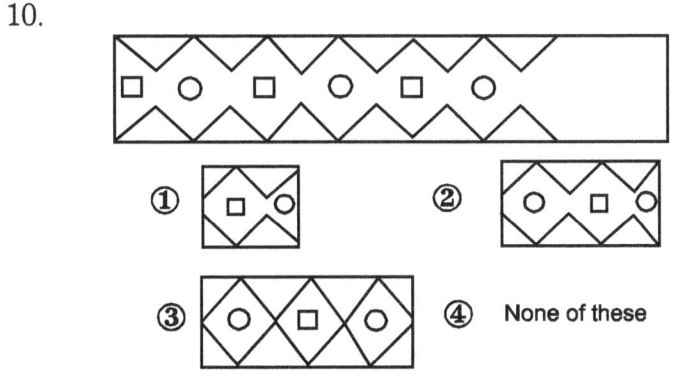

①   ②   ③   ④ None of these

Fig. : 7.24

11.

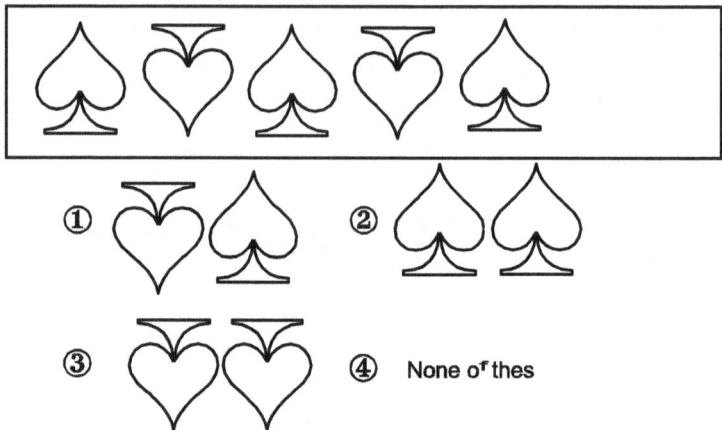

Fig. : 7.25

12. Observe the pattern given below :

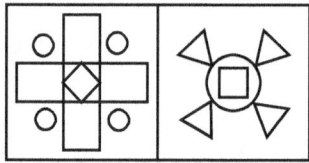

Fig. : 7.26

How many geometrical figures are there in the figure.

① 6   ② 5

③ 4   ④ None of these

13.

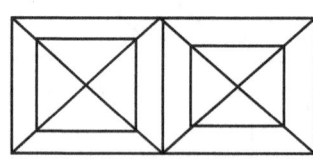

Fig. : 7.27

How many squares and triangles in the figure.

① 4, 24   ② 4, 20

③ 4, 16   ④ None of these

14. Observe the figure given below :

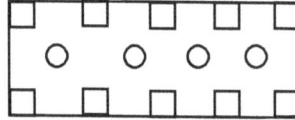

Fig. : 7.28

How many squares and circles in given figure.

① 10, 4   ② 8, 4   ③ 4, 10   ④ None of these

15. Complete the given pattern.

①    ②    ③    ④ None of these

Fig. : 7.29

16.

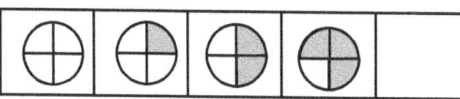

①   ②   ③ 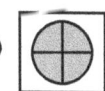   ④ None of these

Fig. : 7.30

Answers

1.	❶	2.	❶	3.	❸	4.	❶	5.(i)	❶
(ii)	❷	6.	❸	7.	❷	8.	❸	9.	❹
10.	❶	11.	❶	12.	❷	13.	❶	14.	❶
15.	❶	16.	❸						

❖ ❖ ❖

Notes :